LETHAL LADIES

Edited by Barbara Collins
& Robert J. Randisi

BERKLEY PRIME CRIME, NEW YORK

LETHAL LADIES

A Berkley Prime Crime Book / published by arrangement with
Barbara Collins and Robert J. Randisi

PRINTING HISTORY
Berkley Prime Crime edition / January 1996

ISBN: 0-425-15141-7

Berkley Prime Crime Books are published
by The Berkley Publishing Group,
200 Madison Avenue, New York, NY 10016.
The name BERKLEY PRIME CRIME and the BERKLEY PRIME CRIME
design are trademarks belonging to Berkley Publishing Corporation.

PRINTED IN THE UNITED STATES OF AMERICA

10 9 8 7 6 5 4 3 2 1

Contents

Introduction

For years the American female private eye was represented in fiction by some one-shot appearances—Rex Stout's Theodolina Bonner, Henry Kane's Marla Trent—and in series by G. G. Fickling's Honey West, who was the female counterpart of Richard S. Prather's Shell Scott. The beauteous Honey appeared in a series of paperbacks in which she usually ended up naked or nearly so, more often than not. While fun, they certainly did nothing to advance the position of women in the P.I. genre. That distinction goes to Marcia Muller. With the publication of the first Sharon McCone novel, *Edwin of the Iron Shoes*, in 1974, she paved the way for Sue Grafton, Sara Paretsky, Linda Barnes, and a host of other fine writers who are now plying their trade chronicling the cases of their respective sleuths, all of whom advance the reputation of the female P.I. with every appearance.

Our intention with this collection is twofold: to showcase some of the finest writing being done in the P.I. field by women, and to illustrate that the Private Eye Writers of America is not the boys club some people might think it is. Here you have stories by sixteen of the best P.I. writers in the field—who just happen to be females.

When Bob Randisi edited *Deadly Allies* with Marilyn Wallace and *Deadly Allies II* with Sue Dunlap their aim—that is, the aim of the editors, PWA, and Sisters in Crime—was to show that both organizations were committed to the same thing—good storytelling . . . and that they were not competitors.

The intention with *Lethal Ladies* is much the same. Within these pages you have great storytelling, and no competition. The men have willingly stepped aside this time to allow the ladies of PWA to show their stuff. When one woman was asked to contribute to this anthology she said she did not write for "gender segregated anthologies." We tried to point out that this project was not such an anthology, but meant to illustrate that PWA is *not* a gender segregated organization. Men and women write P.I. fiction. It's a fact. It's that simple.

Barbara Collins
Muscatine, Iowa

Robert J. Randisi
St. Louis, Missouri

The first line of this story is "Do I look like a corpse to you?" and it takes off from there. San Francisco–based P.I. Jess Randolph is hired by a woman who has read her own obituary. Jess must decide if this woman really isn't dead—that is, if the woman is telling the truth about not being dead—oh, read it yourself. It moves as straight and swift as a bullet. The first Jess Randolph novel was Innocent Stranger.

IDENTITY CRISIS

by Margaret Lucke

"DO I LOOK like a corpse to you?" The young woman leaned forward in my visitor's chair and clutched the corner of my desk.

True, she looked pale and bloodless, and her eyes seemed sunk in shadows. But she was much too fidgety to be dead.

"Not at all," I said. "Based on the evidence in front of me, I'd say you're very much alive."

She nodded. "Exactly. The trouble is, you and I are the only ones who think so. Everywhere I go, people keep telling me I've died. And I can't prove otherwise."

I picked up the sketchbook I use for taking notes. "Maybe you'd better tell me the whole story."

She had already told me her name—Alicia Satterfield.

1

She was in her mid-twenties, but shrouded in an oversized man's shirt, she looked like a fragile child. Limp hair, the beige color of dried grass, drooped to her shoulders.

She had arrived unannounced, peeking timidly through my office door. She smiled with relief when I introduced myself.

"Oh, good. You're the one I'm looking for. See, I'm an artist, too. I saw an article about you a few weeks ago, in the *Chronicle*? I thought, a woman, a painter, and a detective— how perfect. I couldn't remember your name, so I looked up Investigators in the Yellow Pages. I started with the A's and kept calling until someone said, 'Oh, you mean Jess Randolph, she's with Parks and O'Meara.'"

The Parks in Parks and O'Meara—my friend and employer, Tyler—was away at a meeting, but O'Meara came over to say hello, wagging his russet tail. Alicia petted him lavishly, earning instant points in Irish setter heaven. He flopped beside her when she sat down.

Now she touched his soft fur, as if for reassurance. "I guess the story starts two months ago, when my husband and I moved here to San Francisco. I was really thrilled. See, my mother had just died—"

I must have frowned slightly.

"No, I don't mean thrilled about her dying. But she's been sick a long time, a heart condition, it runs in our family. Anyway, we never got along. She always wanted me to do something sensible with my life. To her, that meant anything but painting. But she left me some money. No more being a starving artist."

Alicia had lived with her mother, nursing her and enduring their battles in exchange for room and board. As soon as the older woman died, she married Craig, the boyfriend her mother had disapproved of, and the newlyweds headed for the bright city lights. They found an apartment on Potrero Hill, with a spare room where she could paint.

"Our deal was, I'd make the paintings and Craig would be my agent and take them around to the galleries. It was going to be a dream come true."

She hunched down inside her voluminous shirt. The white oxford cloth was splotched with paint in a rainbow of colors. In the V of the unbuttoned collar, a crystal dangled from a gold chain around her neck.

"But I guess all the changes at once—well, it was a lot of strain. Craig started spending less and less time at home, and when he was home we were fighting. I even began to think he must be seeing someone else, but that was stupid, we didn't know anybody in the city."

So a month ago Alicia packed her paints and blue jeans and retreated to a cabin her mother had owned at Turquoise Lake, up in the Sierra foothills. "I wanted time to myself, to think things over. I just got back yesterday. And that's when everything got weird."

"Weird how?" I asked.

Alicia rubbed a green smear on her sleeve. "When I got home my key wouldn't work. I knocked, and this strange guy answered the door and said he rented the apartment a week ago. I went to the real estate office, Hillside Reality? The lady there told me the previous tenant moved out right after his wife died. She meant Craig. She meant I had died."

"Did she tell you where Craig had gone?"

"She didn't know. And he took all our stuff with him. My paintings and everything."

"What did you do?"

"I didn't know what to do. See, this other weird thing had happened. The day before I left the lake, my purse was stolen. My wallet, checkbook, driver's license—everything with an ID on it. Some of my favorite jewelry was in there, too. Fortunately, I'd hidden some cash in my sleeping bag, or I couldn't have bought gas to drive back."

"Didn't you try to call Craig for help?"

"No. I hadn't decided if I wanted to see him. Then, driving back, I realized—where else could I go?" Her eyes brimmed with tears. "When I couldn't get in the apartment, I went to the Main Library and used their pay phones. I called my bank and the DMV to report what was stolen. They said everything had been canceled because . . . because Alicia Satterfield was deceased."

She started to cry. O'Meara nuzzled her leg, whimpering his concern.

"Then . . . this is the worst part. I went to the Periodical Room and looked through the newspapers. And there it was . . . my obituary. Have you any idea what it's like to read your own obituary? It's . . . it's awful. I have no money left, no way at all to prove who I am."

"What about your friends and family? Surely someone can vouch for you."

"Nobody who could swear I'm me—not in any sort of legal way, an affidavit or whatever." Alicia wiped her eyes on her big sleeve. "I'm an only child, my father left when I was little, I don't even know where he is. Mom and I moved around all the time, she'd get restless after a few months and we'd be off to another town. I never made close friends. And San Francisco . . . we just got here, and I worked at home. I don't know anyone here but Craig."

"Have you gone to the police?"

"I don't want police. They'd just think I'm trying to pull off some crime or other." She gazed at the wall behind my desk. "Did you paint that?"

"Yes." I turned and looked at the big canvas. Olive, aquamarine, splashes of crimson—an abstract inspired by spinnakers on the bay.

"Hope I'm that good someday." Alicia smiled forlornly to reinforce the flattery. "You'll help me, won't you, Jess? It's just some crazy mix-up. You'll find Craig and get it straightened out?"

Twin artistic souls, her body language said. We artists have to stick together. I felt crass asking how she was going to pay for an investigation.

Alicia looked defeated when I mentioned it. "Can't you take the case on a . . . what do lawyers call it?"

"A contingency?"

"That's it."

I hesitated.

"Please," she begged. "If there was any other way, I'd do it. I'll pay you as soon as I can."

O'Meara looked at me pleadingly. It was clear whose side he was on.

What the hell, my schedule was light for once. Nothing pressing that couldn't wait for a day or two.

"Okay," I said. "I'll put in twenty-four hours and see what I can find out. Come back at two o'clock tomorrow. Then we'll decide how to proceed."

Her smile lit her face like a sunbeam. "Oh, thank you! You're a lifesaver." But the light quickly faded. "Uh, Jess, I know that's enough to ask but . . . maybe, could you . . ."

Alicia bent to stroke O'Meara's ear. Her hair fell forward, hiding her expression. I waited.

"See, I don't have anyplace to stay. Last night I slept in my car, but it's scary out there, parked on the street. Could I . . . stay at your place?"

She looked so hopeful, so waiflike, it was hard to say no. But I didn't know Alicia Satterfield. I had no idea if her bizarre story was true, or what she might be up to if it wasn't. Having her move in with me, even for one night, was a bad idea.

There was a homeless shelter I could refer her to. That might be better than sleeping in a car, just barely. Finally, against my better judgment, I took out my wallet. I'd just been to the ATM. The thought crossed my mind that Alicia might have spotted me there and followed me back to the office, concocting a little scam along the way.

But what if she was being straightforward? Friendless, broke, the victim of an appalling fraud. I gave her eighty dollars and directions to a Lombard Street motel where I knew the manager. O'Meara wagged his tail in approval.

Who was it who said only the thinnest line divides saints from fools?

I spent the afternoon checking out Alicia's story. Her bank and the DMV confirmed that a checking account and driver's license in Alicia Satterfield's name had been terminated upon notification of her death.

The manager at Hillside Realty remembered the Satterfields well. "Oh, it's so sad," she said. "Hard to believe the

Good Lord would take someone so young. A heart problem, the husband said. Poor fellow—I never saw anyone in such grief. Just couldn't bear to stay in that apartment, he said. Too many memories."

"Did he say where he was moving to?" I asked.

"No, I can't say he did. Such a pleasant young man, too. I never actually met the wife, poor thing. But I went to the little memorial service he had for her, over in Golden Gate Park."

"Do you remember who was there?" I asked. If I could locate the attendees, they might shed light on all this.

"Couldn't have been more than five or six people. Glad I went, just to swell the crowd a little. There was the husband, of course. The only other one I noticed much was the singer. Lovely dark-haired girl. Real sweet voice, too—she brought tears to my eyes."

I thanked her and hung up. Then, leaving O'Meara with a dog biscuit and instructions to handle any business that might come in, I headed for the Main Library. The clerk in the Periodical Room gave me a stack of recent *Chronicles*. On the third try I found the obituary, dated three weeks earlier. *Alicia Satterfield . . . brief illness . . . survived by her husband . . . donations to the art organization of your choice.*

I left the library and crossed Civic Center Plaza to City Hall. The plaza was adorned with a fountain, rows of trees, and clusters of homeless people who used it as living room, bedroom, even bath. As I passed a tattered gentleman snoring on a bench, I pictured Alicia curled up in her car, and I wondered what she was doing with my eighty dollars.

In the Probate Clerk's office I discovered that, sure enough, Alicia Satterfield had left a will. Her death certificate was also in the file. Cause of death: cardiac failure.

The date of the will was right after her wedding. Most people so young tend not to get around to making one, but perhaps she'd been prompted by her mother's death. I was surprised at the size of Alicia's estate—the legacy from her mother had been substantial. Craig was her sole beneficiary.

Not only that, he was the executor, and the filing documents listed his new address.

Craig Satterfield's new home was an apartment in a brown stucco shoebox at the end of Balboa Street. It was in the fog zone—close enough to the ocean for its walls to be damp and its windows coated with salt, but too far away for a view. Night was falling when I knocked at his door. The sea tang was sharp on the wind.

Craig opened the door just halfway. He was tall and angular, with a forelock of mid-brown hair and glasses over hazel eyes. His only greeting was a look of puzzlement.

I told him my name. "I'm a friend of Alicia's. May I talk to you?"

He bowed his head. When he looked at me again it was with an expression of profound sorrow. "My wife . . . died, three weeks ago."

"I know. I'm sorry." I decided to go along with the story. "May I come in?"

He squeezed his eyes shut, as if forcing back tears. "I really don't want to talk about it. It's too soon, it tears me up just to think about her." He started to close the door.

I leaned against it, keeping it open. "Sometimes talking can make you feel better."

Frowning, he glanced back into the room, then stood aside, permitting me to enter.

The living room was small and plain. An arch opened into a drab kitchen. A closed door hid the rest of the rooms. Faint singing drifted through the walls from the next apartment. The place looked like its occupant was in transition—just moving in, or out. Packing cartons were stacked against one wall. There were no pictures on display—no paintings, no photos. Craig's only memento of his wife was a pair of earrings that sat in an ashtray like a tiny offering to the gods.

"Well, have a seat," Craig gestured aimlessly. "I was just about to pour myself a drink. Want one?" An open bottle of white wine and a couple of glasses were on the coffee table, as if he had been expecting me.

I accepted a glass of wine. The prop would reinforce the

idea that this was a friendly chat. I opened with: "Alicia said she was an artist."

Craig nodded. "She was excited about coming to San Francisco. There's a real art scene here."

"I was hoping to see some of her paintings."

He looked around in bewilderment at the bare walls. "I . . . I burned them."

"You *what*?" I was shocked. Outrage surged through me on Alicia's behalf. How could anyone destroy an artist's work? Alicia would be devastated when she found out.

If she *was* Alicia, my inner voice chided. So far, everything indicated that Alicia was truly dead.

"I had to," Craig said. "Every time I looked at them, I was reminded of . . . of what I'd lost. I couldn't bear it."

"All of them?" I was still quivering with fury.

Craig seemed nonplussed by my vehemence. "Well, maybe not *all*. I was showing them around to galleries, trying to get her a show. I left a couple at the Dorchester Gallery, in North Beach. With everything that's happened, I never thought to go collect them." He took a big gulp of wine.

I said, "I'm a little confused. This afternoon Alicia—or someone claiming to be Alicia—came to see me at my office."

"But that's imposs—oh, no. Don't tell me. What did she look like?"

I described the pale young woman with the dried-grass hair.

"Damn. I knew it. I was afraid she'd show up."

"You mean your wife?"

"No, no. Her name is Carly Michelson. She met Alicia last year when they were both taking art classes at the community college. Alicia dropped out of school, she was so frightened of Carly."

"Frightened? Why?"

"Carly got this insane idea that she and Alicia were related—long-lost twins or something. I admit there was a resemblance, though Alicia was much prettier. Carly was a dabbler—drama classes one semester, art the next. Actually, she should have stuck with the theater. Talk about dramatic—what an actress."

Craig sloshed more wine into his glass. "Then she started dabbling in our lives."

It had seemed innocent enough at first, he explained. Carly admired Alicia's work, and she seemed lonely—it wasn't odd that she would hang around, trying to be friends. Then she began inviting herself over to Alicia's house, pestering her ailing mother if Alicia wasn't home. She followed Alicia and Craig on their dates, and phoned a dozen times a day, often after midnight. She tried to pass off her paintings as Alicia's. Once the cops showed up—Carly, arrested for shoplifting, had insisted her name was Alicia Satterfield.

"That's the real reason we moved here—to escape from Carly. It got really creepy—like she was trying to take over Alicia's life."

I tried to sort out my impressions of the young woman in my office. O'Meara had liked her instantly, and he was usually a good judge of character. But he might be fooled by a good actress with a soft spot for dogs.

"My God!" Craig exclaimed. "You don't think . . ."

"Think what?"

"Carly knew about Alicia's heart problem. She knew if Alicia died, it would be blamed on that."

"Are you suggesting Carly murdered your wife?"

"There's ways she could have done it, aren't there? Killed Alicia, and made it look like her heart?"

"I don't know," I said. Although I could think of possibilities: digitalis, ricin, even caffeine if it were purified and injected in sufficient quantity.

"Jesus! I always figured she was crazy, but—murder!"

"What would she gain from it?" I asked.

"Alicia's mother left her a nice inheritance. Carly must think if she can convince people she's Alicia, she can claim the money."

"But it's yours now, isn't it? Alicia's will—"

"It's mine. As soon as the probate hassle is done with.

God, how could Carly do it? Just kill her in cold blood. I—I can't stand this. I loved Alicia so much."

Craig was trembling. As he lifted his glass, wine splashed over his hand and onto the table. Muttering in annoyance he went into the kitchen.

When he reappeared with a paper towel, his cheeks were wet. The spilled wine might have been a tactic to keep me from seeing him cry. Or, my suspicious inner voice suggested, maybe he rubbed his wine-wet hand across his face to create the illusion.

Either way, his voice was morose. "Please go away now."

I stood, setting down my nearly full glass. "One more thing. Did Carly know about Alicia's mother's cabin at Turquoise Lake?"

"She knew everything." He had his hand at my back, guiding—not quite pushing—me toward the door.

"And you. Did you ever go up there? Say, day before yesterday?"

He gave me an odd look. "Lord, no. I was at work. I've been waiting tables at the Caffe Nonna. It keeps my mind off Alicia."

Craig opened the door. I heard foghorns moaning.

"Look, Jess. One thing, okay? If you see Carly again, don't tell her where to find me. No matter what kind of story she pulls on you. If she killed my wife for her money, I'm the next obstacle."

That night, I was restless, my dreams filled with leaping flames and the stink of burning paint. In the morning I went into the sunporch that doubles as my studio. I needed to see things, to touch them—my easel, my paints, the canvases hanging and the ones stacked against the walls. To reassure myself that everything was still there, still safe.

After the little ritual I felt steady enough to go see—and perhaps rescue—the last of Alicia's art.

The Dorchester Gallery was on Vallejo Street near Columbus, not far from the Parks and O'Meara office.

Walking toward it, I noticed that the Caffe Nonna was in the same block.

The aroma of roasting coffee enticed me in. The front section was an espresso bar; the restaurant was in the rear. I fortified myself with a latte and some chocolate-dipped biscotti before seeking out the manager. She confirmed that Craig Satterfield had worked both lunch and dinner shifts on the day Alicia's purse was stolen one hundred miles away at Turquoise Lake.

The cafe's walls had charming watercolors of Tuscan vineyards. The art on display in the Dorchester was of quite a different breed. The main exhibit was a series of painted checkerboards in colors that made the squares vibrate on the canvas. I watched orange and magenta boxes do a jig and tried to keep from going dizzy.

The clerk glided up to me. She was in her early twenties and very pretty, with brunette hair swept back from her face into a silver clip. Her blue dress was set off by a lapis pendant that somehow looked familiar. A namepin identified her as Noreen Zawicki.

"I see you're admiring these." Her voice was an unctuous ooze. "You have excellent taste. This artist is a wonderful investment, he made such a sensation in New York last year."

But her manner changed when I asked to see Alicia Satterfield's paintings.

"Oh, are you a friend of hers?" She fluttered like a bird; her voice became musical. "Such a shame, her dying like that. The pictures are in back. Just a minute—I'll get them."

The two small paintings she brought out struck me as rough and awkward, but they showed a certain promise. One depicted a vase of flowers, the sort of bouquet you might buy for a few dollars in a supermarket. The other was a landscape, a too-blue lake nestled among pine-studded hills.

"That's Turquoise Lake," Noreen said. "Pretty place, isn't it?"

"You've been there?" I asked.

"Oh, once or twice. Not for a long time, though." She stacked the paintings, preparing to hide them away again.

I put out a hand to stop her. "How much for these?" I asked.

"Well, they're not really for sale. Her husband left them so I could show the gallery owner, but she's on vacation. I sort of forgot we had them."

"In that case, let me take them. I'll return them to Craig." Or to Alicia—unless Alicia was really Carly.

Noreen looked flustered. "I—I don't know if that's a good idea. Maybe I better call him and see what he wants me to do."

She went to an alcove where a desk and computer were set up to create an office. I watched her punch out a phone number. After a moment she frowned and hung up.

"He's not there," she said. "Nothing personal, but after what happened last time I don't dare give these to you."

"Last time? What do you mean?"

"It was really strange. A woman came in and insisted she was Alicia Satterfield. Well, I knew Alicia Satterfield had passed away. I even went to her memorial service."

"What did this woman do?"

Noreen rubbed the blue stone of her necklace. "God, it was spooky. She looked so much like Alicia—Craig showed me his wife's picture, and the resemblance was amazing. She claimed these were her paintings, and when I said I knew the artist had died, she went berserk. I was about to call 911 when she stormed out. When I told Craig, he said some crazy woman had been following his wife around. So you see why I can't let them go without his permission."

"Well, thanks for showing them to me."

"Sure. Here, take one of these flyers. We've having a reception for the artist this weekend."

"Thanks," I said again. "Was this done on your computer over there?"

"That's right," Noreen said proudly. "I designed it. I do all our desktop publishing stuff."

The sun hit my eyes as I walked out of the gallery.

Walking back to the office, I used the flyer as a shade. Checkerboards danced in front of me the entire way.

"That snake! That skunk! That swine!" Alicia—or Carly—ran through a whole menagerie of curses. O'Meara came over and let her pet him because she didn't include Irish setters.

She had arrived at the appointed time, enveloped in the same paint-smeared shirt. I gave her a carefully edited version of my adventures on her behalf.

"I can't believe he burned them!" She was pacing like a caged tiger. "He said he loved me, and then he burned them! He's trying to destroy me! Just erase my whole existence! It's just like he's murdering me, only without bothering to kill me for real!"

"Be glad of that," I said.

"Yeah." Losing steam, she sank onto my visitor's chair. "What am I going to do? Everything's such a mess." She pressed her hands to her eyes, and her shoulders shook with sobs.

It was a convincing performance. But then, Craig said Carly was an excellent actress. O'Meara put his head on her knee, and she bent to hug him. I brought her a cup of tea. Gradually her crying slowed.

"Does the name Carly Michelson mean anything to you?" I asked, once the tea and O'Meara's sympathy had calmed her.

She didn't blink. "No. Who is she?"

Good question—I wished I knew the answer. "Maybe nobody."

"So now what do I do?" she moaned. "Our twenty-four hours is up."

I'd thought about that. "Why don't I keep at it just a little while longer."

"Really? Will you? Oh, thank God." Her sunbeam smiled flashed, then faded. "But what about tonight? The money you gave me is almost gone. Are you sure I can't stay with you? I'd love to see where you live and where you paint. I won't be any trouble, honest."

She reached for me, as if to grab hold and not let go. I felt myself jump back. I wanted to help Alicia Satterfield—but I did not want any Carly Michelson transferring murderous obsessions to me.

"Let me give the investigation the rest of the afternoon. Come back at seven and I'll buy you dinner."

"Okay." Giving O'Meara one more squeeze, she rose from the chair. At the doorway, she turned to me, fingering the crystal on her gold chain.

"Jess? Whatever happens, thanks for helping me."

Then she was gone.

Her gesture with the necklace reminded me: I'd seen Noreen do the same thing. And I realized why the gallery clerk's lapis pendant looked familiar.

It was a busy afternoon. I returned to the Dorchester Gallery with my Polaroid camera, waiting outside the open entrance door until I could snap my shot without being noticed. Then I carried the result over to Potrero Hill.

Back at the office I phoned to invite two more people to dinner. Both parties needed a bit of persuading. One I told the truth to; the other, I confess, I lured with white lies.

Then I called Caffe Nonna. I made a reservation for four, requesting a table in Craig Satterfield's station.

One of my guests was waiting in the espresso bar, nursing a cappuccino, when I arrived with Carly/Alicia in tow. He was a tall man with mahogany skin and a short-cropped frizz of black hair. As he rose to greet us, he aimed a traffic-stopping smile in her direction.

"Alicia Satterfield," I said, "meet Dalton Humphreys. He's a theatrical producer."

"Oh? How nice," she said vaguely—no spark of the interest I would have expected from a former drama student. She didn't seem to notice Humphreys' smile turn to a scowl. Well, I'd warned him I was going to use this little ruse; Alicia had said no police. And surely his Hollywoodish lime-green sports jacket wasn't his usual idea of plain clothes.

"What does a theatrical producer do?" Alicia was trying to make polite conversation. Humphreys stammered something unintelligible. Maybe this wasn't going to work after all.

The situation was saved when my third guest dashed in. Noreen was still in her deep blue dress, but—damn it—she was no longer wearing the lapis pendant.

I introduced her to Humphreys, the theater man. She started gushing at him in her high-priced-art-sales voice, only this time she was marketing herself. He began to relax into his part. It was just what I'd hoped for when I'd phoned her. I had noticed her musical voice, I told her, did she sing? A little, she admitted. Well, I knew a producer who was in town only for tonight, and I thought she might be right for a role he was casting. Was she interested in meeting him? Wow, was she ever!

Noreen didn't even notice Alicia as we were seated at our table. Alicia looked more and more perplexed, but she didn't say a word; she just shrank deeper into her big shirt.

At first I thought what happened next couldn't have timed itself better.

Talking to the Great Producer was making Noreen nervous. She fiddled with the neck of her dress and—bless her—pulled out the pendant.

Alicia's eyes widened at the sight of it.

At that instant our waiter arrived. He hardly looked at us as he set down a loaf of fresh-baked bread, a knife for slicing it, and a crock of butter. "Ciao, my name's Craig, I'll be your server toni—"

"Craig! Goddamn you!" Alicia jumped to her feet. "What are you doing here? What's *she* doing wearing my necklace?"

Noreen turned white. Clutching the blue stone, she moved toward Craig.

"You murderer!" Alicia screamed. "You tried to kill me!"

The dining room fell into abrupt silence. All eyes were on Alicia as she grabbed the bread knife and slashed it across Craig's face. A line of blood appeared, like a streak of red paint from a vandal's brush defiling a canvas.

Humphreys yanked back her arm as she lunged at Noreen.

Humphreys called in a paramedic, plus two uniforms in a black-and-white. They transported Noreen and Craig to the Hall of Justice. He took Alicia in his own car, generously allowing me to ride with her in the backseat.

"I didn't mean to hurt them," she said through tears. She leaned heavily against the door. She'd been shivering, and Humphreys had given her his sports jacket; its long sleeves almost hid the handcuffs that fastened her wrist to the armrest. "It's just . . . when I saw him I got so angry. I never knew a person could feel angry like that."

I tried to murmur something comforting.

"It was seeing that necklace that did it," she said. "It was my mother's. I took it to the lake with me, the earrings, too. They were in my purse when he stole it. How could he give my mother's jewelry to that . . . that . . ."

"Noreen stole your purse," I told her. "They were working together. She did up a fake death certificate on the gallery's computer. Craig had your mother's as a model. They used the false one to establish that you were dead."

"Yeah. Dead." She shuddered. "But they must have known I'd come back."

"They would insist you were Carly Michelson—crazy and dangerous. It might have worked."

"How did you figure it out?"

"Noreen didn't need to look up Craig's number when she phoned him. And the earrings I'd noticed at Craig's apartment matched her necklace. I think she was hiding in the bedroom when I was there. When I took a snapshot of Noreen to Hillside Realty, the manager identified her as the singer at your service."

We made the rest of the journey in silence. Alicia stared out at the bright city lights. Then, as Humphreys pulled into the parking lot, she said something I didn't quite catch.

"What was that?" I asked.

"I really loved him. Why couldn't he love me?" A long pause, and then: "Did he really burn my paintings?"

"I don't know," I said gently. "But I think so."

Humphreys opened the car door on Alicia's side. "All out, ladies. We're here."

Alicia blinked at the lights of the Hall of Justice. Swaddled in the lime-green jacket, she looked fragile and lost. In a way, I thought, Craig had killed his wife after all. He had destroyed her art and her love—two things that defined who she was.

I was left behind as Humphreys took Alicia away to file assault charges against her and book her into jail.

D. C. Brod lives in St. Charles, Illinois, and is the author of the Quint McCauley series. Her most recent McCauley novel was Murder in Store. *"Mission to St. Bride's" finds McCauley on vacation, and if that's not unusual enough, he's in England.*

MISSION TO ST. BRIDE'S

by D. C. Brod

I CAN'T SAY no to old ladies. Not even when I know they're using me. One minute Elsa Turnbull was explaining her problem to me and the next she's telling me how I'm going to fix it. Two days later I'm on a ferry chugging toward a remote little island off the west coast of England in the company of a short, overweight dog of a certain age. His name is Nigel. Nigel Turnbull, I guess. Mine is Quint McCauley. When I'm not tumbling to the spell of some old lady, I try to earn a living as a private detective in a river town west of Chicago.

For me to take a vacation at all is impulsive. But I needed one. Both personal and business matters had left me in a state where I couldn't get my head clear enough to fall asleep until the four a.m. bird was chirping outside my window. Then it was all I could do to drag my ass out of bed in the morning. The idea of walking the Cornwall country-side, refueling with a pint of bitter at a local pub, seemed a likely cure. Then a friend from high school who lived in Truro but took his family to Spain for the winter offered me their flat for a couple weeks. I figured once fate got involved, I shouldn't fight it.

I've been to England before and I like to go in the off-season. Early March definitely qualified as such. I knew I couldn't expect much from the weather, but then I figured if you're going to England for the weather you're deluded anyway.

Once my landlady, Louise Orwell, heard I was visiting her homeland, she made me promise to look up her sister in Penzance. Since I was going to be in Cornwall anyway, that didn't seem to be a problem. Besides, if she was Louise's sister, then I wanted to meet her.

I wasn't disappointed. Elsa Turnbull turned out to be an attractive, energetic woman with an independent streak a mile wide. She was probably a few years older than Louise—which put her in her early seventies—but had that same youthful exuberance and determined carriage. I took her out to dinner and practically had to arm wrestle her for the bill.

After dinner she invited me to join her for tea the next day, and hinted there was something she wanted to talk to me about. I should have known then that my days as a carefree traveler were numbered.

"I'm too much of a lady to go chasing after a man." She poured a steaming cup of tea from a pot speckled with small purple flowers. Then she poised a creamer over the cup and looked up at me, eyebrow arched. I nodded. I wouldn't think of putting anything in my coffee, but there was something about tea that said "drink me white."

Nigel had joined us in the sitting room. He was one of those small, rather corpulent black-and-white dogs with short legs and tiny paws that clicked across tile floor. You see his type with old couples and instantly understand that this family has three members. Now he was settling on the sofa next to Elsa. After a minute, he situated himself on his haunches, legs splayed, and proceeded to stare at me. I wanted to tell him to sit up straight.

Elsa leaned back into the cushion with her own cup and sighed as she gazed at the black-and-white photo on the table next to her. The subject of the photo and her sigh was a round-faced man with wispy white hair and a pleasant smile. He didn't look like a bounder. She nibbled on a scone and returned it to its plate. "I'm really quite good at judging a person's character. I'm sure I wasn't wrong about Elliot."

"You said he went for a week's holiday. Where did he go?"

"St. Bride's. It's an island just west of Cornwall. He was staying at the cottage of a friend." She paused and added, "A male friend."

"Elsa," this was always awkward, "did you loan Elliot any money that he hasn't paid back?"

She appeared genuinely confused as she brushed crumbs from her fingertips. Then her eyes widened. "Oh, I see what you mean." Then she quickly added. "No, I wouldn't do that. Money only muddies a relationship."

"When was he supposed to come back?"

"Last Saturday."

That was five days ago.

"You see," she continued, "he would've had to take a launch to the main island, then a ferry back to Penzance. Neither is very dependable this time of year. So much depends on weather. But I checked and there was both a launch from St. Bride's and a ferry that came back from the big island. He should have been on it."

"Did you try to call Elliot?"

"Yes I did, but there was no answer at the cottage."

I shrugged. "Maybe he decided to extend his vacation on the mainland."

She shook her head. "No. He had promised me we'd go to the theater last Sunday. Elliot is always good as his word." She chewed on her lower lip for a moment. "I'm afraid that something dreadful has happened to him." She stopped talking then, taking a moment to pet Nigel's pointed little head before going back to her tea. "I feel so helpless," she murmured.

Vulnerability seemed out of character for this woman who, the previous night, had made minced meat of our waiter for pouring an inferior glass of port. But I wasn't about to challenge her.

I didn't cherish the thought of boating out to a remote island that was probably windswept and treeless, but I did like this woman. Besides, how could I tell Louise that I'd refused to help her sister? The chair creaked as I shifted my weight. "Would you like me to check out the island?"

Her eyes brightened as she sat up. Even Nigel sat up. "Oh, Quint, would you?"

Like she didn't know all along. "I can spare a few days."

"Oh, that's wonderful." She clapped her hands and glanced at Nigel, who was wagging his wiry little tail. "I've booked a ticket on the ferry for you and Nigel . . ."

I cut her off. "Nigel? Nigel's coming?"

She tilted her head and smiled a smile that would have melted glaciers. "Oh, he so loves the ferry, the sea air. He won't be any trouble. You'll enjoy each other's company."

I managed a grim smile as I returned the cup to its saucer. Perfect.

"You'll love the ferry too," she said.

Wrong. I might have loved the ferry if it had been midsummer and the sea hadn't been so active. I made the mistake of buying a pint of ale when the bar opened. For the remainder of the journey I fixated on its motion in my stomach.

Nigel, however, proved to be quite the trooper. Obviously he'd done this before. While we were waiting to board the ferry, he relieved himself over the side of the pier. I was impressed.

After two and a half hours, we docked at the main island in the early afternoon. It was a bright, clear day with a breeze that cut right through you. Only one other person was heading to St. Bride's. He was a weathered old man with pale, wrinkled skin and cheeks red with broken capillaries from the beating they'd taken by the wind. He nodded at me, but didn't speak. I tried to initiate a conversation, but my attempts were met with noncommittal grunts.

The launch assistant who collected the three pounds this was costing me proved much more sociable. I asked him if he could recommend a place to stay on the island.

"There's two places really." He stood facing me, one leg up on the bench. His face was showing the effects of the wind even though he was barely out of his twenties. He squinted into the sun and continued, "One's a fancy new tourist place with saunas and all that—The Bayside Hotel." He frowned. "Doubt that it's open now. Off-season, y'know. The place is owned and run by folks from the mainland. This time of year there's probably nobody there. The other's a small place with a few rooms and a tiny pub. Not what I'd call luxury, but sure to be open." He chuckled. "With the beating they're getting from the other place, I guess they can't afford to close."

All I wanted was a room. If there was a pub attached, I didn't think a man could ask for much more.

I asked him about the group of islands.

"They get most of their money during the season from the tourist trade. This time of year there's not much going on, I'm afraid."

"How many people live on St. Bride's during off-season?"

"Just a handful. Maybe fifty, sixty. Cars aren't allowed on the island," he added. "Only tourist transports to The Bayside and farm machinery."

"Is this the only launch from St. Bride's to the main island?"

"Sure is."

"So, if anyone had to connect with the ferry, you're the only option?"

"That's right."

Elsa had given me a photo of Elliot—the same one as

was in the frame, only smaller. I took it out now and showed it to the young man. "Do you remember taking him back to the main island?"

He studied it for a moment, frowning to himself. "I remember taking him out a couple weeks ago. But if he came back, it wasn't on the launch."

"I thought you said this was the only way back."

"I said it was the only way to connect to the ferry, but if the weather was all right, he might've taken a helicopter to the mainland." He shrugged. "If he was in a hurry, you know."

"The island has a heliport?"

"Sure. It's by the new hotel." Nodding in that general direction, he added, "Guess those folks are the ones who can afford to fly."

As I returned the photo to my pocket I noticed that I now had the old man's full attention. For the rest of the ride, he never took his eyes from me. By the time we docked at St. Bride's, even Nigel was getting edgy.

The Inn, as it was called, was maybe a quarter of a mile from the pier. Nigel and I walked toward it down a dirt road. On one side was a seawall and the other a row of cottages. The remnants of what looked like an ancient fortress dominated a spit of land jutting out beyond the bay. I was surprised by the sight of a few palm trees in the small yards and the relatively lush vegetation. It was warmer than I imagined it would be, though not balmy by any means, but the effects of the Gulf Stream were in evidence. I passed only one person on my way to The Inn, a middle-aged woman bundled up in a bulky, blue coat and a long, black scarf. She was coming out of one of the cottages and when she saw me, she stopped and stared as I passed. Fifty feet later, I glanced back at her and saw that she was still staring.

The Inn looked much like the cottages, only bigger— gray stone with a rust-colored roof. The pub was, indeed, just a room, with a few comfortable chairs, two tables, and small bar with inverted bottles lining the wall behind it, but judging from the activity behind this room, some serious remodeling was in progress. Off the bar was a hallway with a door on either side and a stairway at the end. In the distance, I heard a telephone ring twice. I tapped a silver, cone-shaped bell, wondering if anyone could hear the "ding" over the sawing and pounding. I dropped my suitcase on the carpeted floor and settled onto a bar stool. When I looked down I saw that Nigel was a pub dog at heart—Elsa would never convince me otherwise. This little guy was curled up around the bar stool. He even appeared mildly interested in his surroundings, such as they were. As I began to think that we might get along after all, one of the doors in the hallway opened and a young woman stepped out. She was smiling as though being visited by some pleasant thought, but when she stepped into the room and saw me, the smile turned into a gape. What was it about this place? I was beginning to feel like Vlad the Impaler.

Since she seemed frozen in time, I figured I'd better initiate the conversation. "Can I get a pint of that Speckled Hen and a room? In that order?"

After a few more seconds of a stare, she pushed a lock of shoulder-length blond hair behind her ear. "I'm afraid there's a problem. We're not open to roomers yet."

"Oh," I said, noting that, despite her horror at the sight of me, she really did seem sorry about there being no room at the inn. I gestured toward the bitter tap. "Is that open?"

She studied me for a moment, apparently considering her options, then stepped behind the bar and took a glass down from a shelf. She was probably in her mid-twenties with clear blue eyes and a nervous smile. Her heavy sweater looked as though it came compliments of one of the sheep that dotted Cornwall's hills.

"Can you suggest a place I can stay? The launch won't be back for two days. Hate to have to camp out on the beach."

She stared into the glass as she drew the Speckled Hen.

My stomach had settled quickly since I'd gotten off the ferry. I helped myself to a bowl of peanuts. "Name's Quint McCauley," I said.

"Cathy," she said, venturing a quick glance at me.

That was a start. "Know where I might stay?" I repeated.

She finished drawing the bitter and set it in front of me, then looked off as though hoping someone would come bail her out of this situation. Finally she said, "Give me a minute," and left.

I drank my bitter, enjoying the taste and sensation as it traveled down my throat. It occurred to me that I hadn't asked about Nigel. I just assumed, this being England, a country where people take their pets very seriously, he would be no problem.

True to her word, Cathy came back a minute later. "Derek'll be out in a minute. He's the manager."

"I'm sorry to cause you trouble," I said, reaching into my shirt pocket, "it's just that I'm on sort of a mission."

She scrunched her eyebrows together. "A mission?"

"Do you remember Elliot Pierce? He was on the island a couple weeks ago." I held the photo out to her, but she didn't look at it.

"I don't think so."

"Here's his picture." I stuck it under her nose.

"Oh," she said, backing off some. "I guess I do. He came in for meals sometimes. Lovely man." (She pronounced it "loovely.")

"He went back on the launch last Saturday." This was a new voice, and I assumed that Derek had joined us. I turned and looked up at a man who filled the archway into the hall. He wore a white shirt with its sleeves rolled up and a small gold hoop earring in his right earlobe. He easily had several inches on my six feet. Judging from the sawdust on his shoulders and in his hair, I figured that, in addition to being the manager, he was also a carpenter. Apparently he didn't need to look at the photo, so I returned it to my pocket.

"I don't think he did," I said. "At least that's what the guy on the launch told me. Said he brought him here but didn't bring him back."

Cathy crossed her arms over her chest. "Might've taken a helicopter," she offered.

The man nodded. "That's probably what he did." He folded his arms over his chest and leaned against the bar.

"Don't mean to be inhospitable, but we aren't exactly prepared for tourists this time of year and, as you can hear, we're a bit of mess right now." He glanced at Cathy, who was wiping the already spotless bar. "Surprised you didn't try the new place first. That's where most Americans like to spend their money." There was no missing the bitterness in that statement.

"Well, the guy on the launch said it probably wasn't open. But when I heard this was the place with a pub, I didn't care if it was open. No contest."

He studied me as though trying to get a reading on the bullshit meter. Finally he shrugged. "Well, guess we can't throw you out on the beach. We'll get a room made up for you."

"I'd appreciate it." I wasn't sure what prompted the change in attitude, but opted to keep my mouth shut. No telling when they might turn on me again.

They put me in a room on the second floor with a view of the road behind The Inn which, Cathy told me, cut across the island to the bay on the opposite side. The room itself was small, but comfortable with the usual amenities. Cathy stood in the door as I began to unpack my one bag. She'd refused a tip, so that wasn't what kept her here. Finally she said, "Are you a friend of Mr. Pierce's?"

"Not really. I'm a friend of a ladyfriend of his. Apparently he never made it home. She's worried."

Cathy frowned and stared at the floor. "Maybe he went to one of the other islands."

"How would he get there?"

She shrugged. "Probably the launch, but if one of the fishermen were going that way, he might've gotten a lift."

"Who can I ask about that?"

"Try down by the pier."

"I'll do that. Thanks."

Nigel and I spent the afternoon walking around the island. It was less than a mile wide and maybe two miles long. Far from being windswept and treeless, the island was lush with vegetation, some of it tropical. I was a little sorry I wasn't in a position to enjoy it. There weren't many shops and hardly any of them were open this time of year. We stopped at the post office/grocery store and I showed Elliot's picture to the woman stocking a bin with small, red potatoes. She allowed that she might have seen Elliot in the store now and then, but offered no more. I flagged down a farmer lumbering down the road on his tractor and held the photo up to him. He just shook his head, then barely gave me time to jump out of his way before he sped up. I asked a few other people I came across. No one was downright rude, but no one was anywhere near helpful either. And no one who recalled Elliot seemed at all distressed or even curious about his disappearance.

The Inn was on the sheltered side of the island. On the other side, the rocks were craggier and the sea more volatile. The Bayside Hotel sprawled out along the bay like a crystal fortress. With all its glass and glitter, it seemed out of place on this island studded with stone houses and crumbling castles. The hotel appeared deserted and there were no boats in sight. The heliport was behind the hotel, but there was no one around to tell me if Elliot had been whisked off the island.

At the pier where the launch had dropped me, I was ignored by one fisherman and sneered at by another who said he'd never seen Elliot, then spat into the water.

"Don't be offended. A man gets used to having no one to talk to during the winter. Takes a while to get the tongue going again."

The raspy voice was coming from a trawler tied to the pier. I looked down and saw a short man with a big belly squatting over the engine. He wiped the grease from his hands onto a soiled, white cloth. "Name's Gordie Miller."

I nodded and introduced myself.

He squinted up at me. "You're asking about that Pierce fellow, aren't you?"

"You remember him?"

"Sure do. Took him over to Wilkes Island 'bout a week ago."

"Why did he want to go there?"

"Puffins. There's a big puffin colony there."

The old puffin story. "How'd he plan to get back?"

Gordie shrugged. "Hitch a ride like he did going out or wait for the launch."

"Don't suppose you'd be headed that way anytime soon?"

"Sorry."

I didn't say anything for a minute, just stared at him. Given the fact that prior to this encounter, no one had offered me the time of day much less their name, I was inclined to be skeptical. "I didn't know Elliot was a bird-watcher."

Gordie smiled, revealing tobacco-stained teeth. "Charming little creatures they are. Hard not to fancy them."

Sure.

I ate dinner in the pub and was served my Cornish pasty by Cathy. As far as I could tell, she and Derek were running the place, probably not an astounding task when no one was there. I was struck by her pleasant manner. Whether I was placing an order or she was picking up my dirty dishes, she'd murmur "lovely" or "thank you." I could do no wrong. Could people this nice be responsible for the disappearance of an innocent old man? Clearly they knew something. None of them—except maybe Gordie—were good actors. Of course, what if Elliot wasn't all that innocent? I only knew him through Elsa's adoring eyes. What if he were involved in drug running or gun smuggling? There was something about this little snatch of islands that harkened back to pirates and ships bearing the Jolly Roger. It was easy to allow the imagination to swim in that direction. Puffin trafficking. Yeah, that was probably it.

I woke at three a.m., and stiffened when I felt something cold on my neck. After a moment I realized it was only Nigel's nose. My relief was tempered by the fact that he was advising me he had to go out. Apparently his bladder wasn't what it used to be. Well, whose was? But he was patient—nothing over the top about Nigel—and watched as I pulled on jeans and a sweatshirt.

It was a clear night, surprisingly mild, and while Nigel

went about his business, I gazed up at the sky full of stars. Amazing. They'd have been even more prominent if the moon weren't almost full, but then I'd have had a lot of trouble seeing where I was going without the moon. God, but it was dark here.

Nigel decided a stroll was in order, and I let him choose the course, which was down the road behind our room toward the new hotel.

We'd been walking for almost twenty minutes when I first heard the voices—shouts in the distance, which increased in volume as we neared the water. I'd taken Nigel off his leash and he trotted a few feet ahead of me. I had images of walking into the midst of a wild beach party, but once we rounded the bend and the bay opened up before us I was stunned by the sight of at least ten fishing boats out in the bay, blazing lights trained down into the water. The boats comprised a huge semicircle as they made their way toward the shore, gradually closing the circle. It looked like they were herding in a school of fish. Or something. I could see them hauling objects out of the water, using nets and pulling them onto the boats. Maybe they were crates of some kind, but there wasn't enough light to be certain. Nigel and I stood and watched as the boats neared the shore, and I could hear voices calling orders to one another. I couldn't make out what they were saying, but I thought I recognized Gordie's raspy voice.

A small creature skittered past us, catching Nigel by surprise. He let out a series of poorly timed, high-pitched yaps. I grabbed him and wrapped my hand around his snout. As he struggled against me, one of the boats turned its light on the shore and pinned us in its glare. I ducked next to the seawall, but it was too late.

The pitch of the voices increased their intensity and two of the boats split off from the rest, heading toward the pier. I tucked Nigel under my arm and ran for it. My instinct was to get off the road, move in toward the center of the island where there was more vegetation, more cover.

I found shelter in a small grove of trees behind the hotel, about fifty feet off the road. From there I could hear activ-

ity on the road—voices, shouting—but unless someone
stumbled on top of us we'd be all right until morning. Not
that I saw any way out of this. We were on an island, so our
options were limited. My guess was that by morning
everyone on the island would be hunting us. All they had to
do was wait us out.

Sometime before morning, I drifted off. I woke, stiff and
damp, and gradually became aware of a crunching sound.
When I sat up and turned, there was a black-and-white goat
calmly chewing twigs. It was tethered to a stake planted in
the middle of someone's yard. So much for great hiding
places. The animal watched me dispassionately, swallowed,
and began foraging for more twigs. Nigel had wandered off.
Probably figured he was better off without me. Probably
right. I considered my options. The launch was due back
tomorrow. I could find a place near the dock to hide, then
make a run for it. Of course, that was precisely what they'd
expect me to do. I brushed myself off and, keeping low to
the ground, moved away from the house. After that I began
to wander, using the rocks and vegetation as cover.

I toyed with the idea of stealing a boat and heading
toward one of the islands visible from St. Bride's. But what
I knew about sailing would fit on a postage stamp. However,
helicopters were something else again. These people might
expect me to try to get a lift off the island from one of the
chopper pilots, but they wouldn't expect me to fly it off
myself. It'd been more years than I cared to recall since I'd
flown choppers during my stint with the army, but I might
remember just enough to get it off the ground and to the
main island. I settled in among a rock formation between the
heliport and the ocean. Sooner or later a chopper was bound
to come. I waited.

I'd positioned myself on high ground so I saw him
coming when he was still a good quarter of a mile away. He
made an occasional side trip, sniffing out a tree or a bush
along the way, but it was uncanny the way Nigel persisted
in my direction. I'd gotten to like the little dog and might
have been genuinely pleased to see him again if he weren't
being followed, at a discreet distance, by Derek and Gordie.

Running seemed pointless. I'd chosen the best cover—
everything else was wide open. There wasn't much I could
do but wait it out.

When Nigel found me, he licked my face. Derek and
Gordie looked down at me like they were really disappointed in me. Then Derek bent over, grabbed my arm, and
pulled me up. "Come on."

I swallowed.

Nigel literally bounded after us as they led me down a
narrow road toward the ocean and the cliffs. Neither Gordie
nor Derek spoke as we made our way up the path. I had
images of Elliot's broken body at the bottom of some cliff
being picked at by the gulls. Thoughts of escape did occur
to me—neither Gordie nor Derek had shown me a weapon—
but again, where was I supposed to go?

At the end of the path was not just a cliff, but a cliff and
a cottage overlooking the bay—a gray stone cottage with a
red door that had been beaten dull by the wind. To my relief
we headed toward the cottage rather than the cliff. Derek
pushed open the door and shoved me inside.

I stumbled into a large room. To the right was a kitchen
and to the left a living area with a great stone fireplace.
Sitting in a recliner facing the fire was Elliot Pierce. He
looked up from the book in his lap and, smiling, toasted me
with a glass of sherry. "Welcome to Dolphin Cottage," he
said.

I glanced behind me to see Gordie shut the door and
position himself in front of it, arms crossed above his belly.

"Does somebody want to tell me what's going on here?"

Derek gestured toward a chair, smaller than Elliot's but
also facing the fire. "Have a seat."

I did. It seemed preferable to being shoved off a cliff.
Derek pulled up a chair from the kitchen table and straddled
it, arms draped over the back. "You know too much."

"Not really," I answered, perhaps too quickly.

I glanced at Gordie who, for some reason, seemed mildly
amused.

"Are you talking about that stuff you were hauling in last

night?" I asked, then blundered on. "Because if you are, then you should know that I didn't see what it was."

Derek told me. "Wood."

I blinked once, twice. "Wood?"

"Pitch pine planks."

I shook my head, still confused. I heard someone chuckling.

"You know that remodeling we're doing?" Derek said. "The bar we're adding, the tables we're building. All the materials are coming from lumber that's washing up on our shores."

"Can you believe it? " Elliot chortled. "Just washed up on the shore!"

"A couple weeks ago a ship—probably somewhere between the Bristol Channel and Biscay—jettisoned its load of lumber. Most of it headed straight for St. Bride's. Washed right up on the shore." Derek smiled at the memory. "Incredible."

"Why would someone jettison their payload?"

"Lots of reasons. Like taking on water in bad weather. Better to lose the load than the ship."

"You don't know whose it was?"

He shook his head. "No. And it doesn't matter. It's ours now. Legally, it belongs to anyone who salvages it." Derek shifted in the chair. "There's a lot of competition for tourists on these islands. We've been hurting since they built The Bayside, which is owned by folks from the mainland who bring in their own staff to run it. The Inn is owned by a bunch of the locals. We were falling way behind. Then this windfall." He opened his arms wide.

"And you don't want to share the wealth?"

"We don't want folks coming from all over fishing lumber out of our waters. That's all."

I turned to Elliot. "And you tumbled on this?"

"Oh, I came here right when it was happening. Didn't catch them in the act. Nothing that exciting. But I did overhear Gordie talking with Derek."

"So, you're stuck here. Until when?"

"Just a few more days," Elliot said. "Five at the most, isn't that what you said, Gordie?"

Gordie nodded. "We just want to make sure we've gotten the full harvest. Besides, there's a crew from the new hotel coming then. Too many people to keep a secret."

"So I'm stuck here too," I said and no one corrected me. Both Derek and Gordie were watching me with straight faces. "This is ridiculous. I'm not going to say anything about this to anyone. Why would I?"

"Sorry," Derek said, his tone matter-of-fact. "We've got too much riding on this to take you at your word."

"Unbelievable," I muttered.

"You walked into it." Derek shrugged.

Nigel walked into it, I thought. I just followed him.

"I just don't like not having choices," I said to him.

Derek stared at the floor for a minute, then looked up at me again. "All right. I'll give you a choice. You can spend the next five days running around the island, maybe freezing to death, or you can stay here. All you can eat."

"And drink?" I asked.

Derek nodded.

Elliot had hauled himself out of the big chair and was rummaging around in the kitchen.

I looked out the window at the cliffs and the beach beyond them. The tide was out and the sea gulls were swooping over the cliffs. I thought I heard one laughing. "Can I walk around if I want to?"

"Sure."

I studied Nigel, who was stretched out by the fire, warming his toes. "Let me see if I have this straight. We sit around for five days, enjoying the scenery? You supply us with food and ale? Once we leave here we're free to talk all we want?"

Derek nodded.

Elliot handed me a sherry glass and filled it.

I looked up at him. "You think Elsa will buy this story?"

He smiled as he refilled his own glass. "We have five days. Plenty of time to dream up another one."

Married to Max Allan Collins, Barbara Collins has recently embarked on her own writing career and has come far fast. Already her stories are staples in the popular Cat Crimes *books, and she also recently appeared in* Murder for Father *and* Murder for Mother. *With "Love Nest" she introduces father-daughter P.I. team Sam and Rebecca Knight and tells the story in both their distinctive voices. This is a giant step forward as a writer, not her first, and definitely not her last.*

LOVE NEST

by Barbara Collins

THE NAME'S SAM Knight, and if you never heard of me, don't worry about it—you will. At least, if my daughter Becky—and don't *you* ever call her that—has her way. And Becky usually gets her way.

Sure, I've done a few jobs over the years that caught some press attention, the most sordid of which was a wife-killed-husband-for-his-money number that got me written up in *People* magazine. But what the hell kind of gauge is that? That article drummed up more crank phone calls than business.

But to hear Becky—Rebecca—talk, you'd think I was Mike Hammer. And let me tell you, there are differences between me and Mike Hammer. First, I've fired a gun, on the job, a grand total of twice. Never killed a man in my life, a proud record I hope to maintain.

Second, Mike Hammer gets laid once in a while.

Becky's my only child. I wanted a son, and it looks like I finally got my wish: my little girl has grown up into a goddamn businessman.

Not that I'm not proud of her—and not that I'm not relieved she got her brains from her mother. The only thing she got from me was some college money, and you don't want to know what those fancy-ass degrees of hers cost me.

We'd never been too close, which is my fault, no question; so I was surprised when she showed up on my doorstep last Christmas after being fired from that company she worked for in Minneapolis. I was proud of her, though, for not putting up with those conniving bastards.

They had tried to get her to use information culled from one client to the advantage of another, better-paying client.

"That's not my idea of ethics," she had said grandly.

"In my game," I told her, nodding, "you treat a client like a priest treats a confessor."

She seemed to like the sound of that as much as I liked the sound of a word like "ethics" coming from her.

Anyway, we sat around the kitchen table, me mostly keeping my mouth shut, her yakking, trying to figure out what she was going to do. . . .

She kept mentioning needing a product . . . something she could use her experience, her know-how, to market herself. I bobbed my head up and down, like I knew what the hell she was talking about, but was just trying to give her a little support. Little late for me to act like a father, but I guess till the final whistle blows, you're still in the game.

Then she looked at me with her mother's big brown eyes and said that I'd never realized my full potential . . . never taken advantage of my reputation. That *I* could be that "product" she was looking for.

"Is that what I am to you?" I asked her. "A potential 'product'? A Popiel Pocket Fisherman for the nineties?"

That stopped her cold; she didn't say a word—but the look on her face was so damn pitiful.

I'd slapped her once, when she was little, for some terrible infraction, like spilling a soft drink or dropping a jam-covered spoon. She hadn't cried. What was she, ten? She'd just looked at me quiveringly with a hurt that had nothing to do with pain.

I had never hit her again, no matter how deeply drowning in my cups I was.

But now here she was, all grown up, giving me that same quiveringly hurt look.

Maybe I saw this as a shot at reconciliation. A chance to be there for her, when I hadn't been while she was growing up, when I was too busy working and drinking and running around on her mother. She was out of the house by the time I cleaned up my act. At least her mother, God rest her soul, had a few good years with a sober, faithful husband.

But as a father to the little girl she'd been, and to this would-be big businesswoman she'd grown up into, I stunk.

So—before the whistle blew—I figured I better go along with her, and her half-baked scheme. Only I was underestimating my daughter—her scheme was fully baked, all right.

Six months ago, I closed the office over on Sixth and University where I'd been for twenty years, and we moved into a pretentious marble tombstone of a building downtown, where the rent is about equal to my total billings last year.

But I'll be damned if we aren't making a go of it.

She hired a secretary—a heavyset woman with no sense of humor and the face of Ernest Borgnine (I had interviewed just the right blonde for the job, but Becky said overweight women were often prejudiced against)—and a computer nerd, and two inexperienced minority graduates from Drake University. All of whom, including Ms. Borgnine, are doing a hell of a job.

Becky knows how to run a business, all right. But she doesn't know jack shit about the detective game.

Me, I'm mostly a figurehead, putting in a cameo appearance each day before hitting the rubber-chicken circuit. Otherwise, you can find me at Barney's Pub, watching

ESPN on the big screen, pretending an O'Doul's is a real beer.

My big bitch with Becky is this snobbish attitude she has about who our clientele should be . . . not wanting to "deal with trivial matters."

"People don't come to private detectives for 'trivial' reasons," I said.

"We don't want to deal with people," Becky said. "We want to deal with corporations."

Becky, like most liberals, has great compassion for the masses and complete contempt for individual human beings.

I thought it was time she learned what our business was really about—flesh and blood . . . people with problems that need solving, not bottom lines or high profiles or market shares.

So, yesterday, after I'd come back from Barney's to discover she was out getting a perm, I took just the sort of case she would have turned her turned-up nose at.

The sort of case that would really curl her hair.

Rebecca Knight is the name, though it's unlikely you've ever heard of me. But it's a safe bet you've heard of *Sam* Knight—my father.

The Satariano case? The Hollingsworth murder trial? The Sniper of Keo Way? Any of those ring a bell?

I thought as much. After all, *People* magazine called him "the most famous real-life Sam Spade alive."

Recently we've gone into business together, operating *Knight and Associates* out of an elegant modern marble Art Deco building in downtown Des Moines. It's high-rise and high rent, but then so is the profile it provides.

You may be thinking I'm using my father's reputation to make a name for myself. Wrong. Following in my father's flatfoot-steps was *never* an ambition of mine. For one thing, I wear a size six; and for another, neither Dad nor Nancy Drew was my role model.

I'm strictly a businesswoman: BA from the University of Iowa; MBA from the University of Minnesota. I held a

position in marketing at a prestigious Minneapolis corporation (which shall remain nameless for legal reasons); but a
year ago I resigned—I got tired of being verbally pawed by
sexists and bumping up against the glass ceiling.

On a holiday visit home, I told my father I'd quit, and that
what I really wanted was to go into business for myself, to
be my *own* boss. I had the skills, and the background—all
I needed was the right product to promote.

Imagine my surprise when Dad suggested that *he* should
be the "product"!

Still, stunned as I was, I could immediately see the
potential. We would capitalize on *his* reputation and *my*
business skills, and turn a run-down, antiquated one-man
operation into a state-of-the-art, thriving investigative firm!

That was six months ago. Dad moved out of his tiny
office in a distressed section of town, and we moved into
our suite of offices at towering 801 Grand. I hired a
receptionist, a computer whiz, a couple of topflight young
investigators.

I run the day-to-day operations. Dad's in the office a
couple of hours each day, but mostly he's out in the field, or
drumming up business. And I've listed him with a speaker's
bureau, so he's often out giving nostalgic talks about his big
cases before the Kiwanis and other business groups.

Our biggest area of disagreement (politics doesn't count)
is the direction of the business. *I* feel the greatest percentage
of our cases should come from the many nationally prominent insurance companies situated here in Iowa's capital
city. The work is steady, clean, and lucrative.

But *he* seems to feel that just about any financially or
emotionally impaired person that might wander through our
doors deserves our immediate and full attention.

Which is why we're barely speaking right now.

It was the middle of the afternoon when I returned to the
office after a very successful meeting with the CEO of
Mutual Insurance. Coming out our glass door was a woman
with long stringy blond hair. I guessed her age to be about
thirty. Her face was pretty, but hard; the kind of hard a

woman gets from too much smoking or drinking or both. She wore torn cutoff jeans and a tight polka-dot top with the shoulders cut out; the outfit might have been cute on someone younger and thinner.

The woman looked right at me, yet through me, then disappeared down the hall.

Inside, I asked Evie, our receptionist, "Who was that?"

"A new client," she answered, fingers clicking on the keyboard.

"That was a *client*? Of *ours*?"

Evie stopped typing and looked up at me. "According to your father," she said, arching an eyebrow. Then she shrugged and returned to her work.

I turned and marched down the carpeted corridor to his office.

He was lying on the couch, shoes off, crossed feet in well-worn socks, a cigarette in one hand, ashes dotting the front of his not-so-white shirt, reading the sports section of the *Des Moines Register*.

"I'm back," I said, forcibly cheerful.

"Oh . . . ah . . . hello, pumpkin," my father said. He sat up on the couch, ashes and newspapers falling to the floor.

Pumpkin? He *never* calls me that.

I narrowed my eyes.

He cleared his throat.

"I took on a new client while you were gone," he told me, "and . . ." He stopped and sniffed the air. "You get a perm again?"

"Never mind," I said irritably. "I want to hear about this client."

He gestured for me to sit next to him on the couch, but I remained standing.

"Look," he explained, "I just couldn't turn the poor kid down. . . ."

"Poor is right. And she hasn't been a 'kid' since *Mary Tyler Moore* wasn't a rerun."

His eyes flared—a hint of the rage he could summon that I remembered all too well from childhood. He was doing his best to keep it in check when he said, "Damn it, Becky, when are you going to realize this business isn't just about money?"

"Okay. Fine. Just please tell me this isn't a marital surveillance job."

He began putting on his shoes, brown Florsheim wingtips. "The folder's on the desk with a picture of the husband," he said.

I sighed. "Well, it's *your* time."

He was standing now, reaching for his coat on the back of the couch. "She insisted the surveillance start tonight," he went on, "and, unfortunately, you've got me speaking to some damn PLO or PEO club this evening."

"*What?*" I was beginning to smell a rat, a big one in Florsheim shoes. "So you'll cancel the talk," I suggested.

Snugging his tie—a Nichole Miller print I'd given him last Christmas—he stopped to look at me. "And disappoint a bunch of little old ladies who are dying to meet me?" he asked. "Now how would that look?" He paused, then added, "Word'll get around your 'product' is unreliable."

He was making me furious. I said, "Then put one of the other investigators on the surveillance!"

My father shook his head. "They're both working over-time on that embezzlement case that goes to court next week . . . *you* know that." His expression turned concil-iatory, and he patted my shoulder. "Everything you'll need is in the folder."

"But . . ."

"See you tomorrow, pumpkin." He smiled, going out the door, doing that magic trick every card-carrying parent can perform so well.

". . . *Da-ad!*"

Turning me back into a five-year-old.

I was not happy, hiding in my car in the parking lot of a country-western bar on Euclid. Still in my jacket and skirt from work, I was feeling grungy, even if they were Armani.

It was almost midnight, and the bar—Heartthrob—had stayed busy all evening, the tuneless, twanging music from inside leaching out every time someone entered or left the dilapidated building; men and women of all shapes and sizes in country-style apparel that seemed more like costumes than clothing, looking for a little laughter, a little love, a little lust. . . .

Tired, I leaned back against the headrest and closed my eyes. In my mind I could see the photo "our" client had given us of her husband and herself.

His name was Lyle. He was tall, muscular, confident, with sandy hair and a charismatic, if smirky, grin. The wife's name was Mary, and she was smiling at him, obviously in love, one arm around his waist, a little too tight, as if she instinctively knew how hard it would be holding onto this one. Still, if the picture had appeared in a tabloid, the caption would have read, *In happier times*.

But I wondered if there really had been any happier times for her, or simply the illusion of it, because she'd always been afraid of losing him to someone taller, thinner, prettier. . . .

I opened my eyes and he was standing just outside the door to the bar, kissing the neck of a woman who looked a lot like his wife.

Only taller, thinner, prettier.

I shrank behind the wheel of my Buick, an unwilling, embarrassed voyeur, as the two pawed at each other, doing a drunken mating dance, like some kind of new country two-step, until suddenly he grabbed her roughly by the hand and pulled her toward his truck.

They got in the cab of the black Chevy, and I was wondering if they were going to stay in there all night, when he started the engine and pulled out of the parking lot.

I followed him, as I had earlier when he'd gotten off work at Kafer Welding Company.

We were traveling east on Euclid, when he moved into an outer lane to catch Interstate 35 going north.

I groaned. Couldn't they settle for a motel in the city?

A few miles on the other side of Ankeny, a small community north of Des Moines, the truck turned off onto a secondary road and headed east; we'd been driving for an endless half an hour.

Ten minutes later, he swerved onto a gravel road and I ate his dust for another five, when suddenly the dust vanished and along with it, the truck.

I panicked and slammed on my brakes, stopping in the middle of the road; everything ahead was dark and still.

Driving forward again, I passed a small clapboard farm-house that sat near the road on my left, and saw the Chevy parked down the short, dirt lane.

I went on by.

About a mile further on the gravel road, I turned around and doubled back, headlights out.

Slowly I pulled up alongside the mailbox on the road in front of the farmhouse, which was partially obstructed from view by a thin row of scraggly pines.

There was no name on the box, just numbers.

I turned off the car and got out a small steno pad and pen from the glove compartment and wrote the address down, then recorded the county road numbers we'd taken, so I could remember how to get back to Des Moines. It was getting stuffy in the car, so I hit the button and eased my window down.

A cool night breeze wafted in, instantly revitalizing me from my sleepy state. I looked through the rustling pines toward the house. A front room light was on. The back was dark.

I was sure in the morning I'd find out the house was rented by Lyle. *A safe, easy love nest to bring his . . . dates,* I thought.

My hand was on the ignition key, when I heard a loud thump from the direction of the house. The noise was more than a door slamming. . . . Like a piece of furniture being overturned.

I sat still. The sounds of whispering pines and squeaking bugs returned, and my hand went back to the ignition key.

Before I could turn it, a muffled scream shattered the solitude.

I froze. It was a woman—and she was *not* crying out in ecstasy. . . .

I didn't know what to do; unlike my father, I don't carry a firearm.

All I had was a flashlight in the glove compartment, and I grabbed it as a feeble form of protection and slid silently out of the Buick.

A three-quarter moon hung in the sky, showing me the way as I hurried down the dirt lane. Approaching the side of the house I could see that the back bedroom window was open; flashes of white lace curtains fluttered against the screen in the breeze. The room itself was dark.

Looking inside (I didn't dare use the flashlight) I could make out, from light from another room, a bed with its rumpled sheets, a dresser, and an overturned nightstand, with the lamp on its side on the floor.

My attention was drawn to noises now coming from somewhere else in the house: a man's angry voice.

Presumably, my client's husband. . . .

I moved along the clapboard to a side front window. It was closed, shade drawn, but there was light behind it. The sides of the cheap, plastic shade had curled from exposure to the sun and heat, and that allowed me to peek inside.

She was tied in a wooden chair, in the kitchen, hands behind her back, wearing just panties and a bra, head hung, blond hair covering her face.

He was standing before her, in jeans sans shirt, yelling, shaking a butcher knife at the woman. I couldn't hear what he was saying, but I didn't have to be a trained lip-reader to make out his mouth forming words like "bitch" and "whore."

I stepped back from the window, mouth hanging open. This was more than a simple one-night stand: this was a guy with a real attitude problem. And this was a special kind of love nest—the kind with bodies buried in the basement.

I glanced toward my Buick, thinking of the car phone. . . . But by the time help could get here it would be too late.

Retracing my steps to the bedroom window, I pushed on

the old screen and it popped inward, onto the floor, and I hitched my skirt up and climbed in.

I moved through the dark bedroom, toward the light of the kitchen, then down a short narrow hallway, hugging the wall.

Lyle was still shouting at her, but now pacing back and forth.

"Who the *fuck* do you think you are!" he yelled, knife gripped in one hand.

Beyond him I could see the poor woman, motionless, head hung, apparently unconscious.

Lyle halted in front of her, his back to the hallway. "I have to decide what to do with you," he growled.

I had already decided what to do with him. I lurched forward and slugged Lyle on the side of the head with my flashlight as hard as I could.

He stiffened, and for one horrifying moment I thought he might just rub his skull, turn, and look at me with a scowl . . . but then his legs went out from under him, the knife tumbling from his hand, and he went down, rattling the floorboards, and lay still.

I let out a big quavering breath of air I'd been holding for the past few minutes. My knees were knocking, but I ran to the woman and untied her hands, which were bound with the western blouse I'd seen her in earlier.

She moaned a little, and lifted her head, and her face was swollen and bruised.

"Who . . . who are you?" she asked.

I told her I was a private investigator hired to follow the jerk who'd just tried to kill her.

"Oh" was all she said.

After finding a dish towel on the kitchen counter, I went over to the unconscious Lyle, got on my knees, and began tying his hands behind his back with the cloth. I was wondering what to use to bind his legs, when out of the corner of my eye I saw the woman rise out of the chair and stoop to pick up the knife.

Maybe it was her somnolent state—which I had attributed to shock—or maybe it was the look in her eyes—cold and so very dead—but the hair on the back of my neck stood up.

Still on my knees by the fallen Lyle, I sat back on my haunches.

She approached me slowly with the knife in one hand, held down by her side.

"I'm grateful you saved me," she said, with a small haunted smile, "but I'm afraid I don't have any choice . . ."

Now the blade in her hand went up, poised over her head, and I pushed off with my legs as the knife came swishing down, glinting in the kitchen light, and I lunged with both of my hands at her arm, twisting it around her back. . . . And three hundred and twenty dollars of karate lessons went out the window as I threw myself on her, bringing her down on the floor, lying on top of the woman like I was a beached whale, my fingernails digging into her wrist, feeling the weapon come loose in her hand.

I didn't know why she'd said what she'd said, or did what she'd done, and I wasn't about to discuss it. I had the knife now, and I grabbed the western blouse that had been discarded nearby and tied her hands behind her back with it again. She lay sobbing on the floor.

There wasn't a phone, so I went out the front door and hurried down the short, dirt lane to use the one in my car.

A figure stepped out of the darkness.

I shrieked and jumped a mile.

"I've already called the police," my father said.

I stared at him.

"How long have you been here?" I demanded.

"Awhile."

My mouth fell open. "And you did *nothing*?!"

"You handled yourself just fine," he said.

"I could have been *killed*!" I screamed at him. "Why didn't you *help* me?"

He put both hands on my shoulders and looked me right in the eye. "Because I won't always be there to help you, pumpkin," he said softly.

And I leaned my head against his chest and wept.

* * *

Sam Knight's the name, though you've probably never heard of me. But I'll bet you've heard of *Rebecca* Knight, my daughter.

People magazine said Becky was "fearless, in the face of a female mass murderer," and that she was "a new breed of woman detective, with brains, brawn, and beauty." Now, that's some kind of gauge!

Just why "The Cutthroat Cowgirl"—so dubbed by the media—felt the need to lure men to her rented farmhouse and slit their throats is beyond me. . . . That's for the shrinks to discover. But you can bet ol' Lyle will think twice before picking up another woman. . . .

Becky's head's gotten a little big lately, with all the publicity. So what. Let her have her moment. I haven't had the heart to tell her I was in the hallway with my gun that night. . . .

I'm proud of my daughter.

And when she reads this, she'll finally know.

Janet Dawson was the fourth winner of the PWA/St. Martin's Press First Private Eye Novel Contest with her Jeri Howard novel Kindred Crimes *(SMP, 1991). The most recent was* Don't Turn Your Back on the Ocean *(Ballantine, 1994). The novels are becoming longer, more complex, and more impressive as she develops as a writer, and her detective, Jeri Howard, develops as a character. Here Jeri is hired to track down the provenance of a '61 Corvette that has only . . . 800 miles on it?*

LITTLE RED CORVETTE

by Janet Dawson

"I SN'T SHE A beauty?" Acey Collins asked, admiration in his eyes and voice. "A '61 Cherry."

I looked at him, exasperated. We were standing on the corner of Thirty-sixth and Broadway, in the heart of Oakland's Auto Row, just after noon on a blustery March day. Acey gazed at the repair shop on the corner with a look he usually reserved for his wife, his kids, or his Harley-Davidson. I followed the direction of his eyes and finally figured out that "she" was a car, a cherry-red Chevrolet Corvette convertible, the car I associated with Tod and Buzz and all those black-and-white reruns of *Route 66*.

"I wonder what the insurance would run on a car like that?"

My companion glared at me as though I'd committed heresy. He shook his head in disgust and folded his tattooed arms over his stringy chest. "You got no soul."

"What I do have is a limited amount of time, Acey. It's chilly, the wind is blowing. You brought me here to look at a car?"

"You got anything better to do?"

"It's lunchtime, Acey. Eating comes to mind."

"So I'll buy you a hot dog."

"Yech. What's the gig, Acey?" I looked at my watch. "I have an appointment in thirty minutes. I'm a private investigator who drives a six-year-old Toyota. Why did you drag me away from my office to show me a little red Corvette?"

"The Toyota could use a tune-up, you know." Acey tossed his head, setting his long gray-blond ponytail moving. He gave me a sly look, pale blue eyes glittering in his bearded face. "I heard it knocking when you pulled up. Those brakes were squealing some too."

"Is this leading somewhere?" I tapped both my foot and the face of my utilitarian Timex.

"I'm a good mechanic, Jeri. You do this for me, I'll work on your car."

That got my attention. The Toyota needed new shocks and I didn't like that sound the brakes made. I'd put off having any major work done because at the moment I had a cash flow problem. Acey's trade-off sounded good to me.

I pushed away seductive thoughts of new points and plugs. "What do I have to do?" I asked, suspicious.

"You're an investigator. I want you to investigate."

"A car? Back up and start at the beginning."

Acey took my arm and nudged me away from the corner like a Border collie taking charge of a wayward sheep. "Come on, I don't want Musetta to see us." We moved back down Thirty-sixth to where my Toyota was parked. I looked at its grimy paint and promised myself a trip to the car wash. *After* Acey worked on it.

"I'm in Musetta's shop a couple of days ago, looking to

buy some parts," Acey said. "I see the Corvette. It's beautiful, a classic. Only eight hundred miles on it."

"A car that old?"

"Yeah. That's one anomaly."

Hearing the word "anomaly" come out of the mouth of this aging biker took me by surprise. "There are others?"

"Plenty. I know Del Musetta, from way back. His brother was at Folsom the same time I was doin' that stretch for receiving stolen property. The criminal gene runs deep in this family. I know what I'm talking about here."

"So how did Musetta get the Corvette in the first place? You think he stole it?"

"Maybe." Acey jerked his bearded chin back toward the repair shop. "He tells me the Corvette was left at the shop to be repaired, five years ago. Says nobody ever came to claim it. Says he got tired of it sitting around his shop, so he decided to sell it."

"How much is he asking?"

Acey named a figure, several times what I'd paid for my Toyota, that made me wince. "That's a bundle."

"No, it ain't." Acey spoke with authority. "Not for that car. I could turn around and sell that Corvette for twice what he's asking. *If* Musetta is telling the truth, it's a good buy. But before I lay out that kind of money for that car, I want to know the deal is on the up-and-up."

He patted my trusty Toyota on the fender, tilted his head and squinted at me and smiled like a fisherman who'd just hooked a big one.

"You do this for me, Jeri, I'll fix this car so it purrs like a cat."

"You've got yourself a deal."

I returned to the repair shop that afternoon, after a spin through the California Civil Code. If the Corvette had been left at Musetta's for repairs and never claimed, the shop owner had what was called a possessory lien on the car. He was entitled to compensation for making repairs, performing labor, furnishing supplies, and storing the vehicle. The lien dated from the time a written statement of charges for the completed work was presented to the Corvette's registered owner.

First question. Did Musetta ever try to find the owner?

The owner could extinguish the lien on the car by presenting the repairman with a cashier's check for the amount owed. If that didn't happen, Musetta could go to court or apply for authorization to conduct a lien sale within thirty days after the lien had arisen.

Second question. Had Musetta obtained authorization within the legal time limit?

For that he had to go to the Department of Motor Vehicles. It should be easy enough to check whether he'd made the request and paid the filing fee.

Acey said the garage owner told him the Corvette had been sitting at the garage for five years. That brought me to the third question. If Musetta had the legal right to sell the car, why had he waited so long?

The Corvette stood to one side of Musetta's shop, under an overhang. Seen this close, I had to agree with Acey. It was a beauty. Paint like a fat ripe cherry, glossy and shiny, complemented by gleaming chrome. Not a mark on it. I circled the car slowly, then I heard someone behind me. I turned and saw a bulky dark-haired man. He was about six feet tall and he carried a lot of excess weight around his middle. He wore a set of grimy blue coveralls with the name "Del" stitched in red above the left breast pocket.

"I couldn't resist a closer look," I said. "What a gorgeous car. Is it for sale?"

"Yeah, it is." He grinned. "You interested?"

"Well, that would depend on the price."

He named a figure, considerably higher than the one Acey had mentioned. First anomaly, I thought. Of course, Acey knows more about cars and what they're worth than I do, and the garage owner knew it. I looked like a better mark, someone who'd pay more for this flashy car.

"You don't normally sell cars, do you?" I looked around, then focused on Del, giving him a flirtatious smile. "How did you happen on this one?"

Del laughed, a big belly-rumbling sound. "There's a story

about that. The guy just left the car here, coupla years back, for a tune-up and a brake job. I told him he could pick it up the next day. He never picked it up."

"How long ago was this?" I asked, frowning. "I mean, doesn't this person still own the car? How can you sell it?"

He rubbed a stubby fingered hand across his bristly chin. "Oh, yeah, I got a lien. Unless the owner shows up and pays me what he owes me, the car belongs to me. Damn thing's been sitting here for three years."

Anomaly number two, I thought. He had told Acey he'd had the car five years.

"I thought about keeping it myself, but . . ." Del stopped and slapped his considerable girth. "It ain't my kinda car. I can't get this belly behind the wheel of a little sports job two-seater. Besides, I looked it up in the Blue Book. It's worth quite a bit. I'd just as soon sell it and get the money."

"It's my kind of car," I said, running a finger over the bright red finish, dangling the possibility that I might be willing to whip out my checkbook this very minute. "Didn't you ever try to find the owner?"

Now Musetta backpedaled. "Well, I called the phone number he left. Buncha times. Even went by his place, but there wasn't anyone there."

I had a feeling the garage owner's efforts to find the Corvette's owner had been somewhat desultory and limited to right after the car was left at the garage. I let a bit of this show on my face. "Do you still have the work request?"

Musetta looked surprised. "Well, yeah. It's in the filing cabinet somewheres. Why?"

"Let me take a look at it."

"What you want to do that for?"

"I'm really interested in buying the car," I said, stroking my handbag as though it contained a large wad of cash. "But I'd feel much better if I tried to contact the owner myself."

Musetta frowned. "I told you, I called his place. Even went by there."

"Just for my own peace of mind." I flashed him a bright smile. "I really couldn't buy the car unless I was sure everything was legal."

"I'm telling ya, I got a lien on this car," Musetta protested. I sighed, shook my head, and turned to go back to my Toyota. "Wait a minute. I guess there's no harm in letting you see it. Just proves my point."

I followed him into the grimy office of the repair shop, where the decor ran to calendars featuring flashy cars and naked female body parts. He opened the second drawer of a brown metal filing cabinet and rummaged through the contents. Finally he pulled out the work request and held it out for me to examine. He looked dismayed when I gently plucked it from his hand.

I quickly glanced at the total for the work performed. It was a hefty repair bill, but a fraction of what Musetta hoped to get by selling the Corvette. The date was smudged, but it looked like April, three years ago. The person who left the Corvette to be repaired was one Raleigh Lambert. He lived at an address on Sea View Avenue in Piedmont, a small city completely surrounded by Oakland, where big well-tended houses hold court on the hills that rise above the city flatlands.

I wrote down the address and phone number. Then I handed the work request back to Musetta, gave him a big smile, and told him I'd be back.

Whoever had named the street Sea View wasn't kidding. Big bucks, I thought, to go with the spectacular panorama of San Francisco Bay visible from the front porch of Raleigh Lambert's gray stone house. I rang the bell. No answer. What had once been a well-tended English garden needed some work, I thought as I walked back down the steps to the curved driveway that led to a detached double garage. No cars, no movement behind the curtains on any of the big glass windows. It didn't look like anyone was home. The place had an aura of neglect.

I repaired to the Alameda County Courthouse for a stroll through the assessor's records. For the past two years, the property taxes on the Piedmont address had been paid by one Harold Baldwin. Three years ago they'd been paid by Raleigh Lambert. Had Lambert sold the house to Baldwin? When I went to the recorder's office to take a look at the real

estate transactions, I didn't find one for the Sea View
address.

I looked up from the microfilm reader and thought for a
moment. Maybe Baldwin inherited the house from Lambert.
I switched my search to the probate records. That's where I
hit pay dirt. Raleigh Lambert was dead, and among the
beneficiaries listed on his will was a nephew, Harold
Baldwin.

Now I had the date of Lambert's death to compare with
the smudged date on Musetta's work request. Lambert left
the Corvette for repairs a week before he died. When I
called the Department of Motor Vehicles, there was no
record of any authorization issued to the garage owner to
conduct a lien sale. Musetta had no right to sell the car. In
fact, he could be charged with conversion. Harold Baldwin
was the legal owner of that little red Corvette.

It was past five when I parked on the street outside the
house on Sea View, with a clear view of the porch and
garage. Fifteen minutes later a silver Jaguar approached and
turned into the curved driveway. By the time the driver was
out of the car and walking toward the house, I was there to
intercept him.

"Harold Baldwin?"

He was medium all over, height, weight, and age, with
short brown hair and brown eyes, wearing gray slacks and
a blue sweater, both of which looked expensive but didn't fit
him very well. He smiled politely and looked a bit wary at
being accosted by a strange woman in his own driveway.
"Yes?"

"It's about your uncle and a car," I began. Then I stopped.

There had to be some reason for the look that flickered in
the man's eyes. Maybe it was my imagination, or a trick of
the light on this March evening. But I was sure his
expression had migrated from polite disinterest to something else. Could it be panic?

Right now Baldwin had masked whatever it was and gone
back to the polite smile. "My uncle and a car?" he repeated.

I did a quick edit on my words. "Your uncle is Raleigh
Lambert?"

"Was. Uncle Raleigh died three years ago."

"Well, that explains it," I said cheerfully. "He left a car at a repair shop on Broadway. A red Corvette. And he never picked it up." Harold Baldwin looked blank. "You didn't know?"

"My uncle was something of a collector." Baldwin frowned. It made him look sulky. "He had so many cars. I do seem to recall a Corvette. I assumed he'd sold it. Who are you?"

"Jeri Howard." I decided not to mention I was a private investigator. "I saw the car at the repair shop and the owner told me it was for sale. He claims he owns it because it was left there and no one picked it up. The work request gave me Mr. Lambert's name and address. So I guess you really own the car, as long as you pay the repair bill."

I smiled again and hoped Harold Baldwin wouldn't ask how I'd figured out he was Raleigh Lambert's nephew and heir to the red Corvette. As it was he seemed preoccupied by what I'd just told him.

"How did your uncle die?" I asked. "It must have been quite unexpected."

"An accident."

I made a sympathetic noise and looked at Baldwin expectantly, waiting for details. With any luck I'd unnerved him to the point that he would say almost anything, just in the hope that I'd go away.

"Yes, right here at the house." He peered at his gold Rolex. "I really must go, Ms. . . . ?"

"Howard."

"Yes, uh, where is this repair shop? I'll have my attorney look into the matter."

I gave him Musetta's name and address, regretting a bit that the cat was out of that particular bag. But since I'd already mentioned it at the outset, there didn't seem to be any way to avoid it.

The next morning I left my Adams Point apartment and headed for the Oakland Public Library where copies of the Oakland *Tribune* were available on microfilm. I backtracked to April, three years ago, hoping that whatever tragic accident had taken Raleigh Lambert's life had rated a mention. If it hadn't I would be reduced to poring through the obituary notices.

I was saved from that fate by a front-page headline informing me that the previous owner of the red Corvette had met the Grim Reaper at the wheel of another of his classic cars, this one a '65 Mustang. But he hadn't been on the streets of Piedmont. Instead, the 72-year-old Lambert had driven the car into the garage, lowered the door, and died of carbon monoxide poisoning.

Lambert was described by the *Tribune* as a retired Oakland businessman. From what I read, he was considered quite the man-about-town. He collected fine porcelain and classic cars. On a Thursday evening in early April, he'd attended a dance at the Claremont Hotel with Mrs. Patricia Wong, described as an old family friend. The body had been found Friday morning by another friend, Teo Martinez. Nephew Harold told the police that his uncle had recently been diagnosed with liver cancer. Lambert's physician confirmed this.

Accident or suicide? I wondered. I moved the microfilm forward but didn't find any other articles about Lambert's death, just the obituary notice which gave the time and date of his funeral.

Small as it is, Piedmont does have its own police force. Sergeant Fleming, the officer who'd investigated Lambert's death, looked like a yuppie lawyer rather than a detective. He was quite bemused when I told him I was a private investigator.

"Most of my time I deal with burglaries and nuisance complaints," he said. "Don't see many dead bodies up here."

"I read the initial report of the incident in the *Tribune*. There seemed to be some question whether it was accidental or suicide."

"We finally ruled that an accidental death. There was alcohol in his system, he was elderly, coming home from a dance, so he may have been tired and less alert than he normally would have been. Lambert had one of those gizmos that opened and closed his garage door. It looked like he'd hit it before he got out of the car and had been overcome by the carbon monoxide. I think he probably hit that garage door button by mistake and didn't even realize what was happening."

"But the nephew, Harold Baldwin, thought it might be suicide."

Fleming nodded. "Lambert's doctor said the cancer would have killed him in a year or eighteen months. So he could have committed suicide, even if his lady friend insisted that was impossible."

"Is that Mrs. Wong, the woman he was with the night he died?"

"Yeah. Lived around the corner from him, on Farragut Avenue. She said he wouldn't have killed himself. I didn't have a note to indicate a suicidal state of mind. Why are you asking about the Lambert case?"

"Any chance it might be murder?"

"Murder?" Fleming's eyebrows shot up. "We haven't had a murder in, oh, twenty, twenty-five years. Was before my time, anyway."

The rich are different, I told myself, and Piedmont really was a world apart from Oakland. Fleming dropped the laid-back yuppie persona. "What makes you think anyone killed Raleigh Lambert?"

"My suspicious nature, I guess. Tell me, where was Harold Baldwin the night his uncle died?"

"At home, in his apartment in Concord. He worked as a salesman, wholesaling electronics."

Baldwin didn't need to work anymore, judging from the figures I'd seen in Uncle Raleigh's probated will. "He's come up in the world, hasn't he? Any witnesses? To his being home in Concord?"

"I took his word for it. Didn't have any reason to doubt it. Do you?"

"Just a hunch."

"A hunch and a buck will get you a lottery ticket," Fleming declared. "You get lucky on either, you let me know."

Patricia Wong's house on Farragut Avenue was a small, pleasantly proportioned stucco, blue with white trim. It had a well-kept garden and it was obvious that Mrs. Wong did the keeping. I found her at the side of the house pruning an azalea, with a sedate black standard poodle for company. As I approached the house, the poodle got up from its spot on the grass and walked over to inspect me.

"He won't hurt you," Mrs. Wong said, with a friendly smile. She was in her early sixties, dressed in blue jeans and a blue work shirt. Today the sun shone and it was warmer than it had been earlier in the week. The poodle sniffed my shoes, legs, and hand, then wagged its short tail to indicate I was okay. Mrs. Wong set down her pruning shears and removed her straw hat. I saw that she had shoulder-length hair, streaked liberally with silver.

"My name is Jeri Howard," I told her. "I'm a private investigator. I'd like to ask you some questions about Raleigh Lambert."

The smile left her face, replaced by sadness in her large brown eyes. "Why?"

"Are you satisfied that his death was an accident?"

She didn't even stop to consider. Instead she shook her head resolutely. "Not at all. But he wouldn't have killed himself either."

Fifteen minutes later we were in Mrs. Wong's living room, seated on a rosewood sofa. She'd made tea, and the strong jasmine scent filled the air. The poodle stretched out at our feet and sighed with contentment.

"Tell me about Raleigh Lambert," I said.

Patricia Wong smiled. "Raleigh was the most charming man. Dapper, handsome, debonair. I don't think I would be exaggerating if I compared him to Cary Grant or Fred Astaire. Not in looks, really. But he had that air about him. Let me show you a picture."

She stood and crossed the room to a shelf which held numerous framed photographs and returned with one, which she handed to me.

I examined it and grinned. I could see Lambert robbing a casino and romancing Grace Kelly in *To Catch a Thief*, or dancing with Cyd Charisse and total aplomb in *The Band Wagon*. He looked like a pistol, his long thoroughbred's face topped by a full head of white hair. Incredibly bright blue eyes smiled out from a tanned face. In this head-and-shoulders shot, Lambert wore a white shirt and I saw what looked like a tennis racquet propped on one shoulder.

"That was taken at the National Senior Games, five years ago," Mrs. Wong said, "Raleigh won gold medals in both singles and doubles. He was so alive. I just can't believe he'd take his own life. Nor can I believe he would be so careless as to lower the garage door before he'd turned off the engine."

"Where does that leave us?" I asked, not yet ready to say the word I'd been thinking ever since I saw that flicker of panic in Harold Baldwin's eyes when I'd mentioned dear Uncle Raleigh. Murder?

Mrs. Wong wasn't ready to say it either. Instead she reached for her jasmine tea. "Why are you asking these questions?"

I decided I wouldn't tell her about that strange look in Harold Baldwin's eyes. At least not right now. "A week before he died, Raleigh Lambert left his Corvette at a repair shop in Oakland. He never picked it up."

"The Corvette," she mused. "I wondered what happened to it. Raleigh and I used to tool down Highway One in that Corvette, playing the radio and singing along." She sighed. "Raleigh loved old cars. He stored most of them in Oakland, but he had several at the house. There was a T-Bird, a Packard. He even had an Edsel."

She looked as though she were having such a wonderful time reliving the past with Raleigh that I hated to bring her into the present. "Now the garage owner is trying to sell the Corvette. He does have a lien, because the repairs were never paid for. But he hasn't taken the legal steps that would enable him to sell the vehicle. A friend of mine is interested in buying the car, so I started checking into it. That's how I stumbled into this. I got curious about why no one ever claimed such a valuable car."

"Harold must not have known it was in the shop." Mrs.

Wong freshened our tea. "I suppose now that he does, your friend will have to buy the Corvette from Harold instead of the garage owner. Harold got rid of all of the cars, except the Jaguar. I think he sold them to a museum or another collector." She sighed. "Harold couldn't wait to trade up from his green beat-up Honda and his one-bedroom apartment in Concord. He's let both the house and garden go to seed. He may have Raleigh's money, but he'll never have Raleigh's style."

"How long had you known Raleigh?"

"Over twenty years," she said. "He and my late husband both loved tennis. I knew his wife Felicia. She died a long time ago. When we were both widowed we started seeing more of each other. Raleigh and I talked about marriage, but we decided we were quite happy just keeping company."

"How would your families have reacted to a marriage?"

"My children wouldn't have minded it. In fact, my daughter used to ask me when Raleigh and I were going to elope. I think Harold was afraid I'd do just that and get his inheritance. Raleigh and Felicia never had any children, you see. Harold's mother was Raleigh's only sister."

I nodded. "Tell me about that night."

"We'd been to a ballroom dance contest at the Claremont. We won first place. I still have the trophy." She smiled fondly at his photograph. "Raleigh was the only man of my acquaintance who could tango. Does that sound like a man who would kill himself the same night?"

"No, it doesn't. But he did have liver cancer."

"I realize that. He told me the day he was diagnosed." Mrs. Wong sipped her tea. "You see, Felicia died of ovarian cancer. A very long and painful death. Raleigh told me he wouldn't go that way. I think he would have killed himself before he became totally incapacitated. But he wasn't. He'd only found out about the cancer a month before. He was going to try radiation and chemotherapy. He would have fought the disease hard before giving in to it."

"Had he been drinking that night?"

"Well, yes," she said, a tad reluctantly. "We both had. But he certainly wasn't drunk. Raleigh held his liquor like the gentleman he was. I didn't detect any sign of intoxication while we were driving home."

"What time did you get here?"

"About ten. He saw me to the door. I invited him in for a nightcap, but he declined. It was a Thursday night. Raleigh had a tennis match at nine Friday morning, and I was taking a class. Besides, I think we were both tired from all that dancing."

I had to agree with her that it didn't sound as though Lambert had killed himself. Maybe he was more intoxicated than she'd thought. "Who found the body?" I asked.

"Teo Martinez, Raleigh's doubles partner. When Raleigh didn't show up for their tennis match, Teo called and didn't get any answer. Finally he went by the house. He heard the car running in the garage as he walked up the driveway." Mrs. Wong shuddered. "Poor Teo."

"So there was no one there besides Raleigh. He didn't have a housekeeper?"

Patricia Wong shook her head. "No household help. He had a cleaning service that came in once a week, on Monday. And he liked to cook for himself."

When I drove into the parking lot of Musetta's repair shop the little red Corvette was gone. I went looking for Del, who glared at me from his grubby lair.

"You got some nerve showing your face around here, lady. I got a hotshot lawyer threatening to hand me over to the cops, charge me with conversion or some damn thing. All because you stuck your nose in." He stared glumly at the spot where the Corvette had been. "Why couldn't you have just bought it?"

"I wasn't really interested in buying the car, Musetta. I'm a private investigator. Besides, it's your own fault. You should have made more of an effort to contact the legal owner. Did you know Lambert?"

"Never met him till he brought that Corvette in here. He said his regular mechanic had retired, and he'd heard I did good work. Told me he collected cars and if I did a good job on the Corvette, maybe we'd have us a long-term arrangement."

"But a week later he was dead. You must have known that, must have seen the article in the *Tribune*." I waved away his protests. "You figured his heir wouldn't miss one car out of half a dozen. So you waited a couple of years before selling it. You should have gone to the DMV for an authorization for lien sale. But they might have tumbled to the fact that you hadn't made any effort to contact Lambert that the repairs were done. Or his heir."

"Swear to God, I did try," Musetta insisted. "I called three, four times. I left messages on his answering machine. I even went by the house twice."

"When?"

"A week after he left the car. I drove up to Piedmont one night after I closed the shop. Made another trip the very next morning, hoping I'd catch him before he left the house."

My ears picked up. "What day of the week was that?"

Musetta sighed. "Lambert left the car here on a Friday. Only reason I remember that is I was planning to cut out early and go fishing. I told him I couldn't get to it until Monday. He said that was fine and to call him when it was ready. I finished the work late Monday afternoon. Called, left a message. Same thing the next three days. I start to wonder if the guy's out of town. Finally I went by the house, Thursday. I know it was Thursday, 'cause that's my bowling night."

Thursday was the night Lambert had squired Mrs. Wong to the dance contest at the Claremont. "Who did you talk with? What did you see?"

"Nothing," Musetta said. "There wasn't anyone home. Not even a maid, in a big house like that. I rang the doorbell. So I figured I'd swing by there Friday morning, before I came over here to open the shop."

So Musetta had been at the Sea View address again Friday morning, the same morning Lambert's body had been found by his friend Teo. "I want you to think very carefully," I told him. "About that Thursday evening when you went to Lambert's house. Were there any cars in the driveway?"

Musetta screwed up his face as he looked back three

years. He nodded. "A couple, covered up. Couldn't tell what make they were. There was this beat-up Honda at the side of the garage. I figured it belonged to the household help. That's why I was surprised when no one answered the door. I thought . . ." He paused and looked confused. "I thought someone was there. That's it. I looked in the window when I rang the bell. Coulda sworn I saw someone in the house. But no one answered the door."

"Was the Honda there when you came back Friday morning?" Musetta hesitated. "Think. What time? You were on your way to the shop, so it must have been—" I broke off and looked at the hours listed on the repair shop's door. "You open at seven, so it must have been six-thirty, quarter to seven."

Musetta nodded. "Yeah, it was just getting light. I didn't go to the door. I sat in my car at the curb, where I could see the porch and the garage, till I saw someone come out. It wasn't Lambert, though."

No, it couldn't have been Raleigh Lambert. He was sitting behind the wheel of his '65 Mustang in that detached garage, dead from carbon monoxide poisoning. If Musetta had walked up the driveway he'd have heard the Mustang's engine. It was still running, as it had been all night, when Teo Martinez found the body later that morning. So whoever had left Lambert's house while Musetta was parked at the curb must have heard that car. Unless that person was dead—or chose to ignore it.

I probed Musetta's memory enough to get an adequate description of the person he'd seen that morning. Then I went up to Piedmont.

Harold Baldwin didn't look any happier to see me this time than he had the last. While he stood at the door, I strolled past him, through the foyer to take a look at the living room. I didn't see any of the fine porcelain Raleigh Lambert was supposed to have collected. Maybe his nephew had sold it all, the way he had the classic cars.

He followed me into the room. "What are you doing here?"

"The little red Corvette. The one that was left at the garage."

"You wanted to buy it? My lawyer is taking care of it. If you still want to buy the car you can get in touch with him." He rattled off a name and phone number. I didn't bother to write it down.

"Such a shame about your uncle dying that way." Baldwin frowned at me. "I understand he killed himself."

"He had cancer," Baldwin said with a shrug. "My aunt died of cancer. I guess he just didn't want to go that way."

"So you knew it was coming. Still, it must have been quite a shock when you found him."

"I didn't find him. His doubles partner found him."

"So you weren't here at all, either Thursday or Friday."

"Of course not. I lived in Concord then. I was at home."

"Right. I suppose you sold that Mustang. Must have had all sorts of unpleasant connotations, what with Uncle Raleigh dying in it. You sold all his cars, except the Jag and the Corvette. But you didn't know about the Corvette. When did you unload the Honda?"

"What Honda?" That look was back, the one I'd seen in Baldwin's eyes the first time I mentioned his uncle and a car.

"According to Patricia Wong, you used to drive a little green Honda. After Raleigh's will was probated you couldn't wait to shed your one-bedroom apartment in Concord and your old car. She was right. You may have Raleigh's money, but you sure as hell don't have his style."

"I don't know what you're talking about," Baldwin stuttered.

"Sure you do. You came out of the house, got into your beat-up Honda, and drove off. But not before you checked the garage to make sure Raleigh was dead. You might have gotten away with it, if it hadn't been for that little red Corvette. Someone saw you that morning—the garage owner. He wanted to catch the owner. I guess he just did."

I picked up the phone and called Sergeant Fleming. "I got lucky," I told him. "And I'm not talking about the lottery."

Marele Day's The Last Tango of Delores Delgado *won the PAW SHAMUS Award for Best Paperback P.I. Novel of 1992. The book featured her series P.I., Claudia Valentine, and was the third in the series.*

This story does not feature Claudia. It is a historical tale—set in the American West—*that first appeared in an Australian anthology called* Crosstown Traffic *in 1993. The Australians are avid readers of hard-boiled fiction, and Marele Day, along with Peter Corriss, is one of the most popular of Australia's crime writers.*

THE KID AND THE MAN FROM PINKERTONS

by Marele Day

Somewhere, out in the borderlands,
these things happen.

IT WAS EARLY morning. The man from Pinkertons headed west. He looked odd out here driving along in a trench coat and a city hat, but that didn't worry him none. He knew how to track his man, the city was the same kind of wilderness as the West. A wasteland full of the same kind of desperadoes, same corrupt cattle barons, same sheriffs working for them.

He stopped. There were hoof marks leading away from the remains of a campfire. He got out of the car. The Kid couldn't be too far ahead, judging by the still-warm embers.

The man from Pinkertons raised the binoculars to his eyes. A flurry of dust up ahead. It had to be the Kid. Nineteen years old and he'd killed thirty-seven men already. There was a price on his head as big as Texas. Not that the man from Pinkertons was thinking about that. He had a job to do, was all.

He got back in the car, adjusted the tilt of his hat, and thought of the motto he worked by—"the eye that never sleeps." He fingered the sleek metal shaft of the gun in his pocket and smiled to himself.

The car had done well. No roads to speak of, but the ground was rock-hard. Course there weren't any gas stations either, but the man had come well-equipped. Enough gas in the trunk to get from here to South America. Last longer than the Kid's horse. And the car wouldn't skitter at the sound of gunshots. All the man had to do was remember not to smoke round the trunk area.

It was hot out here and getting hotter. He loosened his tie. He decided against taking his coat off. If he took his coat off there was no telling where it might end.

He was gaining on the Kid. Better to ease up a little. Wait till the Kid had camped for the night. Come roaring in with those big headlights on high beam, like a great monstrous night animal. Spook the Kid. The man chuckled. Getting the Kid in his headlights like a frightened rabbit. Slam on the handcuffs, take him back to town. Or shoot him. Self-defense. The office would never know what had really happened out here. He fingered the gun in his pocket again. It was all up to him. He could take him back or shoot him on the spot. The man savored the thought as he drove along. One hand on the wheel, one hand on the gun.

He wondered what the Kid looked like up close. A thin-faced kid, they'd told him, eyes blue as the Pacific Ocean, bum fluff on his face. Laughs in a strange high-pitched way when he shoots a man. Remember that, they told him. The man kept remembering it. Only a kid but he'd killed thirty-seven men. Laughed at every one of them. The man straightened his tie, despite the heat. Can't afford to get sentimental—the Kid was a killer.

*   *   *

At 1:30 precisely by his watch the man from Pinkertons pulled a sandwich out of the glove compartment. Corned beef on rye. It was more convenient than shooting a jackrabbit. He finished it off with a slug of whiskey from his quart bottle. That'd kill anything that was starting to fester in the meat. Just one slug, that's all he allowed himself during the day, while he was on the job. There had to be rules. Even if they were your own rules.

He picked up the binoculars again. The Kid didn't seem like he was stopping to shoot a jackrabbit for lunch, he just kept on riding. Didn't he ever get hungry?

All afternoon they rode; the Kid on his horse, the man in his car. The one following the other.

At dusk the Kid stopped. By a dry riverbed. Not much chance of water, but at least the sand would be soft. The Kid waited and listened. No sound of horse hooves behind him. But there was still that dull faraway rumble. What the hell was that anyways? Sorta like a thunderstorm brewing up but not a cloud in the sky. Still, the Kid didn't have anything to fear from nature, it was men you had to look out for. Like the men who'd kilt his ma.

It had always been him and Ma. He never knew his pa. Ma said he was a gentleman and wore fine clothes. The Kid had a picture of a knight. A picture from the book Ma used to read him stories from. The knight was wearing a suit of armor, with the helmet down over his face. The Kid used to pretend his pa was inside that suit of armor. Ma would say: Maybe he is, Son.

The horse snorted, the night air was beginning to chill. The Kid got some dead branches and kindling together and made a fire. He heated up some beans. It sure gave him wind eating beans night after night. One good thing 'bout riding alone—you could fart to your heart's content.

He didn't seem to feel the need of company too much and if he did there was always that little place down in Mexico. The senoritas would sit him in a tub and bathe him, then lie down with him afterwards. He liked their wide smiles and

white teeth, the way their breasts reached out for him. Best
of all he liked how they didn't ask questions about what he
was doing and where he was going.

Because the Kid didn't know where he was going. He had
only one direction—away. Seemed to him the only place he
was safe was out here.

The horse snorted. There was that sound again, that dull
rumble like thunder. Then he saw something out there, like
a lamplight only round like a small moon. Two of them,
both the same. Then the lights disappeared and the noise
stopped.

The Kid listened, his gun cocked. Maybe he'd been out
here too long, seeing and hearing things. Something super-
natural. Maybe he ought to go to church or something. He
watched the horse. Horses can tell when there's something
strange going on. But the horse was quiet, just standing
there. The Kid went back to eating his beans. When he
finished them he took out a stick of candy. He liked candy
like some men like liquor.

The Kid stopped chewing—there was a different noise.
This one he knew. The dry snap of a twig. Not a breath of
wind in the night. Silently the Kid moved away, got down
behind a rock. Both guns out.

More twigs snapped and another sound, kinda crunchy
like a big barrel being rolled over the ground.

Then this big black shape came lumbering in. The Kid
was bug-eyed, strangest thing he ever saw. It looked like
some piece of farm machinery. With glass windows. It
stopped about three feet away from the fire. The Kid could
see now it was made of metal, a little dusty. The fire lit up
a man's face in the window.

Slowly the Kid stood up, his guns pointing toward the
thing, wary but kinda fascinated at the same time. One of
the glass windows lowered all by itself and disappeared
somewhere inside the piece of machinery.

"Howdy. Mind if I join you?"

The Kid watched as the door opened and the man stepped
out. The man lit a cigarette, threw the match into the fire.

"Mind if I ask you your business?" said the Kid, measuring up to him.

"I'm a travelin' salesman." The man smiled.

"What do you sell?"

"Space." He made the word sound long and wide.

The Kid pointed the guns at him. "You can't sell space, don't belong t'anyone."

The man didn't seem to pay the guns any mind. "Newspaper space does. I sell newspaper space to people wanting to advertise their wares. You want to sell something, you put an advertisement in the newspaper."

The man took the quart bottle and offered it to the Kid. The Kid shook his head. "I don't hold with hard liquor."

The man shook his head too, as if that was a goddamn shame. He unscrewed the lid and held the bottle up. "Here's lookin' at you, kid."

Before he could put the bottle to his lips, the Kid shot it out of his hand. "How come you know my name?" the Kid asked, a little jittery now.

The man could have had the Kid on the ground in two seconds flat, guns or no guns, but he bided his time. "That wasn't a very polite gesture. That's my only bottle."

"Mister, you didn't answer my question."

The man looked at him, took a little time before he answered. "Kid? Is that your name? I call everyone kid."

"Out here I'm the only one they call Kid," said the Kid. "You remember that."

"I'll remember," said the man, indulging him, a whisper of a smile. The firelight seemed to make the Kid's eyes even bluer, his downy face even softer. Once he took them pearl-handled guns away from him, the Kid would be no problem. Right there and then the man from Pinkertons decided he'd take the Kid back alive. It'd be a symbolic gesture—taming the wild West.

While the man from Pinkertons was making up his mind about the Kid, the Kid was making up his mind about the man. The man wasn't wearing guns, didn't seem like he was going to do any harm. City man, just passing through, in that weird contraption. Hell, he'd be no trouble. The Kid put one gun away. "You want some beans?" he asked the man.

The man shook his head. He knew better than to eat beans. "I got some food in the car."

"Cart?" the Kid misrepeated. "You call that thing a cart?"

"It's a car. Motorcar. Automobile." The Kid was curious. "Better than forty horses," added the man. It always worked. No kid could resist a car.

"No sort of company for you, not like a horse," the Kid said, trying to think of something bad to say about it.

"I don't need company," said the man.

Something flared up in the fire and the Kid saw himself reflected in the man's eyes. It spooked him. "You don't need company, you don't need to share my campfire," he said. "You can git in your cart and skedaddle."

"Don't mean anything by it," said the man. "I won't be any trouble to you." The man got back in the car, stretched his legs out along the seat, and leaned his head against the window. "See you in the morning."

Yeah, thought the Kid. You may see me in the morning, but I'll be watching you all night, Mr. Space Salesman.

The man arranged his hat at an angle that made him look like he was bunking down for the night; same angle that allowed him to never take his eyes off the Kid. He was from Pinkertons. The eye that never sleeps.

At first light the man got out of the car. The Kid watched him. The man turned away and started fiddling with his pants. Just relieving hisself. A good time for the Kid to do the same. Shoot, the man wasn't going to try anything while he was holding his dick in his hand.

They stood there urinating into the soft sand, backs to each other. The man shook off the last few drops. Then he started to do up his pants, casual-like. But his zip was faster than the Kid's buttons.

Much faster. The Kid felt the small round pressure in the middle of his back and the lightness at his hips as the man deftly removed the pearl-handled guns from the holsters.

"The slightest movement and I'll blast a hole clean through your body," the man breathed down his neck.

From the outside it appeared as if the Kid was rooted to the spot. But inside the blood was whipping round his body as if he was about the leap into a ravine. He wasn't afraid of dying, but he didn't want to be shot in the back. Goddamn city man, didn't he know the rules? Thirty-seven men he'd killed. He didn't want to be shot in the back by a goddamn city man.

Behind his back the man was doing something. "OK," said the man, "you turn around nice and slow."

The Kid turned around nice and slow. The man was pointing a gun at him. As well as that, the Kid's pearl-handled guns were stuck down his trousers. From out of his coat pocket he produced a pair of handcuffs. "OK," he said, "you put your hands out nice and easy."

The Kid put his hands out nice and easy, just like he was told. The man slapped on the cuffs.

"Now you and I are going to take a little ride in my car."

The last thing the Kid wanted to do was get in that goddamn cart. "What about my horse?"

"No room for the horse," said the man, untying the animal. "It can take care of itself." He slapped the horse on the rump and fired a coupla shots in the air. The horse hightailed it out of there.

Shit, thought the Kid. Now the horse was gone. If he refused to get in the cart would he die alone out here in the desert? He knew what happened if the job wasn't done properly. If the man shot him a coupla times and just left him here the vultures would come circling. And vultures didn't wait till a man was properly dead. He didn't want to watch the flesh being picked off his own bones. But better to die out here a man than let himself be captured.

"You want me to git in that thing, you gonna have to put me in it yourself," he challenged the man. The Kid kicked a flurry of sand up into the man's face.

The only other time someone had kicked sand in the man's face was when he was a boy of fourteen. That very same day he sent away for the Charles Atlas bodybuilding

course. No one but no one did that to him anymore. He
knocked the Kid to the ground and beat him till he was
unconscious.

Far far out on the horizon the man made out the toylike
buildings of the city. He put away the binoculars and felt for
a pulse on the Kid's neck. The man smiled. It had been a
piece of cake. The Kid may have been pretty tough with his
pearl-handled guns in tow, but he didn't look too tough
sitting there trussed up like a Thanksgiving turkey, eyes
closed and mouth open. He was only a kid, no match for the
man from Pinkertons. Maybe the thirty-seven men was all
hogwash. Maybe he'd only killed two or three. All the
stories are tall out West.

The car started shuddering then petered to a halt. Out of
gas. A bad sign. The man should have been watching,
should have filled the tank up again before it had got this
low. Keeping his eye on the Kid, he opened the door. He
watched the eyelids. Except for the pulse, the Kid coulda
been dead. Satisfied, the man got out of the car.

It was awful quiet. Just the occasional sound from the
engine cooling down and the wind. Strange sort of sound.
Almost as if it was whispering his name.

He opened the trunk, took out a jerry can of gas. Only one
more can of gas to go. He squinted toward the horizon
again. It'd probably hold. There was a gas station at
Bordertown. He could fill up there, then do the final leg
back to the city. He was looking forward to getting back.
Get his suit pressed, wash the desert dust off. Hand the Kid
over to the proper authorities. Have the mayor make a
speech. Pick up the reward.

He unscrewed the top off the jerry can and started
pouring. A little gasoline spilled onto the man's shoe. He
bent down to wipe it off.

When he stood up again his trousers fell down. How the
hell had that happened?

"You should have checked me for knives."

It was the Kid. Directly behind him. On the ground
between the man's legs lay the Kid's pearl-handled guns.

"You bend down to pick up them guns, mister, you ain't going to be able to sit down for days. More'n likely, you'll bleed to death." The Kid had the man in a very awkward position. The man stood there staring into the black hole of the gas tank, his pants down round his ankles. Hell, how'd he let this happen?

Deftly the Kid hooked his foot around one gun then the other. "OK, now turn around."

Slowly the man turned around.

"Didn't they tell you I was just a skinny kid? Didn't they tell you I've slipped out of handcuffs before? Ain't you ever seen a fox get in and out of a chicken coop? He can make hisself real thin." The Kid was grinning now, building up for a laugh. The man remembered what they'd told him. He knew what happened when the Kid laughed.

"Listen," said the man, "maybe we can do a deal. I was just doing my job. I can let you go, say I never found you."

"What's the point of dealing? Seems I'm the one holding all the cards, Mr. 'Space Salesman.'"

"Then you'd better grab hold of this!" Quick as lightning the man threw the jerry can at the Kid.

The Kid started firing. He didn't want to do it sudden like this, but it was the man's own fault, he shouldn'ta thrown that thing at him.

He watched the man twitching on the ground. It was a comical sight, but for the first time he didn't feel like laughing. Somehow with a city man it was different. He seemed to be taking a long time to die, but never once did he look at the Kid or beg him.

The Kid emptied the barrel into the man's chest.

When he was sure the man was dead, the Kid bent down to him. He felt in his pockets and pulled out a wallet. The Kid knew he wasn't no space salesman, but he wanted to know whether he was a lone bounty hunter or whether he was working for the county. Inside the wallet was an engraved card. On the top of the card it said *Pinkertons Detective Agency*, then a picture of an eye and underneath *The eye that never sleeps*.

Insects started to buzz around the body. The vultures

wouldn't be long in coming. Normally the Kid would have just rode out of there and let nature take its course. But it didn't seem fitting for a city man.

The Kid started kicking the ground till he found a piece that was soft and yielding. He kicked all he could, then got down on the ground and started scraping away with his hands. When he thought it was big enough he dragged the man's body into the shallow grave. He tried to remember the prayers of the Mexican girls. *Vaya con Dios* was all he recalled.

He picked up the man's hat and put it on. It was a little roomy but better than nothing. You needed a hat out here, and the Kid had lost his the same place he'd lost his horse. That had been the man's doing. He picked up the coat as well—nights get mighty cold out in the desert. He took one last hard look at the grave, then turned his back on it.

First thing the Kid had to do was go back and find his horse. He finished off the job of pouring gasoline into the tank, then got into the car. He started the car up. All the time he'd been trussed up he'd been watching the man, watching him press down on them pedals, maneuver that wheel. He made a few false moves, but he soon got the hang of it. He turned the car back in the direction they'd come from.

The tracks were clearly visible.

The Kid hadn't gone far when he realized he'd forgotten one thing. It might take days to find the horse and that fuel the man was putting in the car wasn't going to last forever. He was going to have to get some more of it. The Kid turned the car round again.

The Kid had been driving a coupla hours maybe when he saw a building. Out front was a sign—BORDERTOWN GAS STATION. The Kid looked around. There was no town here, just this one building. The Kid drove past slowly. Something caught his eye. A notice on the wall of the building. If the desert had taught him one thing it was being able to pick things out at a distance. He didn't have to look too hard to know it was a WANTED sign and that he was the one who was wanted. A man came out, but the kid drove right on by.

Further up the road he stopped. He had to go back there. He wasn't going to get anyplace without that fuel. But the man would recognize him. The Kid would have to shoot him. Is that the way he was going to spend his life, shooting every man who looked at him?

The Kid sat there thinking about it. He had to do something. In the mirror he could see the man looking his way.

On the backseat of the car lay the coat. The Kid leaned over for it and put it on. It was an odd-looking coat, but somehow it seemed to go with the hat. It made him feel kinda invincible, like the knight in his suit of armor. The Kid went round to the trunk, got the can out, and walked back to the gas station.

"Run out of gas, did you?" said the gas station man lazily.

"Yes," said the Kid, holding out the can.

"You want a refill?"

"Yes," said the Kid.

The gas station man took the can and filled it. "That'll be two dollars."

The Kid gave the gas station man two dollars. "You got some way I can get a message to town?"

"Sure. You can use the phone."

"You do it for me," said the Kid.

The gas station man gave him a funny look, but he went to the phone and turned the handle a coupla times. He did it again, then came away shaking his head. "Velma must be having her lunch," he said.

"I gotta be on my way," said the Kid. "When Velma's finished her lunch I want you to call the sheriff's office."

"What's the message?" asked the gas station man, not really interested.

"Tell him the Kid is dead." The gas station man dropped his pencil. "Out there in the desert," the Kid added before the man could start asking questions.

"You mean . . . ?"

The Kid didn't have to explain what he meant. He tore the

WANTED sign off the wall. "You won't be needing this anymore."

The gas station man realized that the stranger wasn't someone you messed with. "Who shall I say the message is from, sir?" All nice and polite now.

"The man from Pinkertons. Thanks for the gas." The Kid put another two dollars down on the counter and walked away.

*"Death and Diamonds," featuring P.I. Kiernan
O'Shaughnessy, first appeared in Sara Paretsky's land-
mark anthology* A Woman's Eye. *Susan was also the
coeditor on* Deadly Allies II. *Along with Kiernan she has
two other series featuring meter reader V. J. Haskell and
policewoman Jill Smith. "Death and Diamonds" is a
clever little cat-and-mouse game that showcases Susan
Dunlap's talent.*

DEATH AND DIAMONDS

by Susan Dunlap

"THE THING I love most about being a private investigator is the thrill of the game. I trained in gymnastics as
a kid. I love cases with lots of action. But, alas, you
can't always have what you love." Kiernan O'Shaughnessy
glanced down at her thickly bandaged foot and the crutches
propped beside it.

"Kicked a little too much ass, huh?" The man in the seat
beside her at the Southwest Airlines gate grinned. There was
an impish quality to him. Average height, sleekly muscled,
with the too-dark tan of one who doesn't worry about the
future. He was over forty, but the lines around his bright
green eyes and mouth suggested quick scowls, sudden
bursts of laughter, rather than the folds of age setting in.

Amidst the San Diegans in shorts and T-shirts proclaiming
the Zoo, Tijuana, and the Chargers, he seemed almost
formal in his chinos and sports jacket and the forest-green
polo shirt. He crossed, then recrossed his long legs, and
glanced impatiently at the purser standing guard at the end
of the ramp.

The gate ten waiting area was jammed with tanned
families ready to fly from sunny San Diego to sunnier
Phoenix. The rumble of conversations was broken by
children's shrill whines and exasperated parents barking
their names in warning.

*We are now boarding all passengers for Southwest
Airlines flight twelve forty-four to Oakland, through gate
nine.*

A mob of the Oakland-bound crowded closer to their
gate, clutching their blue plastic boarding passes.

Beside Kiernan the man sighed. But there was a twinkle
in his eyes. "Lucky them. I hate waiting around like this. It's
not something I'm good at. One of the reasons I like flying
Southwest is their open seating. If you move fast you can
get whatever seat you want."

"Which seat is your favorite?"

"One B or C. So I can get off fast. *If* they ever let us *on.*"

The Phoenix-bound flight was half an hour late. With
each announcement of a Southwest departure to some other
destination, the level of grumbling in the Phoenix-bound
area had grown till the air seemed thick with frustration, and
at the same time old and overused, as if it had held just
enough oxygen for the scheduled waiting period, and now,
half an hour later, the tired air only served to dry out noses,
make throats raspy, and tempers short.

The loudspeaker announced the Albuquerque flight was
ready for boarding. A woman in a rhinestone-encrusted
denim jacket ran by racing toward the Albuquerque gate.
Rhinestones. Hardly diamonds, but close enough to bring
the picture of Melissa Jessup to Kiernan's mind. When
she'd last seen her Melissa Jessup had been dead six

months, beaten, stabbed, her corpse left outside to decompose. Gone were her mother's diamonds, the diamonds her mother had left her as security. Melissa hadn't yet been able to bring herself to sell them, even to finance her escape from a life turned fearful, and a man who preferred them to her. It all proved, as Kiernan reminded herself each time the memory of Melissa invaded her thoughts, that diamonds are *not* a girl's best friend, that mother (or at least a mother who says "don't sell them") does *not* know best, and that a woman should never get involved with a man she works with. Melissa Jessup had made all the wrong decisions. Her lover had followed her, killed her, taken her mother's diamonds, and left not one piece of evidence. Melissa's brother had hired Kiernan, hoping with her background in forensic pathology she would find some clue in the autopsy report, or that once she could view Melissa's body she would spot something the local medical examiner had missed. She hadn't. The key that would nail Melissa's killer was not in her corpse, but with the diamonds. Finding those diamonds, and the killer with them, had turned into the most frustrating case of Kiernan's career.

She pushed the picture of Melissa Jessup out of her mind. This was no time for anger or any of the emotions that the thought of Melissa's death brought up. The issue now was getting this suitcase into the right hands in Phoenix. Turning back to the man beside her, she said, "The job I'm on right now is baby-sitting this suitcase from San Diego to Phoenix. This trip is not going to be 'a kick.'"

"Couldn't you have waited till you were off the crutches?" he said, looking down at her bandaged right foot.

"Crime doesn't wait." She smiled, focusing her full attention on the conversation now. "Besides, courier work is perfect for a hobbled lady, don't you think, Mr. . . . uh?"

He glanced down at the plain black suitcase, then back at her. "Detecting all the time, huh?" There was a definite twinkle in his eyes as he laughed. "Well, this one's easy. Getting my name is not going to prove whether you're any good as a detective. I'm Jeff Siebert. And you are?"

"Kiernan O'Shaughnessy. But I can't let that challenge

pass. Anyone can get a name. A professional investigator can do better than that. For a start, I surmise you're single."

He laughed, the delighted laugh of the little boy who's just beaten his parent in rummy. "No wedding ring, no white line on my finger to show I've taken the ring off. Right?"

"Admittedly, that was one factor. But you're wearing a red belt. Since it's nowhere near Christmas, I assume the combination of red belt and green polo shirt is not intentional. You're color-blind."

"Well, yeah," he said, buttoning his jacket over the offending belt. "But they don't ask you to tell red from green before they'll give you a marriage license. So?"

"If you were married, your wife might not check you over before you left each morning, but chances are she would organize your accessories so you could get dressed by yourself, and not have strange women like me commenting on your belt."

This is the final call for boarding Southwest Airlines flight twelve forty-four to Oakland at gate nine.

Kiernan glanced enviously at the last three Oakland-bound passengers as they passed through gate nine. If the Phoenix flight were not so late, she would be in the air now and that much closer to getting the suitcase in the right hands. Turning back to Siebert, she said, "By the same token, I'd guess you have been married or involved with a woman about my size. A blonde."

He sat back down in his seat, and for the first time was still.

"Got your attention, huh?" Kiernan laughed. "I really shouldn't show off like that. It unnerves some people. Others, like you, it just quiets down. Actually, this was pretty easy. You've got a tiny spot of lavender eye shadow on the edge of your lapel. I had a boyfriend your height, and he ended up sending a number of jackets to the cleaners. But no one but me would think to look at the edge of your lapel, and you could have that jacket for years and not notice that."

"But why did you say a blonde?"

"Blondes tend to wear violet eye shadow."
He smiled, clearly relieved.

Flight seventeen sixty-seven departing gate ten with service to Phoenix will begin boarding in just a few minutes. We thank you for your patience.

He groaned. "We'll see how few those minutes are." Across from them a woman with an elephantine carry-on bag pulled it closer to her. Siebert turned to Kiernan, and giving her that intimate grin she was beginning to think of as *his look*, Siebert said, "You seem to be having a good time being a detective."

The picture of Melissa Jessup popped up in her mind. Melissa Jessup had let herself be attracted to a thief. She'd ignored her suspicions about him until it was too late to sell her mother's jewels and she could only grab what was at hand and run. Kiernan pushed the thought away. Pulling her suitcase closer, she said, "Investigating can be a lot of fun if you like strange hours and the thrill of having everything hang on one maneuver. I'll tell you the truth, it appeals to the adolescent in me, particularly if I can pretend to be something or someone else. It's fun to see if I can pull that off."

"How do I know you're not someone else?"

"I could show you ID, but, of course, that wouldn't prove anything." She laughed. "You'll just have to trust me, as I am you. After all *you* did choose to sit down next to me."

"Well, that's because you were the best-looking woman here sitting by herself."

"Or at least the one nearest the hallway where you came in. And this is the only spot around where you have room to pace. You look to be a serious pacer." She laughed again. "But I like your explanation better."

Shrieking, a small girl in yellow raced in front of the seats. Whooping gleefully, a slightly larger male version of herself sprinted by. He lunged for his sister, caught his foot on Kiernan's crutch, and sent it toppling back as he lurched forward, and crashed into a man at the end of the check-in line. His sister skidded to a stop. "Serves you right, Jason. Mom, look what Jason did!"

Siebert bent over and righted Kiernan's crutch. "Travel can be dangerous, huh?"

"Damn crutches! It's like they've got urges all their own," she said. "Like one of them sees an attractive crutch across the room and all of a sudden it's gone. They virtually seduce underage boys."

He laughed, his green eyes twinkling impishly. "They'll come home to you. There's not a crutch in the room that can hold a *crutch* to you."

She hesitated a moment before saying, "My crutches and I thank you." This was, she thought, the kind of chatter that had been wonderfully seductive when she was nineteen. And Jeff Siebert was the restless, impulsive type of man who had personified freedom then. But nearly twenty years of mistakes—her own and more deadly ones like Melissa Jessup's—had shown her the inevitable end of such flirtations.

Siebert stood up and rested a foot against the edge of the table. "So what else is fun about investigating?"

She shifted the suitcase between her feet. "Well, trying to figure out people, like I was doing with you. A lot is common sense, like assuming that you are probably not a patient driver. Perhaps you've passed in a No Passing zone, or even have gotten a speeding ticket."

He nodded, abruptly.

"On the other hand," she went on, "sometimes I know facts beforehand, and then I can fake a Sherlock Holmes and produce anything-but-elementary deductions. The danger with that is getting cocky and blurting out conclusions before you've been given 'evidence' for them."

"Has that happened to you?"

She laughed and looked meaningfully down at her foot. "But I wouldn't want my client to come to that conclusion. We had a long discussion about whether a woman on crutches could handle his delivery."

"Client?" he said, shouting over the announcement of the Yuma flight at the next gate. In a normal voice, he added,

"In your courier work, you mean? What's in that bag of your client's that's so very valuable?"

She moved her feet till they were touching the sides of the suitcase. He leaned in closer. He was definitely the type of man destined to be trouble, she thought, but that little-boy grin, that conspiratorial tone was seductive, particularly in a place like this where any diversion was a boon. She wasn't surprised he had been attracted to her; clearly he was a man who liked little women. She glanced around, pleased that no one else had been drawn to this spot. The nearest travelers were a young couple seated six feet away and too involved in each other to waste time listening to strangers' conversation. "I didn't pack the bag. I'm just delivering it."

He bent down, ear near the side of the suitcase. "Well, at least it's not ticking." Sitting up, he said, "But seriously, isn't that a little dangerous? Women carrying bags for strangers, that's how terrorists have gotten bombs on planes."

"No!" she snapped. "I'm not carrying it for a lover with an M-1. I'm a bonded courier."

The casual observer might not have noticed Siebert's shoulders tensing, slightly, briefly, in anger at her rebuff. Silently, he looked down at her suitcase. "How much does courier work pay?"

"Not a whole lot, particularly compared to the value of what I have to carry. But then there's not much work involved. The chances of theft are minuscule. And I do get to travel. Last fall I drove a package up north. That was a good deal since I had to go up there anyway to check motel registrations in a case I'm working on. It took me a week to do the motels and then I came up empty." An entire week to discover that Melissa's killer had not stopped at a motel or hotel between San Diego and Eureka. "The whole thing would have been a bust if it hadn't been for the courier work."

He glanced down at the suitcase. She suspected he would have been appalled to know how visible was his covetous look. Finally he said, "What was in that package, the one you delivered?"

She glanced over at the young couple. No danger from

them. Still Kiernan lowered her voice. "Diamonds. Untraceable. That's really the only reason to go to the expense of hiring a courier."

"Untraceable, huh?" he said, grinning. "Didn't you even consider taking off over the border with them?"

"Maybe," she said slowly, "if I had known they were worth enough to set me up for the rest of my actuarial allotment, I might have."

We will begin pre-boarding Southwest Airlines flight seventeen sixty-seven with service to Phoenix momentarily. Please keep your seats until pre-boarding has been completed.

She pushed herself up, and positioned the crutches under her arms. It was a moment before he jerked his gaze away from the suitcase and stood, his foot tapping impatiently on the carpet. All around them families were hoisting luggage and positioning toddlers for the charge to the gate. He sighed loudly. "I hope you're good with your elbows."

She laughed and settled back on the arm of the seat.

His gaze went back to the suitcase. He said, "I thought couriers were handcuffed to their packages."

"You've been watching too much TV." She lowered her voice. "Handcuffs play havoc with the metal detector. The last thing you want in this business is buzzers going off and guards racing in from all directions. I go for the low-key approach. Always keep the suitcase in sight. Always be within lunging range."

He took a playful swipe at it. "What would happen if, say, that bag were to get stolen?"

"Stolen!" She pulled the suitcase closer to her. "Well, for starters, I wouldn't get a repeat job. If the goods were insured that might be the end of it. But if it were something untraceable"—she glanced at the suitcase—"it could be a lot worse." With a grin that matched his own, she said, "You're not a thief, are you?"

He shrugged. "Do I look like a thief?"

"You look like the most attractive man here." She paused

long enough to catch his eye. "Of course, looks can be deceiving." She didn't say it, but she could picture him pocketing a necklace carelessly left in a jewelry box during a big party, or a Seiko watch from under a poolside towel. She didn't imagine him planning a heist, but just taking what came his way.

Returning her smile, he said, "When you transport something that can't be traced, don't they even provide you a backup?"

"No! I'm a professional. I don't need backup."

"But with your foot like that?"

"I'm good with the crutches. And besides, the crutches provide camouflage. Who'd think a woman on crutches carrying a battered suitcase had anything worth half a mi— Watch out! The little girl and her brother are loose again." She pulled her crutches closer as the duo raced through the aisle in front of them.

We are ready to begin boarding Southwest Airlines flight number seventeen sixty-seven to Phoenix. Any passengers traveling with small children, or those needing a little extra time may begin boarding now.

The passengers applauded. It was amazing, she thought, how much sarcasm could be carried by a nonverbal sound.

She leaned down for the suitcase. "Pre-boarding. That's me."

"Are you going to be able to handle the crutches and the suitcase?" he asked.

"You're really fascinated with this bag, aren't you?"

"Guilty." He grinned. "Should I dare to offer to carry it? I'd stay within lunging range."

She hesitated.

In the aisle a woman in cerise shorts, carrying twin bags, herded twin toddlers toward the gate. Ahead of her an elderly man leaned precariously on a cane. The family with the boy and girl were still assembling luggage.

He said, "You'd be doing me a big favor letting me

pre-board with you. I like to cadge a seat in the first row on the aisle."

"The seat for the guy who can't wait?"

"Right. But I got here so late that I'm in the last boarding group. I'm never going to snag One B or One C. So help me out. I promise," he said, grinning, "I won't steal."

"Well . . . I wouldn't want my employer to see this. I assured him I wouldn't need any help. But . . ." She shrugged. "No time to waver now. There's already a mob of pre-boarders ahead of us."

He picked up the bag. "Some heavy diamonds."

"Good camouflage, don't you think? Of course, not everything's diamonds."

"Just something untraceable?"

She gave him a half wink. "It may not be untraceable. It may not even be valuable."

"And you may be just a regular mail carrier," he said, starting toward the gate.

She swung after him. The crutches were no problem and the thickly taped right ankle looked worse than it was. Still, it made things much smoother to have Siebert carrying the suitcase. If the opportunity arose, he might be tempted to steal it, but not in a crowded gate at the airport with guards and airline personnel around. He moved slowly, staying right in front of her, running interference. As they neared the gate, a blond man carrying a jumpy toddler hurried in front of them. The gate phone buzzed. The airline rep picked it up and nodded at it. To the blond man and the elderly couple who had settled in behind him, Kiernan, and Siebert, he said, "Sorry, folks. The cleaning crew's a little slow. It'll just be a minute."

Siebert's face scrunched in anger. "What's 'cleaning crew' a euphemism for? A tire fell off and they're looking for it? They've spotted a crack in the engine block and they're trying to figure out if they can avoid telling us?"

Kiernan laughed. "I'll bet people don't travel with you twice."

He laughed. "I just hate being at someone else's mercy. But since we're going to be standing here awhile, why don't you do what you love more than diamonds, Investigator: tell me what you've deduced about me."

"Like reading your palm?" The crutches poked into her armpits; she shifted them back, putting more weight on her bandaged foot. Slowly she surveyed his lanky body, his thin agile hands, con man's hands, hands that were never quite still, always past *Ready*, coming out of *Set*. "Okay. You're traveling from San Diego to Phoenix on the Friday evening flight, so chances are you were here on business. But you don't have on cowboy boots or a Stetson. You're tan, but it's not that dry tan you get in the desert. In fact you could pass for a San Diegan. I would have guessed that you travel for a living, but you're too impatient for that, and if you'd taken this flight once or twice before you wouldn't be surprised that it's late. You'd have a report to read, or a newspaper. No, you do something where you don't take orders, and you don't put up with much." She grinned. "How's that?"

"That's pretty elementary, Sherlock," he said with only a slight edge to his voice. He tapped his fingers against his leg. But all in all he looked only a little warier than any other person in the waiting area would as his secrets were unveiled.

Southwest Airlines flight number seventeen sixty-seven with service to Phoenix is now ready for pre-boarding.

"Okay, folks," the gate attendant called. "Sorry for the delay."

The man with the jittery toddler thrust his boarding pass at the gate attendant and strode down the ramp. The child screamed. The elderly couple moved haltingly, hoisting and readjusting their open sacks with each step. A family squeezed in in front of them, causing the old man to stop dead and move his bag to the other shoulder. Siebert shifted foot to foot.

Stretching up to whisper in his ear, Kiernan said, "It would look bad if you shoved the old people out of your way."

"How bad?" he muttered, grinning, then handed his boarding pass to the attendant.

As she surrendered hers, she said to Siebert, "Go ahead, hurry. I'll meet you in One C and D."

"Thanks." He patted her shoulder.

She watched him stride down the empty ramp. His tan jacket had caught on one hip as he balanced her suitcase and his own. But he neither slowed his pace nor made an attempt to free the jacket; clutching tight to her suitcase he hurried around the elderly couple, moving with the strong stride of a hiker. By the time she got down the ramp the elderly couple and a family with two toddlers and an infant that sucked loudly on a pacifier crowded behind Siebert.

Kiernan watched irritably as the stewardess eyed first Siebert then her big suitcase. The head stewardess has the final word on carry-on luggage, she knew. With all the hassle that was involved with this business anyway, she didn't want to add a confrontation with the stewardess. She dropped the crutches and banged backward into the wall, flailing for purchase as she slipped down to the floor. The stewardess caught her before she hit bottom. "Are you okay?"

"Embarrassed," Kiernan said truthfully. She hated to look clumsy, even if it was an act, even if it allowed Siebert and her suitcase to get on the plane unquestioned. "I'm having an awful time getting used to these things."

"You sure you're okay? Let me help you up," the stewardess said. "I'll have to keep your crutches in the hanging luggage compartment up front while we're in flight. But you go ahead now; I'll come and get them from you."

"That's okay. I'll leave them there and just sit in one of the front seats," she said, taking the crutches and swinging herself on board the plane. From the luggage compartment it took only one long step on her left foot to get to row one. She swung around Siebert, who was hoisting his own suitcase into the overhead bin beside hers, and dropped into One D, by the window. The elderly couple was settling into One A and One B. In another minute Southwest would call the first thirty passengers, and the herd would stampede down the ramp, stuffing approved carryons in overhead compartments, and grabbing the thirty most prized seats.

"That was a smooth move with the stewardess," Siebert said, as he settled into his coveted aisle seat.

"That suitcase is just about the limit of what they'll let you carry on. I've had a few hassles. I could see this one coming. And I suspected that you"—she patted his arm—"were not the patient person to deal with that type of problem. You moved around her pretty smartly yourself. I'd say that merits a drink from my client."

He smiled and rested a hand on hers. "Maybe," he said, leaning closer, "we could have it in Phoenix."

For the first time she had a viscerally queasy feeling about him. Freeing her hand from his, she gave a mock salute. "Maybe so." She looked past him at the elderly couple.

Siebert's gaze followed hers. He grinned as he said, "Do you think they're thieves? After your loot? Little old sprinters?"

"Probably not. But it pays to be alert." She forced a laugh. "I'm afraid constant suspicion is a side effect of my job."

The first wave of passengers hurried past. Already the air in the plane had the sere feel and slightly rancid smell of having been dragged through the filters too many times. By tacit consent they watched the passengers hurry on board, pause, survey their options, and rush on. Kiernan thought fondly of that drink in Phoenix. She would be sitting at a small table, looking out a tinted window, the trip would be over, the case delivered into the proper hands, and she would feel the tension that knotted her back releasing with each swallow of scotch. Or so she hoped. The whole frustrating case depended on this delivery. There was no fallback position. If she screwed up, Melissa Jessup's murderer disappeared.

That tension was what normally made the game fun. But this case was no longer a game. This time she had allowed herself to go beyond her regular rules, to call her former colleagues from the days when she had been a forensic pathologist, looking for some new test that would prove culpability. She had hoped the lab in San Diego could find something. They hadn't. The fact was that the diamonds were the only "something" that would trap the killer, Melissa's lover, who valued them much more than her, a man who might not have bothered going after her had it not been for them. Affairs might be brief, but diamonds, after all, are forever. They would lead her to the murderer's safe house, and the evidence that would tie him to Melissa. *If* she was careful.

She shoved the tongue of the seat belt into the latch and braced her feet as the plane taxied toward the runway. Siebert was tapping his finger on the armrest. The engines whirred, the plane shifted forward momentarily, then flung them back against their seats as it raced down the short runway.

The *fasten seat belt* sign went off. The old man across the aisle pushed himself up and edged toward the front bathroom. Siebert's belt was already unbuckled. Muttering, "Be right back," he jumped up, stood hunched under the overhead bin while the old man cleared the aisle. Then Siebert headed full-out toward the back of the plane. Kiernan slid over and watched him as he strode down the aisle, steps firmer, steadier than she'd have expected of a man racing to the bathroom in a swaying airplane. She could easily imagine him hiking in the redwood forest with someone like her, a small, slight woman. The blond woman with the violet eye shadow. She in jeans and one of those soft Patagonia jackets Kiernan had spotted in the L. L. Bean catalog, violet with blue trim. He in jeans, turtleneck, a forest-green down jacket on his rangy body. Forest-green would pick up the color of his eyes and accent his dark, curly hair. In her picture, his hair was tinted with the first flecks of autumn snow and the ground still soft like the spongy airplane carpeting beneath his feet.

When he got back he made no mention of his hurried trip. He'd barely settled down when the stewardess leaned over him and said, "Would you care for something to drink?"

Kiernan put a hand on his arm. "This one's on my client."

"For that client who insisted you carry his package while you're still on crutches I'm sorry it can't be Lafitte Rothschild. Gin and tonic will have to do." He grinned at the stewardess. Kiernan could picture him in a bar, flashing that grin at a tall redhead, or maybe another small blonde. She could imagine him with the sweat of a San Diego summer still on his brow, his skin brown from too many days at an ocean beach that is too great a temptation for those who grab their pleasures.

"Scotch and water," Kiernan ordered. To him, she said, "I notice that while I'm the investigator, it's you who are asking all the questions. So what about you, what do you do for a living?"

"I quit my job in San Diego and I'm moving back to Phoenix. So I'm not taking the first Friday night flight to get back home, I'm taking it to get to my new home. I had good times in San Diego: the beach, the sailing, Balboa Park. When I came there a couple years ago I thought I'd stay forever. But the draw of the desert is too great. I miss the red rock of Sedona, the pines of the Mogollon Rim, and the high desert outside Tucson." He laughed. "Too much soft California life."

It was easy to picture him outside of Show Low on the Mogollon Rim with the pine trees all around him, some chopped for firewood, the axe lying on a stump, a shovel in his hand. Or in a cabin near Sedona lifting a hatch in the floorboards.

The stewardess brought the drinks and the little bags of peanuts, giving Jeff Siebert the kind of smile Kiernan knew would have driven her crazy had she been Siebert's girlfriend. How often had that type of thing happened? Had his charm brought that reaction so automatically that for him it had seemed merely the way women behave? Had complaints from a girlfriend seemed at first unreasonable, then melodramatic, then infuriating? He was an impatient man, quick to anger. Had liquor made it quicker, like the rhyme said? And the prospect of unsplit profit salved his conscience?

He poured the little bottle of gin over the ice and added tonic. "Cheers."

She touched glasses, then drank. "Are you going to be in Phoenix long?"

"Probably not. I've come into a little money and I figure I'll just travel around, sort of like you do. Find some place I like."

"So we'll just have time for our drink in town then?"

He rested his hand back on hers. "Well, now I may have reason to come back in a while. Or to San Diego. I just need to cut loose for a while."

She forced herself to remain still, not to cringe at his touch. *Cut loose*—what an apt term for him to use. She pictured his sun-browned hand wrapped around the hilt of a chef's knife, working it up and down, up and down, cutting across pink flesh till it no longer looked like flesh, till the flesh mixed with the blood and the organ tissue, till the knife cut down to the bone and the metal point stuck in the breastbone. She pictured Melissa Jessup's blond hair pink from the blood.

She didn't have to picture her body lying out in the woods outside Eureka in northern California. She had seen photos of it. She didn't have to imagine what the cracked ribs and broken clavicle and the sternum marked from the knife point looked like now. Jeff Siebert had seen that too, and had denied what Melissa's brother and the Eureka sheriff all knew—knew in their hearts but could not prove—that Melissa had not gone to Eureka camping by herself as he'd insisted, but had only stopped overnight at the campground she and Jeff had been to the previous summer because she had no money, and hadn't been able to bring herself to sell the diamonds her mother had left her. Instead of a rest on the way to freedom, she'd found Siebert there.

Now Siebert was flying to Phoenix to vanish. He'd pick up Melissa's diamonds wherever he'd stashed them, then he'd be gone.

"What about your client?" he asked. "Will he be meeting you at the airport?"

"No. No one will meet me. I'll just deliver my goods to

the van, collect my money, and be free. What about you?"

"No. No one's waiting for me either. At least I'll be able to give you a hand with that bag. There's no ramp to the terminal in Phoenix. You have to climb down to the tarmac there. Getting down those metal steps with a suitcase and two crutches would be a real balancing act."

All she had to do was get it in the right hands. She shook her head. "Thanks. But I'll have to lug it through the airport just in case. My client didn't handcuff the suitcase to me, but he does expect I'll keep hold of it."

He grinned. "Like you said, you'll be in lunging range all the time."

"No," she said firmly. "I appreciate your offer, Jeff; the bag weighs a ton. But I'm afraid it's got to be in my hand."

Those green eyes of his that had twinkled with laughter narrowed, and his lips pressed together. "Okay," he said slowly. Then his face relaxed almost back to that seductively impish smile that once might have charmed her, as it had Melissa Jessup. "I want you to know that I'll still find you attractive even if the bag yanks your shoulder out of its socket." He gave her hand a pat, then shifted in his seat so his upper arm rested next to hers.

The stewardess collected the glasses. The plane jolted and began its descent. Kiernan braced her feet. Through his jacket, she felt the heat of his arm, the arm that had dug that chef's knife into Melissa Jessup's body. She breathed slowly and did not move.

To Kiernan, he said, "There's a great bar right here in Sky Harbor Airport, the Sky Lounge. Shall we have our drink there?"

She nodded, her mouth suddenly too dry for speech.

The plane bumped down and in a moment the aisles were jammed with passengers ignoring the stewardess's entreaty to stay in their seats. Siebert stood up and pulled his bag out of the overhead compartment and then lifted hers onto his empty seat. "I'll get your crutches," he said, as the elderly man across the aisle pushed his way out in front of him. Siebert shook his head. Picking up both suitcases, he maneuvered around the man and around the corner to the luggage compartment.

Siebert had taken her suitcase. *You don't need to take both suitcases to pick up the crutches.* Kiernan stared after him, her shoulders tensing, her hands clutching the armrests. Her throat was so constricted she could barely breathe. For an instant, she shared the terror that must have paralyzed Melissa Jessup just before he stabbed her.

"Jeff!" she called after him, a trace of panic evident in her voice. He didn't answer her. Instead, she heard a great thump, then him muttering and the stewardess's voice placating.

The airplane door opened. The elderly man moved out into the aisle in front of Kiernan, motioning his wife to go ahead of him, then they moved slowly toward the door.

Kiernan yanked the bandage off her foot, stepped into the aisle. "Excuse me," she said to the couple. Pushing by them as Siebert had so wanted to do, she rounded the corner to the exit.

The stewardess was lifting up a garment bag. Four more bags lay on the floor. So that was the thump she'd heard. A crutch was beside them.

She half heard the stewardess's entreaties to wait, her mutterings about the clumsy man. She looked out the door down onto the tarmac.

Jeffrey Siebert and the suitcase were gone. In those few seconds he had raced down the metal steps and was disappearing into the terminal. By the time she could make it to the Sky Lounge he would be halfway to Show Low, or Sedona.

Now she felt a different type of panic. *This* wasn't in the plan. She couldn't lose Siebert. She jumped over the bags, grabbed one crutch, hurried outside to the top of the stairs, and thrust the crutch across the handrails behind her to make a seat. As the crutch slid down the railings, she kept her knees bent high into her chest to keep from landing and bucking forward onto her head. Instead the momentum propelled her on her feet, as it had in gymnastics. In those routines, she'd had to fight the momentum, now she went with it and ran, full-out.

She ran through the corridor toward the main building, pushing past businessmen, between parents carrying children. Siebert would be running ahead. But no one would stop him, not in an airport. People ran through airports all the time. Beside the metal detectors she saw a man in a tan jacket. Not him. By the luggage pickup another look-alike. She didn't spot him till he was racing out the door to the parking lot.

Siebert raced across the roadway. A van screeched to a halt. Before Kiernan could cross through the traffic a hotel bus eased in front of her. She skirted behind it. She could sense a man following her now. But there was no time to deal with that. Siebert was halfway down the lane of cars. Bent low, she ran down the next lane, the hot dusty desert air drying her throat. By the time she came abreast of Siebert, he was in a light blue Chevy pickup backing out of the parking slot. He hit the gas and, wheels squealing, drove off.

She reached toward the truck with both arms. Siebert didn't stop. She stood watching as Jeffrey Siebert drove off into the sunset.

There was no one behind her as she sauntered into the terminal to the Sky Lounge. She ordered the two drinks Siebert had suggested, and when they came, she tapped "her" glass on "his," and took a drink for Melissa Jessup. Then she swallowed the rest of the drink in two gulps.

By this time Jeff Siebert would be on the freeway. He'd be fighting to stay close to the speed limit, balancing his thief's wariness of the highway patrol against his gnawing urge to force the lock on the suitcase. Jeffrey Siebert was an impatient man, a man who had nevertheless made himself wait nearly a year before leaving California. His stash of self-control would be virtually empty. But he would wait awhile before daring to stop. Then he'd jam a knife between the top and bottom of the suitcase, pry and twist it till the case fell open. He would find diamonds. More diamonds.

Diamonds to take along while he picked up Melissa Jessup's from the spot where he'd hidden them.

She wished Melissa Jessup could see him when he compared the two collections, and realized the new ones he'd stolen were fakes. She wished she herself could see his face when he realized that a woman on crutches had made it out of the plane in time to follow him to point out the blue pickup truck.

Kiernan picked up "Jeff's" glass and drank more slowly. How sweet it would be if Melissa could see that grin of his fade as the surveillance team surrounded him, drawn by the beepers concealed in those fake diamonds. He'd be clutching the evidence that would send him to jail. Just for life, not forever. As Melissa could have told him, only death and diamonds are forever.

*Jan Grape is another PWA member whose short stories
are becoming more in demand by anthology editors. She
has appeared previously in* Deadly Allies I & II, *some of
the* Cat Crimes *anthologies, as well as* Murder for Santa
and Partners in Crime. *Here her P.I. partners C.J. and
Jenny take on a "One-Day Job" that somehow becomes
more complicated than it sounds.*

A ONE-DAY JOB

by Jan Grape

EVEN WITH DEEP creases around her mouth and eyes, and
skin that was leathery—tanned by wind and sun—
something about her presence told me Mrs. Gillingwater would be equally at home astride a horse or at a fancy
dress ball. Her hair, pulled back in a long ponytail, was
dishwater blond streaked with gray. "Ms. Gordon, I just
don't know what to do or where to turn. Those people won't
even talk to me, although I guess I can't blame them. They
think Cord is responsible for Tyler's . . ." Her voice broke,
but for only a moment, then she was back in control again.
". . . for their son's death." Worry was obvious in the line
between her brows, and pain was even stronger in her
pecan-colored eyes.

A woman obviously used to adversity, I had the feeling she could handle anything from a sick calf to a hailstorm destroying their cotton crop. She was descended from that breed of West Texas pioneer women I used to read about, the kind whose grandmothers fought smallpox and Indians and the stark landscape of early Texas.

Maudie Rae Gillingwater had come into C & G Investigations a few minutes earlier saying an Austin homicide lieutenant named Larry Hays had suggested she talk to us. He told her my partner and I might not be the best known private eyes in Austin, but we *were* good investigators.

Larry Hays had been my late husband's friend and partner for ten years before Tommy left the police department and opened an investigator's office. Larry had never been too generous with praise, but his attitude was changing in recent months. And now he even referred clients to us sometimes.

"And you think, Mrs. Gillingwater, that these people know where your daughter is?" I asked.

"Please call me Maudie Rae," she said.

"Okay, Maudie Rae, and I'm Jenny."

"The Kents *have* to know where Megan is. She's been staying with them. But I'm also sure she told them Cord kicked her out and to keep us away from her." She was sitting on the edge of the chair as if she might leap up and walk out at any moment.

I wondered if she was uncomfortable talking to me or if she just had trouble relaxing period. I decided it was probably a little of both.

Suddenly, she blurted out, "All right, I'll admit I was the one who kicked her out, not Cord. But I didn't seriously mean it and Megan knows that. She and I hadn't been getting along even before she got pregnant."

"How far along is she?"

"Almost six months." She shook her head. "Has it only been a month since we found out she was expecting? Seems like this thing has gone on forever."

I'd heard about the case, of course, it had been a hot topic for days. It began four weeks ago in Chisholm, Texas, when the Gillingwaters' daughter turned up pregnant. A few days after that her father had accosted young Kent in front of a witness at the high school, threatening to kill the boy. And the two youngsters had run away—from the small West Texas town to Austin, where the boy's parents lived.

The night they left, Gillingwater was again overheard threatening the boy. Two days after arriving in Austin, Tyler Kent had been shot and killed, and yesterday Cordell Gillingwater had been arrested for the boy's murder.

The fact that Tyler Kent and Megan Gillingwater were sixteen years old had drawn a sympathetic press like stink on a hog pen. Austin's news media had a feeding frenzy—the star-crossed lovers, a modern-day Romeo and Juliet—hinted of tabloid-headline-type news, and reporters have always loved an underdog.

"How did Megan get involved with a boy from Austin?"

"Tyler was living with his grandmother in Chisholm. I don't know the details, but he and his father were in Chisholm taking care of some family business, and then the father left and the boy stayed and started high school. He and Megan started dating during football season. Both parents came to Chisholm at Thanksgiving. Megan had dinner with them.

"That's when my daughter and I first had harsh words over Tyler. I thought she was too young to get serious over any one boy. She didn't want to hear what I thought."

How can mothers and daughters get so angry at each other and say such horrid things? (But what do I know about motherhood? I grew up without mine.) "And your daughter's only sixteen. That's underage, isn't it? Can't you force her to come back?"

"Legally, yes. I talked to your Lieutenant Hayes about it," said Maudie Rae. "I learned I could go to court—get a writ of habeas corpus or some big legal term, and the Kents would have to show up in court with Megan. But all that legal stuff costs money, and I've already had to sell off a good-sized herd of cattle to hire a competent defense lawyer for Cordell."

"Who did you get?"

"Bulldog Porter."

"He's good, maybe even the best defense lawyer in the whole state," I said with a smile.

"I sure hope so for what he's costing."

"I'm surprised you were able to get him to take the case. He's been semiretired for several months." Bulldog's seventy-eight years had finally begun to show after a case we'd helped him with a few months ago turned sour. The lawyer had had strong emotional ties to the young man involved, and C.J. and I had worried about Bulldog ever since—not knowing if he would ever snap back to his former self.

"Mr. Porter went to elementary and junior high school with my mother-in-law down in Galveston. They haven't seen each other for something like sixty years, but she asked for his help. He talked to Cord and afterward said he'd defend him." She cleared her throat. "But he also wanted a ten-thousand-dollar cashier's check for deposit up front."

"That's probably standard."

"Even for the son of an old girlfriend? Looks to me like he'd be a little more trusting."

"One thing I know about Bulldog is that he always manages to get more serious about a case when someone is willing to put their money on the line."

"Maybe things are done like that in a big city, but out in Chisholm, Texas, a man's word counts for something."

"It is different in Austin, Maudie Rae. People get jaded and cynical in cities."

"Well, whatever. I did raise the money for Mr. Porter's fee, but it wouldn't be easy to scrape up another fee like that for another lawyer to get the Kents and Megan into court. I mean, we have the money, but Porter thinks he can get Cord's bond reduced and I'll need ten percent of however much that is to get him out of jail." She leaned back in the chair, rubbed her eyes, and scratched the end of her nose with her thumb. "Oh, if worst comes to worst I can get cash from Mother Gillingwater, but Lordy, Lordy, that woman makes you pay two lifetimes of making up when she does a favor for you."

"I had a grandmother like that," I said. "Did you ask Mr.

Porter if he could do the writ for you? Maybe for a reduced fee?"

"Yes, but he suggested I talk to you and Ms. Gunn, first."

"And you've tried talking to the Kents yourself without . . ."

"I went over to the Kents' house, but Mr. Kent, I think his name is Gene, said he didn't know where Megan was and for me to get the hell off his property before he called the cops." She asked if I minded if she smoked and when I said "no" she opened her purse and pulled out one of those thin cigarillos and lit it.

I opened a drawer and pushed an ashtray over to the edge of my desk for her as Maudie Rae continued talking.

"Mr. Kent was quite belligerent, cussing me out, and I left because I was afraid he'd stroke out or I would. I've also called four times, but each time they hang up when they discover who's calling. If you'd be willing to find and talk to Megan, maybe you can talk some sense into that girl. The idea that she thinks her father would kill anyone is absolutely beyond belief."

"The police have charged him . . ."

"I know, but there's no way in hell that Cordell Gillingwater could have killed that boy, and Megan ought to be the first to admit it. He's the most tenderhearted man I've ever known. Everyone knows how he cries and leaves home just because it's time to cut the steers.

"Besides, we had just arrived in Austin the night Tyler was killed. Cord was exhausted. We had dinner in our rooms and went to sleep early."

"The police didn't believe you?"

"They said if I was asleep how did I know Cord didn't leave the room."

"And . . ."

"When you've been sleeping next to a man as long as I've been sleeping next to Cord, one thing is for certain—you might not wake up every time he goes to take a leak, but you sure as hell know when the bed is empty for more than five or ten minutes."

Her story had a ring of truth. Tommy and I had been

married for ten years before he died, and although he was a cop and worked different shifts through the years, I'd always had trouble sleeping soundly in an empty bed. It was months after his death before I was able to sleep more than twenty or thirty minutes at a time.

My partner, an ex-policewoman named Cinnamon Jemima Gunn, better known as C.J., chose that moment to walk into the office. C.J. had been in Dallas conducting a seminar on tracing financial assets by computer. I introduced her to Mrs. Gillingwater and filled her in on what we were being asked to do.

Maudie Rae wanted to know what we'd charge to try to find Megan, and since C.J.'s the one who keeps our books, I usually defer those decisions to her.

"Two hundred a day plus expenses," said C.J. "It shouldn't take more than two or three days." She pulled out a contract from the file cabinet, handing it to Maudie Rae. "We'll need a deposit."

I watched Maudie Rae's face as she grimaced and I spoke up. "Two hundred will be just fine, Mrs. Gillingwater." I ignored C.J.'s pointed stare.

Mrs. Gillingwater said she was staying at the Executive Suites Hotel as she gave C.J. the check. She signed the contract with a flourish and then opened her purse and gave us a photograph of her daughter. "When you find Megan, please, tell her I love her. Tell her where I'm staying if she needs me."

As soon as the woman walked out the door, C.J.'s kola-nut-colored face got that haughty Nefertiti look that I hate. She reminds me of that actress who played Lieutenant Uhura on the original *Star Trek*, but when she puts on the Egyptian queen's face—I'm in trouble. "Why did you butt in? You should always ask for a two-day minimum. When will you ever learn?"

My partner is six feet tall in her stocking feet, modeled in New York and Paris in her late teens before she became a cop. Normally she moves as gracefully as a panther, but when she's mad she stomps around like a linebacker. She stalked out to the front reception room to her desk and sat in her swivel chair.

I followed her and sat opposite. "I just felt sorry for her—the legal fees are eating her up already."

"Jenny, if what I've heard is true those people have oil and cattle running out the yazoo. Not to mention cotton and . . ."

"And her pregnant sixteen-year-old daughter doesn't want to talk to her and her husband is in jail for murder."

"Sheesh. Hard-luck stories always make you act . . ."

"All you think about is money."

"Someone has to, you obviously never do."

"We've paid the rent this month. We've paid all the bills and took out our salaries—what more do you want?"

"I'd like to be a little ahead instead of always scrambling. I'd like to be able to save . . ."

I started laughing. "Holy cow. Would you listen to us? We sound like an old married couple."

C.J. could never keep a straight face when I got tickled. "You ain't never lied and you ain't even my type." Lapsing into the uneducated dialogue really set me off, because C.J.'s a college graduate.

When I could talk again I said, "Okay. Look, two hundred is a one-day charge and if the lady has assets like you say, she's good for the rest."

"Maybe. I'll know more when I run some computer checks on her." She turned on her computer and started her nimble fingers to work. "But next time when we get to the money part with a client—keep your mouth shut, bitch."

I walked into my inner office without saying anything, but when I reached the doorway, I turned and stuck my tongue out at her back.

"I saw that. Tacky, tacky."

"Bitches do things like that." How had she known?

She turned off the computer and opened the bottom drawer in her desk. "Get your purse and beeper, turn the answering machine on, and let's go see if we can talk to Megan Gillingwater."

The Kents' house was on the edge of the Hyde Park area

of central Austin. One of the oldest neighborhoods in the city, it still retains a genteel charm. The address we wanted was a house made of native rock, burnished a muddy brown by the weather, but freshly painted white shutters brightened it considerably. Oleanders bloomed at each corner, and the flower beds which ran the length of the front were full of the bright colors of petunias, marigolds, zinnias, pansies, and roses.

Native pecan trees and one huge magnolia loaded with white full flowers gave the front yard shade, a welcome addition to the ninety-degree weather of early May. A long driveway led to the back and a detached two-car garage.

I rang the doorbell, which was quickly answered by a tiny woman about my age (thirty-five) with fuzzy blond hair. She wore a white T-shirt emblazoned with Mickey Mouse and a pair of black denim shorts. She was barefoot. "Mrs. Kent?" I asked.

"Yes, yes. Come on in. I know I promised you an hour, but I really don't have that much time today." She turned and was halfway down the hall before I could answer.

C.J. and I looked at each other, shrugged, and followed the woman, who led us to a family room at the back of the house.

She gestured to the French doors which opened to a wide expanse of a St. Augustine lawn edged by crepe myrtle and mimosas, each in full bloom. Someone had spent many hours taking care of the outside. "We can go out back after you've seen the house."

"I beg your pardon?" said C.J.

"Mrs. Kent? I think there's been some mis . . ."

She looked at us expectantly and nodded toward the kitchen, "We might as well start in there. Are you taking photographs, too?"

". . . take. I don't think we're who you expected," I said.

"You mean you're not from Century Twenty-one?" she asked. "We're selling this house and . . ." She stopped. "Who are you, then?"

A slender teenage girl whose abdomen pooched with pregnancy walked out of the kitchen and into the family room drinking a large glass of milk. It was Megan Gillingwater.

"Megan," I said. "I'm Jenny Gordon and this is C.J. Gunn. We're private investigators. Your mother hired us to find . . ."

"Get them out of here," Megan said, but she didn't yell or actually speak much louder than a stage whisper. "I don't want them anywhere near me." She paused, looking like a deer caught in the bright beams of an automobile, then ran across the room passing directly in front of me. I put out my arm to stop her, but she brushed it aside and headed into the hallway.

Mrs. Kent started yelling, "How dare you come into my house!"

"Let's just everyone calm down and see if we can have a nice conversation here." I heard C.J.'s placating tone as I started after Megan, leaving C.J. to deal with Mrs. Kent.

I caught up with the girl when she reached a bedroom off to her right. She darted into the room, with me right behind, and flung herself down on a big four-poster bed covered with a patchwork quilt.

"Megan. I only want to talk to you." The girl's shoulders shook with emotion.

"Please don't cry. Listen a minute and if you don't like what I'm saying, I promise I won't bother you anymore."

I thought she was going to ignore me, but finally she rolled over, sat up, showing me a profile.

Her hair was long, almost to her waist, and looked like a honey-blond waterfall, cascading around her head. Her dark blue eyes were bright in her pale face.

She glanced at me, but let her eyes slide off mine and looked somewhere off to my left. She still didn't speak.

"Megan, your mother wanted me to tell you that your father did not kill Tyler. She says if you think about it rationally, you'll know she's telling the truth. That your father isn't capable of murder. She doesn't know who killed him, but please stop thinking it was your father."

"I don't want to hear any more. Please leave now." She turned her back to me in obvious dismissal.

"I'll go, but your mother wanted me to tell you if you need anything or if you want to talk she's staying at the Executive Suites Hotel."

Her voice was muffled at first when she said, "I will never, ever want anything from my mother." Her eyes flashed with defiance, but she still wouldn't look directly at me. "You tell her that, lady." Her voice was monotonic and I strained to hear.

"And I never ever want to see her again either. Tell her to leave me alone," she said.

She tried but failed to convince me that she meant it. That's when I saw the teardrop fall and watched as she brushed her cheek. I wanted to keep her talking. Something was going on here, but I didn't know what. "If that's what you want me to tell her, okay, but that's no way to treat the grandmother of your baby. Little kids need . . ."

The love-hate relationship with her mother took over and she spoke up. "Don't throw that grandmother crap at me. She's not ready to be a grandmother yet. Said she was much too young."

"I'm sure she didn't mean it."

"Oh, she meant it. She made it perfectly clear. My mother never says something she doesn't mean." She got up from the bed and walked over to turn on a television. "Something else you should know about my mother. She leads my dad around by the balls. She tells him what to do and he does it. He can't wipe his ass without her permission. If she told Daddy to do something about Tyler, my dad would probably do it."

"Do you think your mother would say something like that to your dad?"

"I guess so, I don't know," she whispered. Her flash of rebellion was obviously over.

Suddenly loud voices came from the family room where I'd left C.J. and Mrs. Kent. Gene Kent had come home in a bad mood or maybe that's how he always was. "My wife asked you to leave and Megan asked you to leave. I want you people out of this house right now or I'm throwing you out."

C.J. wouldn't take threats like that from anyone. She was a black belt in TuKong martial arts and had a quick temper. And if he even tried to make her leave before she was ready, he might find himself on the floor looking up in stunned surprise.

I reached the room, just in time to see what I'd been afraid of happening happen. I saw Kent grab C.J.'s shoulder as if to propel her out and next he was on the floor writhing in pain before I could intervene. It was hard to tell with him lying prone, but he looked to be a fairly good-sized man. A brawny construction-worker type. Size didn't matter to C.J.—she'd take on anyone if necessary.

Mrs. Kent stood in the doorway to the kitchen, hand over her mouth, but I thought I saw a brief flash of satisfaction on her face before a mask dropped down.

Megan, who had been close on my heels, hurried to Mrs. Kent. There was no mistaking the fear I saw in their eyes as they stood, arms around each other, looking down at the man of the house.

"C.J. Haven't I told you to ignore clods like that? Let's get out of here before things seriously escalate." I took one arm which she tried to shake off, but I got a vice grip and began steering her to the front door. "I'm sorry, Mrs. Kent. Please offer my apologies to your husband, too," I called back over my shoulder.

I managed to get C.J. inside my car. "Damn it, C.J., the man might file assault charges against you." I started the engine and we drove away.

"No. An asshole like Kent wouldn't ever want to admit he was bested by a woman." She was under control except for her voice.

"Something else happened before the shouting started." And I knew the answer before she told me. The signs had been there in both Megan and Mrs. Kent.

She was rubbing her arm where I had held on to drag her outside. "Kent came in," she said. "When his wife said who we were and what was going on, he knocked the tar out of her."

"But I didn't see any evidence . . ."

"You know the type; hits where it never shows. He got her in the stomach and alongside her head—around her ears—before coming after me."

"Then I'm glad you laid the bastard out." I headed the car to ADP headquarters. We needed details on the Kent boy's case directly from Lieutenant Larry Hays.

We entered headquarters by the front door. There's a circular counter in the atrium lobby which looks more like a hotel or office building lobby. The cops all call it "the donut." Brick terrazzo covers the floor, and the walls are beige and burnt orange. After calling upstairs for Larry to escort us, the officer in the donut ignored us. I walked over to look at the old photographs of police cars and officers of Austin in the past.

After Larry greeted us, he led us to the third floor, where Homicide occupies the south side. Things have changed since Tommy worked here. Most noticeable are the movable panels about five feet high which are covered appropriately in blood-red carpet and divide desks into cubicles. It was a strange feeling to be in this department where my husband had often spent more hours in a day than he had with me.

We filled Larry in on what had happened at the Kents, and when I got to the part about C.J.'s demolition woman moves, he stifled a cough that I felt sure was a disguised laugh. "C.J., you're going to regret this in a day or two."

"It was worth it no matter what happens," she said.

"You know she seldom thinks before she acts," I said. "Look, I know you don't have much time, but what can you tell us about the case and what evidence is there against Cordell Gillingwater?"

"Since the case is still active, I can only tell you what's already public knowledge. The murder weapon was found under the front seat of his car. No fingerprints. He had a strong motive, and he'd threatened the kid."

"And he doesn't have a strong alibi," I said.

"I'm much more interested in Mr. Kent," said C.J. "Hell, I never even saw him before today, but I'll bet he's got a rap sheet."

Larry nodded. "Several family disturbances, assaults, drunk and disorderly. No convictions."

"Long history of violence. Could be something there between him and the son," I said.

"We looked at Kent closely, but there was nothing to connect him to his son's death," said Larry.

"Well, I'd look again if I were you." C.J.'s voice was harsh as she walked out, heading for the elevators.

"Tell her to keep that temper under control." Larry smiled. "I'd hate to have to arrest her."

"I don't tell C.J. anything. I sometimes ask and sometimes plead, but . . ."

"I know, but remind her that just because she doesn't like that asshole is no reason to arrest him for murder."

I caught up with C.J. at the elevator. "Let's go to the Hyatt and have a couple of beers and a bunch of fajitas."

She smiled. "Sounds like my kind of evening."

The telephone woke me at six a.m. It was Lieutenant Hays and his voice was grim. "Megan Gillingwater tried to kill herself. You want to meet me at Brackenridge Hospital?"

"I'll be there in thirty minutes." I hung up and called C.J.

"I knew something's going on with those people, but I haven't been able to figure all the ins and outs yet," she said. "Pick me up on your way?"

Larry Hays was sitting beside Maudie Rae Gillingwater in the ICU waiting room. "How is Megan?" I asked.

"They think she'll be okay," said Larry. "She took some pills."

"The biggest worry is for the baby," said Maudie Rae. Our client's face showed she'd been crying, but she was holding up pretty well. "I'm waiting to go in to see her," said Maudie Rae. I gave her a hug and tears filled her eyes briefly. Then a nurse came and said she could go see her daughter.

C.J. went to find some coffee and Larry and I walked out into the corridor. Several people were in the waiting room and we wanted to be able to talk without bothering them.

"Where's Mrs. Kent?"

"Home, I guess. I think she's the one who called 911, but I'm not sure."

"This is her dead son's girlfriend here. The baby is her grandchild, too. You'd think she'd want to be here."

"Nothing about any of these people seems right to me," he said.

"You mean the Kents?"

"I mean both the Kents and the Gillingwaters."

"Maudie Rae seems like a pretty good old gal. I haven't met Cordell."

"He's about like you'd imagine a West Texas rancher to be—strong and silent. But I think she's capable of most anything."

"Ms. Gordon?" It was Maudie Rae. "Megan wants to see you."

Larry turned to go, too, but the nurse in the pale pink scrub suit who was waiting to escort me to Megan's bedside said, "She said only Ms. Gordon."

The private room Megan Gillingwater had was small, and there was a window with a desk-type ledge and a pass-through box on one side of the door. The nurses could stand outside to do their paperwork and keep an eye on the patient at the same time.

The girl was pale against the bed sheets and looked about twelve. Her blond hair was matted, and there were plastic tubes leading to veins and one to her bladder. Wires ran to machines and a blood-pressure cuff was wrapped around her right arm. I could see a green pulsing light on one monitor and another one had red numbers that kept flashing, and the blipping noises sounded loud. That's when I realized it was monitoring the baby's heart and pulse rate.

Her eyes were closed, but she opened them when the nurse told her she had company.

"Hello, Megan."

She licked her lips and stammered a little. "Uh, sorry. I wanted to, uh, talk to you."

"Okay, Megan. You're doing just fine."

The nurse said I could stay five minutes and pushed a

chair over for me before leaving. She could see us through the Plexiglas window and watch the machines which also monitored Megan's heart rate and blood pressure.

Megan spoke hesitantly and the words came out in broken sentences. "I couldn't get away from him, uh, I tried but he hit me again and again. In the stomach."

"Mr. Kent?"

She nodded. "The only way to get help was to take the pills. He said he would kill me, my baby, and his wife, too, if I told anyone or left the house.

"Gene raped me," she said. "The baby's not Tyler's, but Tyler found out." Tears ran down her cheeks and splashed on the hospital gown.

It was something out of a nightmare. Poor kid was raped, assaulted, and intimidated.

"My father didn't kill Tyler either," she said. "But I saw him die. His father did it."

"Mr. Kent killed his own son?"

She nodded and great heaving sobs began which set off an alarm on the machine.

The nurse came in and started talking soothingly to Megan.

"I didn't do anything," I told the nurse.

"I know. She's agitated herself." She smoothed back Megan's hair and said, "Take slow, long breaths. Think about lying back on fluffy white clouds and floating in a warm summer breeze. Breathe, breathe."

The heartbeat sounds slowed, and the nurse told Megan to keep taking the rhythmic breaths. "Maybe you should talk to Ms. Gordon a little later, Megan."

"No. Have to tell, uh, before something else happens. I didn't want to come down here, but Tyler insisted we confront his father about the rape. That's when Gene Kent killed Tyler. Then he wouldn't let me leave the house or talk to anyone. And I'm still scared because . . ."

"Mrs. Kent's in danger?"

She nodded and closed her eyes.

"Okay, honey," I said. "I'll take care of it." I stood, but

she opened her eyes and her look of despair was almost tangible.

Suddenly she began twisting and turning. "Owww, it hurts. My belly hurts. He hurt my baby." The alarm on the monitor went off again. Another nurse rushed in and said I'd have to leave.

I overheard one nurse, I didn't know which, say in a stage whisper, "She's getting ready to abort."

What should I tell Maudie Rae? That Megan had cleared Cordell? And what about the baby? I certainly didn't feel qualified to say that Megan might lose the baby.

For the time being, I decided the less said the better. When I got back to the waiting room I told Maudie Rae that Megan was fine, but that I needed to talk to Lieutenant Hays alone for a few moments. I could tell she wanted more details, but she'd wait if necessary.

Larry and C.J. knew me well enough to know what I had to say was important and followed me into the hallway without asking any questions. C.J. handed me a Styrofoam cup with coffee as we moved far enough away to keep from being overheard.

I told them what Megan had said, and C.J. said, "I just had a feeling that scumbag was bad news."

Larry said, "I'd better send a patrol car over to check on Mrs. Kent." He said he'd fill us in later and took off.

When we got back to the ICU waiting room, a nurse was talking to Maudie Rae. When I heard the news that Megan had lost the baby, I couldn't help feeling some relief for the girl. Things will be much better this way, I thought.

Later that evening, as C.J. and I sat outside on my patio, Larry Hays telephoned to say Mrs. Kent had disappeared, but Gene Kent had been arrested.

"Do you think he killed her?" I asked.

"I think it's highly probable. I think when Megan went to the hospital Kent knew it was all unraveling and maybe the wife said something about going to the police. We may never find out what happened and we may never find her unless Kent decides to confess."

"Ask Larry about Gillingwater," C.J. said.

"I heard her," he said. "We've released him and I imagine he's at the hospital with his family."

I hung up the receiver and turned to C.J. "We cleared this up in one day. Now, aren't you glad I didn't get any more than two hundred dollars from Maudie Rae? I know how you hate to refund money."

"Lucked into it this time, didn't you? But next time . . ."

"I'll keep my mouth shut when it's time to discuss money."

I leaned back in my lounge chair, feeling pretty satisfied with myself, took another sip of my beer and watched some thunderheads rolling in from West Texas.

While compiling Deadly Allies *together, editors Bob Randisi and Marilyn Wallace both saw this story after the volume was full. When Bob told Marilyn that he wanted to buy it for his next PWA anthology, she replied, "Too late, I already bought it for the next* Sisters in Crime *anthology." It appeared in* Sisters in Crime 4, *and features her P.I. Catherine Sayler. We think you'll see why two editors were ready to fight over it.*

LAST RITES

by Linda Grant

Monday

SOMEWHERE AROUND THIRTY-FIVE the future shrinks, and you realize you won't live forever. Not long after that you begin to look at old people with newfound interest. I was between those two points when my aunt Janet broke her hip and summoned me to her bedside to solve a murder.

Janet is not one of my favorite people. Timid and rather querulous, she is the sort who gives old women a bad name. Show her a rose; she'll notice the aphids. I try not to blame her. Hannah Sayler couldn't have been an easy mother to have, God knows she wasn't even an easy grandmother.

The Chinese bound their daughters' feet; Hannah bound their spirits.

My dad and his brother escaped somehow. They got all the humor, life, and spirit in the family, leaving Janet to peek behind the closet door for imagined dangers and sit in thin-lipped judgment of the many forms of human frailty. She's fond of commenting on the deficiencies of women like myself who don't know their place and can't seem to settle down with a husband and children, and after twelve years, she still regards my decision to become a private investigator as a passing whim that will go away when I grow up. Janet and I don't have a whole lot to talk about.

I hadn't seen Janet in years, despite my mother's urgings, and I knew I ought to feel guilty but I didn't. She lived at Laurel Heights, which my mother informed me was not an old folks home but a retirement community. It looked like a high-rise apartment house to me, the only noticeable difference being that the average age of the tenants was around seventy.

Janet was in the nursing wing, a modern one-story building connected to the main building by a corridor from the lobby. The decor was the same in the two buildings, but the difference was apparent as soon as you stepped through the connecting door.

The nursing wing had that unmistakable institutional feel to it. It could have been a hospital or psych ward, but it was not a place you went by choice. A middle-aged woman in a white uniform sat behind a large semicircular desk. She looked up from the clipboard on which she was writing and seemed surprised to see me.

"Can I help you?" she asked.

"I've come to see Janet Fenney," I said. "I'm her niece."

"Oh, visitors usually come through the front door," she said in a tone I remembered from my third-grade teacher. "You'll need to sign in at the front desk."

She allowed me to walk unsupervised from her station to the front desk, though I had a feeling she was keeping an eye on me all the way. The front desk was next to a large sunny room where about twenty women and a couple of

men sat in a circle of wheelchairs while an impossibly
cheerful blond woman read to them from the newspaper.

A white card in the doorway proclaimed in large print,
"Current Events — 2:00." Some of the audience listened and
appeared to understand; others looked like they'd been
parked there for a nap. One woman who seemed at least a
hundred and ten was slumped forward in her chair with her
mouth hanging open. The man next to her stared into space,
his face a complete blank.

I don't much like to think about old age, especially now
that I realize it might happen to me, so I hurried off to
Janet's room as quickly as I could.

She was sitting up in bed in a room that was split exactly
in half. Each half had a bed, nightstand, chair, and television
set. The half near the window was furnished in heavy
mahogany pieces from a bedroom set. Janet's half was
strictly institutional modern.

Janet was heavier than I remembered her, and her face
was a mass of tiny wrinkles. The skin on the back of her
hands was so thin it looked like it might tear. She's twelve
years older than my dad, and she's been old since I was a
kid. But then anyone over thirty is old to a child.

I was prepared to make small talk. Janet was not. She got
to the point immediately. "We don't have long before my
roommate gets back from therapy. I don't want anyone to
know I suspect anything."

Oh, boy, I thought, galloping paranoia.

She must have read my thoughts on my face because she
said quiet sharply, "I am here because I broke my hip,
Catherine, not because there's anything wrong with my
mind."

She proceeded to prove her point by giving me a clear
and detailed explanation of why she believed that the
woman across the hall, Mary Norton, had been the victim of
foul play. Mary had suffered a massive stroke six weeks
earlier and had never regained consciousness. Two weeks
ago on a Thursday morning, the nurse who checked her
room found her dead. Cause of death was determined to be
heart failure.

It was a perfectly credible cause of death in a woman of seventy-six who had just suffered a massive stroke. The piece that didn't fit was that Janet had heard someone going into Mary's room around two a.m.

"You just don't sleep as well when you get to my age," she informed me. "That's why they pass out those little orange pills, to help people sleep. I don't take them; I figure I'll be sleeping all the time soon enough."

Without the little orange pills, Janet was awake from one to three most mornings. To entertain herself she reconstructed exactly what was happening outside her room from the sounds that reached her through the partially open door. She could tell who was on duty not only from the sound of their voices but from the things they did; trips to the coffee machine, television programs they watched or music they listened to. She knew the routine of the entire night.

The night that Mary died, that routine was altered. Someone buzzed for the nurse, and he walked down the hall. That wasn't so unusual, but the sound of the door across the hall snapping closed was. Janet explained that Mary's door had a distinctive sound because the spring didn't work quite right and it always closed harder than the other doors.

"In this section, they don't check on us between twelve and seven," she explained. "Down in the infirmary, they check every four hours, but here they let us sleep. So you see there was no reason for anyone to go into Mary's room."

"Maybe she rang for the nurse?" I suggested.

"She was unconscious," Janet reminded me, "and she was alone in the room."

"Maybe he decided to check on her?"

"He could have, but why did he deny it? I heard them out in the hall the next morning when they found her. The director, Mrs. Hiller, wanted to know exactly where everyone had been and if anyone had gone into her room. Juan was on duty, and he said he hadn't gone in the room. Mrs. Hiller said the other nurses hadn't either."

Aunt Janet had been reading too many mystery novels, but I couldn't tell her that. I also couldn't tell her that I don't do murders. My clients are banks and big corporations; their problems usually involve employees with sticky fingers or loose lips—embezzlement, creative fraud, industrial espionage—that sort of thing. Murder, I leave to the police.

Janet was not going to accept that, and neither was my mother. I've confronted crooks and even a hired killer, but I wasn't about to take on Janet and my mom. I had no choice but to investigate. It was enough to make me wish that private investigators, like doctors, weren't allowed to work for relatives.

I asked my partner Jesse to do the background work. I'd have loved to stick him with the undercover part, but there are limits to what you can ask of a partner and still have one.

I needed to spend time at Laurel Heights, to get to know people there and to become familiar enough that no one would notice me too much. Since Janet regarded my profession as on the wrong side of decent, I could rely on her not to tell anyone about it. She was delighted that I planned to present myself as an English teacher volunteering to teach a class in oral history. In her eyes, it was as close to respectability as I'd come since high school.

Thursday

Jesse didn't get a lot from his official visit to Laurel Heights. The staff was neither more nor less helpful than others we've interviewed. Asking people what they know that might implicate a friend or coworker in a serious crime doesn't endear you to them, but they don't dare misbehave too badly lest you become suspicious of them.

Three nurses had been on duty the night Mary Norton died—Clarence Jones, Juan Morales, and Dorothy Waters. Morales had been at Station A, just down from Janet's room, Jones at Station B down from the infirmary, Waters in the infirmary. The outside doors were locked at nine, and anyone entering after that had to ring the bell and sign in. No one had signed in after eleven. The only keys to the outside doors were kept by the director, Audrey Hiller, and the Chief of Security for the entire Laurel Heights complex.

Mary Norton's body had been discovered by a nurse on the morning shift. The doctor estimated that she'd died between midnight and three a.m. No autopsy had been performed.

Three nurses and one administrator wasn't bad for a list of suspects, especially when you didn't know if you had a crime.

It was a stroke of luck that all three nurses were on the day shift at present. Laurel Heights rotated their staff every week, one week of day duty, one of p.m. shift, and one of night duty. Janet pointed the nurses out to me and gave me her assessment of each of them—two stinkers and one who might be all right.

I met the director, Audrey Hiller, when I volunteered to teach the oral history class. She was a stern-looking woman in her fifties with gray eyes set in a long face that seemed always to wear an expression of mild irritation. She warned me not to expect too much of my students. "Patience is very important with older people," she said. "In some ways it's like working with children."

Tuesday

There were eleven people in the class, all women. Seven came from the regular retirement community, and four from the nursing facility. As I entered the dayroom where the class was to be held, I felt an attack of self-consciousness. I had no idea what to expect from these women. Some looked so old and frail that I wasn't sure they'd be capable of participating. How would I ever get them to function as a class?

I needn't have worried. They all knew each other, and oral history was a large part of their normal conversation. I didn't have to do more than give them some topics and turn on the tape recorder. Even Laura Mosher who suffered from Alzheimer's and was often confused about the present remembered her childhood with startling clarity.

We began with "an event that changed your life" as the

topic, and Emma Warren volunteered to go first. She was a large woman who looked like she belonged in a rocker on the front porch of a Kansas farmhouse. Her body was sturdy and solid, but her hands were so gnarled by arthritis that they looked like old wood.

She told of being on her own for the first time in her life when her husband went to war. Her story was a reminder of how much things have changed for women in a generation. She had moved from her father's house to her husband's farm, knowing exactly what was expected of her and fitting herself to that role. War had redefined the rules and brought an unexpected sense of freedom.

I looked down at the back of my hand and noticed the brown spots that looked like large freckles. The woman next to me had the same spots, only larger and far more obvious against the porcelain whiteness of her skin. Grandma Sayler had had the same spots. I hated them.

"By the time Ross came home from the South Pacific, we had a one-year-old daughter that he'd never seen," Emma Warren said. "I remember him holding her and saying, 'I'm glad she's a girl so she'll never have to go to war.' It was a good thing he felt that way since we ended up with five daughters."

The circle of women laughed, none harder than Emma Warren. It was a comfortably female group. All had outlived the men they'd married and in a couple of cases, the children they'd borne. They had come to Laurel Heights to finish out their lives, but they maintained a rebellious vitality that I found endearing. I hoped that when I reached their age I'd still be able to laugh as Emma Warren did.

Beyond the circle of women a small man in a white coat hurried down the hall. His skin was the color of light chocolate, and his black hair was flecked with gray and receded from a smooth expanse of forehead. I recognized him from Jesse's description as Clarence Jones, one of the nurses on duty the night Mary Norton died. I couldn't see his face, but I knew it probably wore the same slightly anxious look that Jesse had described.

He was a shy man, more comfortable, I suspected,

counting pills and filling out schedules than interacting with his elderly patients. He was a hard worker, but a silent one, and he was not very popular with the women.

"A little field mouse, that one," Betty Katzen said.

"He's such an old woman," Emma Warren said, laughing her warm, earthy laugh. They all laughed then, pleased by the idea that Clarence Jones was more an old woman than any of them. I wondered how they'd react if they knew he was a murder suspect.

I could see that across the circle Sarah Meyers was tiring. Her eyes lost their focus and her head drooped. She was still recovering from the stroke that had forced her into a wheelchair six months earlier, and the struggle to make herself understood exhausted her quickly.

Aimee Girault also noticed. "Sarah's tired," she said. "Someone must take her back to her room." Aimee understood better than the others the exhausting work of rebuilding a life shattered by stroke. Two years earlier she had suffered a massive stroke that cost her the use of her left arm and leg and exiled her from her comfortable apartment in the Adult Community Building to a shared room in the convalescent hospital.

I went to the nurses' station to find someone to take Sarah to her room. Juan Morales, suspect number two, sat reading a newspaper. He greeted me with a broad smile.

"Sarah, she tired? Sure I take her to her room. She work so hard, that lady. She's a fighter."

He followed me back to the circle and wheeled Sarah off, chatting as he went.

"He's such a nice boy," Emma said. "So friendly."

"He's from El Salvador," another woman said. "He was active in the trade unions. They killed his brother and his uncle, and he had to flee into the countryside. He's always worried they'll deport him. The immigration doesn't accept that he's a political refugee."

"They're Nazis," Aimee said with uncharacteristic bitterness.

When class ended I watched the seven "healthy" members of the group head off down the hall that connected the nursing wing to the rest of Laurel Heights. Beyond the double doors, they stepped into a normal life where privacy and independence were still available, where each had a key to her own apartment, meals could be cooked in her own kitchen, and the day's activities were a matter of choice.

As nursing homes go, Laurel Heights was probably one of the better ones. The lobby was cheerful, the rooms reasonably large, and friends from the adult community were close at hand. But it was a place defined by loss—the loss of health, mobility, or mental acuity, of independence and privacy. For some the loss of the past, for all the loss of the future.

With class over, I headed for the director's office. Hiller was attending a conference on geriatric care and would be out all day.

My position as volunteer teacher was a license to snoop. Since Jesse had found no one on the staff willing to cooperate, snooping was all we had left. It's tough to start an investigation from your fallback position.

I let myself in to the director's office with a credit card. I'd checked the lock earlier when everyone was occupied with breakfast and found that it was little more than decoration. I don't enjoy this sort of thing. I gives me the same jagged adrenaline surge as a roller coaster ride and there's no one at the switch.

I looked around for someplace to hide if someone decided to check on the office. A door behind the desk opened into a small closet. I hoped I wouldn't need it.

Hiller struck me as the kind of person for whom a sloppy file drawer was a sign of moral turpitude, and as I expected, I found her office organized to the point of compulsiveness, a nice trait in someone whose files you want to search. It took only a few minutes to find the files of the three who had been working the night that Mary Norton died.

Clarence Jones had been employed in the nursing facility for six years. Before that he'd been an attendant in a convalescent hospital in Newark, N.J. He was taking courses for a nursing credential.

Juan Morales's file contained a surprise. It indicated that

he was a U.S. citizen, raised in Los Angeles. He'd been at the nursing home just over a year. I scanned the file and wondered which of Juan's histories were correct, and why he'd given his employer a different story from the one he'd told the women.

Dorothy Waters's file revealed that she'd worked at Laurel Heights for three years. The listing of previous employment included stints at numerous other nursing facilities and before that jobs in food service.

I hadn't met Waters, but I remembered complaints about her. She was a woman who vacillated between warm good humor and dark moods of rough irritation. Janet complained that you never knew what to expect; one day she was full of laughter and smiles, doing extra favors without being asked; the next she was angry and sullen, snarling at anyone who rang for help and handling patients with a roughness that bordered on abuse. Janet also suspected she was a thief.

There was one letter from the son of a patient who believed Waters was responsible for the disappearance of his mother's watch and silver picture frame. An attached note indicated that results of an investigation of the charges had been inconclusive. I copied some information from each of the files so that I could check on it later and put them back in the drawer. Then I went looking for Mary Norton's file. It resided in a bottom drawer marked deceased. I do love organized people. No one would have found anything this easily in my office.

I was opening Mary's file when a sound at the door turned my stomach to stone. I slid the file drawer closed and jumped for the closet. It wasn't much bigger than the average coffin, and there was no place to hide if someone opened the door. My body ran through its embarrassing set of reactions to danger—pounding heart, lump in the throat, icy hands, while I tried to keep my breathing light so I didn't puff like a steam engine.

I don't know who came in or what they did. I heard the office door open, a drawer slide out then close, and the door snap shut again. When I finally emerged from the closet, the room appeared unchanged. If someone besides Hiller had the key, I didn't want to stick around.

Janet invited me for lunch, but I couldn't face another ten minutes at Laurel Heights. I gave her what I hoped was a satisfactory excuse. Then I headed home, changed my clothes, and went for a long, satisfying run.

I've been studying the martial art of aikido for ten years. I usually train on Monday and Wednesday nights and skip Tuesdays, but that night I was at the dojo fifteen minutes early. I partnered with the youngest, strongest black belts and trained hard.

Thursday

Today was Aimee Girault's turn. Her stroke had robbed her of the use of the left side of her body, and her left hand lay stiff and clawlike in her lap. She was a tiny woman, probably no more than five three in her prime, and age and two years in a wheelchair had shrunk her to the size of a ten-year-old.

While other patients favored sweat suits and housedresses or robes chosen to be easy to put on, Aimee wore dark slacks and a tailored blouse that gave her an air of elegance. I wondered how she disciplined her uncooperative limbs to get them into such clothes.

She was the leader of the nursing facility women. When Sarah Meyers felt too tired to come to class, Aimee fussed over her and cajoled until she came. She could tell us exactly what kind of shape Laura or any of the other Alzheimer's patients was in that day. She reminded me of my mom's mother, sweet and kindly, gentle and strong.

The story she told us was anything but sweet or gentle. The topic was still an event that changed your life, and Aimee's event took place during the war. When the Germans swept into France, she was in her early twenties and still living on her family's farm. Her immediate reaction to the occupation was to join the Resistance.

"We put as little as possible in writing," she said, "but sometimes we had to write. Then I was the courier; I rode my bicycle to the next town every week so the Germans got used to seeing me. If there was a message, I carried it tucked in my skirt, under my blouse.

"One week I had something very important so I went one day early. At the bridge outside of town was a new soldier. He stopped me and asked me questions. I acted friendly so he wouldn't get suspicious, but then he started flirting. I said no and tried to get back on my bike, but he grabbed me and pulled me into the woods at the side of the road.

"He was trying to kiss me and putting his hands on me. I broke away to run, but he grabbed me and pushed me to the ground. Later I realized he was going to rape me, but then all I could think of was the paper. He was pulling at my clothes, and I was struggling, and then the paper fell to the ground. When he reached down for it, I knew that we were all dead.

"I looked for some weapon, and there was a rock. I grabbed it and I hit him as hard as I could in the head. He didn't fall, and I hit him again and then again. There was blood everywhere, but I couldn't be sure he was dead. He had a knife in his belt so I turned him over and pulled it free, and I cut his throat."

The circle was absolutely still as Aimee looked up at us. I stared at the tiny fragile woman and tried to imagine her slitting the throat of a soldier. She looked around the circle.

"It had to be done," she said.

The group erupted in questions. It was clear that Aimee had never told this story to her friends, but it surprised them far less than it did me. Aimee described how she had hidden the soldier's body and his motorcycle under the bridge and covered the area of the struggle with dry leaves, then sneaked home to change her bloodstained clothes and to get her friends to help her make sure the soldier would never be found.

I stayed for lunch, against my better judgment. I make it a point to avoid places that routinely put their food through a blender. The meal reminded me that there are things worse than dieting.

After lunch I went looking for Dorothy Waters. I found her at the nurses' station. She was complaining loudly to another nurse about one of the patients. "She just don't remember when to go, and she don't ask in time, and then it's oops, all over the place. I seen two-year-olds could do better."

Just down the hall beyond the desk, one of my students, Sarah Meyers, sat in her wheelchair. Tears ran silently down her face. Rage burned in my throat. I wanted to strangle the insensitive nurse. I went to Sarah, wiped her eyes, and tried to console her.

Then I turned on Waters. "I've seen two-year-olds with more tact," I said to her. "I think Mrs. Meyers would like to be somewhere else," I told the other nurse. "Find out where she'd like to go and take her there." The woman took one look at my face and went to Sarah.

"Who the hell are you?" Waters asked.

"I could be from State Unemployment at the rate you're going."

"What the hell? You threatening me?"

"I *never* threaten," I said. I made no attempt to keep the anger out of my voice.

I watched the belligerence fade to uncertainty. "I didn't mean nothing," she said. "I take good care of Sarah."

I softened my tone. "It might help to remember that inside she has the same feelings you do."

"Who're you to be talking about feelings and telling me what to do?" she demanded.

"I just started recently. I work with the program director," I said, hoping that gave me enough status to command cooperation. "I'll bet it isn't easy taking care of all these folks."

She shook her head. "Half of them are off their heads. They ask for something; you get it; they just keep asking. Can't remember you ever brought it. It's 'Nurse, this' and 'Nurse, that,' till you want to scream. I shoulda stayed in food service."

"It was probably easier," I said, settling into the chair next to her desk.

"Sure was." She looked tired now. "I wanted the night work so I could be home in the day with my granddaughter. Then they started this stupid rotation business. Every week's a different schedule, so's you never get used to it. And I gotta leave the child with a neighbor who got no more sense than she has. I'm here taking care of someone else's parents, can't even take care of my own grandchild."

Anxious to justify herself to me, she poured out her story. I learned more than I wanted to know about her cocaine-addicted daughter, her son in the army, her diabetic mother who could no longer live by herself, and her four-year-old grandchild. She also covered her pinched nerve, gastric ulcer, and various other aches and pains.

I steered her to the subject of Laurel Heights and got a list of grievances against administrators, coworkers, and patients. No single piece of it was relevant to Mary Norton's death, yet taken together it gave me a sense of the frustrating, sometimes infuriating work it is to care for others when no one is caring for you. None of the employees of Laurel Heights would ever sleep in its beds. Their elderly parents had to be kept at home or in cheaper, shabbier facilities where welfare paid the tab. It wasn't hard to see how that could make a person bitter.

The results of the background checks on the three nurses and the director were beginning to come in. So far, we didn't have anything more than a few traffic tickets and a squabble with a neighbor. Jesse had discovered one interesting thing. The contract for Laurel Heights stated that once individuals moved into the community, they would be taken care of for the rest of their lives. There was an extra charge for care in the nursing facility, but residents who ran through their savings were kept on at the home's expense.

"Could provide some incentive to hurry along those who are terminal," Jesse said.

"We're all terminal, Jesse," I said, "and the police frown on hurrying people along."

Tuesday

I arrived fifteen minutes before class to discover that it had been canceled. Betty Katzen, one of the women from the adult community, met me in the lounge and told me that Emma Warren was in intensive care at Providence Hospital. "She always showered first thing in the morning, and she must have fallen then, on Saturday; but most of us were going on a field trip to the Flower Show downtown, so we didn't notice until dinnertime. They think she hit her head when she fell, and by the time they found her, she'd been unconscious for over ten hours."

"Has she regained consciousness?" I asked, afraid to hear the answer.

Betty shook her head. "No, and she isn't going to." She paused to gain control of the tears that threatened to break through. "They've done a brain scan; it's flat." At that she began to sob and I put my arm around her and stopped fighting back my own tears.

It took us several minutes to regain control of ourselves. Betty shook her head as she wiped her eyes. "She's gone. Her body's still there, but Emma's gone."

I found Audrey Hiller, the administrator, in the little room the staff used as a lounge. She confirmed Betty's diagnosis. "There's no brain activity," she said. "She can breathe without a respirator and her heart's strong. They'll bring her back here this afternoon, but there's nothing we can do but feed her. I've seen cases like this where they go on for years."

Dorothy Waters sat nearby reading the paper. She should have been home, but she'd been working double shifts lately. "That woman'd been better off if the fall'd killed her outright," she said. "Then her soul'd gone to the Lord instead of hanging around this place."

"Dorothy," Audrey Hiller said sharply, "I don't like that kind of talk."

Dorothy nodded sullenly, but her expression suggested that we all knew she was right.

Thursday

I wasn't sure the women would feel like meeting, but Betty Katzen had assured me that they could use something to take their minds off Emma's accident, so I'd told the recreation director to schedule the class.

The lounge was empty when I arrived and the chairs hadn't been set out for class. With a growing sense of unease, I headed for Audrey Hiller's office only to meet her in the hall. She looked surprised to see me, then realized why I was there and apologized for not calling to tell me that class had been canceled. In a tone completely devoid of emotion, she informed me that Emma Warren had died the night before.

I wondered aloud how a woman she had said could "go on for years" had died so quickly. She gave me a glib and unsatisfactory answer and tried to excuse herself. I pretended not to understand. My questions met with something more than resistance. Was it fear?

I stopped by to see Aimee and found her staring out her window.

"I'm so sorry about Emma," I said, feeling the inadequacy of the words.

"We'll miss her," Aimee said, "but she had a full life, and it didn't end too badly." Her bright eyes studied my face. "She wasn't afraid of death, you know," she said.

Like the grandmother she reminded me of, she was more at ease offering comfort than receiving it. How many friends and relatives had she lost, I wondered. She was of an age when those losses become frequent. Did they become any easier for that? Her face was calm, not serene but certainly not grief-racked. I suspected that she feared death far less than I.

"Her death came so suddenly," I said, searching for a way to ask the questions I needed answers to. "Does it seem at all strange to you?"

Aimee shook her head. "People die for more reasons than the doctors understand, Catherine. She was a vegetable; maybe some part of her wanted to die. You knew her. She was so strong and robust; she'd have hated being stuck in a bed, completely dependent on people."

I nodded and decided not to press matters. It was unfair to arouse fears in Aimee when she had to remain in what might well be a dangerous situation.

I did get Aimee to tell me that Emma had a daughter in Oakland, and I asked the receptionist at Laurel Heights for the address and phone number so that I could express my condolences.

Finding Emma's daughter's house and telling her of my suspicions was a lot harder than convincing her to request an autopsy. She was a nurse, and she knew how easy it is to give a patient the wrong medication.

Monday

The results took a couple of days, and when they came back they didn't make any of us happy. Emma had died from a heavy dose of Seconal, the medication that the nursing facility used to help patients sleep. There was no indication of a needle puncture, so they assumed it had been administered in liquid form.

Having the cops called into the case put me in an awkward position. My ex-husband, Dan Walker, is in Homicide, so no matter who got the case, it'd be someone who knew I wasn't a schoolteacher. Dan wasn't going to be thrilled to hear that I was involved. He never likes civilian involvement, and he likes it even less when I'm the civilian.

All the tricks I'd have used on any other cop would be wasted on Dan, so I brought out the heavy guns. I told him everything I knew about the case and asked if he'd object if I remained undercover in order to reassure my parents. Dan gets along with my parents slightly better than I do, but I knew he wouldn't want to deal with them on this any more than I did. Sure enough, he agreed not to blow my cover. In return, he extracted a promise that I would tell him anything I discovered. He did not make a reciprocal offer.

Tuesday

Our next class meeting took place in the middle of the police investigation. Sober-looking men in dark suits and uniformed officers measured and inspected Emma's room and questioned all the employees.

We had the lounge to ourselves, but it was hard to ignore what was going on just outside the door. I was glad that it was Betty Katzen's turn. She had a strong, clear voice that carried well and a calm manner that helped focus the group. Betty was the Hallmark grandmother—slightly stout with an ample lap for grandchildren to crawl into, apple-red cheeks, and a full head of thick white hair.

Her story, too, dealt with an event that changed her life; and like Emma's and Aimee's, it was a war story. Betty had been an army nurse assigned to a hospital in the Philippines, and was evacuated just before the islands were invaded. She was a direct, plainspoken woman, and her descriptions of some of the things she'd seen made the other women wince.

I was only half listening when the expression of the woman opposite me brought my attention back to the circle. Betty was describing the agonizing decision to let the most seriously injured die in order to be able to treat those who might benefit. "Some of them were so young, and they looked like the kid down the street, but you knew it'd take a team all day to put them back together and even then they probably wouldn't make it. I tried not to look at their faces, just their wounds."

Triage, doing what you must to save the maximum number of lives. I wondered if the Laurel Heights killer thought he or she was practicing triage.

There weren't many questions that day, and the women seemed to feel the same relief I did when I dismissed class. I didn't have a good excuse for hanging around, but no one was paying much attention to me so it didn't matter. I watched the police question not only the nurses but the maintenance man, the delivery people, and the food service workers. The only people they didn't talk to were the patients.

Aimee and Sarah sat in the lounge and chatted. Laura was having a good day and seemed quite lucid if you didn't notice that she repeated herself. They were friends of Emma's; Aimee's room was down the hall from the one where Emma had died, yet no one asked them anything. It was as if they were invisible.

"When you're in a wheelchair people treat you different," Aimee told me. "They think your mind is as weak as your body." Her voice had uncharacteristic bitterness to it.

"Do you have any suspicions of who the killer might be?" I asked.

All three women shook their heads. "I worry about Juan," Aimee said. "Not because he did anything, but because of the immigration."

I worried about Juan, too, but for other reasons. I'd done some checking and found that the story he told the women was true, which meant that he'd lied on his application. It wouldn't take the police long to discover that he was not a U.S. citizen, and the fact that he was hiding his immigration status might well mean he'd fail a lie detector test.

Unless they found something I'd missed, the police would realize fairly quickly that only the nurses and the administrators with keys had access to the nursing facility. They'd also realize that the same set of nurses had been on duty when Mary and Emma died. Juan was in for a rough time.

I was concerned that the women must feel very threatened with a murderer loose in their midst. I knew Janet was terrified. I started to reassure them that the killer probably wouldn't strike now that the police were investigating, but Aimee just shook her head. "We're not afraid of dying, Catherine," she said. "There are things far worse than death."

I went back to Laurel Heights at nine that night, just to test the security. Dorothy Waters answered the door, admitted me, and had me sign the book. I expressed surprise at finding her there, and she explained that she was subbing for someone else. She acted far less interested in my presence there than I was in hers.

The lounge, so sunny and inviting during the day, was still and empty, a shadowy world of angular shapes. In the hall the doors had been left open, perhaps to protect the patients from deeds best done out of sight.

I walked down the hall, past the room where a frail female voice called out for help. When I'd first heard her pleas three weeks ago, I'd been haunted by them. Now I barely heard them. Past room 108, which was shared by two men. The one near the door was little more than a skeleton with skin stretched tight over its frame. His mouth hung open as he slept. I had never seen him awake. The other sat in his bed holding the television remote control and flicking through the channels. He never watched anything for more than a few seconds.

I'd gotten used to the days at Laurel Heights; nights were different. The hall was an empty tunnel under the harsh glare of fluorescent light. Most of the rooms were dark, illuminated only by the pale flickering of a television screen. I could hear snatches of a dozen television shows mixed with other voices, frail and querulous.

A tiny woman with thin gray hair sat in a wheelchair holding a rag doll. Her hands moved constantly, picking at the blanket that covered her lap. She smiled sweetly at me, and said something I didn't understand, then held her doll up to show me.

I forced myself to smile back, but it was a pasted-on smile. The messy sludge of emotions coalesced into my old friend, fear. Laurel Heights scared me. Hell, it terrified me. I've faced men with knives and guns and none of it was anywhere nearly as frightening as the thought of ending up in this place.

I looked down at the old woman with the rag doll. She'd returned to her own world, her eyes dull but her hands constantly working. I wondered what she'd looked like when she was *my* age. Once she'd been young, probably had her time of love and romance. I wanted to imagine that she'd been frail, that somehow she'd been different from me, but the biographies of my oral history group had robbed me of that comforting thought.

These were not weak women. In their youth they had been daring and resourceful. Emma Warren had run a farm by herself while her husband went to war. Betty Katzen had been among the last Americans out of the Philippines. And Aimee Girault had stood against the Nazi soldiers and risked torture and death only to end her life imprisoned in a wheelchair, betrayed by her own body.

I imagined myself as a resident of this place, with a roommate whose mind was drawing her ever backwards into a final infancy, and minimum wage attendants who were at best overworked and at worst brutal. There was no privacy here, strangers stripped off your clothes and bathed your body as if it were an inanimate object to be scrubbed and dried and then returned to its shelf. You shared a room with a person you didn't choose and might very well find objectionable. You ate what you were served or went hungry. You did what you were told or suffered subtle and not so subtle forms of punishment. Prisoners in the county jail were better off; and this was a "good" facility.

My chest was so tight that I could hardly breathe, and the walls seemed to be closing in on me. I simply couldn't stay in the building any longer. Instead of turning down the hall to the infirmary, I headed for the front door.

It took all my self-control to walk through the lobby and out the door. My body wanted desperately to run. Once outside, I took great gulping breaths of air. I leaned against a tree trunk and stared up at the dark, starless sky. The bands around my chest loosened slightly, but I still felt the panic pressing in on me.

I needed to move, to feel my legs swing and my feet meet the ground. I turned to the right and began walking with no destination other than away from Laurel Heights.

I walked for over an hour, more aware of movement than thought, and as I headed back for Laurel Heights, I knew who'd killed Mary and Emma.

Wednesday

Betty Katzen's apartment was on the fifth floor of the main building. She looked surprised to find me at her door.

"Catherine, this is Wednesday, isn't it? We don't have class today."

I asked if I could come in, and she ushered me into a living area with a couch and chair upholstered in a bright floral print. "I know who killed Emma," I said.

Her gaze never faltered. "Really."

I nodded and said nothing.

"Why are you telling me?" she asked. "Surely that's information for the police."

"I guess I wanted to hear about it from you first."

She sighed. "You're not really a teacher, are you?"

"No," I said. "I'm a private investigator."

She nodded. "Aimee wondered about you. You were always watching. You were different from the other volunteers." She paused. "We knew we'd have to do something, of course, if they arrested one of the nurses. But we hoped they wouldn't have enough evidence to accuse anyone."

"And you knew they'd never think of you."

"A bunch of sweet old ladies. Never."

"How long has this been going on?" I asked.

"It started four years ago. A friend, Claire Meltzor, got Alzheimer's. It went very fast, and she was beyond us before we knew how bad it was. We watched as she deteriorated, first her mind, then her body. It was awful.

"She used up all her money. She'd wanted to give her granddaughter something for college, but it all went for nursing. We were all horrified that it could happen to us. That was when we got the idea. No one wanted to be a vegetable, and no one wanted to end up with the mind of a two-year-old. Pain doesn't scare any of us so much, but being like Claire was at the end, that we couldn't face. You probably think we're cowards."

I shook my head. "I think you're among the bravest people I know."

"Aimee is, and Sarah. When Aimee came out of that stroke, she couldn't even roll over. She works every day just to be able to feed herself or hold a book. I've seen her so tired she can't reach up to wipe the tears from her face. But how did you figure it out?"

"I spent some time in the nursing wing last night and got a healthy case of claustrophobia. It made me start to think about how it was for Aimee and the others. Then I realized that there was one door to the nursing facility that everyone had ignored, the one from the retirement center. That door isn't locked at night. It would have been quite easy for Aimee or one of the others to ring for the nurse and draw him away from the nurses' station while someone else came through that door and went down to Mary's or Emma's room.

"And as a nurse, you'd have known how to manage things—what drugs, the necessary dosage, maybe even how to get them."

She sat silently for a moment. Her usually animated face was masklike and the color was gone from her cheeks. I felt like I'd just mugged my Sunday school teacher.

"I guess I am the logical one, and I'm willing to confess, but *not* to implicate my friends. I'm sorry for the trouble we've caused Juan and the other nurses. We can't let one of them be blamed."

I thought of Betty Katzen in prison. Or in a courtroom. And I thought of what I'd have done in her situation. I knew I'd have joined the pact, and having done that, I would have had to fulfill my promise to the others.

I took a deep breath. I was about to make myself an accessory to murder. "I don't really think that's necessary," I said. "The police don't have enough to charge anyone. Juan may have to flee immigration, but your confession wouldn't have any effect on that."

"You won't tell them?"

"Tell them what, that a group of consenting adults are taking care of each other's last wishes?"

She looked skeptical. "But you came here to solve the crime. Can you leave with it unsolved?"

"I came to assure my aunt that she would not be murdered in her bed. I can do that. I've done my job."

We've continued with the oral history class, and we even have a couple of new members. My mother is terribly proud of me for taking time to visit Janet and the other old ladies. She wouldn't understand if I told her that in this class, I'm the student.

Wendi Lee's first P.I. novel, The Good Daughter, *appeared from St. Martin's Press in November of 1994. It featured Boston-based P.I. Angela Matelli, who also appears in this story. Going back as far as Mickey Spillane's Mike Hammer, it seems to be very difficult for P.I.'s to keep their business and private lives separate. Angela finds this to be especially true when she takes on a decoy job for a colleague, against her better judgment.*

CHECK UP

by Wendi Lee

S OMETIMES YOU HAVE to do things you really don't want to do. And sometimes, you get a feeling that something's not going to work out right, but you can't help it—you are drawn to disaster.

That was my instinct the minute Chuck Eddy called, asking me to do him a favor. Eddy was a private investigator, but until recently, not a very successful one. About a year ago, Eddy discovered that the lucrative decoy market hadn't been tapped here in Boston.

When he first decided to specialize, Eddy had given me a call. He figured it would be good for business to have a broad as a partner. But it was an area of investigation that didn't interest me, and since I was doing well enough in my

141

own line of investigation—mostly repos and investigating insurance scams with an occasional truly interesting case thrown in the mix—I passed on the partnership.

The way it works is, a husband or wife comes into an agency because they want to find out if their spouse is capable of cheating on them. The private investigator turns a decoy with a tape recorder, sometimes even a hidden camera, loose on the spouse. The decoy, usually an attractive young man or woman, strikes up a conversation with the mark. Sometimes the sucker takes the bait, sometimes he or she doesn't.

When the phone rang, I was hammering a nail into the wall behind the desk, intending to hang a print I'd recently bought of a duck sitting in a beach chair, a cool drink in his feathered hand, with two bullet holes in the wall behind him. It was by some French artist and I just liked it. So sue me for bad taste.

I answered the phone with my usual, "Angela Matelli Investigations. May I help you?" and immediately heard, "Angela, I need a small favor." I recognized Chuck Eddy's voice and immediately got the feeling that the favor wasn't going to be so small.

"Okay, Chuck. I'll bite," I replied, swinging around to lean against the wall. Unfortunately, the hammer was old and the head was loose enough to fall off and onto my foot. "Ow!" I said.

"Angie? Are you okay?" Eddy asked.

"Uh, yeah. So what's the favor, Chuck?"

"Well, see, I know you don't like this kind of work, but, see, I'm in a bind. I promised this client, see, that I'd get a decoy on her hubby."

I groaned.

Eddy paused and asked, "Are you sure you're all right?"

"Yeah, Chuck. Let me guess. You need a decoy."

"Well, see, I had one all lined up," he said apologetically, "but she called a few minutes ago to tell me she's got an impacted wisdom tooth and is having emergency oral surgery tonight."

"You don't have a list of alternate decoys?"

"Sorry, Angie. Val was the last one. It's been so busy around here," Eddy said, his voice smug, "even the decoys on the alternate list have been working steadily." He couldn't resist adding, "You should have partnered with me when you had the chance. So, would you do me a favor and play decoy tonight?"

I closed my eyes. I didn't need the money, but it would be a good excuse to cruise the bar scene. My latest love interest, Joe, had unceremoniously dumped me when he made the decision to go back to his wife. I hadn't had much luck with men since I left the Marines. Joe had been my longest relationship—almost two months. Before Joe, I'd had a series of month-long relationships. It got to the point where I was forgetting their names and, in the company of my sisters, would call them by the month in which we were dating. Bob had been Mr. May, Rick had been Mr. July, and Joe had been Mr. August, until I realized that we were still going out in September.

It wasn't like I'd started picking out a china pattern or anything like that, but I'd had hopes for Joe. He was ex-military like me—a lieutenant commander in the Navy—and was working as an insurance investigator. So we had a lot in common. He was a little older—forty, to be exact—and separated with two kids. But I had enjoyed his company, he was a good lover, and Ma was happy for a change.

"Angie! I'm so relieved you found someone who would make a good husband," she told me last Sunday at dinner. "So he's a little older and not Italian. At least he's Catholic." She conveniently forgot the divorce thing and, by the end of dinner, she had us married and living nearby in Malden with two kids of our own.

"Ma. Give me a chance to get to know him before we throw the net over him," I replied.

My younger sister Rosa covered her mouth and giggled while Sophia and my three brothers just rolled their eyes.

"Angie?" Eddy's voice sounded tinny on the phone. "Angie? You still there?" Eddy always did that to me—he could talk and talk and I'd just drift off, thinking about something completely different.

"Yeah, I'll do it, Chuck. When and where?"

It was a hotel lounge, of all places, called L'Aubergine, which is French for eggplant. Don't ask me why they called it that. Some bozo in the head office probably decided that it had a worldly ring to it.

I sprinted home to change into something resembling sophisticated. Decoys are usually coed material. I was, well, a little long in the tooth to pass for a coed, but Chuck assured me that the mark was in his mid-forties and would probably be flattered that a woman my age (a little over twenty-nine) would show interest in him.

Most of my work is done in jeans and T-shirts, so I had to borrow something to wear from Rosa. I went downstairs— Rosa has the apartment on the second floor—and knocked on her door. Fortunately, Rosa was there and when I explained what I needed and why, she immediately went to her closet and started tossing dresses out on her bed.

"It's about time you went out."

"It's a job, Rosa, not a date."

She threw me a look over her shoulder. "Yeah, maybe a job, but you've got to look nice and maybe after you get what you're after, you'll stick around and meet a nice guy."

I laughed. "At a bar? I don't think so."

"L'Aubergine is not just a bar. It's a bar in a five-star hotel where rich businessmen stay."

"Rich, married businessmen," I reminded her as I sorted through the dresses on the bed. I started to hold up one to see if the color was right when Rosa stopped me. "I think you should try this one on first." She was holding a little electric blue number. "Little" is the operative word here.

"You've got to be kidding. I couldn't slither into that with a can of Crisco and a shoehorn." I took it from her and held it up, but it didn't even cover ten percent of me.

"Try it on," my younger sister said.

Half an hour later, Rosa stepped back from my face, mascara brush in her hand. "There. You're done. And if I do say so myself, you look fabulous."

I turned to inspect the finished product and gasped. "I look like a high-class hooker." My hair was fluffed up and sprayed so high, I thought I'd have trouble walking through doorways. My body was encased in what amounted to be a shocking blue sausage casing that barely covered my tush, and my makeup was courtesy of Barnum & Bailey.

"You look like most upper-class women these days. The hooker look is still in," Rosa replied, unruffled by my reaction.

I tottered to the doorway in the matching three-inch blue stiletto heels.

"You have to work on your walk," Rosa added. "Try to thrust your hips forward and slink."

"You've got to be kidding," I replied for the second time in an hour. I managed to make it to the car and drive away with some dignity intact.

Thirty minutes later, I was sitting in Chuck Eddy's black van, waiting for Mr. Wrong to show up.

"I gotta tell you, Angie," Eddy said, "you look hot."

"I am hot. Turn the air-conditioning on, Chuck," I replied.

"No, I mean you look really good. I don't suppose when this case is through, you'd wanna go out to dinner with me?"

It didn't surprise me that a guy like Eddy would think this was what a real woman should look like. I scanned Chuck Eddy's puffy body, sparse beard, and mashed-in nose. "Uh, thanks for the offer, Chuck, but we really don't have anything in common. Besides, I was just dumped and I'm trying to get over it."

He shrugged as if it was my loss. "Well, if you ever change your mind—" He turned the binoculars on a dark Mercedes sports coupe that was pulling into the lot. "Well, there's our boy. Your recorder's on?"

Eddy had actually invested in small video recorders and mine fit in a small evening bag. After testing it, I clambered out of the van and wobbled to the entrance, promising myself that as soon as I got into the bar, I'd find a seat and stay there all evening. Lover Boy would have to come to me. His name was Dick MacAfee and his wife suspected him of cheating on her. She thought it was just one-night stands, and that was where I came in. As soon as he picked me up and voiced his intentions, I could make an excuse and leave.

The man who got out of the Mercedes was good-looking in a middle-aged, receding hairline, "I got the money, baby, if you got the time" kind of way. I maneuvered myself into his path and bumped into him. Actually, the bumping into him part was not planned, but it got his attention.

"Well, excuse me," he said with a smile, one hand lightly on my elbow. "Are you going in here?"

I returned the smile. "Yes, I've heard the band is good here."

He looked a bit puzzled. "I didn't know there was a band tonight."

The bar was upscale with lots of blond oak trim surrounding dark green walls and frosted glass. In the kind of bar I frequent, the assorted barflies wear Timexes, drink Miller, and talk about the latest sure bet. These barflies wore Rolexes, drank Stoli on the rocks, and talked about the latest sure bet. The difference was that in my bar, the sure bet is at Suffolk Down and in L'Aubergine, it's on Wall Street.

He escorted me to an unoccupied table in a corner. Fortunately, there was a small jazz band playing. Apparently on Thursday nights, there's usually canned music. I ordered a black Russian and he went up to the bar to get my drink and his own, a whiskey neat. We exchanged names—I lied and said my name was Sherri—and made small talk. He asked what I did for a living—I lied and said I was a secretary—and where I grew up—I lied again, mostly because I was enjoying being another person.

He told me his name was Dick, he was head of a large sportswear corporation, and he was single. Truth, truth, lie. I batted my eyelashes. The atmosphere was humid and I hoped my mascara hadn't melted, which would make me look like a raccoon. Several times, I had to lean toward him so I could furtively sneak a look at the recorder, just to make sure it was still running. I noticed that every time I did this, Dick's eyes zeroed in on my cleavage. He didn't even pretend to look elsewhere.

As I leaned over for the fourth time, I noticed a man on

the far side of the room who looked an awful lot like Joe. In fact, I realized it was Joe. He was sitting at a table with a girl who looked to be about thirteen. Upon closer inspection, I decided she was probably in her early twenties, but she had that beautiful anorexic Kate Moss body and large Oxfam eyes. I knew it wasn't his wife, and I knew he didn't have any daughters that age.

"Sherri?" I felt Dick's hand touch mine. I smiled again. I knew I'd wake up tomorrow with sore facial muscles. I never smiled this much.

"Oh, uh, sorry. I saw someone across the room who looked like my, uh, brother." I was seething inside. Joe hadn't even had the decency to tell me he wanted someone younger, the son of a bitch. Well, as soon as this little job of mine was finished, I'd damn well go over and give him a piece of my mind. I looked at Dick and turned my smile up a notch. "You were telling me that last quarter's returns were enough for a bonus that allowed you to buy that beautiful sports car I saw out in the lot, right?"

He beamed at me and nodded. "I have my own helicopter, too."

"Ooooh," I cooed.

"Maybe I can take you for a ride in it tonight." He leaned toward me, his eyes zeroed in on my cleavage, his voice suddenly husky with desire. I must have leaned over the table once too much.

"Gosh," I replied in a squeaky voice, "that sounds like fun." I glanced over at Joe and wondered if Dick would suspect anything if I requested that we buzz the Burlingame area where Joe lived and put a spotlight on his apartment.

Whack! The sound came out of nowhere. Dick's head hit the table with the force of a tsunami. At first, I thought it was gunfire and I jumped up, ready for action—until I remembered that I didn't have my gun with me and I was wearing stiletto heels. I staggered into the next table, spilling drinks all over the place.

"You bum!" a loud woman's voice shouted over the jazz band's rendition of Duke Ellington's "Do Nothing Till You Hear From Me." "You son of a bitch! What're you doin' with this tootsie?" The owner of the voice was a large, handsome woman. She gestured savagely toward me with her purse, the weapon that whacked the back of Dick's head. He was holding the back of his head as he glanced from me to her. Taking in the frightened rabbit look in his eyes, I felt sorry for him for a moment.

Then I got up and walked toward her. My intention was to take her gently by the elbow and ask her what she thought she was doing. After all, she *had* hired Chuck Eddy to get the goods on her husband. For that matter, where was Eddy? He should have seen her enter the bar. My mistake was thinking I could handle this situation discreetly. The moment I tried to take her elbow, she screeched, "Get your mitts offa me, you, you slut!"

"Sweetie pie," Dick said to her in a placating tone, "she doesn't mean a thing to me—"

This scene was, of course, the center of everyone's attention. I could see Joe getting up and coming toward me. Dick stood up and, avoiding my eyes, started toward his wife.

"Angie!" Joe said, concern in his eyes and a sheepish expression on his face. "What're you doing here?" He glanced at Dick's wife, who was still glaring at me, then to Dick, who was shrinking as fast as Alice after she polished off the DRINK ME bottle.

"Who the hell are you," Dick's wife aimed her rasping voice at Joe, "her pimp?"

I scowled at her. "For your information, lady," I said, "I am *not* a call girl." I resisted the urge to hit her. The lady had a mean right hook with her handbag.

"Angie? I thought your name was Sherri," Dick said to me before his wife thumped the back of his head again.

"Ow!" Dick cringed for a moment, then straightened up and faced his wife. "You know, I'm getting really tired of that. Stop it."

She looked at him with no expression on her face, then whacked him upside the head again. "As soon as you stop hitting on anything that's wearing a tube dress," she said calmly, "I'll stop hitting you."

Joe's waiflike tootsie came up behind him to cling to his arm. "What's going on, Joe?" she asked in a velvet voice. She looked at me. "Who's this, your sister?"

Where the hell was Eddy? I wondered. This was fast becoming a disaster and I wanted out. I turned away for a moment to see if the recorder had done its stuff and found that it was, indeed, still working. I figured the rest of the evening was a loss. A large building was moving toward us. When it got close enough, I realized it was a bouncer.

"Is there a problem here, miss?" he asked, his eyes skimming me like I was a plate of prime rib.

"No," I replied, "nothing I can't handle. I'll call if I need you."

"I'll be right over there," he said, indicating a vague direction. I nodded and thanked him again.

When I finally had a chance to turn around, Dick and his wife were gone, but Joe was still there. I glowered at him and his coed.

"You okay, Angie?"

"What the hell do you care?" I snarled.

Joe suddenly realized that he had this unexplained appendage growing out of his arm. He had the decency to look embarrassed. "Oh, uh, Angela, this is, uh, Mariel." He avoided my eyes suddenly. A lot of men had been doing that to me lately.

"It must not have worked out with your wife," I said dryly, crossing my arms.

Mariel looked up at him, her chin quivering. "Wife? You're married?"

"Uh, well, I'm, uh, separated right now," Joe replied. His eyes looked for an escape route.

"Gee, Joe, it only took you three days to decide that it wasn't working between you two?" I leaned toward Mariel in a confidential manner. "You see, less than a week ago, I was going out with him. Then, three days ago, he told me that he was going back to his wife."

Joe turned red. "Now, Angela, that's not exactly what happened—" Before we could hear his explanation, his sweet little waif grabbed Dick's watery whiskey and dumped it all over Joe's head before marching out of the joint.

I smiled for the first time since Dick's wife spoiled the party. When I left the bar, Joe was still mopping the whiskey off his face and shirt.

I churned outside, ready to rip Eddy's lungs out for his sloppy surveillance. Eddy came out of the van before I got to it, a narrow look on his face.

"What the hell happened, Angie? You went in with the guy, I thought you had it all sewn up. Then I see him leaving with some other broad."

"What do you mean, some other broad?" I returned. "That was his wife, the woman who hired you."

Eddy pulled up short and blinked rapidly, then shook his head. "Naw, that wasn't his wife. His wife came into my office and—" He stopped and slapped the side of his head. I was witnessing an awful lot of slapstick violence this evening. "Geez, could that one tonight be a girlfriend?"

I shook my head slowly. "This is your mess to sort out, Chuck." I took the tape out of my evening bag and handed it to him. "I got what you want. I'm calling it a night. Drop my check in the mail." I stumbled to my car, my feet screaming with each step. Just as I unlocked the car, I turned to Eddy. "And Chuck?"

He looked up from examining the tape recorder. "Yeah, Angie?"

"Don't call me for another one of these gigs. I've just retired." I pulled the high heels off and tossed them in back of my car, then got in and drove, barefoot, back to my place in East Boston.

Christine Matthews first introduced Omaha P.I. Robbie Stanton in "Gentle Insanities," which appeared in 1994's Deadly Allies II *and was very well received. It was also her first mystery short story, after years of writing in the horror field under another name. Between the two Robbie stories, she has published in* Ellery Queen's Mystery Magazine *and the anthology* Mickey Spillane's Vengeance Is Hers.*

In "Promises Made and Broken" her "crazy" lady P.I. returns to discover that while promises may not actually be made to be broken, they too often are.

PROMISES MADE AND BROKEN

by Christine Matthews

CRAZY SURE AIN'T what it used to be.

Remember all those old movies glamorizing insanity? They usually starred Loretta Young, who played the beautiful wife of a highly respected physician. Some terrible trauma befalls her perfect life and she crumbles . . . ever so daintily into a beautiful heap. Reclining on a velvet settee, holding the back of one hand to her brow, she clutches a frilly hanky in the other. Her eyes plead into the camera and then she sighs, retreating into her private world. The lens stays fixed on those beautiful eyes so filled with pain. A violin section orchestrates her breakdown.

Fade to black.

But that was then, and these are the nineties. Your

modern-day crazy lady is a whole different breed. Therapy sessions, work schedules, exercise programs. No swooning allowed. Busy, busy. No time to apply makeup or even have my hair done. Work hard and melt back into society. But I wasn't the wife of a wealthy anybody.

When my extension rang, I jumped. I hadn't had a phone within arm's reach in a year.

"Ms. Stanton?"

"Yes, who's this?"

"You probably don't remember me; we met last year during your interview for the Donahue show. I'm the associate producer, Julie Wilson."

"Sure, I remember you." The other guests and I used to joke that Ms. Wilson was so uptight her suit creaked.

"Good. Well, we're doing an update show. You know, what ever happened to so-and-so? It's been a year since your segment: 'Daring People—Exciting Occupations.' I've managed to track down . . ."

"Wait a minute. You want me to go back on television? Don't you think that's a little . . ." I was trying to figure out how I felt.

"Exciting!"

"For who? Look, I came on the show originally to talk about being a female P.I. I did not, nor do I, intend to talk about my personal life." I realized I felt put-upon and it made me angry.

"But, but our viewers feel so . . . connected to you. First they see you on the show, a respected professional. Then they read about a doctor in Chicago getting murdered right after your father threatened to kill him. The news reports you hired a hitman and tried to frame your own father for the murder. 'A Current Affair' does a whole hour on your troubled childhood, your father's abusive behavior toward you and your sister. Next comes a trial and the insanity verdict. We get letters wanting to know about you every day."

"Gee, I'm a celebrity." Neither one of us laughed.

"Maybe. But you could be such an inspiration to our

viewers." She was trying to appeal to my altruism. Right now that tank was empty.

"I'm sorry, Ms. Wilson, but I don't want to inspire anyone. I just want to figure out where I'm going to live at the end of the week. I lost my apartment; my things are in storage somewhere and I can't even afford to get them out should I find someplace to live. I'm tired and lonely . . ." I stopped, hearing how pathetic I sounded. I wanted to hang the phone up and treat myself to a cry. Then a hot fudge sundae.

"Look, Julie, I didn't mean to dump all this on you. The truth is, I don't think my appearance would be very inspiring. I think your viewers would watch with the same curiosity that would make them slow down to gawk at an accident. And when it was over, they'd give thanks they weren't me."

She released a long sigh. "I understand. I won't press you. But, I do have a message from one of the other guests. Do you remember Hazel Franklin?"

"The eighty-seven-year-old, sky-diving great-grandmother?" What a character. We'd had lunch the day of the taping and never stopped talking.

"Yes. She asked for your phone number or an address. We keep that information confidential. But I told her I'd be calling you today, and she asked that I give you her number. She said it was important. Do you want to take it down?"

I sat up and grabbed the hotel pen and small notepad lying by the phone. "Okay, I'm ready."

Julie repeated each number clearly and carefully. She would have made a great operator. "Hazel lives outside of Nashville. And while you're at it, here's my number, in case you change your mind."

The urge to cry disappeared but the need for ice cream and chocolate persisted. Neither stress nor joy affected my appetite. I liked hospital food, airplane snacks, school lunches as well as haute cuisine.

While I calculated how many calories would be expended walking across the parking lot to Denny's, my hands patted my hips. I bent to touch my toes, then scanned my tight Levis on the way back up. Not bad. Could be better, but then everything could stand some improvement. I decided to call Hazel and wait out the craving for extra whipped cream.

She answered on the third ring. "KPRM: Home of Country Music."

Hesitating, I asked, "Hazel Franklin?"

"That's me. Did I win anything?"

"No, Hazel, it's Roberta Stanton."

"Oh, Robbie darlin', you must think I'm crazy. There's this contest on one of the radio stations; the grand prize is a week in Can-Coon. You just have to answer the phone with their slogan. I'll be glad when the fool thing's over with."

If there was such a thing as reincarnation, and I loved to believe there was, then I'd known Hazel in another life. And I'm certain she made me laugh the same way back then.

"Julie Wilson from the Donahue show told me you were trying to get in touch. Are you okay?"

"You're still the same sweet thing. Askin' me about my ole troubles when your life has been a livin' hell. I swear, honey, you make me want to cry."

I plopped down on the bed, getting comfortable. She wanted to know all my news, and I was surprised that I wanted to tell her everything.

We'd been talking for about twenty minutes when she asked, "So, where do you go from here? I mean, there . . . in Omaha. Are you back in your old place or gonna stay with your sister?"

"I'm at a Hampton Inn for now. My father died right after the trial. His insurance money went to Delia; everything went to her. She insists on giving me part of it, but she's still dealing with a lot of anger and guilt. I don't know . . ."

"You're comin' down here! I have this big ole place all to myself."

"You're very generous . . ."

"Generous, hell, I'm lonely and need your help with somethin'."

The change in Hazel's tone intrigued me. "What?"

"Just say you'll come down and I'll tell you the whole story."

I'd never been comfortable spending even one night in someone else's house. Never liked slumber parties when I was a kid. But now I tried imagining myself in Hazel's home. The fact that we'd gotten along so well, in such a short period of time, did make the prospect very inviting. There would only be the two of us; I could relax. A warm friendly environment, time to spend with this funny lady, it all made me promise to fly to Nashville.

It had taken two weeks, but I'd gotten a good price on a round-trip ticket and now sat in the Nashville airport waiting for Hazel Franklin to pick me up. I fidgeted and watched the people whose cameras gave their tourist status away. A video ran continually, urging travelers to come visit Opryland. Elvis souvenirs and Music City T-shirts filled the window of a nearby gift shop.

I had just noticed a petite woman in white who I swore was Dolly Parton, when Hazel tapped me on the shoulder. "Robbie! Sweetie pie!" She hugged me and I could smell her lilac perfume.

"Hazel. You look wonderful."

Her denim jacket matched the stone-washed shade of her jeans and was embellished with silver studs. Her hair, colored a chestnut brown, was sprayed and pinned on top of her head in a bouquet of curls. A white scarf camouflaged the loose skin of her neck. Her makeup had been applied a little extravagantly to cover wrinkles beneath her eyes. But all things considered, this eighty-eight-year-old woman could easily have passed for a girl of seventy.

"Sorry for bein' late. There was a limo blockin' things up. I heard someone say it belonged to Dolly Parton."

I knew it.

"We'll just get your suitcase and we're outta here."

I held up a large carry-on bag. "This is it."

"Travelin' light these days, huh?" Her smile told me she understood my need to simplify my life now. "The car's right out front. Another five minutes and the cops'll ticket 'er. Well, that's what they threaten to do until I go into my old lady routine." She started down the corridor and I hurried behind.

It took an hour to get from Nashville to Shelbyville. Signs posted near the city limits declared it "The Walking Horse Capital." It was after midnight and as we circled the square, only a full moon lit the way.

"Just round the bend here." Hazel pointed. "The big one, third from the corner." She pulled her car into the driveway of number forty-nine.

The three-story house was painted white with slate blue trim. Lace curtains covered each window and a warm yellow light glowed from inside. As I reached in the backseat for my bag, I felt an immediate calm.

Hazel slammed her door and walked over to my side of the car. "You okay, honey? Are you tired?"

"I feel great. Must be the Tennessee air."

"Good. I was hopin' you weren't one of those early to bed, earlier to risers. I've always loved the night. Get twice as much done after the sun sets."

Inside the Franklin house was what I'd expected . . . sort of. Crocheted doilies were pinned to the back of an overstuffed couch and chair, but the far wall of the living room was covered with a large-screen television set. An entertainment center took up another wall.

"Come on, I'll show you your room. It used to be Alice's, my youngest."

We walked up a small staircase to the second floor. The narrow hallway led to three bedrooms; Hazel stopped at the last door and turned the knob.

"Alice had scads of shows at the Thornwell Gallery in Memphis. Even got a scholarship to study in France. Each time she'd come home, she'd bring a print by some artist she admired or a new paintin' of her own. I thought you'd enjoy how excitin' this room is. It's reelin' with energy."

Colors bombarded my eyes then my brain. I had never seen paintings hung floor to ceiling, there had to have been at least one hundred frames.

"It's . . . very unusual."

"Glad you like it. Now, how 'bout some coffee? Tea? I've got soda or beer. You name it."

I grabbed at any excuse to shut the door on Alice's Gallery. "Tea. I'd love a cup."

The kitchen was cozy and painted pale yellow. A large wooden table sat in the middle of the room, covered with a yellow and white embroidered tablecloth. Its simplicity was complemented by a teapot collection that filled shelves, corner countertops, and windowsills. It instantly became my favorite room.

Hazel poured water into a copper teakettle and I finally asked, "What's wrong? Why do you need my help?"

Arranging cookies on a china plate she spoke with her back to me. "Do me a favor, Robbie, will ya?" She turned and set the plate on the table. "Never get old."

"I'll try. Real hard." I laughed and patted her hand.

"I've always been lucky, ya know? Had my health and my brain is sharper than ever. But the way some folks treat me brings on old age."

Hazel got out two mugs, dropped a tea bag in each, and poured the boiling water. She deposited the mugs on the table and herself into the chair next to me.

"For eight years now I've belonged to this sky-divin' club—The Screamin' Seniors. That's where I met Tucker." Her smile gave all her feelings away. "Tuck was so handsome, probably the finest man I've ever known. We never ran out of words. There was talkin' and laughin' from start to finish."

For the second time, Hazel used the word "was." Past tense.

I shoved a cookie in my mouth. She didn't say a word while I chewed. Finally I swallowed and asked, "What happened to Tucker?"

Staring into her tea, she said, "I'm supposed to believe it was an accident. That his chute just didn't open. Over and out. The end."

"Hazel, I'm so sorry, but . . ."

"Tuck had been a paratrooper durin' the war and after that

an instructor. He'd kid me all the time that he was born with wings."

". . . accidents happen even to the best people," I finished.

Ignoring my wise observation, Hazel eagerly continued. "I went straight to the airfield and cornered Pete, he runs the place. I asked him if he could tell me about Tucker's accident. He knew Tuck and I had been datin'. He was all sweet and sorry till I wanted to see the logbook and anythin' else filled out for the FAA. Then ole Pete started treatin' me like a senile biddy. Once he got past his cooin' and carin' he tells me I wouldn't understand the forms, they were too complicated, and I shouldn't worry myself with all the details. Even went so far as to take me by the hand and walk me to my car. Damn little snot ass." She slammed her hands on the table and stood up.

"I need you, Robbie. I need you to do the runnin' and talkin'. Look at yourself. You're smart an' young; you know all the right things to ask. It's your job."

"Was my job," I corrected. "I'll probably never get licensed again."

"Pish. What the hell does a piece of ole paper mean? If you don't have a birth certificate that don't mean you ain't been born. You have what counts: common sense and good instincts. I remember you tellin' me about some of the cases you worked on. You were good then—you'll be good now."

"Thank you," was all I got out before I heard something drag across the floor upstairs. A loud moan followed.

"What's that?" I held my breath.

Hazel grinned. "Oh, it's just Tucker. Don't get scared or nothin'. He hasn't quite adjusted to bein' dead yet. An' when he promised he'd never leave me, he meant it. Tuck was known for bein' a man of his word." She offered me another cookie.

As I lay in bed, staring at the pink cherubs painted on Alice's ceiling, I rationalized that this was an old house. Old houses settle. It was February and the cold evenings could warp wood or loosen things. Hazel was almost ninety, certainly entitled to imagine or forget things.

And I guess I was just too tired. Fear would have to be put on hold until I'd had some sleep.

When I stumbled down to the kitchen it was eleven o'clock. Hazel had left a note saying there was coffee in the pot, biscuits and gravy in the refrigerator, and she was at a church meeting down the street. Several newspaper articles concerning Tucker's accident were on the counter along with keys to her car. I poured some coffee, vetoed the biscuits and gravy, and popped two pieces of bread into the toaster. As I spread butter onto my breakfast, I read through the clippings.

Finishing up in the bathroom, I heard a door slam. "Hazel? I'm up here."

Footsteps dragged across the living room floor; the door at the bottom of the staircase opened.

"I was just getting ready to leave. Thought I'd start at the airport."

Slow, heavy feet walked the stairs and stopped outside the bathroom.

I opened the door. "I think it would be best if . . ."

The hallway was empty.

I dashed across the floor, setting a new record for stair sprinting. The kitchen was unoccupied as were the dining room and living room. I could feel my heart throbbing clear up into my ears.

My intellect screamed that I should stay put. But involuntary reactions dragged me back up the stairs, pushing me from room to room, making my hands open doors and flip on light switches.

As I was tapping the wall, feeling silly but hoping to find another entrance, the front door slammed. Again.

This time I leaped down the stairs, colliding with the chair and then Hazel in under thirty seconds.

"God Almighty! What is the matter? You scared the life outta me!"

"I heard someone . . . the door opened," I wheezed. "Then they walked up the stairs. No one was there . . ."

" 'Cept for Tucker." Hazel nodded.

I couldn't think of a comeback.

"Now, tell me what you're up to today." She stood in front of me, smiling, waiting for my grand plan to unfold.

I took a minute to calm myself. "I was going to start at the airport. I think it's best I go alone."

"Whatever you say, you're the darin' P.I." She said it with a straight face and sincere heart. "There's a map in the car; I marked all the important spots for you. The name of our instructor is Pete Hooper. You'll see him comin'; he's a hunk."

"Looks like I have everything. Don't wait dinner for me."

"Oh, tonight's bingo. You'll have to fend for yourself."

Hazel was right. Peter Hooper was a hunk. A well-dressed, tanned, blue-eyed, I-think-I'm-in-love kinda hunk.

"So, this will be your first time?" He was asking me about skydiving. I'd decided to pose as a prospective student.

"Yes." Looking down at the release form, I tried holding back my blush.

"It's pretty standard. We need verification, for our files, that you're of age or"—he winked—"have the consent of your parents or guardian. There's also the danger factor; it's not like you were walking in the park. But we go by the book and our equipment is inspected daily."

"There's no chance that something will go wrong?"

"Oh, it's like anything else, you have to know what you're doing and don't take unnecessary risks." He smiled and my stomach fluttered.

"It's just that I came across a story in the paper a few weeks ago about a man who was killed when his chute didn't open."

"Tucker James."

"You knew him?" I asked in mock surprise.

"He belonged to our seniors' group; Tucker was their leader."

"What a shame. Did he take unnecessary risks?" I looked back at the form, didn't want to seem anxious.

"No. He was just stubborn."

"What do you mean?"

"The guy knew his stuff; he'd been jumping since way before any of us were born. But he was bullheaded, refused to admit he was sick. They get like that, my grandmother was the same way."

"Sick? What was wrong with him?"

"Alzheimer's. When Tuck first told me, I insisted on talking to his doctor. The doc assured me the disease was in its early stage and he'd keep me posted. Also said that because Tucker had been jumping for so many years, it was kinda all reflex to him now anyway."

"But you said he died because he was stubborn?"

"The silly old fool insisted on packing his own chute. That should have been reflex too, I suppose, but apparently he got ahold of one of the old ones we use for a target."

"God, how awful."

"Tell me about it; I was the one who found him. Out there." He pointed to a patch of field by the highway.

"Was he . . . ?"

"Sometimes a person can fall from a great height and end up lookin' like he's asleep. Sort of peaceful. But I knew better than to touch him. Called the police right away."

I'd finished filling out the form and handed it to Peter. "That was all you could do."

"Well, everything looks good. We ask you to watch a short film. Would you like to do that now?"

I hated to leave. Peter Hooper's khaki shirt was unbuttoned just enough, revealing soft curly hairs on his chest.

"No. I'll have to come back next week. I just wanted to check out schedules and prices."

"Okay then. You have our brochure, the phone number and hours are on the back. Give me a call when you're ready."

Boy, was I ready!

I sat in Hazel's car at the A&W, eating a hot dog, drinking root beer from a frosty mug. February had never been like this in Omaha. The sun reflected off a large white house across the street. I wished for a pair of sunglasses while trying to verify lettering on a small sign stuck in the front lawn. HUFFMAN BROTHERS COLONIAL CHAPEL.

Returning my unfinished lunch to the tray, I rummaged through my purse for the newspaper articles. Tucker James had been laid out at the chapel three days after his accident.

I honked for the carhop.

It was cool inside. I looked for a ladies' room, hoping no one would intercept me until I'd figured out what to say. The air was saturated with the scent of carnations and roses; my stomach tightened.

Sobbing came from the last stall. I assumed tears were the norm here. I headed for an end sink; the crier was now using one in the middle.

"Are you all right?"

"Me? Sure."

"Sorry. I didn't mean to intrude."

We now stood in front of the lighted mirror and talked to each other's reflection.

"No, no, it just gets to me."

I spoke in a soft, hopefully comforting voice, "Who did you lose?"

"No one . . . in particular. I work here; this is my father's business. Today they brought in a little boy—he drowned. It's just too sad sometimes."

"I bet."

"Are you here to see Mrs. Russell? She's in the Magnolia Suite."

"No. I'm here . . . a little late. I was out of the country when my uncle, Tucker James, died. The only thing I know for sure is that he had an accident and was brought here." She was buying it and moved a little closer.

"I prepared Mr. James. If there's anything I can tell you . . ."

"Did he have an open casket? He was so claustrophobic. Hated tight spaces. It probably sounds silly, but I just need to know he was . . . okay." I was spreading it on too thick and bit my bottom lip as a reminder to shut up.

"Well, he did fall from an airplane. His parachute malfunctioned; I did my best, but we had to have a closed casket. Just about every bone in his body was broken. If it's any comfort, he didn't suffer."

"I read that sometimes the victim of a fall can come through the whole thing without any obvious signs. That he just looks like he's asleep."

"True, I've seen a few like that. Unfortunately, Tucker looked pretty bad."

"Was there anything else?"

Her pretty long curls fanned out around her head when she turned her full attention on me. "Like what?"

Wishing to restore the chatty mood and alleviate her suspicions I did what I could to throw her off. I cried.

"I don't know. I'm just so upset."

She offered me a tissue. "Of course you are. And here I go on and on about broken bones and caskets. I'm so sorry. But we have a close relationship with the police department. Very close. I've been dating a sergeant for two years." She hoped her little joke would make me laugh, but I decided tears were working better and added a few more sniffles.

"My boyfriend knew Tuck; he filled out the reports himself. The hospital did an autopsy, and I worked on . . . sorry . . . prepared your uncle. His injuries were typical for what I've seen in these types of accidents."

"It's just that I miss him terribly."

"You said you were Tucker's niece?"

I let out a nice long sob. Inching toward the door, I couldn't help noticing the large diamond on her left hand as she handed me another tissue.

"My name's Elizabeth Huffman; call if you need anything."

Finally I stood with my hand on the door. "Thank you for your help. I feel much better now."

"Sure you're all right?"

"Fine."

I left the way I'd come.

*   *   *

The sun was setting when I pulled up in front of forty-nine. Stooping to look at red tulips poking through dirt on either side of the front steps, I wondered where'd I be living next spring. A terrible crash came from the second floor, and I darted up the front steps. Fearing something had happened to Hazel I dug my key into the lock, turned the knob to have it pulled out of my hand as a man came running out onto the porch.

"Hold it!" I screamed, clutching my purse.

Slamming the door, he shouted, "Who the hell are you? And why do you have a key to my grandmother's house?"

"I'm staying with Hazel. Roberta Stanton." I offered my hand.

"Sorry, but you scared the shit outta me. I'm Clay Bowman, her grandson."

"Hazel's at bingo. I assumed that was a regular thing with her."

"It is, I just stopped by to drop off some groceries. She'll go days just eating cookies." He grinned, and I wondered why he held a grocery bag if he'd dropped off things inside.

"Clay! Robbie!" Hazel waved as she got out of a car.

Clay shifted the brown paper bag and waved back. "Hey, Granny!" He appeared to be in his twenties, but I remembered Hazel saying he was thirty-two. His black cowboy hat swallowed up most of his hair except for the blond sideburns.

Hazel ran up the stairs and hugged him. "Doll baby, you look great! Come in and meet Robbie."

Clay looked uncomfortable. "We met. Just now."

"Well, come inside anyway; it's gettin' cold."

We ended up in the kitchen and I surveyed countertops for any sign of the groceries Clay had mentioned.

"Sit! Sit yourselves down. I'm fairly bustin'—tonight I won me fifty bucks. Clay, darlin', take off that ole coat. I'll make some cocoa."

Hazel flew around the kitchen like a bird. Pecking and landing long enough to tell us she was out of cocoa. "Hon, would you remember to pick some up next time you stop by the market?"

Clay hung his jacket over the back of a kitchen chair. "Granny hates the grocery store. Says it's crowded with old people takin' too long an' sample ladies shovin' pizza in your face."

Hazel came up behind her grandson and snatched off his hat. "So my big strong policeman here does the shoppin' for his sweet granny."

"Policeman?"

"Oh, didn't I tell you my Clay is a sergeant?" Hazel tossed the cowboy hat. While mussing his hair she bragged, "Clay graduated at the top of his class, received a commendation last year. He's got himself a condo on the other side of town and is engaged to a beautiful girl."

Clay's expression went from bored to delighted. "Me and Beth have been goin' together for twenty-three months now."

"Elizabeth's a cosmetologist; works for her daddy."

Knowing, but asking anyway, I said, "What's the family do?"

Clay answered, "They own and operate the Huffman Mortuary."

Hazel slowly lowered herself into a chair. "Tucker was laid out there."

Clay stood, snatching the bag from the floor. "Talkin' of Beth reminds me I'm supposed to pick her up in a while." He kissed Hazel goodbye. "It was nice meetin' you, Roberta. Hope to see you again."

He had made it as far as the porch when Hazel noticed the jacket left behind.

"I'll catch him." He was on the sidewalk when I dashed outside. Careful to shut the door behind me, I called to him. "Clay, you forgot this."

When we were both out of Hazel's hearing range, I spoke honestly. "Why were you really here today? There weren't any groceries. What's going on?"

"Look, I don't think it's any business of yours what I do in my grandmother's house."

Even though my license had been suspended, I still had a Photostat of the document. Withdrawing it from my wallet, I held it close to his face. "I'm a private investigator. Your grandmother asked me to look into the death of Tucker James."

He chuckled. "What a gal. A P.I.! I love it!"

I stood with the license still in my hand. "Today I found out you worked on the case."

He took his jacket from me. "Look, Pete called me, said there'd been an accident. It took me five, maybe six minutes to get out there. Poor Tuck was broke up real bad. The parachute was lyin' all around him, shredded to pieces. I took a report from Pete. There was an autopsy. It was ruled an accident."

"It was that simple?"

"Tuck was a great guy. He made Granny very happy. But I guess it was just his time to go."

"I guess. Thanks. Look, if I upset you I'm sorry, but please, don't tell your grandmother you know why I'm here. She wanted this handled discreetly."

"Sure."

When I returned to the kitchen, Hazel was gone. I started for my room and met her on her way down. "You just missed Tucker."

"Hazel, we've got to talk about this . . . this . . . ghost thing."

"I know, sugar. I've been waitin' for you to start in about the house bein' old and the noises comin' from plain ole wood and rust rather than the great beyond."

"Well . . ."

"And you must have been wonderin' about me. We haven't known each other all that long. It's only natural you'd be uneasy. Probably figure my elevator isn't goin' all the way to the top floor."

I had to laugh at her. "No, it's not that."

"Then if the idea of Tucker comin' back, even for a little while, comforts me, what's the harm?"

I felt embarrassed. "I'm sorry."

"No need for apologies, sweetie. If there's one thing I've

learned in this lifetime, it's to be kind to myself. I'm tryin' to get through this god-awful loneliness right now. And if talkin' to a ghost helps, so be it."

I hugged her tight. "So be it."

I decided to pay another visit to Peter Hooper. It was an easy decision to make. I took great care dressing the next morning, even spritzed myself with the last of my vanilla perfume.

A twin engine buzzed the field; it was a gorgeous day, temperatures had to be in the high seventies. I parked the car next to a small hangar made of corrugated metal. A gravel trail led right to Peter Hooper's office.

He flashed a smile that could reinvent the swoon. "You're back!"

A slight breeze ruffled my long skirt and I felt pretty. I could hear Bette Davis repeating, "Peetah, Peetah, Peetah," but my own voice said, "Yes, I am."

"Have a seat, I'll get that film set up for you."

I stood in front of his desk, preferring the superior stance. "I'm not here for that."

He straightened in his chair. "Oh? Why are you here then?"

"For more information about Tucker James and his accident. Hazel Franklin hired me. I'm a private investigator."

We stared at each other for a minute.

"I don't believe this! Why won't Hazel let it go? I told you everything yesterday."

"You were very kind." That blush crept over my cheeks again. "But there were a few details that don't fit."

"Such as?"

"You were the first to find Tucker?"

"Check."

"And you said he looked like he was asleep."

"Check."

"Then why did Sergeant Bowman tell me Tucker looked pretty bad when he arrived on the scene?"

Peter shifted in his chair then stood. He came around the

desk and guided me by my elbow. "This'll take a drink to tell."

The small room served as a lunchroom. Three vending machines offered drinks, sandwiches, and candy. A ceiling fan stirred the air, and we sat at one of the four tables in the empty room.

"I'll be right back."

He returned with a bottle of tequila and two glasses. He poured the drinks and we toasted, "To honesty."

The liquor went down hot. "Why are we drinking tequila at eleven in the morning? What happened?"

"I didn't lie. Tucker was sick. He did pack the wrong chute. I was the first to find him in that field. And he did look untouched. God, how is that possible?"

"So," I prodded, "what did you lie about?"

"Tuck was alive when I got there. He was lying on his back, moaning, in such horrific pain. I have dreams about him crying to me for help. It was awful."

I finished my drink.

"He begged. Have you ever heard anyone beg from the pit of their soul? He begged me to finish him. The pain was that great. He tried getting up and that's when I saw he'd landed on a rock and the back of his head was caved in."

"What did you do?"

"I ran like hell to call the police and when I got back, Tuck was still beggin'."

My attraction for this man was now overshadowed by my compassion.

"I kept tryin' to get him to stay still. He grabbed me, asked me to promise that he wouldn't have to go to the hospital. He moaned and begged and before I knew it I picked up that rock and hit him. Just once."

"And when Sergeant Bowman got there, Tucker was dead."

"Yes."

I didn't know what to say. If Peter Hooper had pulled a plug and never bloodied his hands, would he be considered more humane? Tucker James was dying. If not immediately from a fall, then slowly from an illness. He had enjoyed a full life and died doing what he loved best.

"Do you believe in ghosts?" I finally asked. "Homemade ones?"

"We did drink to honesty . . . and I've come this far. Yes. Clay—Sergeant Bowman—and I cooked up the hauntin' to comfort Hazel. Clay was worried about her mental state and asked that I help. He gave me a key. We take turns. Hazel's fit but she's not fast. So far I've been able to make a few noises, move some furniture. We started doin' it every night, now we're down to every other night. Clay says after she's adjusted we'll stop altogether."

The chair squeaked as I stood. "Thanks. I'd better go have a talk with Hazel."

"You're not gonna tell her about the ghost, are you?"

"No. She just needs to be reassured Tucker died from an accident."

"Tuck was a real gentleman. I respected him greatly. I know he would have helped me the way I . . . helped him."

"Yes, I knew he was sick. But he had a lot of good years in him. And I wanted some of them to be spent with me."

"I know." I wanted to comfort her. "He must want to spend time with you if he keeps coming back at night. You were the love of his life."

"I was, wasn't I?"

"You're lucky, you know. I still haven't found my great love. I envy you."

Grandmother hormones clicked in. "You will, Robbie, you will. When you've been around as long as I have, you see life rolls forward like a wheel. Repeatin' itself. Old is new, new is old, lost is found, and found is . . . lost forever."

"I'd give anything if I could bring Tucker back. But, he had an accident. There are people all over this town who miss him. You're very lucky to have known him."

"You're right, hon, I know you're right." Hazel Franklin lifted her glasses and dabbed at the corners of her eyes.

"Look at me, you've come all this way and done exactly what I asked. You've put your life on hold and now I guess you have to get on with it. Have you thought about where you're goin'?"

Before I could answer, a chair skidded across the floor upstairs. Every night since my arrival, the ghost of Tucker James had visited Hazel. Peter Hooper told me the hauntings were rescheduled to occur every other night.

I ran for the steps.

"Robbie, you'll never see Tucker, he vanishes before even I can catch a glimpse."

By the time I got to the bedroom, Clay Bowman was halfway out the window.

I ran to assure him I knew about his arrangement. "Clay, it's okay, Peter told me everything."

He threw something wrapped in brown paper down to the front lawn. Startled, he came back inside the room.

"Is Granny downstairs?"

"Yes, but don't worry. She won't come up. What did you throw out the window?"

"Nothin'."

"You're lying. You lied last night about dropping groceries off. You were taking something out of this house. And now I find you taking something else. What's going on? Do you want me to ask Hazel?"

"No! I've been all through it with her. This is the only way."

"What is?"

"These are mine." He motioned to the paintings in Alice's room. "Mom told me they would go to me when she died. She promised! But after she passed away, I asked Granny if I could have them. Do you have any idea what these are worth?"

"Sorry, no."

He pointed to a small canvas. "That's a genuine Benton, and that red one, a Warhol. I told Granny, Mom promised I could have the collection. And I wanted them now."

"Hazel would never treat you unfairly; she loves you."

"Oh, she knows the collection is mine, but she wants to

keep it around her, a memory of Alice, she says. Even offered to give me some money instead. Granny doesn't even know what she's got here. It's all just sentimental, not cash value to her. I've been takin' pieces outta here for months now and she hasn't missed one thing."

"Do you intend to take all of them? Leave Hazel with nothing?"

"Granny's got Tucker's life insurance money, and still has some of Granddaddy's money socked away. Besides, she gets social security, and this house has been free and clear for years. What more does she need?"

"Clayton! Get your butt out of there!"

Startled, I looked over Clay's shoulder to see Elizabeth Huffman's head sticking through the half-opened window.

"Hurry up before that old lady finds . . . you. Oh, I thought you were alone."

Annoyed, Clay turned and scolded her in a loud whisper, "Didn't I tell you to wait by the car? You're gonna ruin everything."

Ignoring him, Elizabeth pushed the window the rest of the way up and climbed into the bedroom. I couldn't figure out if it was jealousy or that inbred Southern hospitality, but she walked right over to me and extended a hand. "I'm Clayton's fiancée, Elizabeth. Have we met?"

The candlestick lamp produced more shadows than light. I lifted my chin, offering her a better look. "Yes. Yesterday. At the chapel. In the ladies' room."

"Oh, you're Tucker's niece. I don't believe I caught your name."

"She lied to you. Her name's Roberta Stanton and she's a private investigator. Granny hired her."

Elizabeth looked frightened. "I told you she wouldn't buy the idea of a ghost. I knew she'd miss the paintings. I told you. I told you!"

"Shut up for a minute, will you? Granny hired her to investigate Tucker's death. She's never said a word about the paintings? Has she?"

"No."

"Then we're okay. Right?" Elizabeth looked to Clay for a nod.

"As long as Nancy Drew here keeps quiet about all this."

"You will, won't you?" Elizabeth Huffman seemed more little girl right now than grown-up lady. "We're only takin' what belongs to us . . . him, I mean. The old lady doesn't even miss 'em."

"No matter how you juggle this around in your brain, it's stealing. I can't keep something like this from Hazel; she's my friend. And for God's sake, Clay, she's your grandmother."

"I knew we couldn't expect her to understand." Clay reached inside his jacket and pulled out a police revolver. He pointed it at me while ordering Elizabeth back to the car.

"I'm not leavin' you now." The tension seemed to excite her.

"Suit yourself but stay out of my way."

I stood with my hands at my sides. I'd imagined this moment for years. How I had avoided other guns in other cases always amazed me. And now as I faced this desperate man I stepped outside myself and instead of the victim, became the witness. Dim light, hundreds of eyes staring from inside their frames, it all seemed unreal. I had to say something to snap us out of this scene.

"You're not going to kill anyone. You're a coward and a thief, but not a murderer. Now let's just go downstairs."

"You don't know shit about me! First it was my mother. The artist! The oddball! Now the whole town's talkin' about my grandmother. Sky-divin', datin' younger men. The guys at the station laugh. It's embarrassin'. Now along comes her crazy friend."

"Crazy?" There was that awful word again.

"I did my own investigatin', Ms. Stanton. It wasn't hard to track you from Omaha to the nuthouse. You have a police record, remember? Jesus, what a pair you and the old lady make. Who in their right mind would listen to either one of you? Besides, I'd only be doin' my duty if I killed me a crazy woman caught stealin' Granny's precious paintin's."

"I don't know what is goin' on here but could we please

hurry?" Elizabeth stopped pacing in front of a small canvas. Removing it from the wall she brought it closer to the light; admired the work of art.

"You're right, honey, we ain't got all night." Clay raised the gun level with my nose.

Fear unexpectedly released itself inside my head like a waterfall; my ears flooded with panic. "Wait a minute."

"I'm tired of waitin'!" His hand shook but his eyes never left mine.

We stood, frozen, for a few seconds until Elizabeth Huffman interrupted the quiet with a startled gasp. The painting she held seemed to jerk from her hand. I can't explain how, but I swear the canvas flew at least six feet through the air before chopping Clayton squarely across the forehead. Elizabeth exhaled her surprise. Clay grabbed his head, blood dripping down to his nose as he wailed in pain.

Hazel called from the foot of the stairs. "Robbie? Are you okay?"

I maneuvered a nice kick and the gun went flying across the floor.

Out of the corner of my eye, I saw Elizabeth trip, fall, then scurry for the ladder. I grabbed the gun from the corner where it had landed and called to Hazel, "I'm fine. I'll be right down."

The video for Opryland was still playing as Hazel and I sat in the Nashville airport. "I want to thank you for everythin'. I have your payment right here."

"No, I couldn't." I desperately needed the money but taking it from Hazel seemed wrong. She'd already had so much taken from her.

"You did a job, you get paid." She pulled a small package from her huge shoulder bag. Untying a piece of string and spreading back the brown paper, Hazel held up a small painting. It was a pale blue pond strewn with water lilies. It was also the same Monet Elizabeth Huffman had admired two nights ago.

"I can't accept this, Hazel. It's worth . . ."

"Not nearly as much as you are, Robbie, darlin'." She

wrapped the treasure back up in its plain wrapper and handed it to me. "Hang it on your wall and think of beautiful things. Or, if it'll help more, sell it. Either way, get some enjoyment."

I hugged her and kissed her soft cheek. "Thank you."

"That grandson of mine is after me all the time to sell his mother's collection. That's all he sees when he looks at those beautiful paintin's: money. Poor Clayton. He thinks I don't know he's been takin' a few at a time." She shook her head. "I fooled him, though, hid my favorites in the closet, way in the back. Close as I can figure, he's got enough now to buy that house Elizabeth's naggin' him for. Well, he can consider it a weddin' present from his mother and me. And when he settles down a bit, maybe after he has a baby of his own, I'll give him the rest."

My flight was announced and I stood to get in the boarding line. "I'm still worried about you. You could have been hurt . . ."

"Clayton's all the time talkin' big, but the truth is he's just a traffic cop. Wanted to be assigned to a desk, but they needed him out on the street. Why, up until the other night, he'd never had cause to pull a gun on anyone. They scare the daylights outta him. I know for a fact, the first thing he does when he's off duty is unload his revolver. Thanks for not pressin' charges, sugar, but you were never in any real danger."

The situation between Hazel and Clayton was a family matter. It didn't concern me. Professionally. I struggled to separate my feelings. But I couldn't help voicing my concern. "Just because the gun wasn't loaded doesn't mean he won't hurt someone."

"Pish, darlin', Tucker's around to protect me. He took care of you, didn't he?"

I had to agree with Hazel, even though it sounded crazy. "Yes, he did."

In 1993 Marcia Muller received a well-deserved Life Achievement Award from the Private Eye Writers of America. She was the first—and to date, the only—woman recipient. Although she admits she was not the first to create a successful female P.I., her Sharon McCone series is the longest running of any of the female P.I. series. Her novel, Wolf in the Shadows, *was nominated by PWA as Best Private Eye Novel of 1993.*

Another first . . . maybe: this McCone story might have been the first piece of fiction published after the 1989 San Francisco earthquake that made use of it. It first appeared in The Armchair Detective.

SOMEWHERE IN THE CITY

by Marcia Muller

A T 5:04 P.M. ON OCTOBER 17, 1989, the city of San Francisco was jolted by an earthquake that measured a frightening 7.1 on the Richter Scale. The violent tremors left the Bay Bridge impassable, collapsed a double-decker freeway in nearby Oakland, and toppled or severely damaged countless homes and other buildings. From the Bay Area to the seaside town of Santa Cruz some 100 miles south, 65 people were killed and thousands left homeless. And when the aftershocks subsided, San Francisco entered a new era— one in which things would never be quite the same again. As with all cataclysmic events, the question, "Where were you when?" will forever provoke deeply emotional responses in those of us who lived through it. . . .

*   *   *

Where I was when: the headquarters of the Golden Gate Crisis Hotline in the Noe Valley district. I'd been working a case there—off and on, and mostly in the late afternoon and evening hours, for over two weeks—with very few results and with a good deal of frustration.

The hotline occupied one big windowless room behind a run-down coffeehouse on Twenty-fourth Street. The location, I'd been told, was not so much one of choice as of convenience (meaning the rent was affordable), but had I not known that, I would have considered it a stroke of genius. There was something instantly soothing about entering through the coffeehouse, where the aromas of various blends permeated the air and steam rose from huge stainless-steel urns. The patrons were unthreatening— mostly shabby and relaxed, reading or conversing with their feet propped up on chairs. The pastries displayed in the glass case were comfort food at its purest—reminders of the days when calories and cholesterol didn't count. And the round face of the proprietor, Lloyd Warner, was welcoming and kind as he waved troubled visitors through to the crisis center.

On that Tuesday afternoon I arrived at about twenty to five, answering Lloyd's cheerful greeting and trying to ignore the chocolate-covered doughnuts in the case. I had a dinner date at seven-thirty, had been promised some of the best French cuisine on Russian Hill, and was unwilling to spoil my appetite. The doughnuts called out to me, but I turned a deaf ear and hurried past.

The room beyond the coffeehouse contained an assortment of mismatched furniture: several desks and chairs of all vintages and materials; phones in colors and styles ranging from standard black touchtone to a shocking turquoise Princess; three tattered easy chairs dating back to the fifties; and a card table covered with literature on health and psychological services. Two people manned the desks nearest the door. I went to the desk with the turquoise phone, plunked my briefcase and bag down on it, and turned to face them.

"He call today?" I asked.

Pete Lowry, a slender man with a bandit's mustache who was director of the center, took his booted feet off the desk and swiveled to face me. "Nope. It's been quiet all afternoon."

"Too quiet." This came from Ann Potter, a woman with dark frizzed hair who affected the aging-hippie look in jeans and flamboyant over-blouses. "And this weather—I don't like it one bit."

"Ann's having one of her premonitions of gloom and doom," Pete said. "Evil portents and omens lurk all around us—although most of them went up front for coffee a while ago."

Ann's eyes narrowed to a glare. She possessed very little sense of humor, whereas Pete perhaps possessed too much. To forestall the inevitable spat, I interrupted. "Well, I don't like the weather much myself. It's muggy, and too warm for October. It makes me nervous."

"Why?" Pete asked.

I shrugged. "I don't know, but I've felt edgy all day."

The phone on his desk rang. He reached for the receiver. "Golden Gate Crisis Hotline, Pete speaking."

Ann cast one final glare at his back as she crossed to the desk that had been assigned to me. "It *has* been too quiet," she said defensively. "Hardly anyone's called, not even to inquire about how to deal with a friend or a family member. That's not normal, even for a Tuesday."

"Maybe all the crazies are out enjoying the warm weather."

Ann half-smiled, cocking her head. She wasn't sure if what I'd said was funny or not, and didn't know how to react. After a few seconds her attention was drawn to the file I was removing from my briefcase. "Is that about our problem caller?"

"Uh-huh." I sat down and began rereading my notes silently, hoping she'd go away. I'd meant it when I'd said I felt on edge, and was in no mood for conversation.

The file concerned a series of calls that the hotline had received over the past month—all from the same individual, a man with a distinctive raspy voice. Their content had been more or less the same: an initial plaint of being all alone in the world with no one to care if he lived or died; then a gradual escalating from despair to anger, in spite of the trained counselors' skillful responses; and finally the declaration that he had an assault rifle and was going to kill others and himself. He always ended with some variant on the statement, "I'm going to take a whole lot of people with me."

After three of the calls, Pete had decided to notify the police. A trace was placed on the center's lines, but the results were unsatisfactory; most of the time the caller didn't stay on the phone long enough, and in the instances that the calls could be traced, they turned out to have originated from booths in the Marina district. Finally the trace was taken off, the official conclusion being that the calls were the work of a crank—and possibly one with a grudge against someone connected with the hotline.

The official conclusion did not satisfy Pete, however. By the next morning he was in the office of the hotline's attorney at All Souls Legal Cooperative, where I am chief investigator. And a half an hour after that, I was assigned to work the phones at the hotline as often as my other duties permitted, until I'd identified the caller. Following a crash course from Pete in techniques for dealing with callers in crisis—augmented by some reading of my own—they turned me loose on the turquoise phone.

After the first couple of rocky, sweaty-palmed sessions, I'd gotten into it: become able to distinguish the truly disturbed from the fakers or the merely curious; learned to gauge the responses that would work best with a given individual; succeeded at eliciting information that would permit a crisis team to go out and assess the seriousness of the situation in person. In most cases, the team would merely talk the caller into getting counseling. However, if they felt immediate action was warranted, they would act the SFPD, who had the authority to have the individual held for evaluation at the S.F. General Hospital for up to seventy-two hours.

During the past two weeks the problem caller had been routed to me several times, and with each conversation I became more concerned about him. While his threats were melodramatic, I sensed genuine disturbance and desperation in his voice; the swift escalation of panic and anger seemed much out of proportion to whatever verbal stimuli I offered. And, as Pete had stressed in my orientation, no matter how theatrical or frequently made, any threat of suicide or violence toward others was to be taken with utmost seriousness by the hotline volunteers.

Unfortunately I was able to glean very little information from the man. Whenever I tried to get him to reveal concrete facts about himself, he became sly and would dodge my questions. Still, I could make several assumptions about him: he was youngish, reasonably well-educated, and Caucasian. The traces to the Marina indicated he probably lived in that bayside district—which meant he had to have a good income. He listened to classical music (three times I'd heard it playing in the background) from a transistor radio, by the tinny tonal quality. Once I'd caught the call letters of the FM station—one in the Central Valley town of Fresno. Why Fresno? I'd wondered. Perhaps he was from there? But that wasn't much to go on; there were probably several Fresno transplants in his part of the city.

When I looked up from my folder, Ann had gone back to her desk. Pete was still talking in low, reassuring tones with his caller. Ann's phone rang, and she picked up the receiver. I tensed, knowing the next call would cycle automatically to my phone.

When it rang some minutes later, I glanced at my watch and jotted down the time while reaching over for the receiver. Four-fifty-eight. "Golden Gate Crisis Hotline, Sharon speaking."

The caller hung up—either a wrong number or, more likely, someone who lost his nerve. The phone rang again about twenty seconds later and I answered it in the same manner.

"Sharon. It's me." The greeting was the same as the previous times, the raspy voice unmistakable.

"Hey, how's it going?"

A long pause, labored breathing. In the background I could make out the strains of music—Brahms, I thought. "Not so good. I'm really down today."

"You want to talk about it?"

"There isn't much to say. Just more of the same. I took a walk a while ago, thought it might help. But the people, out there flying their kites, I can't take it."

"Why is that?"

"I used to . . . ah, forget it."

"No, I'm interested."

"Well, they're always in couples, you know."

When he didn't go on, I made an interrogatory sound.

"The whole damn world is in couples. Or families. Even here inside my little cottage I can feel it. There are these apartment buildings on either side, and I can feel them pressing in on me, and I'm here all alone."

He was speaking rapidly now, his voice rising. But as his agitation increased, he'd unwittingly revealed something about his living situation. I made a note about the little cottage between the two apartment buildings.

"This place where the people were flying kites," I said, "do you go there often?"

"Sure—it's only two blocks away." A sudden note of sullenness now entered his voice—a part of the pattern he'd previously exhibited. "Why do you want to know about that?"

"Because . . . I'm sorry, I forget your name."

No response.

"It would help if I knew what to call you."

"Look, bitch, I know what you're trying to do."

"Oh?"

"Yeah. You want to get a name, an address. Send the cops out. Next thing I'm chained to the wall at S.F. General. I've ~~~~~ ~h~t route before. But I know my rights now; I went ~~~~ ~~~~~ ;treet to the Legal Switchboard, and they told

I was distracted from what he was saying by a tapping sound—the stack trays on the desk next to me bumped against the wall. I looked over there, frowning. What was causing that . . . ?

". . . gonna take the people next door with me . . ."

I looked back at the desk in front of me. The lamp was jiggling.

"What the hell?" the man on the phone exclaimed.

My swivel chair shifted. A coffee mug tipped and rolled across the desk and into my lap.

Pete said, "Jesus Christ, we're having an earthquake!"

". . . The ceiling's coming down!" The man's voice was panicked now.

"Get under a door frame!" I clutched the edge of the desk, ignoring my own advice.

I heard a crash from the other end of the line. The man screamed in pain. "Help me! Please help—" And then the line went dead.

For a second or so I merely sat there—longtime San Franciscan, frozen by my own disbelief. All around me formerly inanimate objects were in motion. Pete and Ann were scrambling for the archway that led to the door of the coffeehouse.

"Sharon, get under the desk!" she yelled at me.

And then the electricity cut out, leaving the windowless room in blackness. I dropped the dead receiver, slid off the chair, crawled into the kneehole of the desk. There was a cracking, a violent shifting, as if a giant hand had seized the building and twisted it. Tremors buckled the floor beneath me.

This is a bad one. Maybe the big one that they're always talking about.

The sound of something wrenching apart. Pellets of plaster rained down on the desk above me. Time had telescoped; it seemed as if the quake had been going on for many minutes, when in reality it could not have been more than ten or fifteen seconds.

Make it stop! Please make it stop!

And then, as if whatever powers-that-be had heard my

unspoken plea, the shock waves diminished to shivers, and finally ebbed.

Blackness. Silence. Only bits of plaster bouncing off the desks and the floor.

"Ann?" I said. "Pete?" My voice sounded weak, tentative.

"Sharon?" It was Pete. "You okay?"

"Yes. You?"

"We're fine."

Slowly I began to back out of the kneehole. Something blocked it—the chair. I shoved it aside, and emerged. I couldn't see a thing, but I could feel fragments of plaster and other unidentified debris on the floor. Something cut into my palm; I winced.

"God, it's dark," Ann said. "I've got some matches in my purse. Can you—"

"No matches," I told her. "Who knows what shape the gas mains are in."

". . . Oh, right."

Pete said, "Wait, I'll open the door to the coffeehouse."

On hands and knees I began feeling my way toward the sound of their voices. I banged into one of the desks, overturned a wastebasket, then finally reached the opposite wall. As I stood there, Ann's cold hand reached out to guide me. Behind her I could hear Pete fumbling at the door.

I leaned against the wall. Ann was close beside me, her breathing erratic. Pete said, "Goddamned door's jammed." From behind it came voices of people in the coffeehouse.

Now that the danger was over—at least until the first of the aftershocks—my body sagged against the wall, giving way to tremors of its own manufacture. My thoughts turned to the lover with whom I'd planned to have dinner: where had he been when the quake hit? And what about my cats, my house? My friends and my coworkers at All Souls? Other friends scattered throughout the Bay Area?

And what about a nameless, faceless man somewhere in the city who had screamed for help before the phone went dead?

The door to the coffeehouse burst open, spilling weak light into the room. Lloyd Warner and several of his

customers peered anxiously through it. I prodded Ann—
who seemed to have lapsed into lethargy—toward them.

The coffeehouse was fairly dark, but late-afternoon light
showed beyond the plate-glass windows fronting on the
street. It revealed a floor that was awash in spilled liquid and
littered with broken crockery. Chairs were tipped over—
whether by the quake or the patrons' haste to get to shelter
I couldn't tell. About ten people milled about, talking
noisily.

Ann and Pete joined them, but I moved forward to the
window. Outside, Twenty-fourth Street looked much as
usual, except for the lack of traffic and pedestrians. The
buildings still stood, the sun still shone, the air drifting
through the open door of the coffeehouse was still warm and
muggy. In this part of the city, at least, life went on.

Lloyd's transistor radio had been playing the whole
time—tuned to the station that was carrying the coverage of
the third game of the Bay Area World Series, due to start at
five-thirty. I moved closer, listening.

The sportscaster was saying, "Nobody here knows *what's*
going on. The Giants have wandered over to the A's dugout.
It looks like a softball game where somebody forgot to bring
the ball."

Then the broadcast shifted abruptly to the station's
studios. A newswoman was relaying telephone reports from
the neighborhoods. I was relieved to hear that Bernal
Heights, where All Souls is located, and my own small
district near Glen Park were shaken up but for the most part
undamaged. The broadcaster concluded by warning listen-
ers not to use their phones except in cases of emergency.
Ann snorted and said, "Do as I say but not . . ."

Again the broadcast made an abrupt switch—to the
station's traffic helicopter. "From where we are," the reporter said, "it looks as if part of the upper deck of the
Oakland side of the Bay Bridge has collapsed onto the
bottom deck. Cars are pointing every which way, there may
be some in the water. And on the approaches—" The
transmission broke, then resumed after a number of static-
filled seconds. "It looks as if the Cypress Structure on the

Oakland approach to the bridge has also collapsed. Oh my God, there are cars and people—" This time the transmission broke for good.

It was very quiet in the coffeehouse. We all exchanged looks—fearful, horrified. This was an extremely bad one, if not the catastrophic one they'd been predicting for so long.

Lloyd was the first to speak. He said, "I'd better see if I can insulate the urns in some way, keep the coffee hot as long as possible. People'll need it tonight." He went behind the counter, and in a few seconds a couple of the customers followed.

The studio newscast resumed. ". . . fires burning out of control in the Marina district. We're receiving reports of collapsed buildings there, with people trapped inside . . ."

The Marina district. People trapped.

I thought again of the man who had cried out for help over the phone. Of my suspicion, more or less confirmed by today's conversation, that he lived in the Marina.

Behind the counter Lloyd and the customers were wrapping the urns in dish towels. Here—and in other parts of the city, I was sure—people were already overcoming their shock, gearing up to assist in the relief effort. There was nothing I could do in my present surroundings, but . . .

I hurried to the back room and groped until I found my purse on the floor beside the desk. As I picked it up, an aftershock hit—nothing like the original trembler, but strong enough to make me grab the chair for support. When it stopped, I went shakily out to my car.

Twenty-fourth Street was slowly coming to life. People bunched on the sidewalks, talking and gesturing. A man emerged from one of the shops, walked to the center of the street, and surveyed the facade of his building. In the parking lot of nearby Bell Market, employees and customers gathered by the grocery carts. A man in a butcher's apron looked around, shrugged, and headed for a corner tavern. I got into my MG and took a city map from the side pocket.

The Marina area consists mainly of early twentieth-century stucco homes and apartment buildings built on fill on the shore of the bay—which meant the quake damage there would naturally be bad. The district extends roughly from the Fisherman's Wharf area to the Presidio—not large, but large enough, considering I had few clues as to where within its boundaries my man lived. I spread out the map against the steering wheel and examined it.

The man had said he'd taken a walk that afternoon, to a place two blocks from his home where people were flying kites. That would be the Marina Green near the yacht harbor, famous for the elaborate and often fantastical kites flown there in fine weather. Two blocks placed the man's home somewhere on the far side of North Point Street.

I had one more clue: in his anger at me he'd let it slip that the Legal Switchboard was "down the street." The switchboard, a federally funded assistance group, was headquartered in one of the piers at Fort Mason, at the east end of the Marina. While several streets in that vicinity ended at Fort Mason, I saw that only two—Beach and North Point—were within two blocks of the Green as well.

Of course, I reminded myself, "down the street" and "two blocks" could have been generalizations or exaggerations. But it was somewhere to start. I set the map aside and turned the key in the ignition.

The trip across the city was hampered by near-gridlock traffic on some streets. All the stoplights were out; there were no police to direct the panicked motorists. Citizens helped out: I saw men in three-piece suits, women in heels and business attire, even a ragged man who looked to be straight out of one of the homeless shelters, all playing traffic cop. Sirens keened, emergency vehicles snaked from lane to lane. The car radio kept reporting further destruction; there was another aftershock, and then another, but I scarcely felt them because I was in motion.

As I inched along a major crosstown arterial, I asked myself why I was doing this foolhardy thing. The man was nothing to me, really—merely a voice on the phone, always self-pitying, and often antagonistic and potentially violent. I ought to be checking on my house and the folks at All Souls; if I wanted to help people, my efforts would have been better spent in my own neighborhood or Bernal Heights. But instead I was traveling to the most congested and dangerous part of the city in search of a man I'd never laid eyes on.

As I asked the question, I knew the answer. Over the past two weeks the man had told me about his deepest problems. I'd come to know him in spite of his self-protective secretiveness. And he'd become more to me than just the subject of an investigation; I'd begun to care whether he lived or died. Now we had shared a peculiarly intimate moment—that of being together, if only in voice, when the catastrophe that San Franciscans feared the most had struck. He had called for help; I had heard his terror and pain. A connection had been established that could not be broken.

After twenty minutes and little progress, I cut west and took a less-traveled residential street through Japantown and over the crest of Pacific Heights. From the top of the hill I could see and smell the smoke over the Marina; as I crossed the traffic-snarled intersection with Lombard, I could see the flames. I drove another block, then decided to leave the MG and continue on foot.

All around I could see signs of destruction now: a house was twisted at a tortuous angle, its front porch collapsed and crushing a car parked at the curb; on Beach Street an apartment building's upper story had slid into the street, clogging it with rubble; three bottom floors of another building were flattened, leaving only the top intact.

I stopped at a corner, breathing hard, nearly choking on the thickening smoke. The smell of gas from broken lines was vaguely nauseating—frightening, too, because of the potential for explosions. To my left the street was cordoned off; fire-department hoses played on the blazes—weakly, because of damaged water mains. People congregated everywhere, staring about with horror-struck eyes; they huddled together, clinging to one another; many were crying. Firefighters and police were telling bystanders to go home before dark fell. "You should be looking after your property," I heard one say. "You can count on going seventy-two hours without water or power."

"Longer than that," someone said.

"It's not safe here," the policeman added. "Please go home."

Between sobs, a woman said, "What if you've got no home to go to anymore?"

The cop had no answer for her.

Emotions were flying out of control among the onlookers. It would have been easy to feed into it—to weep, even panic. Instead, I turned my back to the flaming buildings, began walking the other way, toward Fort Mason. If the man's home was beyond the barricades, there was nothing I could do for him. But if it lay in the other direction, where there was a lighter concentration of rescue workers, then my assistance might save his life.

I forced myself to walk slower, to study the buildings on either side of the street. I had one last clue that could lead me to the man: he'd said he lived in a little cottage between two apartment buildings. The homes in this district were mostly of substantial size; there couldn't be too many cottages situated in just that way.

Across the street a house slumped over to one side, its roof canted at a forty-five-degree angle; windows from an apartment house had popped out of their frames, and its iron fire escapes were tangled and twisted like a cat's cradle of yarn. Another home was unrecognizable, merely a heap of rubble. And over there, two four-story apartment buildings leaned together, forming an arch over a much smaller structure . . .

I rushed across the street, pushed through a knot of bystanders. The smaller building was a tumble-down mass of white stucco with a smashed red tile roof and a partially flattened iron fence. It had been a Mediterranean-style cottage with grillwork over high windows; now the grills were bent and pushed outward; the collapsed windows resembled swollen-shut eyes.

The woman standing next to me was cradling a terrified cat under her loose cardigan sweater. I asked her, "Did the man who lives in the cottage get out okay?"

She frowned, tightened her grip on the cat as it burrowed

deeper. "I don't know who lives there. It's always kind of deserted-looking."

A man in front of her said, "I've seen lights, but never anybody coming or going."

I moved closer. The cottage was deep in the shadows of the leaning buildings, eerily silent. From above came a groaning sound, and then a piece of wood sheared off the apartment house to the right, crashing onto what remained of the cottage's roof. I looked up, wondering how long before one or the other of the buildings toppled. Wondering if the man was still alive inside the compacted mass of stucco . . .

A man in jeans and a sweatshirt came up and stood beside me. His face was smudged and abraded; his clothing was smeared with dirt and what looked to be blood; he held his left elbow gingerly in the palm of his hand. "You were asking about Dan?" he said.

So that was the anonymous caller's name. "Yes. Did he get out okay/"

"I don't think he was home. At least, I saw him over at the Green around quarter to five."

"He was home. I was talking with him on the phone when the quake hit."

"Oh, Jesus." The man's face paled under the smudges. "My name's Mel; I live . . . lived next door. Are you a friend of Dan's?"

"Yes," I said, realizing it was true.

"That's a surprise." He stared worriedly up at the place where the two buildings leaned together.

"Why?"

"I thought Dan didn't have any friends left. He's pushed us away ever since the accident."

"Accident?"

"You must be a new friend, or else you'd know. Dan's woman was killed on the freeway last spring. A truck crushed her car."

The word "crushed" seemed to hang in the air between us. I said, "I've got to try to get him out of there," and stepped over the flattened portion of the fence.

Mel said, "I'll go with you."

I looked skeptically at his injured arm.

"It's nothing, really," he told me. "I was helping an old lady out of my building, and a beam grazed me."

"Well—" I broke off as a hail of debris came from the building to the left.

Without further conversation, Mel and I crossed the small front yard, skirting fallen bricks, broken glass, and jagged chunks of wallboard. Dusk was coming on fast now; here in the shadows of the leaning buildings it was darker than on the street. I moved toward where the cottage's front door should have been, but couldn't locate it. The windows, with their protruding grillwork, were impassable.

I said, "Is there another entrance?"

"In the back, off a little service porch."

I glanced to either side. The narrow passages between the cottage and the adjacent buildings were jammed with debris. I could possibly scale the mound at the right, but I was leery of setting up vibrations that might cause more debris to come tumbling down.

Mel said, "You'd better give it up. The way the cottage looks, I doubt he survived."

But I wasn't willing to give it up—not yet. There must be a way to at least locate Dan, see if he was alive. But how?

And then I remembered something else from our phone conversations . . .

I said, "I'm going back there."

"Let me."

"No, stay here. That mound will support my weight, but not yours." I moved toward the side of the cottage before Mel could remind me of the risk I was taking.

The mound was over five feet high. I began to climb cautiously, testing every hand- and foothold. Twice jagged chunks of stucco cut my fingers; a piece of wood left a line of splinters on the back of my hand. When I neared the top, I heard the roar of a helicopter, its rotors flapping overhead. I froze, afraid that the air currents would precipitate more debris, then scrambled down the other side of the mound into a weed-choked backyard.

As I straightened, automatically brushing dirt from my jeans, my foot slipped on the soft, spongy ground, then sank into a puddle. Probably a water main was broken nearby. The helicopter still hovered overhead; I couldn't hear a thing above its racket. Nor could I see much: it was even darker back here. I stood still until my eyes adjusted.

The cottage was not so badly damaged at its rear. The steps to the porch had collapsed, and the rear wall leaned inward, but I could make out a door frame opening into blackness inside. I glanced up in irritation at the helicopter, saw it was going away. Waited, and then listened . . .

And heard what I had been hoping to. The music was now Beethoven—his third symphony, the *Eroica*. Its strains were muted, tinny. Music played by an out-of-area FM station, coming from a transistor radio. A transistor whose batteries were functioning long after the electricity had cut out. Whose batteries might have outlived its owner.

I moved quickly to the porch, grasped the iron rail beside the collapsed steps, and pulled myself up. I still could see nothing inside the cottage. The strains of the *Eroica* continued to pour forth, close by now.

Reflexively I reached into my purse for the small flashlight I usually kept there, then remembered it was at home on the kitchen counter—a reminder for me to replace its weak batteries. I swore softly, then started through the doorway, calling out to Dan.

No answer.

"Dan!"

This time I heard a groan.

I rushed forward into the blackness, following the sound of the music. After a few feet I came up against something solid, banging my shins. I lowered a hand, felt around. It was a wooden beam, wedged crosswise.

"Dan?"

Another groan. From the floor—perhaps under the beam. I squatted and made a wide sweep with my hands. They encountered a wool-clad arm; I slid my fingers down it until I touched the wrist, felt for the pulse. It was strong, although slightly irregular.

"Dan," I said, leaning closer, "it's Sharon, from the hotline. We've got to get you out of here."

"Unh. Sharon?" His voice was groggy, confused. He'd probably been drifting in and out of consciousness since the beam fell on him.

"Can you move?" I asked.

". . . Something on my legs."

"Do they feel broken?"

"No, just pinned."

"I can't see much, but I'm going to try to move this beam off you. When I do, roll out from under."

". . . Okay."

From the position at which the beam was wedged, I could tell it would have to be raised. Balancing on the balls of my feet, I got a good grip on it and shoved upward with all my strength. It moved about six inches and then slipped from my grasp. Dan grunted.

"Are you all right?"

"Yeah. Try it again."

I stood, grasped it, and pulled this time. It yielded a little more, and I heard Dan slide across the floor. "I'm clear," he said—and just in time, because I once more lost my grip. The beam crashed down, setting up a vibration that made plaster fall from the ceiling.

"We've got to get out of here fast," I said. "Give me your hand."

He slipped it into mine—long-fingered, work-roughened. Quickly we went through the door, crossed the porch, jumped to the ground. The radio continued to play forlornly behind us. I glanced briefly at Dan, couldn't make out much more than a tall, slender build and a thatch of pale hair. His face was turned from me, toward the cottage.

"Jesus," he said in an awed voice.

I tugged urgently at his hand. "There's no telling how long those apartment buildings are going to stand."

He turned, looked up at them, said, "Jesus" again. I urged him toward the mound of debris.

This time I opted for speed rather than caution—a mistake, because as we neared the top, a cracking noise came from high above. I gave Dan a push, slid after him. A dark, jagged object hurtled down, missing us only by inches. More plasterboard—deadly at that velocity.

For a moment I sat straddle-legged on the ground, sucking in my breath, releasing it tremulously, gasping for more air. Then hands pulled me to my feet and dragged me across the yard toward the sidewalk—Mel and Dan.

Night had fallen by now. A fire had broken out in the house across the street. Its red-orange flickering showed me the man I'd just rescued: ordinary-looking, with regular features that were now marred by dirt and a long cut on the forehead, from which blood had trickled and dried. His pale eyes were studying me; suddenly he looked abashed and shoved both hands into his jeans pockets.

After a moment he asked, "How did you find me?"

"I put together some of the things you'd said on the phone. Doesn't matter now."

"Why did you even bother?"

"Because I care."

He looked at the ground.

I added, "There never was any assault rifle, was there."

He shook his head.

"You made it up, so someone would pay attention."

". . . Yeah."

I felt anger welling up—irrational, considering the present circumstances, but nonetheless justified. "You didn't have to frighten the people at the hotline. All you had to do was ask them for help. Or ask friends like Mel. He cares. People do, you know."

"Nobody does."

"Enough of that! All you have to do is look around to see how much people care about each other. Look at your friend here." I gestured at Mel, who was standing a couple feet away, staring at us. "He hurt his arm rescuing an old lady from his apartment building. Look at those people over by the burning house—they're doing everything they can to help the firefighters. All over this city people are doing things for one another. Goddamn it, I'd never laid eyes on you, but I risked my life anyway!"

Dan was silent for a long moment. Finally he looked up at me. "I know you did. What can I do in return?"

"For me? Nothing. Just pass it on to someone else."

Dan stared across the street at the flaming building, looked back into the shadows where his cottage lay in ruins. Then he nodded and squared his shoulders. To Mel he said, "Let's go over there, see if there's anything we can do."

He put his arm around my shoulders and hugged me briefly, then he and Mel set off at a trot.

The city is recovering now, as it did in 1906, and as it doubtless will when the next big quake hits. Resiliency is what disaster teaches us, I guess—along with the preciousness of life, no matter how disappointing or burdensome it may often seem.

Dan's recovering, too: he's only called the hotline twice, once for a referral to a therapist, and once to ask for my home number so he could invite me to dinner. I turned the invitation down because neither of us needs dwell on the trauma of October seventeenth, and I was fairly sure I heard a measure of relief in his voice when I did so.

I'll never forget Dan, though—or where I was when. And the strains of Beethoven's Third Symphony will forever remind me of the day after which things would never be quite the same again.

Annette Meyers is best known for her Smith & Wetzon novels, published by Doubleday. Of late she has been collaborating with her husband, Martin, on historical mysteries set in New York City. It is in that vein that this story is written. It might even have been called "The Lodger."

THE BEDFORD STREET LEGACY

by Annette Meyers

1

I CAME TO my senses on a cold clear fall day in the year 1919, after a prolonged period of physical and mental devastation caused by the death of everyone who was dear to me. Everyone but Mattie, who nursed me back to a modicum of health.

The Great War took the life of my dear fiancé, Franklin Prince, and the dreadful influenza epidemic in 1918 took the lives of my guardian Mr. Avery and my beloved tutor, Miss Sarah.

I had been orphaned at an early age and became the ward of Jonas Avery, an elderly bachelor who, though kindly, knew nothing of bringing up a girl child of some precocity. So it was well that Mattie, Mr. Avery's cook and housekeeper, took charge of my care.

My education was put into the sturdy hands of Miss Sarah Parkman, who had taught at the Emma Willard School until her seventieth year. Miss Sarah saw in me a fine clay, and convinced that women would eventually—sooner rather than later—get the vote, she devoted herself to giving her avid pupil a classical education equivalent to that of a young gentleman.

Shortly after my recovery I received a visit from my late guardian's attorney, himself a man of some years, who brought with him a full accounting of my financial status, which though modest, would be adequate for me and Mattie so we would not want of the basic necessities. It was thus the news came to me that my guardian had made me his heir, which in itself meant little, for Mr. Avery had, it seemed, been an inveterate player in the stock market and because of losses had been forced to dip into my principal.

The beautiful old house in which I had spent my formative years would have to be sold, and I would have to resign myself to a more financially circumspect life.

"Or," Mr. Bernhardt explained, "you might consider selling the house on Bedford Street."

"What house on Bedford Street?" I asked, quite confused.

"The house on Bedford Street in New York," he said, thinking perhaps that I had knowledge of it.

Well, of course, this took me by complete surprise. "A house in New York? On Bedford Street? I know nothing of this."

"It belonged to the sister of your grandfather, Oliver Brown, for whom you are named," he said. "Miss Brown passed on while your guardian was ill, and I have received a letter from her attorney in New York notifying me that you are her only living relative and, therefore, her heir."

"New York," I said, feeling the first tingle of curiosity for life since my illness and my terrible losses. "Bedford Street. It sounds lovely, but would it be more costly to live in than to stay here in Albany?"

Mr. Bernhardt looked aghast, being of a very conservative bent. "You would not consider such a move. New York City is not a place for gentle young women alone."

"Is the house not inhabitable, then?"

"Quite the opposite. I understand the house is in fine condition and will bring a pretty penny on sale, except for—"

In my excitement, I must admit I did not at first assimilate the "except for—" in Mr. Bernhardt's reply. Instead, I said, "Perhaps Mattie and I could travel to New York and inspect the house and the area before we make up our minds."

"I hardly think—"

"Forgive me, Mr. Bernhardt, but I am quite overcome with all this news you have presented me. Please tell me about my grandfather's sister. I had no idea I had any living relations, though I understand she's dead now."

"I know little about her," he said primly. "The house, however, comes with its own trust fund and a codicil."

"A trust fund? For a house? Please explain."

"Your great-aunt, Miss Evangeline Brown, left a sum of money in trust for the care and upkeep of the house and the salary of a full-time housekeeper."

I was overjoyed. "Why, Mr. Bernhardt. My great-aunt, whom I never knew, will provide a home for Mattie and me. This is wonderful news. We will put this house on the market, and Mattie and I will begin a new life in New York."

"As you wish," Mr. Bernhardt said with the sourest of expressions. I am certain he did not know what to make of the new generation of young women and our desire to exercise more control over our own lives. "But," said he, his thin lips set in disapproval, "I have not told you of the codicil."

Oh, dear, I thought, he was about to burst my bubble. "Yes, the codicil."

"There is a tenant in the house on the ground floor. He has a private entrance."

"Yes, I see, a tenant. Well, if I am to live in the house, the tenant will have to move."

"That, my dear child, is the codicil. The tenant—an

odd, nocturnal man who seldom makes his appearance in daylight and who has equally odd nocturnal visitors—he is the codicil. According to Miss Evangeline Brown's will, he is to live there for his lifetime."

"Oh, I see. Well, that shouldn't matter. Since he has a private entrance, and is, as you say, nocturnal, I shall see little of him, and the rent will be extra money for our coffers."

The old gentleman looked almost triumphant. "I'm afraid," he said, "there will be none of that, for he is to live rent-free so long as he remains in the house."

"Well, then, so be it," I said most cheerfully, for I looked at this news as a gift from God, as well as from my unknown great-aunt Evangeline. "Still, it is a very odd arrangement."

Little did I imagine just how odd it truly was and as with a tidal wave, would change my life as I knew it forever.

ll

We arrived in New York on a particularly lovely spring day in early April and were filled with awe by the magnificence of Grand Central Station. Light streamed down on us from a lofty skylight, and everywhere one looked were well-dressed ladies and gentlemen in traveling clothes. Porters followed with mounds of luggage and traveling trunks.

Mattie took charge at once, summoning our own porter, and soon we, too, were surrounded by hatboxes and satchels.

"We must wait here for the trunk," Mattie said, still fussing over my health, which I had quite recovered.

"I beg your pardon, but would you be Miss Brown? Miss Olivia Brown?" A tall, very pleasant-faced young man, very properly dressed, stood before me.

"I am. And who might you be?" I had become very direct and incautious since my recovery and may even be, as Mattie insists, "full of beans."

"Thomas Jenner, at your service, Miss Brown." He tipped his hat, giving me just a glimpse of unruly dark hair, and smiled. "I am charged with delivering you, your house-keeper, and your luggage to 73½ Bedford Street. Your attorney, Mr. Lyon Bernhardt, made the arrangements."

So it was that Mattie and I, with our caretaker, Mr. Thomas Jenner, directing the livery cab driver, were ensconced in a livery cab piled high with everything we cared to bring with us from our old life to our new.

We rode down the celebrated Fifth Avenue in magical sunlight. I have never seen so many cars and people all intent on going somewhere. I was dazzled by the beauty of the city, as was Mattie.

"This is Madison Square Park," Mr. Jenner said, pointing to a lovely treed area as we rode by. "And this is the famous Flatiron Building, which as you can see looks as it is."

Union Square and then the beautiful homes and tall buildings of lower Fifth Avenue, Washington Square with its great arch. I confess that Mattie and I were soon overwhelmed, so it was a relief when Mr. Jenner tapped our driver on the shoulder.

"Between Morton and Commerce streets," he said. "73½."

When we turned off Fifth Avenue we found ourselves in the heart of Greenwich Village, where small shops and charming brick town houses stood side by side on the narrow streets.

Our driver stopped before a narrow three-story house of red brick with peeling white trim. Small shrubs filled a handkerchief-sized area in front that was fenced in by a black ornate wrought-iron fence. A fine oak door with brass trim led to a small vestibule with two doors.

The two large set-in windows on the ground floor obviously belonged to my tenant in perpetuity, and I admit to being very curious, particularly since those windows were shuttered.

I raised my eyes to the two floors that would be my new home, and I was most inordinately pleased. Who would not be? On the second floor, three tall windows, and on the third, four windows, taller still.

Our escort saw to the unloading of our luggage and

produced a shiny key from his inside pocket, while our livery driver waited impatiently to complete his task and receive his payment.

And I? I fairly danced into the vestibule of my new home. And stopped. Which door was mine? Not the door to the right, for a small brass plate set beside that door informed me of my tenant in perpetuity. It said:

H. MELVILLE

PRIVATE INVESTIGATIONS
(Confidentiality Assured)

lll

Our journey proved more tiring than I had imagined, and the enthusiasm with which I greeted our new situation left me feverish and weak. In spite of Mattie's insistence that I go to bed at once, I prevailed. I wanted a tour of our new home even if it was a cursory one.

Mr. Jenner left us at this point, saying he was at our service, this time presenting Mattie with one of his cards.

It was obvious that the little house had been thoroughly cleaned and aired, although there still remained a faintly musty odor mixed with lemon oil and wax. There were also fresh lilacs in a vase on a table in the snug little parlor filled with the elegant furniture I recognized as that made by the Stickley Brothers of New York.

A large Oriental rug in earthen hues lay on the floor. The parlor, separated by sliding doors, led to a large living room and a small dining room with one of Mr. Tiffany's magnificent chandeliers hanging over the round oak table, on which sat a vase with more lilacs.

I wandered over to the French doors, opened them, and found a cunning stone terrace with steps leading to a courtyard with flowering trees, dogwood and cherry. Faintly, I could hear Mattie oohing and aahing over her kitchen, and when I pushed back the swinging doors, found her filling a kettle. She set it on a huge iron stove, struck a match. When the flames came up, she exclaimed, "We're in business, dearie.

Tea will be ready shortly." Then, seeing how tired I was, Mattie rushed me into a chair and helped me out of my coat.

I was much renewed after tea and biscuits, but Mattie insisted I go to bed, and so to bed I went. My new bedroom was a large and airy room facing Bedford Street. A small sitting room, a dressing room, and connecting bath took up the rest of the floor. There was a bedroom and bath for Mattie on the top floor, which she refused to let me inspect.

No sooner was I in my cotton nighty and resting under the lovely patchwork quilts that lay over the double bed, to my surprise, my eyes closed and I fell into a deep sleep, with only a flickering thought of my codicil and the meaning of the term, private investigations.

I don't know what woke me, the dream perhaps, for in it I was on horseback riding through strange narrow streets. Hooves on cobblestones. Or was it a door slamming? Or the backfire of an automobile? But wake I did, and for the first few moments I had no memory of where I was. I lay there with no sense of danger as my eyes acclimated to the darkness.

The small fire in the grate gave off just enough light, and my memory returned and I was perfectly at peace. I stretched under my bedclothes, dislodging a hot water bottle which fell to the floor with a loud thump.

As if in response, there occurred a peculiar noise, possibly the one that woke me initially. It came from below, in the street or possibly from the apartment of my tenant. I recalled then Mr. Bernhardt's dire warning of nocturnal traffic.

I found my shawl at the foot of the bed where Mattie always left it and threw it around me as I walked to the windows. When I drew back the draperies, I could see below quite clearly. A street lamp not in view nevertheless lit the area.

As I watched, a door slammed and a dark figure rushed into the street, stumbled, caught himself, threw his arms into the air, and returned to the house. The street returned to empty.

Oh, my, I thought, listening. Not a sound ensued. Then I

heard a door close. Now I was wide-awake and my innate curiosity took charge. I adjusted the shawl, which dear Mattie had knitted for me, and lit the candle in the stand beside the bed, placing the globe over it. Listening all the while, I crept, barefoot, I confess, down the stairs to the kitchen.

Old houses have definite personalities marked by how they settle on their foundations, and this one certainly had. It sighed rather than creaked, as the house in Albany had. It sighed softly when I stopped at the enormous hat and umbrella stand in my front hall. My lamp showed me the shadow of a cane among the umbrellas, and I reached for it without much thought of what I would do with it.

Down the stairs I went, cane and skirt of my nightdress clenched in one hand, lamp in the other, the wool of the Oriental runner crisp on my bare feet. I felt suddenly more alive than I had felt in years, and my heart thudded in my chest, sending my lifeblood coursing through my veins. I was positively ecstatic, and was treasuring the feeling as I opened our door tentatively.

The lock of my tenant's door had been removed, leaving a gaping hole. I peered into the hole, but it was black as tar inside. And still. I put the lamp near the hole and looked into the room again.

I was rewarded with a fierce growl that took my breath away, then the door swung open inward, and a voice said, "Douse that bloody light."

IV

So startled was I that I near dropped the lamp. The cane clattered to the floor from my shaking hand. Still, I did as I was told, but tried to catch a sight of the speaker before doing so. Alas, I failed.

"Don't just stand there. Come in and shut the door." The words were terse, but the speaker's tone was resonant and not unfriendly. His accent was quality American with a faint undertone of something else I couldn't quite catch. Throwing caution to the wind, for after all, I was in Greenwich

Village and it was 1920, I entered and shut the door behind me.

The room was quite cold and I hugged my shawl around me, waiting for I knew not what. And then the room was so bathed in light that I had to hold my hand over my eyes for a short time until I was able to see clearly.

When I removed my hand I saw a large room with wood paneling and a carpet of feathers. Light came from an overhead fixture, which I suddenly realized had been electrified. The room also contained what must be a Murphy bed, whose mattress was cut into shreds and whose pillows provided for what I had originally thought was the feather carpet. In an alcove I saw a rolltop desk the drawers of which were open, the contents strewn everywhere. The other objects in the room were a lumpy sofa and two side chairs about to lose their springs, and a file cabinet whose drawers had been upended onto the floor.

My host was bent over the fireplace coaxing a fire from one lonesome log. When he straightened and faced me, I saw a man in his middle years, broad of shoulder, though not more than my height, which was five feet four in shoes, which were not at present on my feet. His hair was fine and light, to his shoulders, and on his forehead he bore a lump the size of a walnut and a bruise that had broken the skin.

"Oh, my," I said. "You've been hurt."

He stared at me and laughed full out. "You must be the old girl's niece."

"I am," I said, at once aware of my own condition, barefoot, dressed as I was in my long white cotton night-dress and wrapped in my multicolored shawl. My auburn hair hung in a long, thick braid down my back to my waist. "Olivia Brown."

"Green eyes must run in the family, Niece," he said, looking me over thoroughly.

"Excuse me," I said, flustered. I began to back toward the damaged door. "I didn't mean to intrude."

"You're here now so you might as well stay." His appraisal of me was most disconcerting. How I wished for

my shoes. "Take a seat," he said. He gestured toward the
sofa on which were piled papers and folders of every sort
and size, in no particular order. He did not clear a space.

Once more, curiosity overcame my apprehension. I moved
a snarl of loose papers carefully to the floor, straightening
them as I did so, and sat. Everywhere one looked about the
floor one saw stacks of files and papers in no particular
order, some of which had come from the file cabinet and
desk, but others, I felt certain, were filed by H. Melville on
the floor.

"You are H. Melville, Private Investigations, then?" I
said. "My codicil," I added.

"The very same." He removed a bottle of Scotch whisky
from a desk drawer, poured some of the liquid onto a
handkerchief, which looked none too clean, and placed it
over his bruised forehead, wincing. He lifted the bottle to
his lips and took a long drink. Then he offered the bottle to
me. "You look like you could use it."

"No, thank you," I said, more primly than I would have
wished, for I knew change was slower to come to Albany
than to Greenwich Village, and I wanted to be of my time,
not of the past.

"Your loss," he said. He set the bottle down and lit a
cigarette. "Vangie could put it away with me, swig for
swig." He seemed amused at my expense, his coal-black
eyes showing no pupils.

"Vangie? You mean Great-aunt Evangeline?" I said,
astonished that he could be so familiar about her.

He took another long drink and squinted at me. "This was
her business," he said. "She brought me in and trained me.
We worked together for twenty years until Miss Alice died
and Vangie's health started to go."

It was all getting so confusing I was having trouble
following. "You mean Great-aunt Evangeline was a private
investigator?"

"I do."

"And who was Miss Alice?"

"Bloody hell, I'm not here to explain the birds and the

bees to you. The two old girls lived together. You know. Like man and wife."

Well, I confess I was so shocked I slid off the sofa to the floor. And I was too shocked to move.

"Welcome to Greenwich Village, Cuz. All the laundry hangs out on the line here."

"A Boston marriage," I murmured, for I had read about this. Two women. Lesbians. I began to understand why my father never spoke of his aunt.

H. Melville was laughing at me again. He didn't offer his hand, so I struggled to my feet and stood, swaying slightly. "I'm sorry to have troubled you," I said, with as much dignity as I could muster. I moved to the door, sliding on the feathers, but he was faster than me. He stood in front of the door, blocking my passage. He reeked so of whisky and tobacco that my eyes teared.

"What did you see?" he demanded. "What did you hear?"

"Excuse me?"

"It's important. I'm in the middle of an assignment and some crucial papers were stolen from me tonight. I surprised the thief and got this for my trouble."

"I've been ill," I said, beginning to feel weak. My knees wobbled terribly. "Could I have a cup of tea?"

He took my elbow and steered me back to the sofa, where I collapsed and tried to gather my thoughts. H. Melville disappeared into another room and soon I heard a kettle come to the boil.

I may have dozed for several minutes, for he shook my shoulder gently and offered me a cup of strong tea colored only slightly by a dollop of milk. "Sugar?" he asked.

"Yes, please."

He reached into the pocket of his jacket and offered me four lumps of sugar in the palm of his hand. I took all four and dropped them into my tea wondering how I would stir them, when he produced a bent silver-plated spoon. So I stirred the sugar into my tea and sipped.

Satisfied, he pulled over a chair and watched me with an intensity that made me quite uncomfortable. As if he were trying to see into my brain. "Tell me," he said.

It was then that I remembered the horse.

V

When I awoke that first sun-bright morning in my new home, I did not remember my encounter with my exotic tenant. I lay back feeling blessed and listened to the pale sounds of the Village awakening around me.

I am free, I thought. My own person at last. In my own home. Just Mattie and me. And then, as if I had summoned her, there came a soft rap on the door and Mattie appeared with a cup of coffee, her eyes shining with laughter and two bright spots on her cheeks.

"I've drawn your bath," she said. "We have a visitor. He's waiting downstairs."

I blushed at that news, for it had to be Mr. Jenner come to call on us, and so I said, but Mattie smiled and made a hasty retreat.

Ah, well, thought I, she is as overwhelmed by all the newness as I. What will she say when I tell her about Great-aunt Evangeline? I was in my bath when it all came to me and I near drowned and came up sputtering. Had I dreamed it?

If I was undecided before, when I followed the cheerful voices to the kitchen, I knew even as I entered that my visitor was H. Melville, Private Investigations.

He made a halfhearted attempt to stand, but he was really more interested in the fat omelet with the thick slab of bacon and fried potatoes that Mattie had just placed before him. I noted that a small plaster covered the bruise on his forehead and that his eyes were bloodshot. There were cigarette stubs in the ashtray that Mattie was fastidiously emptying.

I sat down opposite Mr. Melville, and Mattie filled my bowl with uninspiring oatmeal and poured coffee into three cups.

"Harry tells me you met last night," Mattie said. "Under unusual circumstances."

"Harry?" I said, as I dusted my oatmeal with sugar and added a spot of cream. Harry indeed, I thought. I looked resentfully down at my oatmeal and across at Harry's omelet, which he was devouring with abandon. Why did I have to suffer through this detestable mess because it was good for me, when I could be eating bacon and eggs? "Unusual circumstances? Yes, I would say so . . . Harry." I resolved I would never touch oatmeal again.

"Harry, it is," he said. He was wiping up his plate with a thick chunk of bread.

In the light that streamed through our kitchen window I saw that his hair was the color of sand, that he wore it long and tied in the back with what appeared to be a shoelace. His eyes were truly black with sheer lashes that gave him the odd aspect of having no lashes at all.

I became conscious of Mattie standing behind me, hovering over both of us. "Oh, do sit down, Mattie," I said irritably, "I feel as if a bird is sitting on my shoulder."

Mattie sat down at once and Harry pushed back his plate and offered her a cigarette, which to my everlasting astonishment, she accepted. When he offered me one, I declined, of course, although I was not a stranger to cigarettes. He waited until after he had lit his and Mattie's, then he fixed me with his eyes and said, "I would like you to come with me."

"Where?"

"To see my client. Explanations are in order, and I think perhaps that you hold in your mind a piece of vital information."

VI

Which is how I found myself less than one hour later riding uptown in a taxicab driven by someone named Jake, a man with a shaved head, outstanding ears, and huge shoulders and arms. Harry Melville was sitting in the front seat next to Jake while I sat in the back.

"But what am I supposed to do?" I asked.

"If I tell you, you will practice how you answer. Just be natural." He turned back to Jake and they began an animated conversation about a woman who was found murdered in the courtyard outside Chumley's, a speakeasy in the Village frequented by artists, writers, and actors.

"Excuse me," I said, thoroughly annoyed. "But if you don't give me more information, I must request that you take me home."

Again he fixed me with those eyes. "I will tell you only that my client married an extremely wealthy man two years ago. Prior to her marriage she had a lover to whom she wrote letters of a particular, vulgar nature. After her lover's mysterious death, the letters fell into the hands of a blackmailer. That will have to do for the nonce," he said.

Well, I thought, this was New York and this was the life I'd wanted, full of surprises. As the car rode up Fifth Avenue, I looked out the window at the stylish women in their short skirts, bobbed hair, and cloche hats, and suddenly I felt dowdy. My dress was too long, my hat too big, and I had entirely too much hair. Perhaps a change was desirable to go with my new venue.

We arrived in front of a carved stone mansion on the corner of Fifth Avenue and Seventy-second Street. The imposing residence was built in an architectural style popular at the turn of the century. A boy messenger in a gray uniform was coming down the steps. He walked to a bicycle and prepared to mount it when Harry Melville jumped from the taxi and approached him. Jake, our driver, opened my door and offered me his arm, which I took, and then I was standing on the street.

Melville patted the boy on the shoulder, took a coin from his inside pocket, and presented him with it. The boy got on his bicycle and peddled off, and Melville returned to my side. "Let's go," he said.

A frog-faced butler let us into a formal gallery with marble floors and elegant French furniture. "Good morning, Mr. Melville," he said. He held in his hand a brightly wrapped package, which he set down on a shallow side table when he took Melville's card.

"Good morning, Abel," Melville said. I was astonished to see him surreptitiously motion me to the package, and I realized after a moment that he was interested in knowing to whom it was addressed. So I sidled over to the table, pretending to inspect my image in the magnificent gold leaf mirror that hung over the table.

When Abel showed us into a lovely room, filled almost entirely by a piano, and bright with sunlight and fresh flowers, I whispered to Melville, "Lanford Ebbing the second."

"Are you certain?" was his response. He studied the small fire in the hearth, then walked over to a piano, and I followed him. A large silver trophy of a rider on a horse held a silk shawl cover to the piano. The trophy bore the name Lanford Ebbing III.

"Of course, I'm certain."

"The second, you say? Not the third?"

"The second."

He gave me a look of sublime satisfaction and sat down at the piano, letting his fingers touch the keys. I prayed he wouldn't suddenly begin to play, as it would be a breach of good manners. I put my attention instead to the tapestries of medieval pastoral scenes hanging from the walls. The ceiling above was beautifully ornamented with carved plaster flowers.

I gave him a stern look and sat myself on a sofa upholstered in rose-colored striped damask and listened to the song of two lovebirds in a large gilded cage that hung from the ceiling near the front window. I found the birds rather engaging, although Melville did not, for he flapped his arms and growled at them in an effort to get them to stop.

Finally, when I was about to scold him for his rudeness, we were interrupted by the arrival of three individuals. The first, Mrs. Dorothea Ebbing, an aging beauty in her forties, wearing a mauve silk day dress. Her skirt, which was much shorter than mine, stopped at midcalf and revealed slim legs and well-turned ankles in silk hose. Her hair was golden, almost too golden, and marcelled and shingled in the latest fashion. In direct opposition to her dress, her face was ravaged. Dark circles pouched under her eyes and her skin was sallow. She seemed frail and ill and leaned on the arm of a well-dressed, attractive young man. I felt quite sorry for her.

"My stepson, Lanford Ebbing the third, and my secretary, Miss Savage."

Miss Savage was a plain woman, her brown hair in a tight bun, her eyes distorted by thick glasses. She wore a drab, ill-fitting brown dress, wrinkled cotton hose, and sensible shoes, but I confess my attention went to the dark-haired young man.

"My associate, Miss Olivia Brown," Melville said casually, waving the line in the air like a flourish.

Associate, thought I. I was surprised and more than a little pleased.

After the how-do-you-do's were concluded, and everyone was seated, Mrs. Ebbing said, "My letters. Have you got them?"

"No, ma'am," Melville said. "But I know where they are."

Everyone froze in place for a moment, until Mrs. Ebbing, poor lady, gave a cry of pain and collapsed against her stepson, who patted her hand. "But what good will it do me if they are not in my hands?"

I caught a faint exchange between Mr. Ebbing III and Miss Savage, then Miss Savage rose and, removing a package of powder from her pocket, dusted it into a glass sitting on a silver tray on the sideboard. She filled the glass with water from a silver pitcher. When she carried it to her employer, Mrs. Ebbing waved her away. "Not now, dear."

Again I caught an almost imperceptible exchange between the stepson and the secretary. I began to wonder how Miss Savage would look without her glasses and in a different hairdo.

"Your letters are in this house at this very moment, Mrs. Ebbing," Melville said.

"Oh," she said, quite startled. "How can they be if they're not in my possession?" I could see her thinking this through, as I had, coming to a terrifying conclusion. "Dear God, my husband—"

"Your letters were in my possession, Mrs. Ebbing, for

only a few hours, when I was hit on the head and they were stolen from me."

"But if they are in this house—"

"Doro, don't you think you should lie down, or at least take the sedative Miss Savage has prepared for you?" Mr. Ebbing looked very concerned, almost fearful.

"They were delivered to this house not thirty minutes ago by messenger."

"Oh, no! Then my husband has seen them."

"That's enough, Melville," young Lanford Ebbing said, jumping to his feet. "You've failed in your task. It's time you were gone."

"Ring for your butler, Mrs. Ebbing," Melville said. He ran his fingers on the keys of the piano and by this time I was too fascinated to be embarrassed. "Ask him to bring you the package that arrived this morning addressed to your husband."

"No, Doro!" The young man stood near the door. When the butler arrived, he grabbed for the package, but Abel tossed it to Melville, who caught it with a grin.

"Ah," Melville said. "And perhaps you were out riding in the Village last night, Mr. Ebbing, and by happenstance, found yourself in my neighborhood and thought you'd drop in on me and relieve me of your stepmother's burden. You see, my associate, Miss Brown, heard the sound of a rider, hooves on cobblestones."

"No, Lanny, no."

I found myself watching, not Mrs. Ebbing or the stepson, or even Melville, but Miss Savage. Her face had turned pasty white. She was creeping away, aiming to disappear. I stood up and walked to the door, placing my back against it.

"Whose idea was it, yours or Miss Savage's?" Melville asked. He stepped over to the grate and tossed his package into the fire. There was utter silence as the letters burned. "Miss Savage," Melville said, "I would suggest you leave these parts, or we will swear out a complaint against you. I believe you are the blackmailer, are you not?"

I stepped away from the door, because I'm certain her fury was such that she would have plunged through me.

"Lanny," Mrs. Ebbing said, "I can't believe this of you."

"I'm sorry, Doro." He fell to his knees and buried his head in her lap.

When we took our leave, she was stroking his hair and soothing him.

"A gutless creature," Melville said. "He'll never amount to anything."

VII

Feeling very jolly, for he had earned himself a wondrous fee, or so he said, Melville took me to Chumley's, off Barrow Street, behind a dark door, through the flagstoned courtyard where the young woman had been found murdered, and into the real life of Greenwich Village. I was introduced to Eugene O'Neill, who at once bought me a beer, and then to Max Eastman, Edna Millay, and Edmund Wilson, with whom Melville had gone to college.

"Princeton," Mr. Wilson said.

Princeton, indeed, I thought. And when they asked if I would like to be in their plays at the Provincetown Playhouse, I said, "Oh, yes, yes, yes."

And when I went home, I cut my hair.

This is Donna Murray's first published fiction, but after selling it she did not rest on her laurels. Not only has she recently sold her first novel, but she's signed a three-book deal with St. Martin's Press. In this story she introduces Pennsylvania-based P.I. Sandy "Rainy" McGuinn, who is working as a decoy to find a killer.

HEELS

by Donna Huston Murray

WHEN I STRAIGHTENED up from fixing my high heel, Wilson DeVrie, the bartender, slid me another crooked smile. He had presumed leering privileges when I ordered my first drink.

"Champagne cocktail. Hold the champagne," I whispered, glancing left and right before adding, "I'm working." Couldn't have an old acquaintance blow my cover before I quizzed even one out-of-towner.

Wil gave my wink a bemused stare, very frank and rude, clearly delighted to have something on me that gave him the upper hand. I refrained from glaring back. As I said, I was working; and the idea of a large man at arm's length keeping tabs on the bozos was comforting, even with Scarp and a

213

backup right out in the parking lot. When you've been hired to attract a murderer, extra insurance is always a comfort.

"What the hell am I supposed to use?" my high school acquaintance asked. "Pepsi?"

"Jeez, Wil," I said. "You're the bartender. Wrap a towel around a bottle of 7-Up." Willy DeVrie had not been the class valedictorian.

Come to think of it, neither had I. My best subject was Teenaged Malcontents of the Opposite Sex, an expertise that has proven useful well into my twenties—in my personal life as well as my business.

I'm a private investigator in a small Pennsylvania town. The living is marginal at best, but I refuse to move. Doing a little moonlighting for the local police department made sense, but pride and easier offers have kept me from approaching my old friend, Scarp Poletta, until this morning. Pride isn't much use when there's a murderer loose in your town. Soon after I read about it I slapped my newspaper on Scarp's cigarette-scarred desk. It was so early that his coffee smelled leftover.

"What if we get a thunderstorm while you're working for me?" he responded to my pitch.

The way he actually waited for an answer reminded me that I was talking to a professional cop, not just my old partner from eleventh grade woodworking shop.

"I do what needs doing, Scarp. You know that."

He tucked his chin tight into the V of his summer uniform shirt but permitted a small smile to soften his eyes. "Hell, that probably means you shower at the Y after you're through teaching aerobics."

I grinned to thank him. It was a true friend who made you sound brave for fighting off a phobia. "If the department took me on, I could quit the Y."

Scarp grunted. "You still got the card?"

He referred to the hypnotherapist's phone number I refuse to use. Knowing my eight-month-old brother drowned in a rainstorm is bad enough. Who in their right mind would want to remember the graphic details?

"Come on, Scarp," I coaxed. "The police department's

stretched to the limit. I'm free lance. No benefits. The comptroller's got to love it." I leaned in for the kill. "Also, the only female on the force does her nails every day at noon."

Scarp ran his eyes over my chest, which was presently dusting his desk top. "You are in better shape than Irene."

Suggestive humor, our method of handling the sexual tension, but I couldn't joke back. Not now. This was a job interview after all. I said, "I have more guts, too."

He smirked. "Unless it rains."

I said nothing to that. Scarp's one of the few people I allow to tease me about personal things. If either of us had any common sense, we might have been lovers by now. But then we would have parted company long ago, too.

"People know you around here," he complained. "You'll be useless undercover."

I pulled a face at his wording, which brought a smile and a slight blush. "You know what I mean, Rainy."

"That's where you're wrong. I belong. I blend. Plus all the evidence in this case points toward an outsider who wouldn't know me from Eve."

"Yeah?" Scarp said, cocking his chin, needling me to continue.

"Yeah," I said, going along. "The motel attached to Wil's bar is booked solid with conventioneers. Wil saw Cathy with a guy wearing a name tag, and her body was discovered within carrying distance of the motel."

A farmer plowing past a copse of trees had noticed a bright color out of the corner of his eye, the short magenta dress Cathy Tervoorst had replaced after having sex. Everything was there in the newspaper, if you looked. Even the hint that the victim brought on her own strangling by threatening blackmail. Why else had she died fully dressed if not during negotiation time?

Out of consideration for her family, the article did refrain from mentioning the young woman's reputation. Although she never considered herself a pro, she drank in conventioneers' bars and accepted monetary "gifts" exactly like one.

Scarp stood to stare out his chicken-wired window. He abruptly turned. "Okay," he said. "Get yourself up like white trash and I'll wire you with a mike at your place. Sam and me'll listen from a blue laundry van out in Wil's parking lot."

"That's it?"

"We'll use you tonight and tomorrow night from nine until closing. I want you to learn everything you can before those supermarket managers go home Sunday afternoon. After that, we'll have to nail the sucker on the regular payroll."

We shook on it, Scarp looking grim.

"Evenin', gorgeous," a baldie with a pink smirk muttered into my ear. He'd come up quietly, or maybe the bar's sultry radio music was louder than I realized.

Inches from my face the guy's lips shone with spit. I forced a smile, twisted a fist into my stomach to squeeze out the lump, and hooked a hip over the edge of my bar stool. The leg that remained floor-bound in a three-inch pump lost skirt it could scarcely afford, and Baldie was quick to appreciate the effect. My legs are Spandex-approved; just check my aerobics contract under benefits.

"Hi," I said, filling the word with meaning.

"Buy you a drink?"

"That would be lovely," I breathed. Thursday night Wil had been too shorthanded to remember what the suspect with Cathy looked like or what the name tag said, but he thought maybe the guy drank beer.

I glanced at the beverage in Baldie's fist. Amber fluid on the rocks. Also, no name tag, a problem I should quickly remedy.

"You here with the convention?" I asked.

Baldie straightened and blushed, proud of his managerial status.

"Yes."

"You have a name?"

"Mike."

I raised an eyebrow to push for a last name, but "Mike" didn't respond.

I stuck out a hand and lied. "I'm Kit."

"Like in Carson?" he quipped.

I treated him to a little laugh. "Exactly."

"Some sort of rough rider, wasn't he?"

I rolled a shoulder to avoid ruining my blond bimbo image. How could Cathy find the money remotely worth it?

Her memory chastened me; we all do what we have to to get by.

"I'm glad you came over," I said.

Mike appeared pleasantly surprised. "Yeah?"

"Maybe you can help me."

Baldie turned down the heat a notch, his mind-set obviously directed more toward how I could help him. "How's that?"

"I'm on sort of a sentimental mission."

Bald Mike the Manager subtly repositioned himself for escape.

"You see, my girlfriend was the one they found near here, and I would love to talk to somebody who spoke to her last night. She was my roomie."

Mike stood erect as a post. "Sorry, kid. I wasn't here." He moved off.

I scouted the room for another flirt. A lanky guy in a plaid shirt leaning on his elbows met my eyes, smiled that smile.

I tilted my chin, raised my left eyebrow, and reeled him in.

"How ya doin', sweet hips?" he drawled. I shifted the referred-to hips and raised both eyebrows. Then I drained my fruit juice and 7-Up and told him I was thirsty.

"Those things expensive?" Tex asked.

"Yeah, but I'm worth it."

Tex raised his eyebrows. "Lord, you northern women are hot. I swear it must be a blessing you get snow."

Wil placed a beer in Tex's wide hand, then shielded his work with his body while he poured me another.

"You here last night?" I asked.

"Yeah, me'n some good old boys. Phew, they can drink. I missed two meetings this mornin' before I even rolled over."

I pretended to perk up. "Then maybe one of you talked to my girlfriend Cathy."

Tex clucked and wagged his head. "Girl got strangled? Horrible thing. We'd've drunk elsewhere tonight, except for the convenience. Looks like it's convenient for half the town." I scanned the room. The crowd was larger than usual for a Friday night.

"Ghouls," I said with sincerity.

"Poor kid. You two real close?"

"She was my roommate."

Tex nodded. "Then you must be Wil's old lady. Whyn't you say so? Hell, I wouldn't go and jump old Wil's claim. You been foolin' with me."

My mouth dropped open. Wil was just delivering my drink, so I switched my attention to him. "Your girlfriend roomed with Cathy Tervoorst?"

The bartender snapped to attention. "Ex-girlfriend," he said vehemently. "*Ex*-girlfriend." Then he proceeded to fill a fistful of beer mugs one after the other.

Tex had returned to the good old boys, who all glanced at me once before concentrating on their drinks.

Throughout the evening I spoke to four or five other men and learned far more than I cared to about stale marriages, managerial headaches, and the expense of orthodontics. Turned out the guy whose kids needed braces actually spoke to Cathy, but he dismissed her as "Dull company," which probably meant she cut off his deadly conversation.

Now and then I made eye contact with Wil. His indifference secured my attention like flypaper. The fluid motions of his hands, his detachment rarely broken by a smile, the tilt of his left eyebrow as he listened to a customer—everything he did started to fascinate me. Sure, getting to know him better might further the case, but that didn't explain my mother's voice saying, "Jesus, Sandy. Would it kill you to go out with a nice guy just once?"

About 1:30 a.m. Wil shooed out the remaining stragglers, and I went outside to Scarp's borrowed laundry truck to return the microphone.

"This thing's been stabbing my boob all night," I remarked.

Scarp was too dejected for banter, so I adjusted my attitude. "Sorry," I said. Disappointment hollowed his eyes, but he tried to shrug it off.

"We'll get him," he said more to himself than to me. Briefly I wondered if Cathy was more of a friend than he cared to admit—his taste in women comparing roughly to mine in men—but it was probably just professional frustration. Lord knew this murder was frustrating enough to account for Scarp's mood. That and the hour.

We agreed on the particulars for Saturday night, and he settled himself in the truck's driver's seat next to Sam. Then he snapped out of it long enough to ask if I wanted them to follow me home.

"Nah," I said a little defiantly. I suppose I didn't care to be an afterthought. "I think I'll . . ." I indicated the back door to the bar with a shoulder.

"Figures," Scarp said with plain disgust. I shouldn't have cared, but I was stung. Maybe Wil wasn't brilliant or anything, but he wasn't a heel either.

My friendly inclinations warmed to a regular glow by the time I settled on a bar stool to watch Wil tidy up.

"You look good doing that," I said. "Like you've been doing it forever."

"I have," he said. "Fix you another champagne cocktail?" There was amusement playing in the corner of his mouth. It was a nice mouth when he let it be.

"Vodka tonic," I suggested instead, "not a lot of ice."

I concentrated on rubbing my temples until Wil startled me by setting down the drink.

"Bad night?" he asked.

"Not bad exactly," I answered. "Just wasted."

Wil's eyes appeared soft with fatigue as well as something I hoped was tenderness.

"It's only your first night, right?"

"Well, yes," I admitted.

"It'll go better," he said, then added, "if you want it to."

My feelings went to mush. My emotional plate had been empty that long.

Wil poured himself a Scotch, neat.

"What happened?" I asked. At that point I couldn't say if I was working or not. But I asked the question just the same.

"With what?"

"You know. Your girl. What happened?"

He looked at me a long moment without much behind it. Then he looked away and answered in a flat, impersonal tone.

"Marcy was pregnant. We argued. She got an abortion. She decided to leave. End of story."

"Where'd she go?"

He shrugged, and I wondered if maybe his voice had become unreliable.

"I'm sorry," was my next line, so I delivered it while watching for more overt evidence of Wil's feelings.

"What about Cathy?" I asked. "Did it bother you when she came around?"

Wil's eyes narrowed slightly. "Why should it?"

"No reason." I could see that his view would be that as long as Cathy frequented his bar, there was a chance one day Marcy would show up.

"Did Cathy have anyone special?"

"You mean a regular boyfriend?" Wil snorted but stopped short of laughter. "Nah. She spread herself around."

That was pretty much what I figured, but having it confirmed eliminated the idea of a jealous boyfriend murdering Cathy over the conventioneer.

Wil was showing me puppy eyes again, so I ran my finger down his cheek and said good night with my fingertip on his lips.

He removed my hand gently by the wrist. "Careful going home," he said.

"Yeah," I agreed. "There could be a supermarket manager behind any bush."

Saturday would be the night. I could feel it in the air pressure. The TV over the bar showed a bitterly fought hockey playoff that looked bad for the home team. The crowd felt restless, too, as if the slightest controversy would set off a brawl. A man's night out. A night to go home drunk and slap the little woman around.

If I'd been what I was supposed to be, the alternative to marital bliss, I'd have run at the first smell of danger.

But I was wired, and Scarp paid me to belly up to every squint-eyed, tight-knuckled lout with money for beer.

There was Norman the hydraulic drill operator whose grasp of my upper arm left red bruises and whose breath was not to be believed. He spoke only with those painful hands punctuated with grunts and spits, but from Wil I learned that Norman had indeed been present on Thursday night.

"Took a carryout, too," he remembered belatedly.

"Show any interest in Cathy?" I asked.

"Same as you're getting." Scorn, in other words. I made a mental note to ask Scarp whether Cathy's upper arms were bruised.

Around Wil's central table, the one that folded away to become dance space, seven conventioneers argued about whose turn it was to pick up the tab. Tex was there, and Bald Mike, who shouted, "No dammit. I got stiffed Thursday night," and with those five incriminating words reinstated himself among the suspects.

Scarp preferred the one who never spoke, a small, swarthy guy who appeared to be from one of those countries where women wear veils. He clamped his eyes on me the second he sat down and violated me from the corner of the room seventeen ways until Sunday.

My skin felt clammy just noticing his stare, but I forced myself to walk over to his table. Scarp is out there, I reminded myself, and Wil is just behind you.

"Evening, fella," I said. "Come to buy me a drink?"

The man's eyes bulged. For a second I thought he was going to swallow his mustache; but after one last gawk at my breasts, he bolted for the front door leaving behind most of a mug of beer.

I almost forgot about him until Scarp asked me to describe him.

"Get a name?" he asked.

"No. No tag."

Scarp nodded, his tongue worrying at his cheek. "He staying here?"

"I don't think so."

His professional's face showed regret. "Never mind. We'll pick him out at the convention."

"What about Bald Mike?" I suggested. "Lied about being here Thursday?"

Scarp wasn't listening. He was still on the silent foreigner. "I like him," he confirmed to his male associate with a smile. "Sexually repressed guy works up the nerve to have it off with a hooker. Gets the guilts and dumps her in the woods. Yeah. Good work, McGuinn," he said with a pat on my bruised arm.

I wagged my head. "I don't know, Scarp. That Mike guy lied about being here Thursday. And that local guy—Norman. Did you get a look at these bruises?"

"Yeah, yeah. You did good tonight, doll. We'll take it from here. You go home and get some sleep." From an impersonal last name to a child's toy in two successive sentences.

"You better quit dehumanizing women before your contract comes up," I snapped. Our present mayor happened to be female. I heard she beheaded men for lesser slurs.

Scarp chose to ignore me.

"Ride home?" he asked.

"No. Thank you." I was puffing a little, fists on my hips.

"Where you going?"

I glared. "Back inside, if it's any of your business." Maybe Wil would remember something else.

"Is it any of my business?"

Scarp wasn't quite as tuned out as I thought.

"No," I hastened to assure him. "I just need to talk to a nice guy for a while."

The admission settled me down. Hell, Scarp could be right about the foreigner. I'd call in the morning, volunteer to pick the guy out of the crowd. Save him a little effort. In the morning. Not right now.

Scarp nodded to indicate he accepted my interest in Wil. Now and then he probably needed to touch base with a decent woman, too.

He slammed the door of the truck. "Take care of yourself," he told me, meaning either everything or nothing.

"I always do." His smile made me feel hollow.

Wil was polishing a glass when I returned. The light of his work area shadowed the bar around him. Chairs upended onto tables aimed their skeletal legs toward the ceiling. Without the crowd the bar felt cold.

"You about done?" I asked. The heat lightning rumbling some distant clouds made me shiver.

"Could be," he conceded. Fatigue pressed his body into that vulnerable slouch that draws me in every time.

"You want some coffee?" he asked.

"Okay."

"Upstairs," Wil directed; and when I hesitated, he said, "Come on," as if only a fool would refuse. It felt like charity, but I went.

Maybe moonlighting for Scarp had been a bad idea, a little more emotionally complex than I expected. Maybe it hadn't been pride that kept me from volunteering before — just good animal instinct. Either that or the thunder was jazzing my nerves.

Wil's apartment was up a stairwell behind the bar. A kitchen/living room area dominated the available space with a bedroom/bath apparently located to the right. My host proceeded to measure coffee into a filter with the detached precision he seemed to use for everything.

I strolled around the dividing green sofa, touching the pleated edge of an off-white lamp shade as I passed. Everything was surprisingly neat for a bachelor. Only a few items cluttered the end tables — newspapers, a baseball hat with the Blue Jays' logo, a little boy's bat and glove under the lamp by an ashtray.

I picked up the little nightstick-sized bat and gave it a swing. "This is cute, Wil. You make it?"

"Why?" Something dark came through in his voice. I

wondered briefly if he regretted inviting me up. Felt invaded like some men do at first.

"Just asking," I said. Then I laughed. "It reminds me of the one Scarp Poletta and me tried making on the school lathe."

Wil turned toward me, an oddly intense expression on his face.

I continued to smile as if I hadn't noticed. "Except ours was more of a toothpick before we gave up."

Wil stepped toward me, wiping his hands on a towel. "What's Scarp Poletta got to do with this?" He tossed the towel toward my face. It landed on the floor.

I caught myself leaning slightly back, my pulse quickened with adrenaline. Animal instinct told me what to say, how to say it. "Nothing. We just did wood shop together back in high school."

Wil's fists pressed against his trouser pockets, flexing his shoulders into a menace. My mind raced to catch up, rapidly packaging questions and answers into complete units.

Why had he reacted so strongly when I mentioned Scarp? The first thing I told him was that I was working undercover for the police. "Champagne cocktail, hold the champagne," I said. "I'm working." Everybody in town knew I was a P.I.

Recognizing the foolishness of my assumption brought on a cold sweat. Wil and I had maintained only a nodding acquaintance since high school, so it was possible—make that probable—that he had no idea what I did for a living.

Seven-Up cocktails and spiked heels. Shit. He'd taken me for the hooker I was pretending to be.

"Put that down," he said, referring to the toy bat in my hand.

"Sure, Wil." What did he think I was going to do with it? "Jeez, it's only a toy." I flicked it onto the sofa.

Wil's shoulders squared like a block of condominiums, his eyes narrowed with menace. "Not to me, it's not."

What the hell was he talking about? It certainly was a toy. About fifteen inches long. Little glove to go with it.

My eyes widened, and Wil correctly guessed that I'd correctly guessed the significance of the bat and glove. I inched backward on my precarious heels as he eased toward me.

"Now take it easy, Wil. This doesn't have to be a problem. I'm sure you were overcome with grief."

When a girl is in trouble, she tells a close friend, a roommate. If the roommate is a Cathy Tervoorst, she takes you to her abortionist. End of problem. Unless the father happens to be Wilson DeVrie.

"Damn right I was out of my mind," he agreed. "I was furious."

Dead simple. I felt like a fool. He wanted his child, fought desperately with the woman carrying that child. And lost.

"They'll understand," I babbled. "Lots of people feel that way about abortion." Not me, but lots of other people. "Cathy killed your . . . your baby, so you killed Cathy. It's a perfectly reasonable defense." Or maybe not, but now was not the time to argue ethics.

Wil agreed. He hadn't listened to a word I'd said.

"This won't hurt much," he told me.

I glanced around for an escape route, then for a weapon. The miniature baseball bat on the sofa was the only loose item around. It was out of reach, and unless I scored a direct hit on Wil's most vulnerable body part, it was useless anyhow.

Wil stepped closer, treated me to a demented grin. I had visions of him pulling wings off insects.

He inched forward. I stumbled back. He caught my left cheekbone with the back of his hand and stretched for a forehanded slap. My eyes swam and the side of my face was numb. I ducked under his next swing and said, "Come on, Wil. You don't want to do this."

He growled and lunged for me with both arms. I scurried around behind him, but he turned abruptly and we were face-to-face again. I inched backward, tripped on a footstool, landed on my rear. I patted the hardwood floor for something—for anything—and came up empty. Wil's sick smile broadened.

Cathy's murderer prepared to lunge for my throat, his huge, graceful hands spread wide.

Street sense said go for the kick. "Women don't possess enough upper body strength or arm extension to punch a man." The Y's self-defense advice was sound. My strength was in my legs.

I used one fraction of a second to shift my right hip toward the left, placing me just off center of Wil's bulk. As his body fell forward, I kicked viciously with my left foot, hoping to knock the wind out of him. My heel connected with the soft flesh under his right rib cage. He expelled air with a loud moan.

"Ayuh," I cried from the pain of the impact.

I completed the shift of my hip and painfully extricated my leg from his weight. I rubbed my sprained ankle and wiped my face with a sleeve.

Then I regulated my breathing and braced myself for more trouble.

Despite reason, my respite continued. Another larger fear set in.

I forced myself to look closely at Wil's face. Wil's openmouthed, open-eyed, unbreathing face pressed against the dusty floor. I checked his neck for a pulse.

The phone was twenty-five feet away. Ignoring my own shudders of shock, I chose not to risk brain damage—I started the CPR right away.

Resuscitation is tough when you're alone. Nobody else to phone for help. Nobody to spell you when you get tired. I stopped when I had to stop, when exhaustion forced me to recognize that there had been not one flicker of response.

I rocked Wil's head in my lap and petted his hair until most of my tears were spent.

Scarp answered the first ring. In ten minutes he was there.

The others came in twelve. While they worked, Scarp held my hand. When he had to move away, he touched my knee coming and going. He told me ten different ways it was a fluke. How would I know a kick like that could cause a traumatic heart attack? "The angle. The spiked heel. Maybe Wil had a bum heart. Fate, Sandy, that's what it was." He said I shouldn't feel guilty, Wil would have fared badly in prison.

He said all that and more, but we both knew they were only words.

After a time, we were alone in the apartment once again.

"Let's go," Scarp told me. He tugged my hand, and I followed. Silently, we drove through the rain, the windows rolled up tight.

He unlocked my apartment door and gestured me inside.

We curled up on top of my covers like children. Scarp held me from behind so I could breathe, his arm across my collarbone and my face uncovered. His breath was warm against my ear, sweet as a baby's. Sweet as my brother Jim's.

When it got light, Scarp kissed my hair and pulled his numb arm out from under. He covered me with the edge of my grandmother's chenille bedspread.

When he left, he closed the door just as quietly as if I'd been asleep.

This story first appeared in P.I. Magazine, *which has since stopped publishing fiction. (No correlation there.) S. J. Rozan's first novel,* China Trade, *was published in 1994 by St. Martin's Press. Both feature the P.I. team of Lydia Chin and Bill Smith.*

It's interesting to note that while this short story was written from the first-person point of view of Bill Smith, her "Film at Eleven," which appeared in Deadly Allies II, *was written from the point of view of Lydia Chin. She's equally adept at both viewpoints. Go out and buy her book and see which one she used there.*

ONCE BURNED

by S. J. Rozan

A SEARING PAIN spiked my side the same moment I heard her voice.

"Let him go," she hissed, behind me.

She twisted the knife. I opened my hands. The kid I'd been holding pulled away.

"Put your hands on the wall," she told me. I did what she said. The four a.m. darkness was full of garbage and gasoline.

"What the hell are you doing?" the kid growled.

"Saving your big ass," she snapped.

"I told you to stay with the bike."

"It's no fun waiting, Joey," she whined.

"This ain't fun. It's business."

This might be all the break I'd get, so I took it. I whipped around, my elbow aimed at her voice.

I hit hard and she howled with pain. The knife tugged from my skin, clattered across the alley.

Another howl: rage this time. Meaty hands grabbed me, spun me around. The kid screamed, "You hurt her!" His hand closed on my jaw, forced my head back. I smashed his wrist away, bent him over, kicked his face.

That slowed him down; but then something slammed the back of my knee. I crumpled. I landed heavily, started to stand. A fist with all the kid's hulking weight behind it threw me hard against a Dumpster which rang with the crash.

I shook my head clear, looked up to see two figures, one huge, one small. The huge one was holding a gun.

The girl would have been small anywhere; next to that human rock pile she was miniature, doll-like. Thick dark hair brushed her shoulders; she wore fingerless lace gloves on her tiny hands. She was smiling. Her left eye was beginning to swell.

The gun was a garden-variety automatic.

My gun was a revolver, a short-barrel .38, but it was under my jacket and my jacket was zipped and that put it on Mars.

"Okay," I rasped. "This round's yours."

"Who's paying you?" the kid demanded.

"Mick Daly. Who the hell's paying you?"

He ignored that, spat blood through a split lip. "Tell that limp dick if he don't sell tomorrow the price goes down. The boss don't want to wait no more."

"Who's the boss? George Trakas?"

"Guess."

"You the guy who's been breaking windows and slashing tires around here?"

"Guess that too. Who're you?"

"Bill Smith. Who's your partner?"

"I got no partner."

"Yes you do." The girl grinned.

"Like hell." The kid grinned too. He pulled her to him, nuzzled her neck, one eye and the gun still on me. "This is a man's game, baby. Little girls can't play. They might get hurt."

"Who the hell pulled your bacon out of the pan just now?" she asked hotly, punching his chest.

The kid sneered. "I could've taken him."

"Yeah, sure," she said. "Anyway, Joey, he hurt me, look." She pouted, tilted her head to show her shiner. "Blow him away for me, Joey?"

"Okay, baby." Joey sounded surprised. "If you want."

"Well," she said doubtfully, "maybe not. You gave him a message for that guy. Maybe blow him away next time you see him."

"Yeah." Joey grinned. "Yeah, that sounds good. How's that sound to you, cowboy?"

"Great," I said. "And tell Trakas something for me. Tell him Mick's not selling. Tell him to take his condos and shove them."

Joey just kept grinning. He patted the girl's bottom. "Go back to the bike, baby. Wait for me."

She flashed me a look of amused contempt. Then she turned and strolled carelessly up the alley.

Joey wet his grinning lips. Then, eyes on me, he crossed to the kitchen door of Daly's Tavern, where I'd caught him with a gasoline can. "Now don't you move, cowboy." Gun in one hand, he picked up the can and splashed the door, the ground below it, poured a semicircle around the Dumpster and me. He backed up the alley, splashing gas wall-to-wall as he went. At the head of the alley he dropped the can. It rang hollowly.

Behind him in the street a car went by, stonily following its headlights like a blindered horse.

Joey lit a cigarette, flicked the match in front of him.

My heart crashed against my chest as flames erupted up the alley, snaked toward me with a ripping sound.

The heat blasted my face; my eyes stung. There was no back way out of this alley, nothing to climb. I drew a breath, flung myself forward as the flames reached Daly's door with a roar.

I slipped, the knee where the girl had cracked me

buckled. I pushed to my feet, disoriented in the heat and hallucinatory dance of flames. Stumbling forward, I hit a wall I didn't see. I felt my way along it, hoping it would lead me out, and just when I'd begun to know it wouldn't and nothing mattered except to breathe, the wall ended. I lurched forward, fell gasping to the sidewalk.

The shifting glow behind me threw sliding shadows, my shadow and the shadow of the man I never did get to meet who pulled me clear of the burning alley and ran down the block to call 911.

After Lt. King from the Arson Squad and Sgt. Romero from the Sixth Precinct and the blond cop who looked like a fourteen-year-old in someone else's mustache had gone, Mick Daly stepped through the curtains around my alcove at St. Vincent's E.R.

"Jesus, Mary, and Joseph," he muttered, peering at me. "I didn't hire you to get yourself killed."

"You're kidding." I coughed. "I got it wrong?"

"As usual. You hurt bad?"

"No."

He regarded me critically. "You used to have eyebrows."

"Is this an improvement?"

"Not by much. What happened?"

"A hulk named Joey thought your place needed a gasoline rinse." I coughed again, added: "He had a message for you: sell by tomorrow or the price goes down."

Mick's eyes narrowed, same for his mouth. "So you were right."

"Christ, Mick, of course I was right!"

"Hey, if you're so goddamn smart what are you doing here?"

"I got sandbagged by Shirley Temple."

Mick cocked an eyebrow. Lucky him. "Shirley Temple?"

"You don't think a three-hundred-pound gorilla did this to me all by himself? I'm a pro, for Chrissake. But he had a girl with him, with little lace gloves."

Mick heaved a sigh, ran a hand through hair that had once

been redder. He sat on the bed, stared at the scuff marks on the floor. "I don't know," he said. "Maybe I should sell."

"Uh-huh. Hand me my pants." I swung my legs over the edge of the bed, winced at the twinge in my side.

"No, I mean it. What's the point? I'm getting old. It's a lot of money."

"Yeah." I stood, tested my knee. "You could move to Florida, play golf."

"Screw that." He scowled.

"Of course, you'd have to sell the piano. But probably you'd get a good price."

"Sell that piano? You crazy?"

"Florida's bad for pianos. Why do you think I left the South?"

"Always wondered. You going to wear that?"

I looked at the shirt in my hand. It had a bloodstain the size of a saucer.

"I think I have to. The jacket's worse." My charred jacket lay limply on the shelf under the bed. Even through the disinfectant I could smell it.

Mick peeled his jacket off, handed it to me wordlessly. I rescued my wallet, threw my jacket and shirt in the trash. I pushed the curtain aside and went about the business of signing myself out.

Out on Seventh Avenue rush hour hadn't started yet. It was a clear, clean September morning. Nice contrast to me.

I asked Mick, "How bad's the damage?"

He grunted. "Could be worse. Kitchen's a wreck, part of the kitchen roof's gone, but that's all. Place smells awful. Kind of like you do."

"Can you open tonight?"

He gave me a long, searching look. Then he grinned. "Goddamn right I can open tonight."

I grinned back. "Who's playing?"

"Bigman Jones."

"Didn't even know he was in town."

"He wanted to lay low awhile. Been sick, you know. But he likes the room."

"Everyone likes the room, Mick. Daly's is every pianist's favorite gig."

Mick pulled out cigarettes, offered me one. He lit them, pretending not to notice when I flinched at the flame.

"Who's there?" I asked.

"At the bar? Your Chinese girl."

"Lydia."

He nodded. "Came in at six to relieve you, saw what'd happened. Seemed to me she wanted to come down to see you, but she said no, she'd stay on the job until you told her different."

"She's a pro too. And don't let her hear you say 'girl.' She'll break your nose." I drew in smoke, streamed it out. "Besides, she is by no stretch of the imagination mine."

"Why not?"

"I'm not her type. Too old, too ugly, too cynical. Too Caucasian."

Mick looked at me appraisingly. "You're not that cynical," he said.

Outside Daly's the sidewalk still glistened wetly in the morning sun. There was a strong odor of burnt wood and under it I thought I smelled gasoline, but that could have been memory.

The building wasn't memory, though, not yet. If Trakas's development went through the whole block would be gone, three- and four-story walk-ups ripped up and thrown away, replaced by a twenty-story tower where handsome young men in suspenders and paisley ties could live comfortably with attractive young women in navy skirts and Nikes. Trakas had options already on all the other buildings, the deli, the barbershop, the liquor store, the laundry. Of course, there'd be stores in the condo tower too: a video rental place, a gourmet take-out, a Gap. Maybe even a bar, with a name like Barnaby's.

Mick paused at the door, looked at the building's face, at the tin cornice and the sharp shadows of the brickwork. "It's not a bad place, is it? Even if it leans a little."

"It's a hundred years old. It's got a right to lean."

From the scorched alley a figure stepped onto the sidewalk, a young Chinese woman with her hands in the pockets of a complicated leather jacket. Her onyx eyes swept the street, then met mine. She walked over, brushed my hand with her fingertips. "Are you all right?" she asked. Her right hand stayed in her pocket. That would be where her gun was.

"It hurts a lot," I said. "Want to kiss it and make it better?"

She smiled almost imperceptibly. "Not even a little." Both hands in the pockets again. "Hi, Mick."

"Hi, Miss Chin. Anything new?"

"It's been quiet," Lydia answered. To me: "What do you want me to do?"

I grinned, but I answered her straight. "What you've been doing. But I'm going to bring in someone else too. I want two people here now, every shift, one inside, one outside."

"How the hell am I going to pay for that?" Mick growled.

"Raise the cover. It won't be long, Mick. Just until the police find this Joey and tie him to Trakas."

"Give me a break," Mick said. "Trakas and the mayor are in bed together. No cop's going to lose sleep over this. Lousy fire at a lousy bar." He didn't meet my eyes, just stared at the face of his building.

"Mick," I said. "If they don't do it, I will."

He said nothing.

"If you want me to. It's not what you hired me for. But tell me to go ahead and I'll take care of it."

"How?" he asked.

"Don't worry about it."

"Bill—"

"I owe you something," I said. "For this." I gestured toward the alley.

"*You* owe *me*?"

"It was my watch."

Over his shoulder the light changed. Cars carrying early-morning commuters flowed noisily down Seventh toward Wall and Broad and all the other streets where important things happen every day.

"C'mon," I said. "Buy me a drink, and then I'll go. I have work to do."

I spent the next hour at the Sixth Precinct going through mug books, because I'd said I would, though I didn't find Joey, as I knew I wouldn't. Wherever Trakas got his talent, it wasn't likely to be as easy to trace as all that. Trakas was a respectable guy.

Then I went home. I stripped and washed, keeping the tape over the stitches dry because I knew to do that, though the doctor at St. Vincent's had forgotten to tell me. I didn't shave because he had remembered to tell me not to do that, not for a few days. Like a bad sunburn, he said. So I hit the street again looking like a boiled lobster with five o'clock shadow. And no eyebrows, but I couldn't remember whether lobsters were supposed to have eyebrows.

I picked up coffee from the place on the corner and my Acura from the lot down the street. I dodged my way across Manhattan, headed uptown to the 59th Street Bridge, and went to Queens.

On a corner of Steinway Street in Astoria the Acropolis diner sat in its parking lot like a patriarch in the village square, keeping a benevolent but clear eye on the wide parkway, the furniture showrooms and electronics outlets, the aluminum-sided houses behind their chain link fences.

I parked by the door, stopped at the cigarette machine for reinforcements. Sharp autumn sunlight cut across the table-top in the red vinyl booth by the window. A waiter appeared with a huge laminated menu I'd memorized years ago.

I ordered fried eggs, sausage, toast, and coffee. "And I want to see Gus."

He nodded. I lit the last Kent from my open pack, drank my coffee when it came. Gus arrived at the table not long after my breakfast did.

"Hey!" he beamed, dropping onto the banquette across from me. His thinning hair had receded a little above his hawkish face since last I'd seen him. "Where you been?" He looked at me more closely. "And what happened there?"

"Sunburn," I said.

"Late in the season." He waited; I didn't answer. He changed the subject. "Hey, I'm a grandpa!"

I put my coffee down, shook his hand. "Congratulations. Diane?"

He nodded.

"Boy or girl?"

"A boy, about a month ago."

"They name him Gus?"

"Damn right," he answered proudly. "So, you come here to discuss my family, or to eat my eggs? Or you looking for some action?"

"Could be."

"Big or small?"

"What've you got?"

"I got the Mets over the Reds at Shea tonight."

"What are you giving?"

"Four to one."

I finished off the eggs. "All right. Half a yard on the Reds."

He cackled. "I knew it! God, you love a loser! Now, you want big? I got a high-stakes poker game I can get you into."

"No, thanks. But there is something else I want."

"What's that?"

I tore the cellophane from the new cigarettes, tapped one out. "If I wanted muscle," I said, "Greek muscle, where would I go?"

Gus's look was carefully blank. "Why would you want Greek muscle?"

"If I were Greek. Muscle work is ethnic work, Gus. Blacks use blacks, Italians use Italians. A Greek is leaning on a friend of mine, so I figure he's using Greek muscle to do it. Plus I've met the muscle, and he doesn't look Jewish."

"What does he look like?"

"A brick outhouse." I described Joey to Gus.

"Don't know him," Gus said, studiedly casual. "It's important?"

"I wouldn't waste your time if it weren't."

"Okay." Gus stood. "If I run across him, I'll let you know."

"Thanks." I shook his hand. "Send my love to Diane and the baby."

Gus disappeared into the kitchen. I signaled the waiter for my check. There wasn't one. I left him a big tip and headed back to Manhattan.

It was harder to park near Trakas's Third Avenue office than in Astoria; in fact, it was impossible, and I ended up putting the car in the lot under the building. There was an empty spot labeled "Mr. Trakas," right up front.

The building was one of those new granite jobs, banded red and gray, bronze windows and a plaza that got it a five-floor bonus. Outside, executives and secretaries and bike messengers perched on planters in the warm autumn sun.

The lobby was granite too, walls and floor, cool as a cave. I rode the wood-paneled elevator to the thirtieth floor. The lobby outside Trakas's office was carpeted in two shades of teal. The same carpet continued inside the heavy glass doors, except there it had roses in the borders.

Inside the glass doors it was very, very quiet. An elegant black woman sat at an elegant teak desk. She wore a shade of lipstick so close to the carpet roses and so perfect on her it made me wonder whether Trakas changed his decor to match his receptionists. Or maybe it was the other way around.

"May I help you?" She smiled icily.

"Bill Smith to see George Trakas, please."

"I'm sorry, I think Mr. Trakas is out. Was he expecting you?"

"No, but he'll want to see me."

"Oh, I'm sure he will," she said, "if he's here." She spoke into the phone: "Lillian, there's a Mr. Smith here to see Mr. Trakas . . . that's what I thought . . . no, not to me . . . thanks." She replaced the sleek receiver in its cradle. "He's out, and he's not expected back today." There was a discreet note of triumph in her smile.

I handed her my card. "When he does come back, tell him I was here. Tell him Joey sent me."

"Why not?" She shrugged. "It worked before."

I paused in the act of turning to walk out. "Before what?"

"Before you."

"And that means what?"

Her eyes were wide and innocent. "Whatever it means is Mr. Trakas's business."

"Would twenty dollars make it my business?" I edged a bill from my wallet, slid it across the desk. I held it down with a finger.

She smiled that flash-frozen smile, put a finger on the twenty also. "Whoever Joey is, he sent someone else to see Mr. Trakas without an appointment. She got invited in."

I took my finger away. "Little girl? Lots of dark hair?"

She nodded, folding the bill.

"This morning?"

Again, a nod.

"Remember her name?"

Another.

I eased another twenty across her desk.

She lifted it delicately, folded it separately from the other. "Marie Aristides. At least, that's what she said. Of course, you said your name was Smith."

"I always do. Know what they talked about?"

A shrug this time.

"Would Lillian?"

"I could ask her." She wagged the bills discreetly.

I nodded. It was going around.

"Lillian," she said into the phone, "that Aristides girl who saw Mr. Trakas this morning . . . yes, right . . . do you know why she was here? . . . No . . . I was just thinking about her . . . no, thanks."

She put the phone down. "She doesn't know."

"If you find someone who does, call me. And I still want to see Mr. Trakas."

"Mr. Trakas can be hard to see. Unless you know when to look."

I slid another twenty from my wallet. "When would you recommend?"

She plucked the bill from my hand, added it to its friends. "Well, I understand he comes in early. I'm told he's often here by seven. Of course, I don't know that myself; I'm never in before nine."

So I left my twenties folded in her manicured hand and went home. Before I retrieved my car I called Gus to give him the girl's name, in case it helped. I gave it to Sgt. Romero at the Sixth Precinct too, but she didn't seem to care very much.

Lousy fire at a lousy bar.

By the time I got home my side and my knee were killing me. I poured an inch of Maker's Mark, went into the bedroom. The blinds were down and I didn't raise them. I put on a CD, Pollini playing Chopin Etudes. I lay down on the bed, finished the bourbon, and was asleep before he hit number four.

It was just before ten, a cool night as clear as the day had been, when I walked back into Daly's. The etched glass door opened onto the purr of conversation and the clink of glasses. Missing was the smell of burgers, fries, pasta sauce; instead there was the dryness of old smoke. The kitchen was dark.

The walls of the narrow room were lined with photos of legendary jazz pianists, most of them autographed to Mick, some in thanks for money advanced or the chance to crash in the office upstairs, no questions asked.

"You're limping," Mick greeted me.

"You're Irish. Bigman here yet?"

"Over there."

I checked in with Ray Diaz, who'd be working the shift with me, and with the two guys coming off. A slow day, they said. I sent Ray outside, started down the bar to where Bigman Jones loomed over a beer.

He spotted me coming. Grinning all over his huge black face, he threw back an arm, roared, "Mr. Smith!" I thought

I remembered that roar as more powerful, but it still made a dozen people look up from their drinks.

"Mr. Jones," I answered.

He clasped my hand with a paw the size of a fielder's mitt. "God *damn*!" he said. "An' I thought you was an ugly mother before!"

"I was," I said. "How've you been, Mr. Jones?"

"Poorly, Mr. Smith. I been poorly. But I thought I best come in and play this place"—he gestured around the room—"'cause it look like this be my last chance."

"The hell it is. This dump'll outlast us all."

"'Specially me," he said morosely. "Don't matter anyway. I'm movin' home."

"Where's home?"

"Apalachicola."

"Florida? You're from Florida?"

"What the hell you laughin' at, white boy? You a cracker too, as I recall. Course, you a hillbilly, so you ignorant." He drained his beer. "Well, jes' so you know, ain't no place like the Gulf. Gulls screamin', salt in the air; settin' watchin' the sunset from your own front porch . . ."

"Have you got a front porch?"

"Well, I got my eye on one. Sweetest little place you ever did see. But places right on the Gulf, they expensive. Prob'ly I'll get me a place in town. That ain't so bad, neither. And it ain't like I'll be there long."

"What do you mean?"

He ignored me. "Know what I'd like, though? I'd like to get my hands on that Trakas bastard 'fore I go. Jes' for old times, understand?"

"My job, Mr. Jones. Your hands are too valuable."

"You?" He coughed suddenly, a hacking cough deep in his chest. He recovered, and he grinned, but now something was in his eyes I hadn't seen before. "You too soft-assed. I bet you still thinkin' the good guys win."

"Me? I don't even think there are any good guys."

"You got that right. Mr. Daly!" he shouted up the bar. "Bring this cracker honky trash somethin' to drink before he have a collapse!"

"No, thanks," I said. "I'm working."

Jones squinted at me. "Since when that stopped you?"

I shrugged. "You hot tonight, Mr. Jones?"

"As the devil hisself. You stayin' for the set?"

"Uh-uh. But do something for me?" I pulled a recorder from my jacket pocket. "Tape it? Maybe I'll learn something."

He hesitated, then took the machine. "You ain't never learned nothin', all the years I've knowed you. Why ain't you stayin'?"

"I'm working the outside," I said. "I wouldn't be able to work in here while you were playing. Couldn't concentrate."

And that was it. That was the mistake, the thing I always do differently in dreams I wake from suddenly, heart pounding, dreams that always, anyway, come out the same.

If I'd been inside I'd have seen her. Even with the tight black dress, the sleek blond wig, maybe I'd have known her. Maybe I could have stopped her.

But Ray didn't know her. In the smoky, crowded bar, he didn't spot her. Where was I when she went in? I don't know. Checking the back, the alley, a car full of guys whose faces I didn't like driving slowly down the street.

When she went in I don't know where I was. But when the explosion came, shock waves and breaking glass, screams and smoke, I was inside in seconds. Fighting against the surge of people, I reached the back just before the fire got serious. I was the one who pulled her from under the wreckage left by the bomb she'd been planting, a homemade bomb that had gone off too soon. I carried her outside, and held her while she died. And maybe I'd have known her, because her tiny hands still wore delicate black lace gloves.

"Mick," I said, "you can't do anything else here tonight." Broken glass crunched underfoot as I crossed the room. Cops, firemen, paramedics, press, all had come and gone. Mick lingered by an upturned table, staring around him at walls whose remaining photos hung crooked, smoke-blackened. Everywhere, water glittered in the light filtering in from the street lamps. "Come on, let's go."

He surveyed the wreckage, spoke slowly. "I'm going to sell."

"Mick—"

He waved an impatient hand. "I know what you're going to say: It's not that bad. The building's sound. I can rebuild. The insurance'll pay. That it?"

"Something like that."

He didn't look at me. He gestured at the piano, let his hand drop. Along one side the case was charred and dull; elsewhere water pooled on the polished wood. "Piano's gone." His voice caught in his throat. "Can't fix this piano, can you?"

"No," I said quietly. "No, I don't think you can."

Something square-edged under the piano caught my eye. I reached down for it. My recorder. I turned it over in my hand, punched the rewind button without much hope, but it worked. I hit "play." Percussive bass chords under an inhumanly fast right hand echoed in the ruined room. Mick stirred, listened. "He was good. Second set was shaping up to be better."

"He'll open for you when you rebuild," I said. "Go home and sleep."

"No. I'll stay for a little. But alone, okay?"

The music stopped abruptly. I turned the machine off. "Okay. Sure. But call me if . . . whatever." I threaded through the debris to the door.

Mick spoke across the room. "Bill?"

I turned.

"You can't fight a guy like Trakas," he said. "It's not your fault."

"Yeah," I said, and left.

Outside, I stood awhile, looking over the block: the brick face of Daly's, the graffitied steel shutter drawn over the liquor store, the gates locked across the deli and the barbershop and the laundry. It was just after four, sparse late-night traffic moving on Seventh and a chill wind blowing from the river. I could go home and sleep, the way I'd told Mick to do; or I could hit an after-hours place, have the drink I hadn't let Bigman Jones buy me, and then another, and maybe after a while I wouldn't hear Daly's piano playing in my head, and I wouldn't feel Marie Aristides's hand clutching my arm, until her grip loosened and her hand slipped away.

I lit a cigarette, hailed a cab, and watched the city slide past me into the night.

Home, I called my service. I had a message. The operator read it to me with the disinterested precision of a professional go-between.

"It says, 'The guy he wants is Joey Theodorou. He works seven to three loading trucks at the UPS place on Greenwich. I don't know where he lives.' It's signed Gus."

I hung up the phone, poured a small bourbon over a lot of ice. I put on a record Bigman Jones had made twenty years ago, settled into a chair, and closed my eyes.

The ringing of the phone snapped me awake. Pale light showed through the front window; the music had stopped. The clock read 5:15. I grabbed for the phone before the service could get it, said "Smith" in a sleep-hoarse voice.

"Bill, it's Lydia. I was getting dressed to come to work and I heard about it on the radio. How bad is it?"

I rubbed a hand over my face. "The girl was killed. The one who knifed me. She was setting the bomb."

"Oh, God," she said softly. Then: "Was anyone else hurt?"

"No. No one else."

She let a breath out. "And the damage?"

"The building's okay, but the room's a wreck. Mostly from water—sprinklers and firehoses." I reached for my bourbon. The glass held nothing but half-melted ice. "The piano's a total loss."

"Oh, no. Poor Mick—that piano was special, wasn't it?"

"Yeah." I swallowed what was in the glass. "It was."

A cautious note crept into her voice. "I don't like the way you sound."

"Hang up," I suggested.

"What are you going to do?"

"Doesn't seem to make much goddamn difference what I do."

"Bill—"

"Don't, Lydia."

A pause. "All right. Just tell me what you're going to do."

"I'm going to find Joey Theodorou."

"Joey, that kid from the other night? You know where to find him?"

"I have a lead."

"Give it to the police."

"You know what they'll do with it?" I said savagely. "They'll pick him up. Ask questions he won't answer. He'll get a lawyer and they'll have to let him go. Trakas'll hand him ten grand and a one-way ticket to anyplace. Case dismissed."

"And if you find him?"

"Something else."

"All right," she said. "But I'm coming with you."

"No."

"You need backup. Two people are always better than one."

"Who told you that?"

"You."

"I never said 'always.' "

"Where should I meet you?"

"No."

"Bill, do you want to be the Marlboro Man or do you want to catch this kid?"

I cursed, groped for a cigarette. When I found one I put the receiver down to light it. I inhaled deeply, shook out the match, picked up the receiver again. "Lydia?"

"I'm still here."

"I'm sorry. You're right."

"It's okay," she said gently.

"There's a diner at Harrison and Hudson. I keep my car near there. I'm going to grab some breakfast. Can you be there by six?"

"I'll come now. I'll have breakfast with you."

"Mmm," I said. "And Lydia? Do one more thing?"

"What's that?"

"Tell me the part about you getting dressed again."

"I'm glad you're feeling better," she said, and hung up.

We sat in my car half a block up from the UPS depot. The air was thin, the sun sharp. I pulled a cigarette from my jacket, put it in my mouth, took it out again, asked, "Will it bother you if I smoke?"

"Not half as much as it'll bother you if you don't." Lydia opened her window. "What makes you think he'll show, after what happened?"

"Maybe he won't. If he doesn't, I'll go to the foreman after the shift starts and get his address."

"If he won't give it to you?"

"I'll send you. He'll give it to you."

"I don't like the way that sounds."

"What?"

"You'll send me. You make it sound as though I work for you."

"You do."

"I free-lance. I hired on for this case."

"So you work for me."

"Maybe, but I don't like the way it sounds."

So we sat, and I smoked, and Joey didn't show. The stream of shift workers swelled to a flood, then thinned to a trickle, dried up. Normal early-morning traffic picked up, and brown trucks started rolling out of the orange-brick building.

"You're right." I stubbed out my third Kent. "He's not coming."

"Would you?" Lydia asked. "If you'd sent your girlfriend on that kind of job, and that had happened to her, would you be up to pretending the next morning that everything was normal?"

"If I'd sent—" I stopped, stared at her.

Her eyes were puzzled. "What is it?"

"Jesus, Smith—!" I switched the car on, shifted fast, cut

into the stream of traffic in front of a silver Mazda whose driver sat on his horn. He had every right.

"Buckle up," I told Lydia.

"Where are we going?"

"To find Joey."

She was too smart to try to talk to me again.

I screeched to a stop at Trakas's Third Avenue building. The lobby was still cool and granite and the elevator was wood and the ride was interminable. On the thirtieth floor I pushed out of the cab, said, "Back me," and yanked open the glass doors.

The teal carpet with the roses was soft and thick. My steps made no sound passing the empty teak desk, which stood waiting for the receptionist who never came in before nine. Down the hall, toward the corner, more by instinct than thought; closed doors, covered office machines, gray rectangles of unlit ceiling lights. Then at the end of the hall an open door, and sounds: a thud, a groan. I stepped through the door, gun drawn, shouted, "Joey! Let him go!"

The hulking back outlined against the window stiffened. The kid swung around, forcing in front of him a smaller man who staggered, face bloody and swollen. Joey's automatic had been on the desk beside him; he grabbed it up now, wrapped his arm around the bloodied man's throat, put the gun to his head.

"Get the hell out of here!" he roared. "Get away, or I'll shoot him! I'll shoot you too!"

"Joey," I said, my voice and my gun level, "you can't shoot any faster than I can. First shot you fire, I'll blow your head off. You won't see him die."

"Doesn't matter." He laughed a wild laugh, tightened his arm against the other man's throat. "Only I didn't want him to die easy. I wanted it to hurt, the way she hurt when she died!"

"For God's sake!" the smaller man's voice croaked. "Shoot him!"

"Why?" I asked. I slipped my left hand into my jacket pocket, moved it around, came out with a cigarette. "I was there when she died, Trakas." I put the cigarette in my mouth, looked around. I inched slowly left, coming no closer to Joey, making no sudden moves. "You didn't send her, did you, Joey?" I moved behind Trakas's sleek rosewood desk, until the window was behind me and I faced the door. Joey kept the gun to Trakas's head, turned to keep Trakas as a shield between him and me. I reached onto the desk for the marble lighter. "No, you didn't send her. You didn't know anything about it. She was free-lancing, wasn't she, Trakas?" I lit my cigarette.

"It wasn't my idea!" the bloodied man blurted. "She came to me! But Joey, she said you sent her! I never would've okayed it, except I thought it was your idea! I swear, Joey, I swear I wouldn't have hired a girl to—"

"Shut up!" Joey howled. "Shut up! You bastard, I'll kill you—!"

"Joey!" I said sharply. He stopped, stared at me, his face contorted. I made my voice soft. "Ever kill a man, Joey? Strange thing happens when you kill a man. He stays with you forever, after that. Hate a man enough to kill him and you never get rid of him. You ready to live with Trakas forever, Joey?"

He didn't answer, just stared.

"She wanted to be your partner, Joey," I went on. "Not just your girl."

"Don't need no partner," Joey half-whispered mechanically.

"Yes, you did, Joey," I said. "Just like I do. My partner's behind you now, Joey, and she's ready to blow a hole in you if you don't put the gun down."

A glint sprang into Joey's eyes. "The hell with that, cowboy. You got no partner."

"I do," I said. "And she's a better shot than I am."

"And I don't have Bill's scruples," Lydia spoke from the doorway behind Joey. "It won't bother me at all to shoot you in the back."

Joey's eyes grew big. There was no movement, no sound, in the carpeted office.

Then Trakas yelled, "What the hell are you waiting for? Shoot him!"

Joey shoved Trakas forward, spun, and fired through the doorway; but Lydia had dropped as soon as he'd moved. His shot went whistling over her head. Hers blew a red hole in the center of his chest.

He stumbled back, fell into a chair. Open-eyed, he slid to the floor. A crimson streak stained the teal fabric.

I strode around the desk, crouched by him. I felt his neck for a pulse, but he was gone. I closed his eyes.

Lydia hadn't moved much since she'd fired. Now she stood, walked slowly over. Her eyes fixed on Joey for a long minute. Then she put her gun away, said in very close to her normal voice, "Shouldn't we call the police?"

Trakas pulled himself into a chair. "Who the hell are you guys? Aren't you the police?"

"No," I said. "We work for Mick Daly."

Trakas's eyes narrowed, glinted a glint like Joey's had. "Oh," he said. "And so what?"

"So I'm going to call the police." I moved to the phone.

"Wait," said Trakas. "What are you going to tell them?"

I put the phone down. "Depends."

"You've got nothing on me, you know."

"I heard a lot of talk about who got hired to do what," I said. "You hear that, Lydia?"

"Yes."

"You heard a lot of nothing." Trakas spoke slowly, through swollen lips. "Here's what happened: Mick Daly sent two enforcers to shake me down. Look at me, see what they did to me. My bodyguard, he tried to protect me, but one of Daly's people, the pretty one"—he smiled at Lydia—"shot him." He settled back in his chair, smiling.

I slid my left hand into my jacket pocket, where the cigarette had come from. I lifted out my recorder, pressed "rewind," pressed "play." At first there were only the flashing notes of Bigman Jones's riff; but suddenly, my voice. "I was there when she died, Trakas." I fast-forwarded, hit "play" again. A different voice: "—never would've okayed it, except I thought it was your idea! I swear, Joey, I swear I wouldn't have hired a girl—" I turned it off.

Trakas's smile disappeared. His face was colorless under the blood and the purple swelling. "You can't take that to court."

"Not to court," I said. "To Channel Five. Channel Nine. The *Times*, the *News*, the *Post*. They'll eat it up. The mayor'll get his balls in an uproar. There'll be an investigation. Probably they'll never prove anything, but you'll sure as hell be through in this town, Trakas. You'll never see another building permit. Nobody will even take your phone calls anymore."

We held each other's eyes, he in his leather chair by the window, me leaning over his rosewood desk. Lydia stood so close to me I could feel her warmth; Joey lay on the floor, growing cold.

"Well," Trakas said. "Stalemate. What do we do?"

"This is what we do." I dropped the recorder in my pocket. "I put this tape in a safe deposit box, with a letter to my lawyer in case anything happens to me. You drop the Seventh Avenue project. Market's bad, anyhow. Condos aren't selling."

"Drop the whole project? I can't do that!"

"Sure you can, Trakas. And one more thing."

"What?"

"There's a piece of real estate in Florida a friend of mine has his eye on. Small potatoes for you: fifty thousand, maybe sixty. Buy it for him."

"You're crazy."

I pressed the button on the machine in my pocket. Trakas jumped at the sound of Joey's scream: "Shut up! Shut up! You bastard, I'll kill you!"

I turned the recorder off.

"Then," I said, "we tell the police what happened. Joey came here to kill you. Maybe he was crazy. I wouldn't know. We were tailing him for a client, followed him here. We tried to talk him down, but he shot at Lydia and she shot back. Isn't that right?"

Trakas turned his chair, stared for a long time out his window at Manhattan spread at his feet.

"Yeah," he said. "Yeah, I guess it is."

A week later I was at the piano in the late afternoon when the phone rang.

"It's Mick. I—it's here. I want you to see it."

"I'm on my way. Is it what you expected?"

"Well, it's a goddamn legend, so I knew, but to see it . . . They carved their names all over it: the legs, the case, the top—just not near the keys. That was Bigman's only rule. So you didn't have to see someone else's name while you played. But they're all here, everyone you ever heard of, everyone you ever heard play. You've got to come see it. I just . . ."

"You just what?"

"I just wish I knew why he gave it to me. Why isn't he taking it with him?"

I said quietly, "He's not going to need it, Mick. And you do. And besides," I added, "Florida's bad for pianos."

Before I left I called Lydia. "I just wanted to see how you were doing," I said. "Are you okay?"

For a moment she didn't answer. Then, "It's true what you said, isn't it? About what happens when you kill someone."

"Yes," I said. "Yes, it's true."

"Mmm." A pause. In a stronger voice: "Then I guess you get used to it."

"You learn to live with it."

More silence. "Lydia, listen," I said. "I'm on my way to Mick's, to take a look at Bigman Jones's piano. Come with me; then I'll take you to dinner."

She said, "I don't know."

"Just dinner. I promise. I'll behave. Just some company."

"All right." Her voice held a ghost of a smile. "I'd like some company."

I closed the piano, shut the lights, walked down the two flights of wooden stairs from my place. I wasn't moving fast; I was too late to catch anything of the sunset except the orange embers banked in rows across the sky.

"At the Old Swimming Hole" first appeared in Mean Streets, *the second PWA anthology. That was 1984. Since that time Sara Paretsky's popularity has soared even higher, despite all that Kathleen Turner tried to do to it. She edited one of the finest anthologies in recent years,* A Woman's Eye, *and her most recent V. I. Warshawski novel,* Tunnel Vision, *is the best-selling—and simply the best— yet.*

Here Warshawski takes charge when a murder occurs at a swimming meet she's attending.

AT THE OLD SWIMMING HOLE

by Sara Paretsky

1

THE GYM WAS dank—chlorine and sweat combined in a hot sticky mass. Shouts from the trainers, from the swimmers, from the spectators bounced from the high metal ceiling and back and forth from the benches lining the pool on two sides. The cacophony set up an unpleasant buzzing in my head.

I was not enjoying myself. My shirt was soaked through with sweat. Anyway, I was too old to sit cheering on a bleacher for two hours. But Alicia had been insistent—I had to be there in person for her to get points on her sponsor card.

Alicia Alonso Dauphine and I had gone through school together, so I knew all her childhood anguish over her parents' decision to bestow a prima ballerina's name on her. Alicia had never had the slightest interest in fine arts. From her earliest years, all she wanted was to muck around with engines. At eighteen off she went to the University of Illinois to study aeronautics.

Despite her lack of interest in dance, Alicia was very athletic. Next to airplanes the only thing she really cared about was competitive swimming. I used to cheer her when she was NCAA swimming champ, always with a bit of irritation about being locked in a dank, noisy gym for hours at a time—swimming is not a great spectator sport. But after all, what are friends for?

When Alicia joined Berman Aircraft as an associate engineer, we drifted our separate ways. We met occasionally at weddings, confirmations, bar mitzvahs. (My, how our friends were aging! Childlessness seemed to suspend us in time, but each new ceremony in their lives marked a new milestone toward old age for the women we had played with in school.)

Then last week I'd gotten a call from Alicia. Berman was mounting a team for a citywide corporate competition— money would be raised through sponsors for the American Cancer Society. Both Alicia's mother and mine had died of cancer—would I sponsor her races? Doubling my contribution if she won? It was only after I'd made the pledge that I realized she expected me there in person. One of her sponsors had to show up to testify that she'd done it and all the others were busy with their homes and children and come on, V.I., what do you do all day long? I need you.

How can you know you're being manipulated and still let it happen? I hunched an impatient shoulder and turned back to the starting blocks.

From where I sat, Alicia was just another bathing-suited body with a cap. Her distinctive cheekbones were softened and flattened by the dim fluorescence. Not a wisp of her thick black hair trailed around her face. She was wearing a bright red tank suit—no extra straps or flounces to slow her down in the water.

The swimmers had been wandering around the side of the pool, swinging their arms to stretch out the muscles, not talking much while the timers argued some inaudible point with the referee. Now a police whistle shrilled faintly about the din and the competitors snapped to attention, moving toward the starting blocks at the far end of the pool.

We were about to watch the fifty-meter freestyle. I looked at the hand-scribbled card Alicia had given me before the meet. After the fifty-meter, she was in a 4 x 50 relay. Then I could leave.

The swimmers were mounting the blocks when someone began complaining again. The woman from the Ajax insurance team was complaining about the marker on the inside of her lane. The referee reshuffled the swimmers, leaving the offending lane empty. The swimmers finally mounted the blocks again. Timers got into position.

Standing to see the start of the race, I no longer knew where Alicia was. Red tanks bent over lanes two, three, and six, their features smoothed by caps and dimmed lighting into anonymity.

The referee raised the starting gun. Arms swung back for the dive. Then the gun and seven bodies flung themselves into the water. Perfect dive in lane six—had to be Alicia, surfacing, pulling away from all but one other swimmer, a fast little woman from the brokerage house of Feldstein, Holtz, and Woods.

Problems for the red-suited woman in lane two. I hadn't seen her dive, but she was having trouble righting herself, couldn't seem to make headway in the lane. Now everyone was noticing her. Whistles were blowing, the man on the loudspeaker tried ineffectually to call for silence.

I pushed my way through the crowds on the benches and vaulted over the barrier dividing the spectators from the water. Useless over the din to order someone into the pool for her. Useless to point out the growing circle of red. I kicked off running shoes and dove from the side. Swimming underwater to the second lane. Not Alicia. Surely not.

Seeing the water turn red around me. Surface. Find the woman. Drag her to the edge where finally a few galvanized hands pulled her out.

I scrambled from the pool and picked out someone in a striped referee's shirt. "Get a fire department ambulance as fast as you can."

He gaped at me stupidly.

"Dial 911, damn it. Do it now!" I pushed him toward the door, hard, and he suddenly broke into a trot.

I knelt beside the woman. She was breathing, but shallowly. I felt her gently. Hard to find the source of bleeding with the wet suit, but I thought it came from the upper back. Demanding help from one of the bystanders, I carefully turned her to her side. Blood was oozing now, not pouring, from a wound below her left shoulder. Pack it with towels, elevate her feet, keep the crowd back. Wait. Wait. Wait. Watch the shallow breathing turn to choking. Mouth-to-mouth does no good. Who knows cardiopulmonary resuscitation? A muscular young man in skimpy bikini shorts comes forward and works at her chest. By the time the paramedics hustle in with stretcher and equipment, the shallow choking breath has stopped. They take her to the hospital, but we all know it's no good.

As the stretcher-bearers trotted away, the rest of the room came back into focus. Alicia was standing at my side, black hair hanging damply to her shoulders, watching me with fierce concentration. Everyone else seemed to be shrieking in unison; the sound re-echoing from the rafters was more unbearable than ever.

I stood up, put my mouth close to Alicia's ear, and asked her to take me to whoever was in charge. She pointed at a man in an Izod T-shirt standing on the other side of the hole left by the dead swimmer's body.

I went over to him. "I'm V. I. Warshawski. I'm a private detective. That woman was murdered—shot through the back. Whoever shot her probably left during the confusion. But you'd better get the cops here now. And tell everyone over your megaphone that no one leaves until the police have seen them."

He looked at my dripping jeans and shirt. "Do you have anything to back up this preposterous statement?"

I held out my hands. "Blood." I grabbed the microphone from him. "May I have your attention, please." My voice bounced around the hollow room. "There has been a serious accident in the pool. Until the police have been here no one can leave this area. I am asking the six timers who were at the far end of the pool to come here now."

There was a brief silence, like a current switched off, before the clamor started up more horrifically than before. A handful of people picked their way along the edge of the pool toward me. The man in the Izod shirt was fulminating, but lacked the guts to try to grab the mike.

When the timers came up I said, "You six are the only ones who definitely could not have killed that woman. I want you to stand at the exits." I tapped each in turn and sent them to a post—two to the doors on the second floor at the top of the bleachers, two to the ground floor exits, and one each to the doors leading to the men's and women's dressing rooms.

"Don't let anyone leave, regardless of *anything* he or she says. If they have to use the bathroom, tough—hold it until the cops get here. Anyone tries to leave, keep them here. If they want to fight, let it go but get as complete a description as you can."

They trotted off to their stations. I gave Izod back his mike, made my way to a pay phone in the corner, and dialed the Eleventh Street homicide number.

11

"You sent the guy to guard the upstairs exit and he waltzed away, probably taking the gun with him. He must be on his knees in some church right now thanking God for sending a pushy private investigator to this race." Sergeant McGonnigal was not fighting sarcasm as hard as he might have.

I bit my lips. He couldn't be angrier with me than I was with myself. I sneezed and shivered in my damp, clammy clothes. "You're right, Sergeant. I wish you'd been at the meet instead of me. You'd probably have had ten uniformed officers with you who could've taken charge as soon as the starting gun was fired and avoided this mess. Do any of the timers know who the man was?"

We were in an office which the school athletic department had given the police for their investigation-scene headquarters. McGonnigal had been questioning all the timers, figuring their closeness to the pool gave them the best angle on what had happened. One was missing, the man I'd sent to the upper balcony exit.

The sergeant grudgingly told me he'd been over that ground with the other timers. None of them knew who the missing man was—each of the companies in the meet had supplied volunteers to do the timing and other odd jobs. Everyone just assumed this man was from someone else's firm. No one had noticed him that closely; their attention was focused on the action in the pool. My brief glance at him gave the police their best description: medium height, short light brown hair, wearing a pale green T-shirt and faded white denim shorts. Yes, baggy enough for a gun to fit in a pocket unnoticed.

"You know, Sergeant, I asked for the six timers at the far end of the pool because they were facing the swimmers, so none of them could have shot the dead woman in the back. This guy came forward. That means there's a timer missing— either the person actually down at the far end was in collusion, or you're missing a body."

McGonnigal made an angry gesture—not at me. Himself for not having thought of it before. He detailed two uniformed cops to round up all the volunteers and find out who the errant timer was.

"Any more information on the dead woman?"

McGonnigal picked up a pad from the paper-littered desk in front of him. "Her name was Louise Carmody. You know that. She was twenty-four. She worked for the Ft. Dearborn Bank and Trust as a junior lending officer. You know that. Her boss is very shocked—you probably could guess that. And she has no enemies. No dead person ever does."

"Was she working on anything sensitive?"

He gave me a withering glance. "What twenty-four-year-old junior loan officer works on anything sensitive?"

"Lots," I said firmly. "No senior person ever does the grubby work. A junior officer crunches numbers, or gathers basic data for crunching. Was she working on any project that someone might not want her to get data for?"

McGonnigal shrugged wearily, but made a note on a second pad—the closest he would come to recognizing I might have a good suggestion.

I sneezed again. "Do you need me for anything else? I'd like to dry off."

"No, go. I'd just as soon you weren't around when Lieutenant Mallory arrives, anyway."

Bobby Mallory was McGonnigal's boss. He was also an old friend of my father, who had been a beat sergeant until his death fifteen years ago. Bobby did not like women on the crime scene in any capacity—victim, perpetrator, or investigator—and he especially did not like his old friend Tony's daughter on the scene. I appreciated McGonnigal's unwillingness to witness any acrimony between his boss and me, and was getting up to leave when the uniformed cops came back.

The sixth timer had been found in a supply closet behind the men's lockers. He was concussed and groggy from a head wound and couldn't remember how he got to where he was. Couldn't remember anything past lunchtime. I waited long enough to hear that and slid from the room.

Alicia was waiting for me at the far end of the hall. She had changed from her suit into jeans and a pullover and was squatting on her heels, staring fiercely at nothing. When she saw me coming she stood up and pushed her black hair out of her eyes.

"You look a mess, V.I."

"Thanks. I'm glad to get help and support from my friends after they've dragged me into a murder investigation."

"Oh, don't get angry—I didn't mean it that way. I'm

sorry I dragged you into a murder investigation. No, I'm
not, actually. I'm glad you were on hand. Can we talk?"

"After I put some dry clothes on and stop looking a
mess."

She offered me her jacket. Since I'm five eight to her five
four, it wasn't much of a cover, but I draped it gratefully
over my shoulders to protect myself from the chilly October
evening.

At my apartment, Alicia followed me into the bathroom
while I turned on the hot water. "Do you know who the dead
woman was? The police wouldn't tell us."

"Yes," I responded irritably. "And if you'll give me
twenty minutes to warm up I'll tell you. Bathing is not a
group sport in this apartment."

She trailed out of the bathroom, her face set in tense lines.
When I joined her in the living room some twenty minutes
later, a towel around my damp hair, she was sitting in front
of the television set changing channels.

"No news yet," she said. "Who was the dead woman?"

"Louise Carmody. Junior loan officer at the Ft. Dearborn.
You know her?"

Alicia shook her head. "Do the police know why she was
shot?"

"They're just starting to investigate. What do you know
about it?"

"Nothing. Are they going to put her name on the news?"

"Probably, if the family's been notified. Why is this
important?"

"No reason. It just seems so ghoulish, reporters hovering
around her dead body and everything."

"Could I have the truth, please?"

She sprang to her feet and glared at me. "It is the truth."

"Screw that. You don't know her name, you spin the TV
dials to see the reports, and now you think it's ghoulish for
the police to hover around? . . . Tell you what I think,
Alicia. I think you know who did the shooting. They
shuffled the swimmers, nobody knew who was in which
lane. You started out in lane two, and you'd be dead if the

woman from Ajax hadn't complained. Who wants to kill you?"

Her black eyes glittered in her white face. "No one. Why don't you have a little empathy, Vic? I might have been killed. There was a madman out there who shot a woman. Why don't you give me some sympathy?"

"I jumped into a pool to pull that woman out. I sat around in wet clothes for two hours talking to the cops. I'm beat. You want sympathy, go someplace else. The little I have is reserved for myself tonight. I'd like to know why I really had to be at the pool, if it wasn't to ward off a potential attacker. And if you'd told me that at the outset, Louise Carmody might still be alive."

"Damn you, Vic, stop doubting every word I say. I told you why I needed you there—someone had to sign the card. Millie works during the day. So does Fredda. Katie has a new baby. Elene is becoming a grandmother for the first time. Get off my goddamn back."

"If you're not going to tell me the truth, and if you're going to scream at me about it, I'd just as soon you left."

She stood silent for a minute. "Sorry, Vic. I'll get a better grip on myself."

"Great. You do that. I'm fixing some supper—want any?"

She shook her head. When I returned with a plate of pasta and olives, Beth Blacksin was just announcing the top local story. Alicia sat with her hands clenched as Beth stated the dead woman's name. After that, she didn't say much. Just asked if she could crash for the night—she lived in Warrenville, a good hour's drive from town, near Berman's aeronautic engineering labs.

I gave her pillows and a blanket for the couch and went to bed. I was pretty angry: I figured she wanted to sleep over because she was scared and it infuriated me she wouldn't talk about it.

When the phone woke me at two-thirty, my throat was raw, the start of a cold brought on by sitting around in wet clothes for so long. A heavy voice asked for Alicia.

"I don't know who you're talking about," I said hoarsely.

"Be your age, Warshawski. She brought you to the gym. She isn't at her own place. She's gotta be with you. You don't want to wake her up, give her a message. She was lucky tonight. We want the money by noon, or she won't be so lucky a second time."

He hung up. I held the receiver a second longer and heard another click. The living room extension. I pulled on a dressing gown and padded down the hallway. The apartment door shut just as I got to the living room. I ran to the top of the stairs; Alicia's footsteps were echoing up and down the stairwell.

"Alicia! Alicia—you can't go out there alone. Come back here!"

The slamming of the entryway door was my only answer.

III

I didn't sleep well, my cold mixing with worry and anger over Alicia. At eight I hoisted my aching body out of bed and sat sneezing over some steaming fruit juice while I tried to force my brain to work. Alicia owed somebody money. That somebody was pissed off enough to kill because he didn't have it. Bankers do not kill wayward loan customers. Loan sharks do, but what could Alicia have done to wrack up so much indebtedness? Berman probably paid her a hundred grand or so a year for the special kinds of designs she did on aircraft wings. And she was the kind of client a bank usually values. So what did she need money for that only a shark would provide?

The clock was ticking. I called her office—she'd phoned in sick; the secretary didn't know where she was calling from, but had assumed home. On a dim chance I tried her home. No answer. Alicia had one brother, Tom, an insurance agent on the far south side. After a few tries I located his office in Flossmoor. He hadn't heard from Alicia for weeks. And no, he didn't know who she might owe money to.

Reluctantly Tom gave me their father's phone number in Florida. Mr. Dauphine hadn't heard from his daughter, either.

"If she calls you, or if she shows up, *please* let me know. She's in trouble up here and the only way I can help her is by knowing where she is." I gave him the number without much expectation of hearing from him again.

I did know someone who might be able to give me a line on her debts. A while back I'd done a major favor for Don Pasquale, a local mob leader. If she owed him money, he might listen to my intercession. If not, he might be able to tell me who she had borrowed from. I just was reluctant to be indebted to him for my information. Sorry, Pasquale— come whistle for your return favor—that kind of response didn't go down too well with a man like him. Still, I didn't know where else to start.

Torfino's, an Elmwood Park restaurant where the don had a part-time office, put me through to his chief assistant Ernesto. A well-remembered gravel voice told me I sounded awful.

"Thank you, Ernesto," I snuffled. "Did you hear about the death of Louise Carmody at the University of Illinois gym last night? She was probably shot by mistake, poor thing. The intended victim was a woman named Alicia Dauphine. We grew up together, so I feel a little solicitous on her behalf. She owes a lot of money to someone—I wondered if you know who."

"Name isn't familiar, Warshawski. I'll check around and call you back."

My cold made me feel as though I was at the bottom of a fishtank. I couldn't think fast enough or hard enough to imagine where Alicia might have gone to ground. Perhaps at her house, believing if she didn't answer the phone no one would think she was home? It wasn't a very clever idea, but it was the best I could do in my muffled snuffled state.

The old farmhouse in Warrenville which Alicia had modernized lay behind a high school. The boys were out practicing football. They were wearing light jerseys since the day was warm; I huddled in my winter coat, my cold making me feel sorry for myself. We were close enough that I could see their mouthpieces, but they paid no attention as I walked around the house looking for signs of life.

Alicia's car was in the garage, but the house looked cold and unoccupied. As I made my way to the back a black-and-white cat darted out from the bushes and began weaving itself around my ankles, mewing piteously. Alicia had three cats. This one wanted something to eat.

Alicia had installed a sophisticated burglar alarm system—she had an office in her home and often worked on preliminary designs there. An expert had gotten through the system into the pantry—some kind of epoxy had been sprayed on the wires to freeze them. Then, somehow disabling the phone link, the intruder had cut through the wires.

My stomach muscles tightened and I wished futilely for the Smith & Wesson locked in my safe at home. My cold really had addled my brains for me not to take it on such an errand. Still, where burglars lead shall P.I.'s hesitate? I opened the window, slid a leg over, and landed on the pantry floor. My feline friend followed more gracefully. She promptly abandoned me to start sniffing at the pantry walls.

Cautiously opening the door I slid into the kitchen. It was deserted, the refrigerator and clock motors humming gently, a dry dishcloth draped over the sink. In the living room another cat joined me and followed me into the electronic wonderland of Alicia's study. She had used built-in bookcases to house her computers and other gadgets. The printers were tucked along a side wall and wires ran everywhere. Whoever had broken in was not interested in merchandise—the street value of her study contents would have brought in a nice return, but they stood unharmed.

By now I was dreading the trek upstairs. The second cat, a tabby, trotted briskly ahead of me, tail waving like a flag. Alicia's bedroom door was shut. I kicked it open with my right leg and pressed myself against the wall. Nothing. Dropping to my knees I looked in. The bed, tidily covered with an old-fashioned white spread, was empty. So was the bathroom. So was the guestroom and an old sun-porch she'd glassed in and converted to a solarium.

The person who broke in had not come to steal—everything was preternaturally tidy. So he (she?) had come to attack Alicia. The hair stood up along the nape of my neck. Where was he? Not in the house. Hiding outside?

I started down the stairs again when I heard a noise, a heavy scraping. I froze, trying to locate the source. A movement caught my eye at the line of vision. The hatch to the crawl space had been shoved open; an arm swung down. For a split second only I stared at the arm and the gun in its grip, then leaped down the stairs two at a time.

A heavy thud—the man jumping onto the upper landing. The crack as the gun fired. A jolt in my left shoulder and I gasped with shock and fell the last few steps to the bottom. Righted myself. Reached for the deadlock on the front door. Heard an outraged squawk, loud swearing, and a crash that sounded like a man falling downstairs. Then I had the door open and was staggering outside while an angry bundle of fur poured past me. One of the cats, a heroine, tripping my assailant and saving my life.

IV

I never really lost consciousness. The football players saw me stagger down the sidewalk and came trouping over. In their concern for me they failed to tackle the gunman, but they got me to a hospital where a young intern removed the slug from my shoulder; the winter coat had protected me from major damage. Between my cold and the gunshot, I was just as happy to let him incarcerate me for a few days.

They tucked me into bed and I fell into a heavy, uneasy sleep. I had jumped into the black waters of Lake Michigan in search of Alicia, trying to reach her ahead of a shark. She was lurking just out of reach. She didn't know that her oxygen tank ran out at noon.

When I woke finally, soaked with sweat, it was dark outside. The room was lit faintly by a fluorescent light over the sink. A lean man in a brown wool business suit was sitting next to the bed. When he saw me looking at him he reached into his coat.

I thought if he was going to shoot me there wasn't a thing

I could do about it—I was too limp from my heavy sleep to move. Instead of a gun, though, he pulled out an ID case.

"Miss Warshawski? Peter Carlton, Federal Bureau of Investigation. I know you're not feeling well, but I need to talk to you about Alicia Dauphine."

"So the shark ate her," I said.

"What?" he demanded sharply. "What does that mean?"

"Nothing. Where is she?"

"We don't know. That's what we want to talk to you about. She went home with you after the swimming meet yesterday. Correct?"

"Gosh, Mr. Carlton. I love watching my tax dollars at work. If you've been following her, you must have a better fix on her whereabouts than I do. I last saw her around two-thirty this morning. If it's still today, that is."

"What did she talk to you about?"

My mind was starting to unfog. "Why is the Bureau interested in Miss Dauphine?"

He didn't want to tell me. All he wanted was every word Alicia had said to me. When I wouldn't budge, he started in on why I was in her house and what had I noticed there.

Finally I said, "Mr. Carlton, if you can't tell me why you're interested in Miss Dauphine, there's no way I can respond to your questions. I don't believe the Bureau—or the police—or anyone, come to that—has any right to pry into the affairs of citizens in the hopes of turning up some scandal. You tell me why you're interested and I'll tell you if I know anything relevant to that interest."

With an ill grace he said, "We believe she has been selling Defense Department secrets to the North Koreans."

"No," I said flatly. "She wouldn't."

"Some wing designs she was working on have disappeared. She's disappeared. And a Korean functionary in St. Charles has disappeared."

"Sounds pretty circumstantial to me. The wing designs might be in her home. They could easily be on a disk someplace—she did all her drafting on computer."

They'd been through her computer files at home and at work and found nothing. Her boss did not have copies of the latest design, only of the early stuff. I thought about the heavy voice on the phone demanding money but loyalty to Alicia made me keep it to myself—give her a chance to tell her story first.

I did give him everything Alicia had said, her nervousness and her sudden departure. That I was worried about her and went to see if she was in her house. And was shot by an intruder hiding in the crawl space. Who might have taken her designs. Although nothing looked pilfered.

He didn't believe me. I don't know if he thought I knew something I wasn't telling, or if he thought I had joined Alicia in selling secrets to the Koreans. But he kept at me for so long that I finally pushed my call-button. When the nurse I arrived I explained that I was worn-out and could she please show my visitor out? He left but promised me that he would return.

Cursing my weakness, I fell asleep again. When I next woke it was morning and both my cold and my shoulder were much improved. When the doctors came by on their morning visit I got their agreement to a discharge. I called my answering service from a phone in the lobby. Ernesto had been in touch. I reached him at Torfino's.

"Saw about your accident in the papers, Warshawski. How you feeling? . . . And Dauphine. Apparently she's signed a note for $750,000 to Art Smollensk. Can't do anything to help you out. The don sends his best wishes for your recovery."

Art Smollensk, gambling king. When I worked for the Public Defender I'd had to defend some of his small-time employees—people at the level of smashing someone's fingers in his car door. The ones who did hits and arson usually could afford their own attorneys.

Alicia as a gambler made no sense to me—but we hadn't been close for over a decade. There were lots of things I didn't know about her.

At home for a change of clothes I stopped in the basement where I store useless mementos in a locked stall. After fifteen minutes of shifting boxes around I was sweating and my left shoulder was throbbing and oozing stickily, but I'd located my high school yearbook. I took it upstairs with me and thumbed through it, trying to gain inspiration on where Alicia might have gone to earth.

None came. I was about to leave again when the phone rang. It was Alicia, talking against a background of noise. "Thank God you're safe, Vic. I saw about the shooting in the paper. Please don't worry about me. I'm okay. Stay away and don't worry."

She hung up before I could ask her anything. I concentrated, not on what she'd said, but what had been in the background. Metal doors banging open and shut. Lots of loud wild talking. Not an airport—the talking was too loud for that and there weren't any intercom announcements in the background. I knew what it was. If I'd just let my mind relax it would come to me.

Idly flipping through the yearbook, I looked for faces Alicia might trust. I found my own staring from a group photo of the girls basketball team. I'd been a guard—Victoria the protectress from way back. On the next page, Alicia smiled fiercely, holding a swimming trophy. Her coach, who also taught Latin, had desperately wanted Alicia to train for the Olympics, but Alicia had her heart set on the U of I and engineering. . . . Suddenly I knew what the clanking was, where Alicia was. No other sound like that exists anywhere on earth.

V

Alicia and I grew up under the shadow of the steel mills in South Chicago. Nowhere else has the deterioration of American industry shown up more clearly. Wisconsin Steel is padlocked shut. The South Works are a shadow of their former monstrous grandeur. Unemployment is almost fifty percent, and the number of jobless youths lounging in the bars and on the streets has grown from the days when I hurried past them to the safety of my mother's house.

The high school was more derelict than I remembered. Many windows were boarded over. The asphalt playground was cracked and covered with litter, and the bleachers around the football field were badly weathered.

The guard at the doorway demanded my business. I showed her my P.I. license and said I needed to talk to the women's gym teacher on confidential business. After some dickering—hostile on her side, snuffly on mine—she gave me a pass. I didn't need directions down the scuffed corridors, past the battered lockers, past the smell of rancid oil coming from the cafeteria, to the noise and life of the gym.

Teenage girls in blue shirts and white shorts—the school colors—were shrieking, jumping, wailing in pursuit of volleyballs. I watched the pandemonium until the buzzer ended the period, then walked up to the instructor.

She was panting and sweating and gave me an incurious glance, looking only briefly at the pass I held out for her. "Yes?"

"You have a new swimming coach, don't you?"

"Just a volunteer. Are you from the union? She isn't drawing a paycheck. But Miss McFarlane, the coach, is desperately shorthanded, she teaches Latin, you know, and this woman is a big help."

"I'm not from the union. I'm her trainer. I need to talk to her—find out why she's dropped out and whether she plans to compete in any of her meets this fall."

The teacher gave me the hard look of someone used to sizing up fabricated excuses. I didn't think she believed me, but she told me I could go into the pool area and talk to the swim coach.

The pool dated to the time when this high school served an affluent neighborhood. It was twenty-five yards long, built with skylights along the outer wall. You reached it through the changing rooms, separate ones with showers for girls and boys. It didn't have an outside hallway entrance.

Alicia was perched alone on the high dive. A few students, boys and girls, were splashing about in the pool, but no organized training was in progress. Alicia was staring at nothing.

I cupped my hands and called up to her, "Do you want me to climb up, or are you going to come down?"

At that she turned and recognized me. "Vic!" Her cry was enough to stop the splashing in the pool. "How—Are you alone?"

"I'm alone. Come down—I took a slug in the shoulder—I'm not climbing up after you."

She shot off the board in a perfect arc, barely rippling the surface of the water. The kids watched with envy. I was pretty jealous, myself—nothing I do is done with that much grace.

She surfaced near me, but looked at the students. "I want you guys swimming laps," she said sharply. "What do you think this is—summer camp?"

They left us reluctantly and began swimming.

"How did you find me?"

"It was easy. I was looking through the yearbook trying to think of someone you would trust. Miss McFarlane was the easy answer—I remembered how you practically lived in her house for two years. You liked to read *Jane Eyre* together and she adored you. You are in deep trouble. Smollensk is after you and so is the FBI. You can't hide here forever. You'd better talk to the Bureau guys. They won't love you, but at least they're not going to shoot you."

"The FBI? Whatever for?"

"Your designs, sweetie pie. Your designs and the Koreans. The FBI are the people who look into that kind of thing."

"Vic. I don't know what you're talking about." The words were said with such slow deliberateness I was almost persuaded.

"The $750,000 you owe Art Smollensk."

She shook her head, then said, "Oh. Yes. That."

"Yes, that. I guess it seems like more money to me than it does to you. Or had you forgotten Louise Carmody getting shot? . . . Anyway, a known Korean spy left Fermilab yesterday or the day before, and you're gone, and some of your wing designs are gone, and the FBI think you've sold them overseas and maybe gone East yourself. I didn't tell them about Art, but they'll probably get there before too long."

"How sure are they that the designs are gone?"

"Your boss can't find them. Maybe you have a duplicate set at home nobody knows about."

She shook her head again. "I don't leave that kind of thing at home. I had them last Saturday, working, but I took the diskettes back . . ."

Her voice trailed off as a look of horror washed across her face. "Oh, no. This is worse than I thought." She hoisted herself out of the pool. "I've got to go. Got to get away before someone else figures out I'm here."

"Alicia, for Christ's sake. What has happened?"

She stopped and looked at me, tears swimming in her black eyes. "If I could tell anyone, it would be you, Vic." Then she was jogging into the girls' changing room, leaving the students in the pool swimming laps.

I stuck with her. "Where are you going? The Feds have a hook on any place you have friends or relations. Smollensk does, too."

That stopped her. "Tom, too?"

"Tom first, last, and foremost. He's the only relative you have in Chicago."

She was starting to shiver in the bare corridor. I grabbed her and shook her. "Tell me the truth, Alicia. I can't fly blind. I already took a bullet in the shoulder."

Suddenly she was sobbing on my chest. "Oh, Vic. It's been so awful. You can't know—you can't understand—you won't believe—" she was hiccoughing.

I led her into the shower room and found a towel. Rubbing her down I got the story in choking bits and pieces.

Tom was the gambler. He'd gotten into it in a small way in high school and college. After he went into business for himself, the habit grew. He'd mortgaged his insurance agency assets, taken out a second mortgage on the house, but couldn't stop.

"He came to me two weeks ago. Told me he was going to start filing false claims with his companies, collect the money." She gave a twisted smile. "He didn't have to put that kind of pressure on—I can't help helping him."

"But, Alicia, why? And how does Art Smollensk have your name?"

"Is that the man Tom owes money to? I think he uses my name—Alonso, my middle name—I know he does, I just don't like to think about it. Someone came around threatening me three years ago. I told Tom never to use my name again and he didn't for a long time, but now I guess he was desperate—$750,000, you know. . . .

"As to why I help him . . . You never had any brothers or sisters, so maybe you can't understand. When Mom died I was thirteen, he was six. I looked after him. Got him out of trouble. All kinds of stuff. It gets to be a habit, I guess. Or an obligation. That's why I've never married, you know, never had any children of my own. I don't want any more responsibilities like this one."

"And the designs?"

She looked horrified again. "He came over for dinner on Saturday. I'd been working all day on the things and he came into the study when I was logging off. I didn't tell him it was Defense Department work, but it's not too hard to figure out what I do is defense-related—after all, that's all Berman does; we don't make commercial aircraft. I haven't had a chance to look at the designs since—I worked out all day Sunday getting ready for that damned meet Monday. Tom must have taken my diskettes and swapped the labels with some others—I've got tons of them lying around."

She gave a twisted smile. "It was a gamble: a gamble that there'd be something valuable on them and a gamble I wouldn't discover the switch before he got rid of them. But he's a gambler."

"I see. . . . Look, Alicia. You can only be responsible for Tom so far. Even if you could bail him out this time—and I don't see how you possibly can—there'll be a next time. And you may not survive this one to help him again. Let's call the FBI."

She squeezed her eyes shut. "You don't understand, Vic. You can't possibly understand."

While I was trying to reason her into phoning the Bureau, Miss McFarlane, swim coach-cum-Latin-teacher, came briskly into the locker room. "Allie! One of the girls came to get me. Are you all—" She did a double take. "Victoria! Good to see you. Have you come to help Allie? I told her she could count on you."

"Have you told her what's going on?" I demanded of Alicia.

Yes, Miss McFarlane knew most of the story. Agreed that it was very worrying, but said Allie could not possibly turn in her own brother. She had given Allie a gym mat and some bedding to sleep on—she could just stay at the gym until the furor died down and they could think of something else to do.

I sat helplessly as Miss McFarlane led Alicia off to get some dry clothes. At last, when they didn't rejoin me, I sought them out, poking through half-remembered halls and doors until I found the staff coaching office. Alicia was alone, looking about fifteen in an old cheerleader's uniform Miss McFarlane had dug up for her.

"Miss McFarlane teaching?" I asked sharply.

Alicia looked guilty but defiant. "Yes. Two-thirty class. Look. The critical thing is to get those diskettes back. I called Tom, explained it to him. Told him I'd try to help him raise the money, but that we couldn't let the Koreans have those things. He agreed, so he's bringing them out here."

The room rocked slightly around me. "No. I know you don't have much sense of humor, but this is a joke, isn't it?"

She didn't understand. Wouldn't understand that if the Koreans had already left the country Tom no longer had the material. That if Tom was coming here she was the scapegoat. At last, despairing, I said, "Where is he meeting you? Here?"

"I told him I'd be at the pool."

"Will you do one thing my way? Will you go to Miss McFarlane's class and conjugate verbs for forty-five minutes and let me meet him at the pool? Please?"

At last, her jaw set stubbornly, she agreed. She still wouldn't let me call the Bureau, though. "Not until I've talked to Tom myself. It may all be a mistake, you know."

We both knew it wasn't, but I saw her into the Latin class without making the phone call I knew it was my duty to make, and returned to the pool. Driving out the two students still splashing around in the water, I put signs on the locker room doors saying the water was contaminated and there would be no swimming until further notice.

I turned out the lights and settled in a corner of the room remote from the outside windows to wait. And go over and over in my mind the story. I believed it. Was I fooling myself? Was that why she wouldn't call the Feds?

At last Tom came in through the men's locker room entrance. "Allie? Allie?" His voice bounced off the high rafters and echoed around me. I was well back in the shadows, my Smith & Wesson in hand; he didn't see me.

After half a minute or so another man joined him. I didn't recognize the stranger, but his baggy clothes marked him as part of Smollensk's group, not the Bureau. He talked softly to Tom for a minute. Then they went into the girl's locker room together.

When they returned I had moved partway up the side of the pool, ready to follow them if they went back into the main part of the high school looking for Alicia.

"Tom!" I called. "It's V. I. Warshawski. I know the whole story. Give me the diskettes."

"Warshawski!" he yelled. "What the hell are you doing here?"

I sensed rather than saw the movement his friend made. I shot at him and dived into the water. His bullet zinged as it hit the tiles where I'd been standing. My wet clothes and my sore shoulder made it hard to move. Another bullet hit the water by my head and I went under again, fumbling with my heavy jacket, getting it free, surfacing, hearing Alicia's sharp voice.

"Tom, why are you shooting at Vic? Stop it now. Stop it and give me back the diskettes."

Another flurry of shots, this time away from me, giving me a chance to get to the side of the pool, to climb out. Alicia lay on the floor near the door to the girls' locker room. Tom stood silently by. The gunman was jamming more bullets into his gun.

As fast as I could in my sodden clothes I lumbered to the hitman, grabbing his arm, squeezing, feeling blood start to seep from my shoulder, stepping on his instep, putting all the force of my body into my leg. Tom, though, Tom was taking the gun from him. Tom was going to shoot me.

"Drop that gun, Tom Dauphine." It was Miss McFarlane. Years of teaching in a tough school gave creditable authority to her; Tom dropped the gun.

VI

Alicia lived long enough to tell the truth to the FBI. It was small comfort to me. Small consolation to see Tom's statement. He hoped he could get Smollensk to kill his sister before she said anything. If that happened, he had a good gamble on her dying a traitor in their eyes—after all, her designs were gone, and her name was in Smollensk's files. Maybe the truth never would have come out. Worth a gamble to a betting man.

The Feds arrived about five minutes after the shooting stopped. They'd been watching Tom, just not closely enough. They were sore they'd let Alicia get shot. So they dumped some charges on me—obstructing federal authorities, not telling them where Alicia was, not calling as soon as I had the truth from her, God knows what else. I spent several days in jail. It seemed like a suitable penance, just not enough of one.

*Livia Washburn is a past winner of the SHAMUS Award
for Best Paperback P.I. Novel with* Wild Night *(Tor, 1986).
The book, like this story, features stuntman, P.I., and
ex-cowboy Lucas Hallam, working in Hollywood in the
1920s. Here he's working on a Tom Mix film and finds
much more than he bargained for.*

LYNCHING IN MIXVILLE

by L. J. Washburn

"**B**UT WERE WE scared?" asked the man in the creamy
white Stetson and fancy beaded shirt. "No, sir, not
one damn bit. There were at least thirty desperadoes
holed up in that cabin, and me with a force of ten deputies.
Well, hell, three-to-one odds ain't nothin'. We charged that
cabin, guns a-blazin', and killed upwards of twenty of them
owlhoots. As for the rest . . ." Tom Mix shrugged. "Well,
we hung 'em. Figured it was best just to save the state the
expense of a trial."

The reporter from the movie magazine was eagerly
making notes as Mix spun the yarn. She glanced up from
time to time, clearly overwhelmed by the charm of the
handsome cowboy actor.

"What about Tony?" the girl asked breathlessly.

Mix patted the big white horse who stood patiently next to him. "Right there with me every step of the way, of course. Man couldn't want a better hoss than ol' Tony here, could he, boy?"

The horse shook his head from side to side, long white mane flying.

The girl broke out laughing. "How precious! Such a smart horse."

Several yards away, one man dressed in range clothes muttered to another, "Horse is smarter than Mix, if you ask me."

They were on the back lot at Mixville, the large studio complex in Glendale where Tom Mix, the King of the Cowboys, made the motion pictures that were thrilling the whole country. The sun was almost directly overhead, and Mix and his crew and actors were taking their lunch break. Never one to shun publicity, Mix was also taking advantage of the break to grant an interview.

Even on a break, the place was busy. Men and women scurried around after finishing the box lunches provided by the studio. Producers conferred with directors, directors conferred with scenarists, scenarists conferred with their own private muses and tried to come up with something else exciting for Tom Mix to do in front of the cameras. There were props to be arranged, lights to be moved, horses to be saddled. The respite would be over before long, and then it would be back to the serious business of creating fantasies.

The only people who didn't seem to be in a hurry were the cowboys.

They were the riding extras and the stuntmen, the horsemen who made up all the posses and outlaw gangs and cavalry troops. All shapes and sizes, they had one thing in common—they were cowboys, and to them a job you couldn't do on horseback usually wasn't worth doing.

They were used to Mix's bragging, and they put no stock in the phony flamboyant biography that somebody—either the studio publicity department or Mix himself—had dreamed up for the star. Mostly, they didn't pay a whole lot of attention to him. He paid well and offered steady work to good riders, and that was the main thing. There was no point in challenging any of the whoppers he told. That would just make him mad, and that was like cutting your nose off to spite your face.

Lucas Hallam had found some shade under a tree, and he was polishing off his lunch out of the hot sun. A big man dressed in buckskins and a floppy-brimmed felt hat, Hallam had the same look of authenticity about him that the other cowboys did. The reason was simple. Like the others, he looked like what he was—an old cowboy.

There was something different about Hallam, though. There was a sharpness in his blue-gray eyes, set deep in the craggy face. They were the eyes of a manhunter.

In his time, he had been sheriff, Ranger, Pinkerton man. He had skirted the fence on the other side of the law, too, as a hired gun. The West had still been wild when he was a young man, and he had been wild along with it. Then the times had changed, and so had he. Like a lot of others, he had found a home of sorts here in Hollywood, doing the sort of work he had done all his life, only now it was for a camera. And he had a license from the state that said he could work as a private investigator when he wanted to, so the skills he had developed as a lawman weren't wasting away from lack of use.

He wasn't thinking about any of that on this hot summer day, though. He was thinking about finishing his lunch and then maybe tipping his hat down over his eyes to catch a snooze before the director called them back to work.

That plan got spoiled.

A high, querulous voice said, "And I'm callin' you a damn liar, Mix! I don't care how big a star you are, boy."

Hallam looked over to see Tom Mix and that gal reporter standing close by Mix's private trailer. He had heard that the girl was interviewing Mix for her magazine, but he hadn't paid much attention to what was going on. Publicity was a common thing on a Mix picture.

There were several cowboys standing close to Mix and the girl, and it was one of them who had done the shouting. He was an old man, stringy thin, and Hallam recognized him as Hank Daniels. As Hallam climbed to his feet and started to amble in that direction, Daniels went on, "No, you're a liar *and* a coward! I'm tired o' listenin' to it, Mix."

"You know what you can do, then," Mix said with a cold stare on his face as Hallam walked up. "You can get the hell off this picture."

"Don't think I won't!" Daniels railed. "I'm gettin' my stuff and clearin' out! But I'm goin' to tell this gal the truth first."

There were three other men standing with Daniels, and they looked uncomfortable. Jack Montgomery, Roy Norwood, and a waddy Hallam knew only as Shorty were all cowboys, and while they didn't want Daniels making Mix mad, they weren't going to stick their noses in another man's business, either. Hallam nodded to Montgomery, who was one of his closest friends in Hollywood, and watched while Daniels continued his ranting.

"Thirty outlaws, my foot!" Daniels snapped. "Twernt but five of 'em, and they put up about as much fuss as a pack o' newborn pups. And there was at least twenty of us in the posse. When them boys in the cabin seen us ridin' up, they throwed out their guns and come out with their hands in the air. I been hearin' you tell about leadin' the posse that caught the famous Ghost River Gang for years, Mix, but you don't know the first damn thing about it. You weren't there!"

Mix had listened to the old man with little change of expression. There was a fire burning in his dark eyes as he said in a low voice, "Are you through, Daniels?"

Daniels spat into the dust. "Reckon I am." He leered at the girl. "One more thing, missy. Mix got one part of it right by accident. We hung them bastards, all right, ever' one of them."

The girl glanced back and forth between Mix and Daniels, obviously torn about which one to believe. Like all the other fans, she wanted to believe Mix and his dashing stories. But there was no denying the sincerity in the old man's voice.

"But why?" she asked. "What did they do?"

"They tried to rob the Ghost River bank," Daniels said.

"Can't let folks get away with things like that. So we hung 'em. Boyd and Devers, Schaefer and Newcomb and the Palo Duro Kid. Hung 'em, every one."

Daniels laughed, a cracked quality to his voice. The girl looked at him, aghast.

This had gone on long enough. Hallam stepped over to Daniels, put a hand on his arm, and said, "Come on now, Hank. You've had your say."

Daniels nodded. "Damn right I did. Had enough o' that fancy dan."

With gentle pressure, Hallam started to lead the old man away. The other three cowboys fell in behind.

Mix suddenly rapped out, "Hallam."

Hallam looked over his shoulder. There was no fear in his eyes as they met Mix's. "What is it, Tom?"

"I meant it when I said I want that old man off the lot."

Hallam nodded. "Know you did."

Daniels was still muttering as the little group headed for the long clapboard bunkhouse that served as a dormitory for the cowboys who had no other place to stay. It was set off away from the soundstages, and there were always at least a dozen men staying there to answer the early morning call of "Roll out or roll up, you sons of bitches!"

As Daniels started up the short flight of steps that led into the bunkhouse, he paused and grabbed at the railing, swaying slightly. Hallam caught his arm and steadied him. "You all right, Hank?" he asked.

"Shore, shore," Daniels said. "Reckon I been out in that hot sun too long. Not as young as I used to be, you know."

Montgomery, Norwood, and Shorty all expressed concern, but Daniels waved them off. "You boys go on back to work," he said. "I'll round up my gear and get out o' here, like Mix wants, soon's I rest up a mite."

Hallam suddenly realized that he didn't know just how old Hank Daniels was. Judging by appearances, he was probably in his late sixties, but when a cowboy got old and leathery, the years probably didn't show up as much. Daniels could have been in his eighties, and that was a lot of years to be carrying around in weather like this.

Hallam knew about carrying around a lot of years. He'd passed the half-century mark himself. And Daniels's talk about the Ghost River Gang had brought back some memories for *him*, too.

As he followed Daniels into the shadowy interior of the bunkhouse, Hallam heard the assistant director bawling for the riding extras to get back to work. Again, Daniels told them to go on, assuring them that he'd be all right. Montgomery, Norwood, and Shorty went, but grudgingly. The cowboys stuck together, because they were the only ones who really understood the reality behind all the playacting.

Hallam stood in the doorway and watched Daniels make his shaky way to his bunk. As the old man sank down on the hard mattress, Hallam said, "You sure you're goin' to be all right, Hank?"

"Dammit, I told you to quit your worryin'!" Daniels barked. "Get back to work, boy. I'll just sit here for a spell. Mix won't mind too much, I reckon."

Hallam nodded slowly. "All right, Hank. Reckon I'll see you around the Waterhole," he said, referring to the Hollywood speakeasy where most of the riding extras gathered to wet their whistles.

"Reckon so," Daniels said. Sitting down, he suddenly looked smaller to Hallam, almost like somebody had stolen his old bones.

Hallam went back out into the glaring sunlight, and as he walked toward the bustling back lot, he thought about his own connection with the Ghost River Gang. He had been a deputy U.S. marshal at the time, and he had ridden into the town of Ghost River on the trail of the Palo Duro Kid. The kid came from a good family in East Texas, according to the information that Hallam had, but that hadn't stopped him from following the lure of a desperado's life. Hallam had arrived too late in Ghost River, though; the aborted bank robbery had occurred the day before, and by the time he caught up with the posse, the members of the youthful gang were already dangling from hemp ropes. Hallam had never held with lynch justice, but in this case there was nothing he could do about it.

He had known, of course, that Tom Mix hadn't had a thing to do with the capture of the Ghost River Gang. At that time, Mix had probably still been back in the coal mines of Pennsylvania. But it made a good story for the actor to tell, especially after it had been fancied up some, and Hallam wasn't one to begrudge a man his tall tales.

Before he could reach the back lot, he saw Mix's big car roaring toward him. Mix brought it to a halt beside Hallam, kicking up a cloud of dust in the process, and said over the smooth purring of the big engine, "Did you get rid of that old coot?"

"He's goin'," Hallam said. "He wasn't feelin' so good, so he's restin' up in the bunkhouse for a little bit. But then he'll be off the lot."

"He'd better be," Mix grunted angrily. "He showed me up in front of that pretty little gal, and I don't like that. Not one damn bit."

Hallam said nothing in reply, and after a moment, Mix gunned off in the direction of the bunkhouse and the offices beyond. He must not have been in any of the next scenes on the shooting schedule, Hallam supposed, or he wouldn't be leaving at a time like this. Usually, he was on the set even for scenes he wasn't in, just so that he could keep an eye on things and make sure that the finished product had his stamp on it.

Once Hallam got back to work, a couple of hours went by quickly. He rode up and down the streets of the back lot town, whooping and hollering and shooting off his big Colt along with the rest of the boys. They were supposed to be an outlaw gang terrorizing the town, and Mix was going to put a stop to that soon enough. He showed up again about an hour after roaring off in his car and went right to work on the next scene that called for his presence. Hallam had just about forgotten the altercation between Mix and Daniels.

Until one of the studio flunkeys came running from the bunkhouse, yelling at the top of his lungs.

The director bounced out of his chair and spun around,

livid at the interruption. But then everyone on the set heard the words "Dead! He's dead!"

Hallam wheeled his horse and put the spurs to it. He was the first one in motion, but the other cowboys were right behind him. He covered the two hundred yards to the bunkhouse in a matter of moments and yanked the horse to a stop in front of the steps. Hallam swung down from the saddle, took the steps two at a time, and burst into the bunkhouse.

He stopped just inside the door, his face hard as granite. He had expected to find Hank Daniels dead, all right, but most likely from a heart attack or a stroke or just plain old age.

He hadn't expected to find him strung up from a ceiling beam, a noose tight around his neck and his booted feet dangling two feet off the floor.

Hank Daniels had been lynched. Just like the Ghost River Gang. . . .

Police investigations were nothing new to Hallam, seeing as how he was in the detective business himself. But to most of the people on the set, being involved in a murder case was a brand-new and not very pleasant experience.

And it *was* murder. That much was plain right off. Nobody could tie their own hands behind their back and then hang themselves.

It was late afternoon before the cops got through questioning everyone. A detective lieutenant named Ben Dunnemore was in charge of the investigation. Hallam knew him fairly well, and the two of them stood under the same tree where Hallam had eaten his lunch.

"Well, Lucas," Dunnemore said, "what do you think?"

Hallam studied the lieutenant a moment before replying. Dunnemore was stocky and middle-aged, with a world-weary look about him, and there was no point in trying to read his expression. He was probably the best poker player Hallam knew.

"About what?" Hallam asked innocently.

"Don't play games with me, Lucas. You were here all

day, you know the people involved. Who do you think killed this old man?"

Hallam shook his head. "The city don't pay me to have opinions on things like that, Ben. Reckon that's your job."

Dunnemore glared at him. "In other words, you don't want to say."

"Most of these folks are friends of mine, Ben."

"What about Daniels? Wasn't he your friend?"

Hallam said nothing.

Dunnemore was right, though; Hallam had his own ideas about what had happened today and why, but he didn't want to say anything about them. This whole business had put him in a damn sorry position.

"All right, then," Dunnemore went on after a moment, "if you don't want to say anything, I'll just tell you how it looks to me." He paused again, but Hallam kept his mouth shut. Dunnemore sighed. "Daniels and Tom Mix had an argument earlier this afternoon. Daniels called Mix a liar, and Mix ordered the old man off the lot. A little later, you told Mix that Daniels was still here, and he drove off in a huff. I've got all this from other witnesses besides you, Lucas, so there's no point in denying any of it."

"You're doin' the talkin'," Hallam said.

"Daniels didn't have any other enemies around here, not according to what I've heard. Nobody seemed to know him real well, because he kept pretty much to himself, but he hadn't had any run-ins with anybody else on the lot. That leaves me with only one good suspect, Lucas."

Hallam shook his head. "You ain't tryin' to say that you're goin' to charge Tom Mix with murder?"

"What choice do I have?" Dunnemore shrugged. "Unless you've got a better idea for a suspect?"

Hallam stared off at the sunlight and rubbed his bristly jaw. Unfortunately, he had come to the same conclusions that Dunnemore had.

As far as opportunity went, a lot of people could have lynched Hank Daniels. He had been alone in the bunkhouse when Hallam left him, and as far as anybody knew, no one else had entered the bunkhouse until the studio man had gone in to post the next day's tentative shooting schedule on the bulletin board. The schedule hadn't gotten posted, because the fella had been too busy running back out and hollering about the dead man.

Around a busy place like a movie set, though, there was almost no way to account for every minute that a person spent. It would have been simple enough for someone to slip into the bunkhouse unseen. Hank Daniels was a tired old man; it wouldn't have taken long to overcome any fight he might have put up. Then it was a matter of seconds to lash his hands behind him, put the noose around his neck, and haul him up to die.

All told, the killer might have been in the bunkhouse only three or four minutes.

And Mix had been off the set for at least an hour.

"Well?" Dunnemore said.

"What's Mix say he was doin' while he was off the set?" Hallam asked.

Dunnemore jerked his head in the direction of the offices and bunkhouse. "He says he was in the offices talking to some of the studio executives. They confirm that he was there, and I've got plenty of witnesses who saw his car parked there. But nobody can swear where Mix was every minute he wasn't on the set. He could have walked over to the bunkhouse, killed the old man, and come back to the set without anybody noticing anything out of the ordinary."

Hallam nodded. Dunnemore was no fool. He had considered the possibilities and come up with the most logical suspect—Tom Mix.

"Seems like a mighty weak motive," Hallam said stubbornly. "They had a few words, but I've heard a heap worse on movie sets."

"Daniels embarrassed Mix in front of a reporter," Dunnemore pointed out. "Publicity's food and drink to that man, and you know it. Besides, the reporter was a pretty girl. I'm sure that didn't help any."

"You're goin' to take him in?"

"I don't see as I have any choice, Lucas. I at least have to take him in for further questioning."

"You do what you think best, Ben," Hallam told him. He knew that Dunnemore didn't want to believe that Tom Mix was a murderer any more than he did. If Mix was arrested, it would shock the whole country. Clean-living cowboy heroes didn't go around killing old men in cold blood.

Not to mention the effect that such a thing would have on the movie industry. This was going to be a bad day, sure enough.

Ben Dunnemore wasn't going to shirk his duty, though. Hallam was as sure of that as he was of anything.

"I told Mix to wait in his trailer," Dunnemore grunted. "Guess I'd better go tell him he'll be coming along with me."

Hallam nodded but didn't say anything. He watched the lieutenant start walking slowly toward the trailer where the King of the Cowboys waited.

Jack Montgomery and Roy Norwood had been lounging in the shade of another tree nearby, and now they came over to Hallam with anxious expressions on their faces. "What's up, Lucas?" Montgomery asked. "What's that lieutenant goin' to do?"

"What he has to," Hallam replied as he saw Dunnemore vanish into the trailer. "He's goin' to arrest Tom Mix."

Shocked exclamations came from both of the other cowboys. "He can't do that!" Norwood moaned. "That'll shut down production, and we'll be up Salt Creek."

"Nothin' else he can do," Hallam said. "Mix is the only suspect he's got."

Montgomery shook his head regretfully. "Damn, I wish we'd put a stop to it when ol' Hank started in on Mix. Me and Roy and Lawson shoulda hustled him away from there."

Hallam frowned. "What?"

"I said we shoulda just got Hank away from Mix."

Hallam's eyes had narrowed in concentration. "You and Roy and who?" he asked, a strange intensity in his voice.

Montgomery stared at him in puzzlement. "Shorty Lawson," he said. "What's the matter with you, Lucas? You losin' your hearin'?"

"Reckon I never heard him called by his full name," Hallam mused. "Just knew him as Shorty."

"I don't for the life of me see why you're worryin' about that," Norwood said impatiently. "I don't know about you, but I *needed* this job."

"Maybe you'll still have it," Hallam said. "Either o' you fellers seen Shorty here lately?"

"He was amblin' down toward the corral last time I saw him," Montgomery said. "What's gotten into you, Lucas? You look a little spooked."

"Just doin' a little rememberin', Jack," Hallam said. "Just a little rememberin'."

He walked off toward the corral, his long legs carrying him along at a good clip, the limp in the right one hardly slowing him down.

He hoped he wasn't too late already.

As he neared the corral, he saw a short, stocky figure hefting a saddle and getting ready to swing it up on the back of a horse tied to the fence. Hallam called out, "Howdy, Lawson. Gettin' ready to do some ridin'?"

Shorty Lawson turned around quickly, holding the heavy saddle between himself and Hallam. There was a startled look on his face that was replaced by a quick, friendly grin.

"Lordy, you spooked me, Lucas," Lawson said. "Didn't know anything was around."

Hallam didn't return the grin. He gestured at the saddle with a big hand. "Asked if you was goin' to be ridin'," he rumbled.

Lawson shrugged. "Anything wrong with that?" The grin was rapidly melting off his face.

Hallam ignored the question and asked another of his own. "You wouldn't be one of the East Texas Lawsons, now would you, Shorty?"

"Could be," Lawson said curtly. He made no pretense of being friendly now. "What's it to you?"

"Well, it's a funny thing. I got to rememberin' another fella name of Lawson. Theodore Lawson, his name was. Young fella, probably not more than twenty or so. Came from a respectable family in East Texas, but goin' into the family business wasn't enough for Theodore. He thought the money would be better and the gettin' it more fun on the owlhoot trail. He picked out another name to go by, so as not to shame the folks back home. Got to give him credit for that. Called himself the Palo Duro Kid."

Lawson took a deep breath. "Mind tellin' me why you're spinnin' this yarn, Hallam? Maybe you should go into the book writin' business, like Zane Grey."

"This is no yarn," Hallam said. "It's the truth, Lawson. There's more to it, though. This young fella, the Palo Duro Kid, came to a bad end. Got himself hung by some vigilantes. I was on his trail at the time, and I wanted to bring him in alive. So I was mighty upset when I found out he'd been lynched. Reckon I wasn't as upset as the boy's older brother, though. I didn't remember the Kid's real name right off, not until I was reminded of it. I don't reckon his brother ever forgot that lynchin', though."

There was about ten feet between the two men. Hallam could see the muscles twitching in Lawson's face. Lawson's voice shook slightly as he said, "They had no right to string him up like that. He was only a kid, goddamn it! And they didn't even get any money from that bank."

Hallam stood with his feet spread wide, his thumbs hooked in his belt. "Why'd you come here, Shorty? Had you heard about Mix claimin' to have been one of the posse?"

Lawson nodded. "Word got back to me a couple of years ago. Somebody who'd worked on a Mix picture heard him tell the story about the Ghost River Gang. I was workin' on a spread in Oklahoma at the time, so as soon as I could, I drifted on out here and got into the picture business." He smiled again, but it wasn't a pleasant expression this time. "I been waitin' for the right time ever since."

"Until today you found out you were after the wrong man," Hallam said. "You heard the truth of it from Hank Daniels."

Lawson's lips pulled back from his teeth even more. "Hell, I knew Mix had to be colorin' it up some. I knew the straight of it, how it happened and all, I just didn't know all the men who were involved." He paused, then said, "I found some of 'em, though. Enough to make a start on payin' 'em back for Teddy."

Hallam felt a chill go through him. He knew what Lawson meant. There were other dead men behind him besides Hank Daniels, men who, over the years, had paid a blood debt to Shorty Lawson.

"Couldn't pass up the chance when ol' Hank confessed right in front of you, could you?" Hallam said. "You knew he was by himself up there in the bunkhouse, so you slipped up there while we were all busy and strung him up. Findin' a lariat around there was no problem. Musta seemed fittin' to you, killin' him that way."

"And I watched him kick his life out," Lawson said savagely. "I watched his eyes and his tongue bulge out just like Teddy's must have when they hung him from that tree. And I laughed, Hallam. It was a damn funny sight."

Hallam sighed and took a step toward him. "You'd best come with me, Shorty. We'll go talk to the lieutenant."

"The hell we will," Lawson grated. "I had a score to settle. Nothin' wrong with that."

"Maybe not in the old days. But times have changed, Shorty."

"Not for me."

He threw the saddle at Hallam as hard as he could.

Hallam tried to duck, but the heavy saddle slammed into him and staggered him. He caught his balance as he went down on one knee.

Lawson jerked the reins of his horse loose and vaulted onto its back in one smooth motion. His heels dug into its sides and sent it spurting away from the corral.

With a muttered curse, Hallam yanked the corral gate open and caught the first horse he laid hands on. There was no time to saddle up, no time for a bridle and bit. All he could do was grab the animal's mane, swing onto its back, and kick it into motion just as Lawson had.

Lawson had a good start, and he was lighter than Hallam. Hallam leaned forward over the neck of his horse, patting it and talking to it in low tones and communicating with it as only a man could who has spent most of his life in partnership with a horse. As they pounded back toward the soundstages, Hallam's mount put on a gallant burst of speed, but he could see that it wasn't going to be enough. Lawson was pulling away.

Lawson flashed past Mix's trailer just as Dunnemore stepped out with the cowboy actor right behind him. Mix looked upset, and both he and Dunnemore leaped back, startled, as Lawson rode by and left a cloud of dust.

"What the hell?" Mix yelled.

Hallam was on them by that time, heeling his horse around and racing past them. "He killed Daniels!" he shouted over the uproar of galloping hooves, and then he was by them.

He heard a faint whistle behind him and glanced over his shoulder to see Mix leaping into Tony's saddle. The big white horse took off like a flash of light, leaving Ben Dunnemore behind to yell, "Hey! Come back here!"

Hallam grinned. Tom Mix was joining the chase.

Lawson's horse was lining out across open country now, having gone past the soundstages, the offices, and the bunkhouse where Hank Daniels had met his Maker. They filmed a lot of chase scenes out here on this back lot, and Hallam knew it well. Still, he had to watch close to keep his horse from stepping in a hole.

He heard the pound of hooves beside him and looked over. Mix had caught up with him. That Tony was some horse, and despite his faults, there was one thing you could say for his rider.

Tom Mix rode like the wind.

Lawson looked over his shoulder and saw them coming. Mix was pulling ahead of Hallam now. He was lighter, a better rider on a better horse. It was only a matter of time until he caught up with Lawson. The fleeing man kept looking back, fear visible on his face even at this distance.

And then Lawson's horse went down.

It was probably the most spectacular horse fall Hallam had ever seen, more brutal than any Running W. The horse must have stepped in a hole, because he went hooves over head with a wild scream. Lawson came off his back and landed hard, and then the horse rolled clean over him.

Miraculously, the horse clambered to its feet as Hallam and Mix rode up and leaped out of their saddles. It seemed to be unhurt, just walleyed and shaken up, which was more than you could say for Lawson.

Lawson was screaming in a high thin voice as Hallam knelt beside him. It took only a second for Hallam to see what had happened. "Back's broke," he said. "No tellin' how bad he's busted up inside. But he'll live long enough to make sure you don't go to jail, Tom."

Mix knelt beside Hallam, the late afternoon sun sparkling on his hat and shirt. "You said he's the killer?"

"That's right. Story goes back a long way, but it can all be checked out, even if Lawson don't confess. He's got a hell of a lot better motive than you, so I don't think you'll be goin' to the hoosegow just yet." Hallam leaned forward and put a calloused hand on the shoulder of the writhing Lawson. "Take it easy, Shorty," he said. "Help's on the way."

Lawson's eyes suddenly rolled up in his head and he went limp. Hallam knew he had fainted from the pain.

Mix and Hallam stood up and watched the crowd of people who were running toward them across the back lot. Mix looked down at Lawson and shook his head. "Hell of a way for a man to end up," he said. "Even a killer."

"So's dancin' at the end of a rope," Hallam said.

Lawson had been right about one thing. The times had changed, but he hadn't. And just like in the old days, the story of the Ghost River Gang had finally come to a violent end.